PEACOCKS AND PARSNIP WINE

Bun and Phipps are staying at the Rectory, looking after their curate cousin, following his wife's riding accident. One evening, they attend a dinner party. A fellow guest is found shot dead in the churchyard next morning.

Several other guests immediately ask the sisters to provide them with respectable alibis. Bun and Phipps, ever ready to oblige their new-found friends, fabricate a suitably involved story which is passed on to the investigating detectives.

Later, Bun and Phipps find the murder weapon and begin their own investigation without bothering the County Constabulary.

A suspect postal package is taken to Bodmin Hospital, by the detectives, for X-ray, but found to contain old rusty horseshoes instead of the expected automatic pistol.

The detectives are attacked by a very angry peacock, when arriving to interview its owners.

Reasons why those false alibis were needed become apparent when extra-marital liasons come to light . . . and bottles of the Rectory cook's famous parsnip wine have everyone legless when they are not exploding like defective hand grenades.

Also by Harriet Hicks
And published by Treviades Press

Trouble in Topsham
(paperback)

Problems in Polperro
(paperback)

Catching the Wind
in
Cabbage Nets
(hardback)

Peacocks and Parsnip Wine

by

Harriet Hicks

TREVIADES **T P** CORNWALL
PRESS TR11 5RG

Copyright © Harriet Hicks

First published in Great Britain 2005
by
Treviades Press, Falmouth, Cornwall,
TR11 5RG

*All characters in this publication are fictitious.
Any resemblance to real persons, living or dead,
is purely coincidental.*

A CIP catalogue record of this book is available
from the British Library.

ISBN 0-9534323-4-3

Printed and bound by T.J.INTERNATIONAL LTD
Padstow, Cornwall, PL28 8RW.

Typesetting and design by Treviades Press.

Notes re: cover pictures

The reader will find that part of the action takes place in a village named St Tudy.

It is located approximately five miles West of the Bodmin Moor and five and a half miles South-West of Camelford.

The author chose this delightful Cornish country village in order to have a genuine picturesque setting for the following story - which is pure fiction from beginning to end.

The original manuscript was completed eight years ago, with photographs being taken at about the same time.

The front cover picture is of the original St Tudy Church of England Rectory . . . which was later put up for sale.

The back cover picture is a view of the village school.

Notes on author

The author is Westcountry born and
bred, first attending Kingskerswell
village school; moving to Torquay at the
age of six; then Paignton, before
settling in Cornwall in May 1940.

Now nearing seventy-five, Harriet Hicks
writes full-time . . . ably hindered by
Polly, a much-loved stray cat, and her
family of three kittens.

CONTENTS

DEDICATION

To: 'Captain Ginger' . . . father of
Jezebel, Darkie Grey
and Little Titch . . .

. . . without whose constant hindrances
this book would have been completed
six months earlier

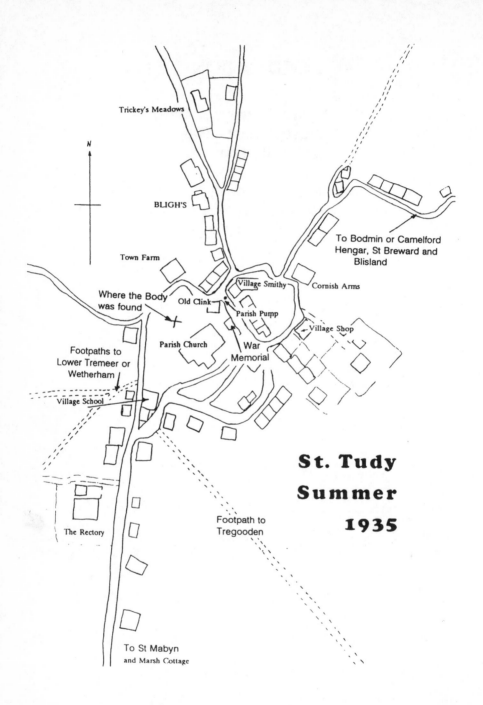

Trickey's Meadows

N

BLIGH'S

Town Farm

To Bodmin or Camelford
Hengar, St Breward and
Blisland

Where the Body
was found

Old Clink

Village Smithy

Cornish Arms

Parish Pump

Village Shop

Footpaths to
Lower Tremeer or
Wetherham

Parish Church

War
Memorial

Village School

St. Tudy
Summer
1935

The Rectory

Footpath to
Tregooden

To St Mabyn
and Marsh Cottage

Morning Tea

A slim, fresh-faced, middle-age woman of slightly less than average height, still clad in her nightie and dressing gown entered the room.

"Hello Bun. Sleep well, dear?" She greeted the other occupant.

Her sister nodded drowsily.

Miss Philippa Hyde, always known as Phipps after her family had declared the original christian name too much of a tongue twister for easy pronunciation, closed the morning-room door, crossed to the table and sat down.

"I've just had a nasty shock," she began tremulously. "Something dreadful's happened!"

The older woman, christened Anthea Eulalia by Victorian parents who had liked the names but failed to consider the consequences to a growing girl, looked up from pouring tea.

Had one of their housemaids suddenly given notice, smashed a piece of Crown Derby, broken a leg or declared herself 'heavy with child'? She wondered aloud.

"Rather more serious than that, Bun." Phipps replied, grimacing momentarily with annoyance at the mention of such mundane domestic trivialities. "You remember that nasty little man who was seated between Dorothy Nunn and myself - at the Knightons' dinner party - last night?"

Her sister sniffed disdainfully.

"Weedy body . . . snakelike eyes?"

"Yes dear, well: he's been found shot!"

"Accident or suicide, old girl?"

1

"Neither. According to the second housemaid, who told me she'd got it more or less first hand from the postman, people are speaking of murder."

Phipps waited impatiently while Bun drank some tea, then thoughtfully replaced cup in saucer, before observing that their short stay in this quiet, off-the-beaten-track Cornish country village of St Tudy might not turn out to be as dull and uneventful as first expected.

Phipps agreed, saying that it wasn't every evening one sat down to dine beside a future murder victim.

"Just as well, I'd say, Phippsie."

The younger sister agreed, adding that prior knowledge could put one off one's feed.

"Do they have any idea who did it?" Bun enquired.

"Not yet dear . . . but they know roughly when: between eight o'clock in the evening and midnight. So we're all suspects!"

Bun, seeking to establish facts - rather than encourage flights of fancy - asked her younger sister if the time of death had been estimated by a local doctor . . . or their friendly chatterbox of a village postman, whose medical knowledge might well be totally inadequate for such a task.

"Doctor MacIlroy, of course," Phipps snapped. "He must have mentioned it to his maid . . . "

" . . . who told the cook, who told the postman, who hurried on his way to tell everyone else in the village," Bun laughed.

"Quicker than writing a letter and cheaper than buying the Cornish Guardian. Can't see why we should be included in the list of suspects though. I never spoke to the fellow. Can't even recall his name. Do you, Phippsie?"

Miss Philippa Hyde replied he was a Mr Everard Wheeler, Clerk to the Magistrates of a nearby town; Clerk to the Rural District Council; Member of a Board of Guardians; Honorary Secretary to the Parochial Church Committee and closely connected to many voluntary organisations . . . with the probably exceptions of The Women's Institute and Young Women's Christian Association . . . though - in each case - he may well have been a co-opted member.

2

Bun shrugged her shoulders. "A finger in too many pies."

Phipps twisted her lips dismissively. "Poking his nose into everybody else's business."

"Men like that have few friends and many enemies," the older woman observed.

Phipps expressed the opinion that in all probability there would have been somebody present at Dudley Knightons' place, on the previous evening, who would have almost certainly crossed swords with a man like Everard Wheeler at one time or another.

"Hmmm. Yes . . . see what y'mean. Could have bumped him off on the way home. But that lets us off the hook, old girl. We've only been staying at the rectory for slightly less than a fortnight."

She reached for the teapot, to refill her cup.

"In any case: ladies prefer to poison their victims," she added after giving the matter more thought. "Shooting's a man's way of solving disagreements which can't be resolved over a couple of pints in the Cornish Arms."

Phipps gave it as her opinion that by then, the mid-1930s, one was just as likely to be shot by a woman as a man . . . thanks to the development of what Americans called the 'handbag gun'.

Bun declared that showing so many American gangster films in public picture houses must also surely help to encourage the use of guns amongst the criminal classes.

"I gather," Phipps began portentously, "from something I've read in library books, that automatic pistols can be made small enough to slip into a woman's stocking top without discomfort."

"Hmmm. Never thought of that, old girl. Didn't the maid tell you the size of the bullet hole, or something?"

Phipps replied no, her information had been confined to the single fact that Mr Wheeler had been found shot; which meant their murderer could have used almost anything from a farmer's rabbiting gun to a Wild West revolver.

Bun finished drinking her cup of tea, then observed visitors could be expected soon, bringing further details.

Phipps jumped up from the table. "In that case, since we're both still in our nightdresses, I think I'll just pop upstairs to get washed and changed."

Bun nodded. "All right. You carry on, while I finish drinking my tea. So long as one of us is presentable, that should be enough to satisfy the conventions and deal with callers."

She watched her sister leave. Although they were both in their early forties, Phippsie seemed to have kept a slim, active-looking figure, with accompanying prettiness and vivacity. Bun glanced down at her own matronly outline, grimacing with resignation. This was what happened to people who spent too many years in sedentary occupations. In her own case: the damage had been done when she was assisting in a Brighton preparatory school.

Oh well: they were retired now. She would have to take herself in hand. Perhaps this visit to Cornwall would help. Nice long tramps across the moors and all that sort of thing.

They were staying in the village rectory as a favour to a second cousin. Crispian's father - when a cathedral canon - had helped further the career of Bun's youngest brother when he took Holy Orders.

Thus: when Crispian Hyde, now curate at St Tudy, had turned up on their doorstep with the sad tale of his wife's riding accident, which would keep her confined to a hospital bed for several weeks, Bun and Phipps had instantly agreed to help.

So here they were, taking over the responsibilities of curate's wife, until Joan's compound fractures healed.

Ordinarily there would have been no need for such panic but the rector - a widower nearing retirement - had been ordered by his bishop to take two months rest, following a severe heart attack. This had left Crispian in sole charge of the parish. As he had reminded Bun and Phipps - themselves daughters of a Sussex parson - they well knew just how much work was done by an incumbent's wife.

However, setting aside family ties, the two unmarried sisters had looked forward to the novelty of having live-in domestic staff once again, for Crispian had mentioned the cook-housekeeper and two maids employed at St Tudy rectory.

Bun and Phipps had lost their last housemaid to Brighton Corporation buses in 1916 - when she became a wartime conductress - and had to manage without servants ever since.

4

The older sister smiled contentedly. It was a delightful novelty to be able to confine one's kitchen visits to discussion about meals which she wouldn't have to cook for herself.

And the village was located near the edge of Bodmin Moor, most convenient for a ramble up Brown Willy or Roughtor.

Not that she had been out that way as yet.

The sisters had found a small, but very friendly social set active in the parish, on their arrival. These people had accepted Bun and Phipps into their midst on the strength of their connection with the rectory, and yesterday's invitation to the Knightons' had been but one in a series of similarly pleasant engagements.

Bun smiled as she recalled Phippsie's current concern: that they must be neglecting the poor of the parish by spending so much time enjoying themselves amongst the better off residents.

These fears had been allayed when Bun pointed out that cultivation of the Upper Classes was the first step in providing charity for the Lower Classes.

Phippsie had seen the sense in this and carried on enjoying herself with a clear conscience.

And now they had a genuine murder in their midst!

Bun hoped it would prove to be a bit of a mystery.

There was nothing quite so irresistible as sudden death to set tongues wagging . . . furthermore: sifting through theory, speculation and wild rumour helped sharpen the mind.

A bell rang in a distant corner of the old building.

Shortly after, one of the maids came into the morning-room.

"Cap'n Holbrook's 'ere. Wants to speak to you, Miss Hyde."

Bun, gesturing at her dressing-gown, pointed out she was quite unfit to receive visitors. He should be shown into the library.

"Then run upstairs and fetch my sister, please."

Now: here was an interesting development.

Roddy Holbrook was a serving officer, attached to the Bodmin Barracks after being sent home from an Indian cantonment, following a severe bout of some tropical disease.

He played excellent tennis, though lacked staying power due to the after effects of his recent illness, and was a stylish swimmer who displayed a muscular body on the sands afterwards.

"A handsome sort of a rogue," Bun murmured, "who will obviously prove to be quite a charmer to younger women."

Unfortunately for Bun and Phipps, the captain was at least ten years their junior . . . so neither entertained any romantic notions on their own behalf.

Bun glanced at her wristlet watch.

Time young Roddy was reporting for duty in the barracks.

Perhaps this visit had something to do with that shooting!

She wished she had dressed.

As it was, she might be missing something. Bun swallowed the remains of her tea and hurried away upstairs. By dressing for speed rather than effect, she might be able to reach the library before too much had been said.

Captain Holbrook needs an Alibi

They met on the upper landing, Phipps shaking her skirt and petticoat straight as she hurried down . . . Bun pausing to catch her breath after rushing up with equal haste.

"Whatever can he want at this time in the morning?"

"Don't know, old girl. But if it's anything to do with that shooting . . . keep him talking about local fatstock prices, his old motorbike or the Duke of Cornwall's Light Infantry until I get down there."

This having been said, each went her separate way.

Phipps was not particularly au fait with the selling price of bulls and bullocks. She didn't know a great deal about the Light Infantry either, so she encouraged Rodney Holbrook to tell her all about his motorcycle. Previous experience had shown that any young man who owned one could speak upon this subject for absolutely ages with great enthusiasm.

She found young Roddy came up to par splendidly.

Even so, by the time she heard her older sister beginning to descend the creaking oak staircase, Phipps had begun to regret her choice.

Young Roddy had unfortunately taken her expression of casual curiosity to indicate that she was as keenly interested in things mechanical as himself . . . with the result that he was now pressing her to come for a 'spin', and appeared most unlikely to accept a negative answer.

Then she thought of a way out.

"All right . . . on one condition!"

"That I promise not to exceed five miles per hour?"

"No. Don't be silly," Phipps snapped in reply. "But . . . having regard to my age, sex and the fact that my late father was a Victorian country parson - when ladies were expected to behave as ladies - I shall require a side-saddle!"

"Oh I think we can arrange that," the Captain replied with a mischievous smile.

Phippsie's heart sank.

"I'll have a few words with our Regimental Transport chap," the young officer said carelessly. "Clever fellow with his hands, our Sergeant Harvey. He'll fix up something to meet with your approval . . . or I'll get him confined to barracks for a week or two. Tell me: will you be free for the trial run sometime after tea? Say . . . between five and seven-ish?"

Phipps, seeing no alternative, admitted she would be available, resolving to pop into the church and pray for rain before the appointed hour.

"Right! See you then. Dress of the day being a thick tweed skirt with not too much flare . . . or the slipstream might wrap it round your neck."

Phipps smiled weakly, silently wondering if it might be safer to develop a high temperature or convincingly sore throat by the evening . . . just in case The Lord was exceptionally busy and failed to receive her supplication from the church pew.

At this point her sister entered the library, too late to save her, and asked Roddy Holbrook what he was doing by paying social calls in St Tudy, when he should have been supervising his licentious soldiery in Bodmin Barracks.

"Ah well: I'm not a company officer. Sort of: a spare hand at present, 'til the M.O. declares me fit and well once again. So I'm attached to the permanent staff on admin duties. As a matter of fact: they've put me in charge of the rifles and ammunition, which is why I've dropped in to see you. Wanted to catch you before you went out. Need to ask a small favour."

Bun sat down in an armchair, giving her sister a quizzical glance which provoked no reaction.

She turned towards their unexpected guest.

"Is there any connection between this favour and rumours of a shooting - currently circulating on the village grapevine - by any chance?"

"Yes. 'Fraid so," Roddy admitted with a disarming smile. "Our police are bound to question all those present at the Knightons' dinner party, last night, because we were probably the last people to see Wheeler alive."

Bun agreed with this and waited to hear more.

Captain Holbrook blurted out that he needed an alibi.

"Been sowing wild oats . . . during the hours of darkness?"

"Something like that."

"And now - if she's a single lady - you fear for her honour while, if she's a married woman, you're more worried about your own skin, I suppose."

Roddy nodded.

Bun shook her head.

"Husbands can be very unrelenting under those circumstances, and one still doesn't need a licence to buy a horsewhip."

The young officer flinched.

"Actually, there's a bit more than a lady's honour at stake," he hastened to explain. "Mother and Wheeler crossed swords over a disputed boundary, not so many moons ago, and I'm afraid that I issued threats."

"To the late Mr Wheeler?"

"Outside the Cornish Arms. Just after closing time . . . so I had a most appreciative audience."

Phipps saw Bun raise her eyebrows.

"I suppose you threatened to shoot him?"

"Say it all the time - in the mess - amongst friends," Roddy admitted with a dismissive shrug. "Nobody takes a blind bit of notice. It has no more significance than telling one of your sergeants that you'll have his guts for garters if he fails to meet your requirements at any time. But it's all different in a village."

Bun agreed, observing that the onlookers would all remember what took place and more than half would rush to tell the police.

"Not because they particularly dislike me," Roddy said, "but simply to give themselves a fleeting moment of self-importance."

9

Phipps turned towards her sister, pointing out Roddy Holbrook's invidious situation.

"Well exactly," he agreed. "I could have borrowed a rifle or service revolver without anyone knowing a thing about it."

"And you must have thousands of bullets," Phipps suggested.

"Nobody would ever know if I swiped a couple."

"Wherewithal, reason and threat. A potent combination!" Bun agreed with a nod of her head. After a moment's thought she said, "You'd better tell the bobbies that you escorted us back to the rectory, after we left the Knightons' place . . ."

" . . . and stopped talking 'til after midnight," Phipps cut in.

"Over a nightcap?" Roddy suggested helpfully.

"Yes. We'll all have to say we didn't realise how late it was," Bun instructed the other two. "Then you left, Roddy, and we went straight upstairs to bed, Phippsie . . . about twenty to one."

"But what about your Curate Cousin?" the Captain asked.

"No need to worry about Crispian. He was staying overnight in Truro so that he could visit Joan, in the Royal Cornwall Infirmary," Bun reassured him.

"She was due to have another minor operation yesterday evening," Phipps added by way of further explanation, "so he wanted to be close enough to give moral support."

Bun's face assumed a darkening expression as she warned Roddy Holbrook not to think this was a grant of absolution for all his sins of the flesh. The alibi was being provided, as an act of expediency, because she did not wish to see the less savoury episodes of his private life becoming public property during any criminal investigations.

"Something is sure to get back to your commanding officer," the older sister continued, "and you could be thrown out of your regiment. It probably wouldn't worry you but that would upset your mother. I shouldn't want that to happen. I like Lady Mary."

Phipps smiled as the young sinner jumped to his feet, relief showing in every movement, thanked them for their help, reminded her that they had a date after tea, and then departed.

Bun regarded her sister with curiosity, asking what was meant by the Captain's final, somewhat daring remark.

Phipps recounted what had happened when young Roddy was talking about his motorcycle . . . and her method of avoiding closer acquaintance with this machine. "You'll see dear, he'll never get a side-saddle fitted in place of his pillion seat. I expect he'll have forgotten all about it by the time he reaches Bodmin."

Bun wanted to know what her sister would do if their gallant captain did manage to procure the necessary side-saddle.

"I shall have to plead a sore throat or severe headache."

"And I shall say that's the first I've heard of it!" Bun replied as she headed for the kitchen to order their breakfast.

She found the maids - Mavis and Mary - a study in still-life.

Mrs Gregory, the cook, was staring fondly at the breadboard, where a robin pecked up crumbs with feverish haste . . . whilst Sooty the cat prowled restlessly between the table legs, gnashing her teeth in very obvious frustration.

Bun paused in the doorway until the bird flew off, leaving a fresh dropping in payment.

Then Mrs Gregory nodded pleasantly.

"Just having his breakfast, dear of him. Comes in, same time, every mornin' an' pecks at the window if I 'aven't got it open."

She turned away, telling Mavis to wash the breadboard and then cut six medium slices for toast. "You'll be wanting your breakfast now, I suppose?" the cook asked, addressing Bun.

"Yes please. I thought eggs, bacon and tomatoes . . . and we shall both be in for luncheon." She glanced through the open window at the beginning of another hot day. "No need to cook anything, in this weather. A salmon salad will do very nicely, and Mr Crispian is expected back during the afternoon. Perhaps you could bake some of your delicious tea-cakes?"

"Yes M'am," Cook agreed then asked, "What about dinner?"

"I'll speak to you later about that. One never knows . . . we may find ourselves entertaining the local Murder Squad by then." Bun glanced around generally. "Have you heard anything further, concerning this business of the shooting?"

Mrs Gregory replied 'no', but they might learn more when old Tom Coote, their jobbing gardener, turned up for work later. "Of course, I could always send one of they girls over to the shop."

"Give Mary sixpence. She can buy a tin of Oxo cubes." Bun turned towards the girl. "And don't rush to get served. The longer you wait, the more gossip you'll hear."

Cook rattled her frying pan, which was heating up on top of the range, shouting over her shoulder that Mary didn't need any instructions in time-wasting. She was a past master at the art.

Mary, putting on her hat and coat, after hanging up her white apron, petulantly swirled her skirts about herself as if to sweep away a pack of lies and flounced out.

A bell rang on the wall. Bun glanced up. More visitors! Telling Mavis not to bother about the front door, she went out herself to see who was there.

Phipps had been quicker. She was ushering in a rather distraught, slim and attractive young woman in her early twenties: Teresa Lockhart, who said she was sorry to be a nuisance, but could she have a word . . . rather urgently?

Miss Lockhart also needs an Alibi

Bun showed Teresa into the breakfast-room, explaining that they were just about to have their meal and could they offer tea or coffee? The girl declined both, assuring them that she only needed a little help.

Phipps, who had already noted the hole in one stocking, a very small ladder starting in the other, muddy brown country brogues which appeared not to have been cleaned for several weeks, and a creased skirt with the frightful contrast of a jumper in quite the wrong colour, decided Miss Lockhart was in need of a great deal of help.

But what could one expect?

According to what Phipps and her sister had gathered in previous conversations with mutual friends, Teresa Lockhart was the result of a union between a gentleman well past marrying age and a much younger woman who had died in childbirth.

Bun and Phipps sat down at the table, having invited their visitor to take a vacant chair, whereupon Teresa came straight to the point.

She had heard Mr Wheeler had been found shot . . . and not before time too, 'cos he was a thoroughly nasty little man.

"Point is: Charlie Keast, our local postman, is going about, telling everyone that it's murder."

She looked at each sister in turn.

They nodded silently.

Teresa rushed on to say that Charlie was putting the time of death at something short of midnight.

13

"So we have heard," Bun replied, "but why does this cause you to have a near nervous breakdown?"

"Because I was out walking - by myself - about that time so I'm afraid the police might think it was my finger on the trigger, once they've had a chance to question some of our neighbours!"

"But can't your father vouch for you, dear?" Bun enquired.

Teresa shook her head.

Phipps winced, hoping nothing unpleasant would be dislodged from those unkempt curls and land in the marmalade.

The girl went on to say that her father had taken his sleeping draught earlier in the evening, so he hadn't even been awake to see her return from the Knightons'.

"I simply crept up to my room, slipped out of my glad rags, threw on an old skirt and jumper, grabbed my coat and beret, then went straight out again."

Bun asked, "What time was this?"

"Don't know. Sorry . . . I didn't notice."

Phipps suggested that perhaps Teresa remembered her time of return, when she might have glanced at a clock in passing by.

"No good. I staggered off to bed without looking at the hall clock. And just my rotten luck . . . I never saw anybody to speak to, while I was out, mooching round the lanes. So you can see, can't you: why I'm a bit desperate for someone to help out, as regards an alibi? Thought you might be prepared to vouch for me. Christian charity and all that sort of thing."

Bun explained that they could not speak of having passed her, whilst out walking, because this would conflict with a previous arrangement.

"So you're in the soup, too? Oh, I say: I am sorry to be bothering you like this."

Phipps patted Teresa's hand reassuringly.

"Anything I can do?" Their visitor asked contritely, then brightened. "Perhaps we could cook up something together?"

When Teresa paused for breath, Bun told her that Phippsie and herself had remained in the rectory, after returning from the Knightons'. Roddy Holbrook had been with them, having come in for a nightcap.

"Stayed until well after midnight," Phipps added poker-faced.

"The only thing I can suggest," Bun continued, "is that you should say you joined the party . . . having noticed a light in the library window."

Phipps reminded them that it was impossible to see that window from the road, because of the height and thickness of the rectory hedge.

Bun nodded agreement, suggesting Teresa should say that she had walked through the gate and made her way some distance up the drive.

Phipps screwed up her face in rejection, violently shaking her head.

"The question which springs to mind is: why?" She enquired.

After rejecting stock reasons involving lost brooches, making plans for a summer bazaar or a mislaid umbrella, it was decided Teresa would say she had felt unusually depressed and come round in hopes of finding somebody to talk to.

"Actually, that's a pretty honest sort of a lie because Doctor MacIlroy can confirm I suffer from depression," the girl admitted wryly. "He prescribes little white pills for it. You know how it is: Father being so old and ill, in a great big empty house which can make one feel frightfully lonely at times . . . well? What can you expect?"

Phipps responded with sympathetic phrases.

Her sister asked precisely what Teresa had done, to make all this connivance necessary. "Surely you haven't been issuing threats of doing bodily harm to this Wheeler person?"

Phipps noted the girl had the grace to look embarrassed, as she admitted that this was the case.

"He once owned land adjacent to our garden. Let it out to a local farmer for sheep grazing. The stupid creatures got through to our vegetables and ate everything in sight one morning, before any of us were out of bed."

"Hard words led to threats?" Bun enquired.

"I wrote him a stinking note . . . in which I stated - in capital letters - that people such as him ought to be 'put down'. Well: that means shooting, doesn't it?"

Bun and Phipps agreed that she had a point, though shooting was not yet an established fact, only wild rumour.

Teresa assured them that Charlie Keast was infallible.

"He seems to have an in-built filter system. Always sorts wheat from chaff before passing anything on to the next person."

"One gathers Mr Wheeler was generally disliked," Bun said.

"Mmmm." Teresa nodded her head in agreement. "He used to let his dogs off the leash, when crossing Bernard Drysdale's fields, then they would chase Millicent's pea-fowl. Our Bernard took to strolling about with a loaded shotgun. Actually fired it, on one occasion. Said later that he'd caught his foot on a molehill and pulled the trigger accidentally. Anyway, it did the trick. Old Wheeler chose a different footpath afterwards!"

Phipps murmured that she hoped the Drysdales wouldn't be coming to the rectory, for help with their alibis, because it would make life rather too complicated.

"No. They're thick as thieves with Dorothy Nunn, so I expect the three of them will arrange something between themselves." Teresa smiled before adding, "We call the Drysdales our secret peacock-eaters . . . because they breed them . . . but what happens to the adult birds?"

"Well of course: the males have a decorative value," Bun said. "So if there's any truth in your rumour, it will be the hens which end up in the oven."

Phipps gave a knowing nod, reminding them that peacocks were members of the pheasant family, but said she wouldn't care to eat one herself.

"They're pets! It would be as heartless as eating one's cat!"

"Wouldn't taste the same though," Bun observed.

Phipps winced and brought their minds back to last night's dinner party, by saying she presumed the old gentleman who had been seated between Teresa and her sister could be left off the list of murder suspects.

"Gee-Gee Danvers, Ah-ree-bah?"

Phipps stared, pop-eyed at this mouthful of gobbledy-gook.

Her older sister remained cool, calm and unflurried.

"Are you speaking about a man, or a Spanish horse, dear?"

16

"Our associate member of the Royal Institute of British Architects. His initials are 'G.G.' though nobody has ever heard Mr Danvers mention his christian names. Must be long gone seventy. Been retired for years."

"So he wouldn't be able to lash out with his fists, if a neighbour did anything to upset him," Phipps mused thoughtfully.

"All the more reason to assume he might resort to shooting," her sister pointed out. Bun asked Teresa if the late Mr Wheeler had ever upset Gee-Gee Danvers.

"Well there was that new servants' wing, which he built on the end of his house. Old Danvers maintained it should have been put at the back because it made the original Georgian structure appear lop-sided."

"An architect who still feels concerned with a lack of aesthetic standards on the part of others may well voice displeasure," Bun agreed cautiously, "but I cannot accept such a difference of opinions could be a reason for shooting one's neighbour, no matter how unpleasant the fellow proves to be."

Teresa said she wouldn't see much point in anyone shooting a man after unsightly building work had been completed. It would be the same as shutting the stable door after the gypsies had made off with one's carriage horses.

Phipps raised the question of why did people - as agreeable as the Knightons - include anyone, such as the odious Mr Wheeler, amongst their dinner guests?

"Word goes round that our Lieutenant-Commander RN Retired was interested in buying a field from Wheeler."

"A case of buttering-up?" Bun suggested.

"Absolutely. The land in question is a small paddock, lying between Dudley Knighton's ground and the Wadebridge Road. It's been said that Patricia feels the need for a longer drive, complete with sweeping curves, to approach her front door."

Phipps asked if Wheeler had owned most of the village.

"Heavens no. The Duchy of Cornwall is our principal landlord, but there are lots of odd bits and pieces - probably given by grant to faithful servants of previous centuries - which come up for sale from time to time."

"When the last surviving member of the original family dies?"

"Yes . . . then our Mr Wheeler was always first in the queue, waving his ever-ready cheque book, as soon as he found out who was handling the probate," Teresa said with a laugh.

"What an unpleasant opportunist," Phipps commented.

Teresa nodded vehemently, saying that Wheeler must have owned plots all over the village at one time or another.

"Always selling them at a handsome profit?" Bun suggested.

Teresa acknowledged this was the generally held opinion.

At that point, conversation was interrupted by a knock on the door. One of the maids came into the room. "Please Miss: Lieutenant-Commander Knighton's on the 'phone. Particularly wants to speak to you, Miss Hyde. Say's it's urgent!"

Dorothy Nunn Plays Safe

Bun hurried into a small cloakroom which housed the old fashioned candlestick telephone, picked up the ear-piece and made her presence known.

"Dudley Knighton here: in a bit of a spot . . . tricky situation. It's about that fellow Wheeler. I'm told some public spirited person has shot the little weasel . . . and a good job too! Trouble is: my having him here to dinner last night. My wife and I rather wanted to soften him up a bit . . . before making an offer on a piece of land."

"The old paddock?" Bun asked.

"That's right. Thought of putting in one of those serpentine carriage drives, with a few hydrangeas to either side. Patricia's very keen. Been reading a lot of Jane Austen recently. Anyway the cantankerous little swine told me his paddock wasn't for sale."

"Obviously hoping to take advantage of your eagerness."

"Well that's what I thought too: jack up the price and make me pay through the nose. I told him what he could do with those sort of tricks, by way of reply . . . "

"In front of witnesses, of course?"

"More fool me . . . a couple of local auctioneers and licensed valuers. My man and Jack Wills, brought over from Camelford, to look after Wheeler's interests. He sat next to you, at dinner, by the way."

"And now you're worried about the police finding out what you felt like doing to the late - but clearly unlamented - Mr Everard Wheeler?" Bun suggested with a dry laugh.

19

Dudley Knighton admitted this was so. He had made no secret of his hopes for the paddock and, now that its owner was dead, he would be able to purchase the land at a fair market price from the executors in due course.

"So I suppose you're afraid the police will think yours was the finger which pulled the trigger?" Bun observed.

"Exactly. Hole in one. Done him in to grab the paddock on the cheap. Sticky business. Patricia thought it might be a good idea to seek help regarding an alibi. Neither of us went out, after you'd all gone home to bed, but one can't prove a negative . . . if you see what I mean."

"So you require an independent witness to vouch for you?"

"If you could see your way clear to oblige friends . . . "

" . . . one of the ladies from the rectory being a first choice because other people do not - as a general rule - associate clergymen's womenfolk with fabricated evidence." Bun suggested with another dry laugh.

"You've put it in a nutshell," the Lieutenant-Commander replied. Hope it doesn't conflict with matters of principal? Didn't seek to offend."

Bun, recalling how two other applicants had already secured the Hydes' complicity for similar reasons, replied that she always saw it as a Christian Duty to help her friends. Dudley Knighton should tell the police that she remained behind to talk about his business of rearing day-old chicks, while her younger sister walked back to the rectory with Captain Holbrook.

"You can make the point of saying you particularly recall them setting off together. It will go a long way to confirming their own alibis."

"Ah yes. See what y'mean: you scratch my back and I'll scratch yours," the Lieutenant-Commander replied. He paused for a moment, then added, "Thank you very much, m'dear. If you don't mind my saying so . . . you'd have made a perfect gentleman if you weren't a natural-born lady."

Bun returned to the breakfast-room muttering about the complications of having a respectable family background when police were expected in the neighbourhood.

"It appears that at least half our new-found friends consider us to be so far above reproach that we must make ideal character witnesses," she observed upon sitting down once again.

Phipps noticed Teresa had the decency to blush.

Bun turned to the girl, explaining there would now be a slight change in their original story. Teresa should say she found Phipps with Roddy Holbrook in the library . . . and Roddy escorted her home when they left at twenty to one.

Bun turned towards her younger sister.

"Phippsie: your story will now be that you waited up for me, but I didn't return until one o'clock, when I was brought home by Dudley Knighton." Bun shook her head with irritation. "And that means I must tell Dudley the time. Completely forgot to mention it when we were on the 'phone, just now."

"You'll have to tell Roddy Holbrook about these changes too, dear," Phipps reminded her sister.

Bun rose from the table with an exasperated sigh, saying that she had better do so at once.

While she was ringing round the countryside, Mavis answered the door bell, and found a very agitated Miss Nunn on the front step, wishing to speak to Miss Hyde.

The maid showed this new caller into the library, just in case Miss Hyde didn't want Miss Nunn meeting Miss Lockhart, then waited in the front hall until her temporary mistress had finished telephoning.

When Bun heard of Dorothy Nunn's arrival she told herself resignedly that this could only mean yet another local acquaintance had rushed round to seek a watertight alibi from somebody whose respectability would be assumed without question. Mavis was thanked, then dismissed with a grim but silent nod.

Then Bun proceeded to the library.

Where she found the slim form of Miss Nunn - a dithery sort of a woman at the best of times - standing beside a high-backed armchair. Her hand moved slowly to and fro over the leather covering, smoothing its shiny surface in much the same way as she might have petted a stray cat.

When she saw Bun come into the room, this hand went rigid, steely fingers gripping the chair as if Dorothy was seeking to extract moral support from the fabric.

As predicted, Bun soon found that the anticipated murder investigation was the sole cause of this unfortunate creature's early morning visit.

Dorothy hoped she wasn't being a frightful nuisance, but she had just called on Dudley Knighton, seeking his advice on how she could convincingly prove that she had gone straight home from the dinner party and remained inside her own cottage until next morning.

"But why are you so concerned?" Bun enquired, gesturing for her uninvited guest to sit down.

Dorothy took a seat, replying with some degree of asperity that, living on her own as she did, there wouldn't be anybody available to corroborate her story . . . except Tiddles who never said much about anything. "And you know what the police are like . . . they'll be bound to question everybody."

"So you went to see Dudley and Patricia?" Bun prompted.

Dorothy gave a wry smile.

"I was hoping they would agree to say that I had stopped talking 'til after midnight, which would have . . . "

"Yes. Yes. We had our post delivered before breakfast. That would have covered you for the time of the shooting," Bun cut Dorothy short with a peremptory wave of her right hand.

"Except that the Knightons told me they had already made a private arrangement with you and your sister." Miss Nunn said with a helpless shrug.

"So you felt that you had no alternative but to come round and ask Phippsie and I to do the same for yourself." Bun said in a soothing tone of voice.

Dorothy Nunn nodded eagerly.

Bun rang for Mavis and asked her to bring their guest a cup of tea, then resumed her seat . . . deep in thought.

If she encouraged Dorothy to say she had remained behind at the Knightons' place, the police might think that was unlikely. There was her cat to be considered.

It could be presumed Dorothy would have hurried home - after the lengthy dinner party - to let the creature out or, if it had been out for several hours, to get Tiddles indoors for the night.

Difficult! Then Victorian morals came to Bun's rescue.

She decided that the latest version of the alibi story should be that Dorothy Nunn accompanied Phipps and young Roddy back to the rectory . . . as a chaperone.

Mavis brought the tea.

Dorothy's shaking hand spilt half of it in her saucer.

Bun outlined her solution.

Dorothy's face lit up so much with relief that Bun almost reached out to pat her on the head and murmur 'there, there dear' . . . but she managed to control this sudden urge.

"Oh yes . . . one more thing: Teresa Lockhart called in and stopped to chat, being escorted home by Roddy Holbrook at twenty minutes to one," Bun explained. "So I suggest we now say that Roddy went home with you at first - after leaving my sister at the rectory - to see if your cat was all right. The pair of you then returned to the rectory, when you were joined by Teresa. Then you finally departed - with Roddy and Teresa - at twenty to one."

"Oh thank you so much. I know I haven't done Old Wheeler any harm but the police can be terribly inquisitive, can't they? That's why I thought it best to play safe."

Miss Nunn couldn't thank her enough.

And Miss Hyde couldn't get rid of her caller quick enough.

As she showed Dorothy Nunn out, Bun casually enquired why she had not made some similar sort of arrangement with Millicent Drysdale. "Surely: that's what close friends are for?"

Dorothy resumed her pathetic expression, replying that she had been too late. "Millie said 'everything was fixed up'. I didn't like to force myself . . . especially knowing the rector and his curate were both away from home. I felt I would prefer to rely upon you and your sister."

Bun thought it fortunate that Phippsie and herself believed in practising a fairly practical form of Christianity, where little white lies were hopefully overlooked on the Day of Judgment - always providing they were told in a good cause.

She smiled as she watched Dorothy walking away from her, down the short curve of the gravel drive. A pear-shaped woman; decently slim above . . . but decided bulbous below the waistline.

Bun compressed her lips and shook her head regretfully. What comes of following a sedentary occupation. Writing articles and short stories for women's magazines might pay well enough, but all that sitting down played havoc with the figure. Look what schoolteaching did to mine, she thought ruefully, smoothing her hands over hips and flanks.

Then, recalling the interior of Dorothy's cottage - it was like something from the pages of House and Garden - Bun concluded writers were paid a great deal more than Brighton preparatory school assistants. Dorothy dressed well, too. Bun shrugged. Perhaps she had private means. That could account for it.

"Oh well . . . back to Teresa . . . then the telephone, yet again! Confuse everyone else before they confuse me," she murmured.

What the Villagers had to Say

Just as Bun reached the breakfast-room door, and stretched out a hand to open it Mary - the maid who had been sent around to the village shop - approached along the back passageway, coming from the direction of the kitchen.

"Police are here, Miss Hyde!" She said gravely. "They come in a car from Bodmin. Two men . . . in plain clothes!" She ended dramatically.

Bun opened the door and waved Mary inside, saying that she expected Miss Philippa would like to hear what the girl had to say. Then the two sisters became a mainly silent audience whilst the maid told them all the latest news . . . with Teresa offering supplementary explanations.

Mr Wheeler had been found in the churchyard by young Billy Penrose, first thing that morning. The lad had been on his way to work at Tregooden.

"Lives in one of those old cottages down the lane leading to Tremeer," Teresa interjected. "Which means he would have walked through the village, then taken a footpath across the fields. What did he say, Mary?"

"Well, according to Mrs Prescott . . . "

"Proper old busy-body. Exaggerates everything . . . "

" . . . the body was lying in a pool of blood!"

Phipps gulped, Teresa grinned weakly and Bun sniffed.

"But Mrs Binham said she'd been told there weren't hardly no blood at all: just a small hole at one side of Mr Wheeler's head, and bits blown out from the opposite side."

Teresa's head nodded approvingly.

"Much more reliable. Her husband's the sexton. Whereabouts was the body lying, Mary?"

"Well . . . some say it were in that corner between the side of the church and the tower . . . but others say he were sitting on the grass, near the War Memorial. You pays your money an' takes your choice!"

Asked by Teresa whether she had been to either location, Mary reminded her audience that the ground in that corner by the tower was all covered in stone or concrete. When she got there, she assured her audience that she had really looked around most carefully, but found no signs of any bloodstains.

"And I don't think he could have been found anywhere near the War Memorial either, 'cos there weren't no one hanging about nearby. The nearest people were a tittle-tattling bunch of old men, down near the Cornish Arms. I noticed Mr Tamblyn and Jan Hosen . . . "

" . . . both perfectly capable of talking the hind leg off your pet donkey, but not one of those old codgers has ever been further afield than the nearest market town in their entire lives," Teresa interrupted once again.

" . . . and there were some women talking together on that there narrow pavement, halfway round the north side of the graveyard," Mary continued, "but I couldn't see anything to look at. So I 'spects they just met up on their way to the shop, an' stopped for a bit of a chat."

Phipps grimaced with disappointment.

Teresa asked the maid if she had by any fortunate chance heard the women mention a gun, or speak of hearing sounds of shooting, during the night.

Mary shook her head, saying she didn't think any gun had been found . . . but there was a story going around that old Miss Pridham had heard a loud 'bang', just after she got into bed and blew the candle out.

Bun enquired whether Miss Pridham's bedtime was known.

Mary shook her head, going on to say, "People in the shop said that 'bang' was heard about eleven o'clock."

Teresa wanted to know if it sounded like a gunshot.

Mary reluctantly admitted some folk had dismissed the noise as a car backfiring.

Bun reminded the girl that she had mentioned plain clothes policemen, and asked what they were doing.

"Dunno Miss. They stopped their car by that pump at the back of the smithy, got out, asked where Constable Pope lived, then drove off."

"Our village bobby," Teresa added somewhat unnecessarily.

"Which means they haven't visited the scene of the crime," Bun pointed out.

She thought about the layout of St Tudy.

Six minor roads converged, becoming three where they met, just before reaching the village. The church occupied a central position, with the village school located at the west end of the original graveyard. A main road ran around beneath its boundary wall from northwest to south. Cottages and their gardens backed on to the eastern limits of the graveyard.

Therefore: most of the old burial ground could be observed by strolling along surrounding county thoroughfares . . . and the rest would be visible from a path, running through the land from a lychgate - by the school - to another gateway down near the War Memorial, more or less opposite the parish pump.

She concluded it could do no harm to let the maids take it in turn to carry out a circuit, during the course of the morning. Eventually: the village doctor and plain clothes detectives were bound to settle for an outdoor conference . . . which could indicate precisely where the late Mr Wheeler had been found.

At this point, Phipps asked what had happened to the body.

"Yes! You haven't mentioned that," Bun prompted.

"Mrs Ernie Gilbert . . . "

" . . . to distinguish her from her sister-in-law - Mrs Eddie Gilbert - they live in adjacent cottages on the road out, just before it splits in two: left branch going off to Hengar. Rowlandson used to stay there; with the Onslows," Teresa digressed.

Bun asked if that particular Rowlandson was the well-known artist, noted for his water-colours of North Cornwall.

Teresa agreed this was so, before rushing on to explain that the other fork crossed the main Bodmin road, which took one out to Blisland, close to the edge of Bodmin Moor.

Mary broke in then, saying that Mrs Gilbert had actually seen the ambulance pass by, "So they must have taken the body down to Truro - for the Royal Cornwall Infirmary . . . unless they only took him to Bodmin Hospital."

Bun returned to the hole in Mr Wheeler's head. Had anyone given some indication as to size?

"Oh yes! I forgot to tell you," Mary exclaimed. "See: they had to get the body over to Doctor MacIlroy's surgery 'cos he didn't want to go poking about where everyone could stand and gawp. So Constable Pope knocked up Mr Binham. Asked him to get out the parish bier . . . "

"A sort of wood frame on four large pram wheels . . . "

"I know," Bun said. "We used to have one at our father's church, back in Sussex. But do go on, Mary."

"Well: Constable Pope stood back an' let our Doctor an' old Mr Binham lift the body - them both being used to dead things - and Mrs Binham told people in the shop that her Ted had picked up the head end . . . so he was able to get a good look at the wound. Said it weren't no bigger than her little finger!"

"Which rules out shotguns," Phipps murmured.

"And there are too many trees in the way, for the killer to have used a rifle from any distance," her sister pointed out.

"So it must have been a pistol!" Teresa concluded.

"And full size," Bun suggested, "because 'handbag guns' only use bullets similar to those fired in fairground shooting galleries. Something called two-two's. A very small bore."

"Which means the murder weapon could have been a service revolver," Phipps said. "No wonder young Roddy was worried."

"And Dudley Knighton, too," her sister added, "because I expect he's got a few old war souvenirs tucked away in the chest of drawers, beneath his seaboot stockings."

Teresa suggested Dudley would be more likely to have one of those famous German automatics, such as a Mauser or Luger, since he was a serving officer during the last war.

Bun asked Mary if she had any more information, received a negative reply then dismissed her.

They heard the hall clock chime, as the maid left the room.

Teresa said she ought to be getting back to her father.

Phipps walked to the front door and showed her out.

When she rejoined Bun, she said that Teresa had gone away without a care in the world, now that they knew a full-sized pistol had been used to shoot Wheeler.

"Huh! There's plenty of automatics being manufactured, which are mid-way between a point two-two and the traditional Wild West forty-five," Bun responded. "I'd say - from what we know of the wound size - that a thirty-eight was used . . . and I don't think your average woman would find one of them too hard to fire, Phippsie. From what I recall seeing at the cinema, one only has to pull back some sort of a sliding device, on top, to cock it ready for the first shot . . . and after that they cock themselves. Hence the term 'automatic'."

Her sister nodded. "Yes. I see what you mean, dear: and when one stops to consider what we've already noticed, both Patricia Knighton and Millicent Drysdale have very firm handshakes, don't they?"

"Comes of helping their husbands with all that chick rearing."

"Carrying buckets of feed, then shovelling out the droppings?"

"Nothing has such a dead weight as a barrow load of fowls' muck, old girl . . . and I'll wager Patricia has wheeled out plenty of that stuff during the last fifteen years, since poor old Dudley got 'the chop' under those Geddes Axe naval economy cuts, back in the 1920s."

Bun stood up, saying she must tell the cook to let one of the maids take a stroll around the village, from time to time, throughout the morning,

"To keep us posted on progress. Then I have to telephone everyone depending on us for their alibis, to let them know the final arrangements."

Phipps, recalling a passage from the Book of Jeremiah, quoted, "'For the heart is deceitful above all things . . . and desperately wicked'. I shouldn't care to be in your shoes on Judgment Day!"

"I haven't told any lies . . . only made suitable adjustments to the truth against possible future eventualities. Anyway: if it will make you feel better, Phippsie, I'll have a bath after I've finished with the 'phone . . . and wash away all my sins."

Some time later, when she had bathed and dressed properly for the day ahead, Bun joined her sister in the library, where Phipps had her head buried in that day's Western Morning News.

She rang for their mid-morning tea to be brought through from the kitchen.

Shortly after this, Mary returned.

Addressing Bun, she said, "Please Miss: the police are in the kitchen . . . and they'd like a word!"

The County Constabulary Arrive

"Well . . . bring them in here, girl!" Bun instructed their hovering maid servant.

Mary scuttled away to the nether regions, reappearing in less than a minute accompanied by two strangers.

Phipps watched apprehensively as the plain-clothes policemen were shown into the library, then Mary waved crossed fingers behind their backs so that Miss Phippsie could see, before going out and closing the door.

Introductions appeared superfluous because the Hyde sisters had met Detective Sergeant Bassett once before, when they were staying in a holiday cottage at Polperro and narrowly escaped being charged with wasting police time, after their casual interference had started a false murder hunt.

The slightly corpulent Bassett stopped in his tracks, clearly amazed to find the Hyde sisters in occupation at this Cornish rectory, then told them that his companion, on this occasion, was Detective Constable Polkinghorne.

Turning towards his younger, more slightly built companion, Detective Sergeant Bassett explained.

"These are the two ladies I told you about." Gesturing right and then left, he said, "Miss Anthea Eulalia Hyde and Miss Philippa Hyde."

Finally, he glared at Bun, wanting to know what the sisters were doing in St Tudy.

She explained about their relationship to the present curate, with a brief reference concerning his wife's riding accident.

Phipps thought of how unnecessary that was, because a few words with the village bobby would have given all this information, together with the latest details of the rector's heart trouble . . . and the day Sooty the cat was expected to produce her next cuddle of kittens, too.

"I take it the curate's not at home?" Bassett muttered.

"Spent the night in Truro," Bun replied.

"His wife was due to have another operation," Phipps added.

Bassett confirmed that a body had been discovered in the churchyard - believed to have been shot - and warned that men from the county force would doubtlessly be carrying out searches.

"We haven't found the gun," Polkinghorne explained.

"Well don't look at us!" Phipps said hurriedly. "We haven't been anywhere near the church this morning."

Bun, inviting the two policemen to sit down, added that none of their parishioners had called at the rectory - to hand in any weapons - either.

There was a pause while everyone eyed each other with what Phipps could only think of as wary speculation.

However, the spell was soon broken when Mary returned with a loaded tray, which she set down on an occasional table. Then Bun took charge and began pouring tea.

Phipps looked across at Bassett, who told her they had about a half an hour's wait before the police pathologist could arrive from his laboratory at Truro.

"So I thought we might pick up a bit of background information. I believe you both attended a small dinner party during the latter part of yesterday evening?"

Phipps agreed, saying that she had actually been seated next to Mr Wheeler.

"Guests of some people called Knighton?"

"Yes. There were a dozen of us and Dorothy Nunn - she writes short stories for magazines - sat on my other side. Much more affable. I don't suppose I exchanged as much as twenty words with Mr Wheeler throughout the entire meal. Quite frankly, though I know one shouldn't speak ill of the dead, I thought him a very sour little man . . . probably crossed in love at a very early age."

"So you wouldn't know why he turned up dead amongst the gravestones?"

"Not really . . . but I suppose he must have been hoping to meet somebody."

"Why do you say that?" Polkinghorne enquired.

"Because he would not have needed to walk through the village in order to reach his own house, after leaving the Knightons' place." Phipps replied with a slight shrug.

Bassett asked if Phipps had overheard Wheeler speaking about a later meeting, during the early part of the evening. "You know what I'm driving at: when people are all milling about, chatting and drinking sherry."

Phipps racked her brains for a few moments before answering that all she could now recall was Millie Drysdale, discussing the price of full-grown peacocks with Jack Wills - a local auctioneer and estate agent - Lady Mary Holbrook giving Dorothy Nunn a few tips on making lime marmalade, and young Roddy flirting with Teresa Lockhart at one time.

Bassett then addressed her sister, asking if any of the men were known to own a pistol.

"Can't say for sure," Bun replied thoughtfully, "but it's fairly certain that Dudley Knighton will have one hidden away beneath his underwear."

"Why do you say that?"

"Because he once told me that there had been times when he was put in charge of boarding parties during The War. He was a naval officer, you know."

"I see. Any other guests with wartime experience?"

"We don't know much about Bernard Drysdale, nobody does, but he's obviously 'Officer and Gentleman' class, so I wouldn't be at all surprised to find he has brought something back from the trenches in Flanders by way of a souvenir . . . possibly a captured German weapon."

Phipps joined in at this point, to mention Captain Holbrook's present duties at Bodmin Barracks.

"He's been put in charge of the rifles and ammunition."

The detectives exchanged meaningful glances.

Then Bassett began counting by tapping the fingers of one hand on his knee. He looked across at Phipps and said, "I believe you mentioned a round dozen?"

She nodded silently.

"If we deduct three from that figure, namely yourselves and the late Mr Wheeler, and take into account the fact that you've told me about three of the gentlemen who were present . . . what about the rest?"

Bun broke in to suggest the police were best suited to find out more about the auctioneers because they were both Cornishmen, with offices in nearby towns.

"Which leaves us with Mr Danvers," Phipps added.

Bun shook her head.

"Shouldn't think there was much violence left in him. A retired architect . . . becoming visibly frail. Don't know his age, but he must be well past seventy. Wouldn't have served in The War, which means he's unlikely to have a pistol."

Polkinghorne suggested that Danvers could have gone out to South Africa with one of the yeomanry regiments, during the Boer War.

Phipps saw Bassett give his companion a severe grimace, almost as if he was reproving Polkinghorne for attempting to make a joke, before pointing out Danvers would have been in his mid-thirties at the turn of the century. "Too old for galloping about the African veldt, in my view."

In the silence which followed this observation, Phipps got up to pass round the plate of biscuits a second time, whilst her sister was refilling teacups.

"So how are you enjoying yourselves - in St Tudy?" Bassett enquired when everyone was settled once again.

Phipps told him of several invitations to tea, swimming parties, picnics at Daymer Bay, and a very exhausting afternoon's tramp all round the old slate quarries near Trebarwith Strand and Port William.

"Not much time spent on parish visits, but at least we're getting to know the lie of the land quite well." Bun commented.

Bassett reminded her that she had spoken of peacocks.

"Oh yes. The Drysdales rear them. One hopes they won't invite us to dinner when roast peacock is on the menu."

Polkinghorne visibly winced.

His superior was made of sterner stuff, merely commenting that a roast peacock always held pride of place at state banquets in the Middle Ages.

"They used to gild the feet and beak, dress the body in full feather - once it was cooked - then carry it into the hall at the head of a solemn procession."

Bassett paused for effect before adding, "Ye Knights of Olde used to swear an oath with one hand on the bird, in much the same way as we would do, when in court, today."

"But using a bible . . . rather than the parson's nose?" Polkinghorne enquired with a very straight face.

Bassett glared.

Phipps bridged the silence by asking where on earth he had heard all this.

"When I was stationed at Tintagel - supposed to be the home of King Arthur. Some Old Dear told me; though I shouldn't have thought they had peacocks in Cornwall as far back as the days of the Round Table and Excalibur."

To which, Polkinghorne replied darkly that from what he had heard, folk up Tintagel way would apparently tell you anything to sell a few more souvenirs.

Bassett said, "Yes . . . well . . . " to bring them all back into the present tense, then asked the Hydes if they could recall their fellow guests' order of departure.

Bun recited part of her alibi story, stopping at the point where her sister set off home, accompanied by Captain Holbrook, with Dorothy Nunn acting as chaperone . . . then gave Phipps a meaningful stare.

"Well . . . Dorothy saw me into the rectory, then carried on home, to make sure her little cat was all right."

Bun coughed suggestively.

"And Captain Holbrook went with her for company. Then, after quite a short time, they both came back to me . . . and stayed 'til twenty minutes to one."

Bun waited a moment, then tut-tutted.

"Oh yes. Goodness me! Nearly forgot:" Phipps hastened to add, "Teresa Lockhart called about a quarter of an hour after Dorothy came back. And all three left together."

Polkinghorne wondered why Miss Lockhart was out so late.

Phipps noticed her sister glaring at her, realised she had forgotten to mention Teresa's tendency towards sleeplessness and depression and hastened to put this right. To her relief, both the detectives and Bun appeared satisfied with that.

Before either man could ask further questions there was a gentle tap on the door and Mary returned to say, "Excuse me, Miss Hyde: there's a Truro gentleman just arrived . . . and he's asking for the detectives."

"Ah," Bassett exclaimed, jumping to his feet. "The pathologist, appointed by our Chief Constable at the beginning of the month to show us Cornish folk how to do our job. Come on!"

Bassett and Polkinghorne Begin Enquiries

Polkinghorne, attempting to soothe his chief's ruffled feelings as they left the rectory, mentioned that he had heard the pathologist's father was born in St Austell, where the grandfather had once been a minister.

"Local church . . . not national government."

Bassett replied grumpily that he supposed - if this new man was half-Cornish - it might possibly be of some assistance in helping them to understand each another.

But he was immediately disarmed when he met the tall, round-faced gentleman - in his early thirties - who introduced himself as Doctor G B H Tresidder.

"Oh yes sir. Grievous Bodily Harm?"

"George Benjamin Herbert actually . . . but I gave up practising on live patients as soon as I qualified, so you'll never have to accuse me of G B H in the legal sense of that phrase."

Detective Sergeant Bassett responded to this cheery greeting with a smile and a nod, first introducing his assistant and then himself, immediately going on to ask where Doctor Tresidder would like to start work.

"Where the body was found! In the churchyard, I believe?"

Bassett gave a short confirmatory nod.

Tresidder explained that he had driven straight up from his home - a few miles outside Truro - and so had not viewed the mortal remains as yet, while they were walking in the direction of the 15th century parish church.

"Said to have been shot, sir," Bassett replied.

"Have you seen where the bullet went . . . after leaving the body?"

"No. Haven't come across the gun either."

Doctor Tresidder reminded the detectives that a .38 pistol could be thrown several yards away from the body, by the effects of normal recoil, if one was shooting one's self.

"The hand muscles - as you would know - lose their grip quite involuntarily . . . immediately the bullet scrambles your brains."

Polkinghorne shuddered.

Bassett assured the pathologist they had made a thorough search through grass and weeds for many feet, without as much as finding a discarded toffee paper.

"Well of course . . . I shouldn't care to express an opinion at this stage but - from what your village constable told me - it does seem possible a .38 pistol was used," Doctor Tresidder murmured thoughtfully.

Then he suddenly twisted his head, an almost birdlike motion, to look directly into Bassett's eyes.

"Was there no spent cartridge to be found, Sergeant?"

"'Fraid not, sir . . . though it would have probably been trodden into the ground by the time we arrived at the scene. There was that chap who found the body in the first place; then Constable Pope; followed by his second visit with Doctor MacIlroy; and finally Pope's third visit when he was accompanied by the sexton complete with parish bier."

"By which time: most traces of evidence would have been all but obliterated, Sergeant."

Tresidder gave a short laugh.

"One might just as well have invited the entire village to drop in for a quick dance round the Maypole before breakfast!"

Bassett pointed out the village bobby had little experience of serious crime.

"Oh I'm not blaming your Constable Pope . . . but you'll have to find that cartridge case - let alone the gun - or no coroner will ever accept suicide as a working proposition. Neither shall I!"

Bassett pulled a long face, visualising many miserable hours spent on hands and knees crawling through the churchyard grass.

The pathologist told him to cheer up. He might have had to look for a dressmaker's pin . . . which would be infinitely more difficult to locate.

"If I were in your place, I should be inclined to question that fellow who found the body. Never know: he may have picked up the cartridge case - because it was made of brass, all nice and shiny - to take home as a memento of the occasion."

The detective sergeant agreed this was a good suggestion, then led the way around to the spot where the late Mr Wheeler had been found.

Tresidder looked over the trampled grass, pausing here and there to line up certain trees, then went off to scrutinise their trunks without finding a spent bullet lodged beneath the bark. Finally, he asked the way to Doctor MacIlroy's surgery, saying he would like to have a quick word with the local GP, before driving back to Truro.

"Going to cut up the body to find out what makes him tick?"

"No Sergeant. Actually . . . I shall be looking for reasons why he has stopped ticking," the pathologist replied with a friendly smile, before striding away to confer with the village doctor.

Bassett nodded at the grass.

"Well: you heard what the gentleman said, Constable. So you'd better bend your knees to look about a bit."

Detective Constable Polkinghorne drooped with dismay.

His boss slapped him on the back, by way of encouragement.

"But I'll get the knees of my trousers filthy, scratching about here, Sarge!"

"Don't worry, Ceddie boy, I need you to help question people in the village. I'll 'phone up Bodmin and get them to send out some help. That's a job for uniformed men, not us specialists."

Cedric Polkinghorne breathed a sigh of relief.

Bassett led the way out of the churchyard, asking his assistant what he thought of the Miss Hydes.

"Nice enough old dears, Sarge. Wouldn't have minded a date with the younger one - if she'd been ten years younger. Neat figure; curly hair - naturally fair, I'd say - and a sweet smile."

"And what about her big sister?"

39

Polkinghorne paused thoughtfully as they passed through the lychgate, then suggested that the older woman looked a bit formidable, didn't she?

"Built like a double-bottomed battleship, Sarge!"

Bassett expressed the thought that possession of a 'cruiser stern' did not qualify its owner for the title of 'battleship'. However, he went on to acknowledge the fact that the lady's bust size made her very suitable as a figurehead for a man o' war.

Standing just outside the village school, Bassett said, "Right! I'll leave you to it, then. Knock on a few cottage doors and make yourself known to the local residents . . . but no sneaking inside for stray cups of tea! I'll send Pope over to give you a hand after I've 'phoned our guv'nor."

Cedric Polkinghorne looked around to get his bearings. It appeared that the road which surrounded the churchyard came up from the direction of the rectory; then bent to its right, almost forming the shape of a shepherd's crook, before one arrived at a short diagonal path from which one would reach the church porch.

There was a narrow grass strip beyond, where several mature trees grew between a scattering of old gravestones, in front of a thick hedge. Polkinghorne went up to look over and found gardens separated - from where he stood - by a footpath.

He returned to the village school, where a single cottage faced him on the opposite side of a tarmac square. Several more cottages - behind him - lined the road between where he stood and the rectory. Polkinghorne crossed to begin knocking on doors, and found another grass-grown burying-ground beyond, as one walked towards the village centre.

Working around the school square area, he failed to obtain any useful information. As was usual in Cornish villages, when the police arrived, nobody admitted hearing or seeing anything.

A lane curved round to his left, as he faced the cottage opposite the school. The detective followed this to discover a converted barn, or workshop, standing between himself and the old churchyard. A row of four cottages overlooked this building from the other side of the lane.

Polkinghorne began calling on these householders . . . thinking it was about time his sergeant returned. "Probably got his size ten feet under Pope's kitchen table, drinking tea," he grumbled to himself. But when he reached number three cottage, the detective finally thought he was getting somewhere.

The woman who came to the door told him she had heard a car draw up in the middle of the night.

"I didn't 'ear nobody speak . . . but doors opened . . . and then slammed shut again!"

However, hope was dashed at number four . . . where the lady of the house said some folk would do anything for a couple of lamb chops. Asked to elaborate, Polkinghorne was informed that the painted hussy, living just round the next corner - whose husband was away doing his territorial training on the Isle of Wight - had got herself a bit of stuff.

"Butcher-bloke from over to Camelford, if what I heard in our village shop is anything to go by. Proper disgraceful . . . comin's an' goin's in the middle of the night. She must think we don't know what's 'appening . . . but we do, m'dear, we do. Make no mistake about that!"

Polkinghorne gravely assured the lady that he most certainly did believe her. Then he walked to the end of this short lane, where he found another group of tiny cottages facing inwards onto a very small square. Equally negative results were obtained by calling on the occupiers.

Polkinghorne had just left the last building - and caught sight of the Cornish Arms at the end of another short lane beyond the village shop - when he heard his sergeant calling from outside a large double-fronted house which had gardens running up beside the old churchyard.

"I thought you'd left me to do it all by myself, Sarge."

Bassett led the way towards the shade of a huge horse chestnut tree, growing on the opposite side of the road from the parish pump, assuring his disgruntled detective constable that he had been calling on all the folk living beside the Bodmin, Camelford, Wadebridge and St Teath roads, which converged just before reaching the Old Clink.

Persistent sounds of man beating iron disturbed this otherwise tranquil setting, and sulphurous fumes from a blacksmith's forge tainted the clean country air.

Bassett suggested they withdraw to the churchyard.

They did so, making themselves comfortable on a tombstone which was so old that its lettering had almost been worn away by nearly two centuries of wind and rain. Bassett disclosed that he had not learned anything to their advantage and asked how Cedric had got on.

"A deafening silence . . . except for a bit of scandal concerning one woman's method of payment for her lamb chops."

"Never mind, boy. Village folk are like this . . . but give 'em twenty-four hours to talk it over amongst themselves, then we'll try again."

"And everyone will come up with the same story!"

Bassett shrugged, pointing out that would be an improvement on no story at all. He was about to say more when Polkinghorne began laughing.

"Hey . . . look at this lot, Sarge!"

Bassett turned: four uniformed constables self-consciously advanced along the churchyard path. Three were carrying reaping hooks whilst the fourth attempted to hold a pair of garden shears in the same position as he might have held his swagger cane, when a gunner with the Royal Field Artillery.

A burly individual, wearing hairy tweeds of an alarming ginger discolouration, brought up the rear.

Bassett stood up, shaking his head and saying some kind soul ought to tell their guv'nor that ginger/orange tweed doesn't suit him at all.

"Oh well . . . best have a word, I suppose."

"About his suit?" Polkinghorne muttered sotto voce.

"And ruin all chances of promotion for the next ten years?"

Superintendent Charles Hawken raised a hand, telling the four uniformed men to halt. Addressing his sergeant, he asked what was required of them.

Bassett pointed to the area of flattened grass and said it had to be thoroughly searched for a pistol or its spent cartridge case.

42

The four men proceeded, muttering amongst themselves.

Hawken discussed the case, so far as it had gone, and grumbled about the village bobby letting the deceased be removed.

Bassett suggested there had been no alternative because - as a result of the pathologist being appointed - a directive had been circulated to the effect that all cadavers had to be sent directly to Truro, in future.

Hawken said he would have that changed.

"If you haven't found the gun or any spent cartridge cases, would it be possible that this Wheeler fellow was killed elsewhere, and the body dumped here afterwards?"

"I am considering that aspect, sir," Bassett lied cheerfully.

"What beats me, in that event, is why dump it in a graveyard?"

"A criminal with a logical mind, sir? I mean: bodies usually end up somewhere like this? Don't they?"

"Meaning: once dead, one has to chuck the body somewhere?"

"Or double-bluff. Our victim - having been killed nearby - is left in St Tudy churchyard in hopes that we'll go off looking further afield, sir."

"Thinking we'll assume no one could be so stupid as to shove their victim's cadaver into the home ground burial plot?"

Polkinghorne joined in, at this point, reminding the other two that few country people owned any form of transport which might be suitable for moving a body from one parish to another.

"You think our killer owned a gun - war souvenir - but not the necessary pony and trap for getting rid of the evidence?"

"On the other hand sir: we know the victim was a weedy type."

"Yes . . . perhaps as little as seven or eight stone. In which case: a chap of normal build could have killed Wheeler while using a silencer - because you tell me no one has reported hearing a gunshot last night - then carried him down here slung over his shoulder like a side of pork," Hawken murmured.

"Or a woman could have done it," Bassett suggested.

"What? On her shoulder?" His superintendent asked.

"No sir . . . but in an ordinary garden wheelbarrow."

"In that case, I suggest you make your first specific enquiries amongst the naval commander's dinner guests.

Superintendent Hawken dragged out a gold watch from his waistcoat pocket, held it up, shook his head at the swift passage of time, explained that he had to get back to Bodmin, and returned to where he had parked his car.

Polkinghorne watched his retreating figure, thinking the guv'nor looked more like a shambling bear which had just escaped from a travelling circus than a senior police officer, then turned towards Bassett.

"You know Sarge: he might be right about that dinner party being mixed up in this business. Perhaps the host deliberately invited Wheeler with the intention of doing him in."

"There are other possibilities, if it turns out to be murder, because one - or both - of the Knightons could have been acting in collusion with a third party . . . for reasons as yet unknown."

"Or one person - be it host, guest or otherwise - simply seized an unexpected opportunity . . . and acted on the spur of the moment," Polkinghorne concluded.

Bassett replied Lieutenant-Commander Dudley Knighton was his first choice . . . with the lady-wife pushing the barrow.

Tricky Moments at 'Trickey's Meadows'

The detectives made their way out of the churchyard, by descending a short flight of stone steps adjacent to the Old Clink, then walked past the village pump and front of the blacksmith's shop, before bearing to their left.

Rounding cottages, they were accosted by a woman leaning out over her half-door.

She shouted, "'Ave you caught that feller who did the shooting, me 'andsome?"

Bassett replied, "No m'dear. But 'tis early days, yet."

Polkinghorne's attention was distracted in the opposite direction, as he admired Churchtown Cottages . . . and counted the net curtains which twitched in their windows.

Bassett led the way past Virginia House, with its long workshop reaching almost to a point where the road divided. A signpost indicated one turned right for St Teath, but kept straight on for Wadebridge.

The detectives took this latter route, Bassett mentioning that Dudley Knighton's place should be no more than a few hundred yards further on.

"A couple of small fields, once owned by a chap called Trickey so I've been told, Ceddie boy. Hence their present name of Trickey's Meadows."

Polkinghorne saw a green-painted lorry come out of a hidden gateway and drive slowly in their direction. As it passed, he noted several sacks of poultry feed and suggested this vehicle had probably just made a delivery to the lieutenant-commander.

45

Bassett agreed before nodding towards a large house on their left. "Wheeler's home," he explained. It was built of the local grey slatestone and stood in its own grounds. Polkinghorne saw the name BLIGH'S and queried its owner's choice.

"Yes. A bit pretentious because I reckon that's a Victorian building, whereas Captain Bligh - of Mutiny on the Bounty - was dead and buried by 1817, when George the Third was still on the throne . . . in a manner of speaking."

"What does that mean, Sarge?"

"Poor old bloke lost his marbles; and the Prince of Wales took over as Regent in 1811."

"Ah. Then why's the house called Bligh's?"

"Perhaps one of the family owned the land, back along. After all: the Blighs are known to have lived in this parish at one time. Didn't you see that plaque, up on the church wall, a bit along from the porch?"

"Oh yes . . . and, come to think of it Sarge, there's an old tombstone with that surname, as well."

"Probably brothers or cousins of the gallant captain," Bassett murmured as they turned in through open double gates, on which a board proclaimed: D. & P. Knighton, Poultry and Day Old Chicks for sale.

An elderly man, riding a large black sit-up-and-beg bicycle called, "Good morning!" as he passed along the road. Polkinghorne remarked that the machine looked very similar to an old police bike.

"Which reminds me: what's happened to our village bobby? You told me you'd send him over to give me a hand, but I haven't seen hide nor hair of Pope."

Bassett explained that their local man had to attend Magistrates Court, in Camelford, to give evidence in a poaching case so he couldn't possibly be available 'til some time in the afternoon.

They stopped at Knighton's front door, where a grey cat was sitting on the step. Bassett knocked and the cat sidled into the house as soon as the door was opened.

Polkinghorne weighed up Knighton as Bassett introduced them.

The retired naval officer was a tall, slim, rather fine looking man, probably in his early forties, with dark wavy hair above a typical patrician face. Someone born to command . . . rather than one of the lower orders . . . trained to jump and obey.

The detectives were ushered into a light, airy sitting-room, asked to excuse the smell of baking, offered fresh currant buns with tea or coffee, and told Mrs Knighton had taken to yeast cookery like the proverbial duck to water since becoming settled in Cornwall.

"Her last home - when I commanded a fleet destroyer - was in Malta . . . but that was before the Geddes Axe chopped our navy into small pieces. Still: mustn't complain. I managed to survive The War . . . and got rapid promotion because of it."

Knighton grimaced regretfully.

"Bit of a wrench to leave though; I might have made Captain in another couple of years. Anyway: what can I do for you?"

Polkinghorne heard his sergeant say that Wheeler had been shot, so they were checking on any guns owned by the dead man's friends. Then a grey-haired woman, with flour on her apron, stepped into the room carrying a tray of tea and buns.

Knighton introduced his wife, who smiled, set her tray down on a convenient side table, then returned to the kitchen.

Bassett reminded their host they had been discussing guns.

Knighton poured tea and offered buns whilst admitting he possessed a Webley .455 service revolver, which he produced from a sideboard drawer. "Don't normally keep it down here," he explained with a smile, "but when I heard about Wheeler I knew the police would be around, so I put this somewhere handy."

Polkinghorne watched his sergeant examine the weapon, then it was passed to him with a comment about the broad arrow mark stamped into the metal.

Knighton admitted it had been government property but claimed right of ownership after losing his own gun at sea.

"It was when I commanded a contraband control vessel - she was a converted steam yacht on loan from one of those Indian maharajahs - which struck a mine while the first lieutenant was away examining a Dutchman's bills of lading. Lost all my kit."

Polkinghorne handed the weapon back, suggesting it fired the wrong sized bullet.

Bassett agreed, swallowed some tea and changed the subject by mentioning the Bligh family gravestone. "Didn't see one for the famous captain though, sir. I suppose he's buried on some exotic South Sea Island?"

Knighton laughed.

"Nothing so romantic; quite sordid actually. After serving with Nelson at the Battle of Copenhagen, he was sent to New South Wales as Governor, eventually coming back to this country and settling in Kent. The poor fellow went up to London for an operation and died in his lodgings . . . so they buried his body in Lambeth!"

The detective sergeant kept to trivialities until he had finished his tea - and a couple of currant buns - then he resumed the role of inquisitioner by asking if the dinner party had been given for any particular reason.

"Not really, though it was all rather odd . . . how it came about. This fellow Wheeler, not quite a gentleman if you follow me, suggested it when I approached him about buying a field which he owned. Said it was so much more civilised to talk business after a good meal, accompanied by the right glass of wine."

"So you took the hint?" Bassett suggested.

"Yes . . . and the damned fellow even told me who to invite! All to no purpose. He named a price, for his bit of land, which was so high that it wasn't even a starting point for negotiations."

"May one ask, sir," Polkinghorne began, trying to be as tactful as possible, "whether your opinion was based upon current valuations in this part of the county . . . or your own - perfectly understandable desire - to obtain a bargain?"

"I had an estate agent present to advise me."

"So Wheeler was simply trying to take advantage of your good nature?" Bassett suggested blandly.

"Exactly . . . and I told him so in no uncertain manner," Knighton admitted. "Trouble is: I lost my temper in front of two completely reliable witnesses - the estate agents - but I didn't threaten to shoot the blighter for all that."

"But, according to information received from Constable Pope, who ought to know what's what through living in St Tudy, there are others who have been less circumspect?" Bassett suggested.

Knighton laughed.

"You're thinking of that business with the shotgun, down in one of Drysdale's footpath fields, aren't you?"

The detective sergeant agreed this was so.

"Shot across the bows stuff," Knighton replied with a dismissive shrug. "I'm sure no real harm was intended. Simply the traditional warning shot . . . though Drysdale always maintained he tripped over a molehill and the gun was discharged accidentally."

"And you tell me that Wheeler asked you to include this gentleman at last night's dinner," Bassett asked incredulously.

Knighton shrugged again, calmly observing that real life happenings were often stranger than fiction.

"According to Constable Pope: a Miss Lockhart once sent Wheeler a threatening letter . . . ?" Bassett said, eyebrows raised.

"Oh that! Well . . . there was a dispute over animal trespass, as far as I remember, and the silly girl used the expression 'ought to be Put Down' . . . but hang it all: she was only having a touch of the hystericals."

Knighton paused, took a deep breath and added, "You know: I don't much care for this. It's a bit like telling tales out of school, sneaking behind your friends' backs, and all that sort of thing."

Bassett sympathised as he pointed out that the young lady in question was present at the previous evening's dinner.

"And you expect me to believe you, when you tell me Wheeler asked to have her included . . . along with this Drysdale fellow who actually discharged a gun when Wheeler was walking across his land?"

Knighton spread his hands apart, shrugged and gave it as his opinion that the unpleasant Mr Wheeler must have turned over a new leaf in his declining years.

"Which did not extend to yourself - the host - and any proposed business dealings," Bassett observed drily.

"That only goes to show one cannot predict the future workings of another man's mind, Sergeant."

"But you had previously spent over twenty years as a naval officer . . . in charge of other men . . . ?"

"And when I found one like Wheeler aboard any vessel which I commanded, I quickly posted him elsewhere," Knighton retorted with a malicious grin.

"But you miss my point, sir. I suggest you did possess sufficient experience to see through people like Wheeler . . . so why go to all this trouble to please him, last night?" Bassett pressed, "When you must have known in advance that you were doomed to fail?"

Knighton pulled a wry face, "I wanted that field. I suppose I let desire cloud my judgement."

Polkinghorne said it would appear that the late Mr Wheeler deliberately got all these people together, last night, in hopes of making them feel thoroughly uncomfortable.

Knighton admitted that - in retrospect - he felt bound to agree.

Bassett changed the subject slightly, asking if it was correct that Miss Anthea Eulalia Hyde stayed behind - after the other guests had departed - at the end of the previous evening.

"Yes. Talking chickens with my wife . . . or rather: their illnesses. My late father-in-law was a vet with an Indian cavalry regiment for most of his service life. Patricia inherited all his text books and tools of the trade, when the old man passed on to meet St Peter."

Knighton paused for a moment, before going on to say that his wife had still got her old man's horse castrators - or whatever one called 'em - amongst other equally gruesome bits and bobs.

"Makes me feel decidedly uncomfortable - about my manly extremities - just to look at them! Pat says: 'One squeeze and they're off'. But I shouldn't think the horse found that much compensation for his loss!"

Polkinghorne had to stifle a laugh as he heard his sergeant reply that a pair of castrators - no matter how antique - were not really suitable for displaying on one's sideboard alongside the family silver, before bringing their conversation back to the matter in hand by asking if Knighton could remember the order in which his guests had departed.

"The younger Miss Hyde - Philippa - went off first."

"On her own, sir?" Polkinghorne prompted, by way of showing his sergeant that he, too, had his wits about him.

"No! Not at that time of night. With Captain Holbrook . . . "

"Who is reported as threatening to shoot Wheeler outside the village pub," Bassett interrupted.

"Yes . . . though there's not an ounce of harm in young Roddy. Just letting off steam."

"Which can result in shots being fired, but please continue, sir."

"Well . . . Dorothy Nunn tagged along, partly because all three would be walking in the same direction, but also because she thought they ought to have a chaperone."

"What a quaint little woman," Bassett murmured.

"Oh she's all of that," Knighton agreed with a laugh, "but a very nice, friendly soul. Now: where was I?"

"About to tell me who left after those three."

"Yes. The two auctioneers - or estate agents - went off together. Bill Rowse has a bit of a reputation as a ladies' man, so he might have dropped in on one of the local widows. Jack Wills is more interested in sea-fishing . . . so he might have driven out to the coast, if the tide was coming in."

"And the Drysdales?" Bassett prompted.

"Came by car. They live about a mile away, down in the valley, beside the road to St Mabyn."

"Give anyone else a lift?" Bassett prompted.

"Only Lady Mary Holbrook - Roddy's mother - who had walked round here, earlier, but said she didn't feel like making the return journey on her own two feet. Wheeler left at about the same time and Teresa - Miss Lockhart - went shortly afterwards. Then old Danvers, quite an authority on church architecture, ambled away to his cottage in Churchtown a few minutes later, when he realised everyone else had disappeared."

"Which means: if we discount Miss Philippa Hyde and old Mr Danvers, one or more of seven people might have lain in wait for Wheeler to walk down the road to Bligh's," Bassett mused aloud.

"Or called on him after he got indoors," Polkinghorne suggested, "if one of your dinner guests is responsible for his death . . . which we hope is not the case."

Lieutenant-Commander Knighton firmly assured the detectives that everyone would be able to account for their movements until they went to bed. "They didn't start leaving 'til nearly half past ten, so they've only got an hour and a half to account for, if our postman is to be believed. He went around telling everyone Wheeler died between eight o'clock and midnight."

Bassett stood up, preparatory to leaving, pointing out the majority of postmen were ill-qualified to form such opinions.

"By the way, sir," Polkinghorne broke in suddenly, "you told us Wheeler selected your guests. What was the connection between him and the ladies at the rectory?"

"None whatever. Some of us have made them welcome and invited them to join us on our normal social occasions. I simply put their names forward and Wheeler raised no objection."

"Ah well . . . that's two off the hook!" Bassett laughed, turning towards the door. "By the way, sir, tell Mrs Knighton the buns were delicious. We'll be back for more if we can time it right."

"Meaning you believe some of my guests could be involved?"

"Something like that," Bassett replied with a wry smile.

Revelations on the Rectory Lawn

Bun and Phipps had also been deep in conversation about the activities - known and unknown - of their fellow guests at Dudley Knighton's dinner party on the previous evening, while comfortably seated in deck-chairs on the rectory's front lawn, when Millicent Drysdale called.

Bun put down her knitting.

Phipps folded their morning newspapers, then pottered around to the kitchen, where she asked the cook to have one of the maids bring out three tumblers and a jug of her fresh lemonade.

On returning to their deck-chairs, Phipps heard Millie Drysdale telling her sister that Bernard and herself had been very fortunate, at the end of the previous evening, in being asked for a lift home by Lady Mary Holbrook.

"Somebody of impeccable reputation to vouch for you in times of trouble . . . like now?" Bun suggested.

"Well yes. What's more: she invited us in, when we reached her place, and I think we must have stayed chatting until something like half past twelve."

"Fancy you noticing the time!" Phipps commented.

"Couldn't be exact to the minute," Millie admitted . . . but I remember glancing at our clock, when we finally reached home, and saw the hands were pointing at twenty to one."

Phipps smiled to herself when she heard her sister remarking upon the fact it was quite surprising how many people felt they needed a cast iron alibi when a fellow dinner guest appeared to have ended his life in mysterious circumstances.

"Well . . . if it had been anyone else, nobody would have given the situation a second's thought," Millie Drysdale replied swiftly.

"But Mr Wheeler has to be seen as a special case?" Bun asked.

"None of us had any cause to like Wheeler. Some had even threatened the nasty little maggot with violence . . . and that includes Bernard!" Millie answered in very positive tones.

"Discharging a loaded shotgun accidentally-on-purpose?"

"Oh! So you've heard about that contretemps in one of our path-fields?"

Bun remarked that it appeared to have been discussed in every village home . . . usually with much laughter.

Millie shrugged.

"Just for the record: Bernard really did trip over a molehill, but no one seems prepared to believe us. Hence our relief at having one of the local aristocracy able to provide the proverbial watertight alibi."

At this point, Mary came out with the lemonade and a plate of biscuits. She set this down, asked if there would be anything else, received a negative answer, and went back to the house.

Bun returned to the subject of alibis, as she poured out from the brimming jug, by observing that others surely did not have such a pressing reason to seek independent corroboration of their after-dinner activities.

Phipps passed the biscuit plate.

Her sister passed the tumblers and Millicent Drysdale laughed.

"Beginning with old Danvers: I'd say he's really the only one of us who has nothing to worry about!"

"Meaning all the rest of you have crossed swords with the late Mr Wheeler at some time or another?" Phipps enquired.

Millicent Drysdale replied that Teresa Lockhart was the most recent example.

"Sheep got into their garden from one of Wheeler's fields - let out to a local farmer - and nibbled the spring cabbages."

"Oh yes, we did hear something . . . ?"

"Hmmm! Silly girl sent Wheeler a snotty letter, then went about telling everyone he ought to be Put Down!"

"But surely she wouldn't have . . . ?" Phipps interjected.

"Probably not . . . but young Tess has a nasty habit of wandering abroad during the hours of darkness. I've seen her once or twice myself, when Bernard and I have been driving home after attending some exciting local theatrical treat: such as an Oscar Wilde play by the amateur dramaticals or the operatic society's latest re-hash of The Pirates of Penzance."

Phipps suggested animal trespass was hardly sufficient grounds for committing murder.

Millicent agreed, but said Teresa was a very 'nervy' sort of girl.

"I can quite imagine her gnawing her fingers to the bone, once she heard that Wheeler's dead body had been discovered in our churchyard."

"'Thus conscience doth make cowards of us all'," Phipps heard her sister murmur.

"My own thoughts, too," Millicent concurred.

Phipps suggested Captain Holbrook should have been placed with G G Danvers - as a non-runner - because he had only recently returned from abroad.

Millicent pounced on this without restraint saying that: men being what they were . . . and everyone knew what she meant by that, young Roddy was making up for lost time since returning to his native soil.

"A bit of a gay dog, eh?" Bun asked with a knowing smile.

"Well . . . I'm positive he's got a bit of fluff somewhere nearby!"

"But he's never accompanied when he comes on picnics," Phipps reminded their informant.

"Which means she's a married woman!" Mrs Drysdale retorted with an abrupt nod by way of visual emphasis.

Bun wondered aloud what made the speaker so sure.

"Well . . . I've happened to see him - in the distance - when shopping in Bodmin a couple of times recently, and he's always been speaking to the same person," Millicent told the two sisters with a shake of the head.

"So you think he was probably out on the tiles, after we left the Knightons?" Phipps asked.

"Pretty safe bet, I should say. D'you know: I'd give anything to be a fly on the wall when the police question young Roddy."

Bun, ignoring all this innuendo, sought to discuss somebody else, saying that she supposed Miss Nunn had little to fear living, as she did, such a visibly blameless life.

Millicent waved a hand disparagingly.

"Don't you believe it, my dears! She's having an affair with a married man, too!"

"Surely not?" Phipps exclaimed wide-eyed at this suggestion.

"Well of course . . . no one knows who he is, but he must be married because none of us have ever clapped eyes on him." Millie replied, almost smacking her lips with relish.

"Another with a guilty conscience in so small a community?" Bun commented, deliberately ignoring the curious fact that people could know a person's sex and marital status without having actually seen the object of their curiosity in the flesh.

Millicent replied that still waters ran deep and she wouldn't mind betting dear Dorothy would be having hysterics at this very moment, now that the police were in the village, and going round questioning everyone.

"You've seen them?" Phipps enquired.

"Oh yes: four in the churchyard grass - looking for the murder weapon - and two plain-clothes men knocking on cottage doors. So Dorothy will be in no doubt that she's going to be asked to account for her movements the same as the rest of us. And she lacks Roddy Holbrook's worldly experience. A sweet, innocent creature - if one puts aside her passionate peccadilloes with another woman's husband - so she'll have the greatest difficulty in concocting a suitable pack of lies if she was committing mortal sin last night . . . all in the name of true love."

Bun supposed that it was reasonable for Miss Dorothy Nunn to avail herself of any chance to obtain a bit of practical experience somehow, if she was earning her living by writing love stories, or they might lack plausibility.

Phipps changed the subject by asking Millie about Lady Mary.

"Can't say for certain . . . but she's had three gardeners leave in as many years. All quite young men, too!"

"D'you think they could have raised a blaze in the Holbrook shrubberies?" Bun enquired.

"Either that . . . or been dismissed for non-cooperation!"

Phipps, seeing nothing to be gained by pursuing that point, turned their conversation towards the land agents.

Millie dismissed Jack Wills, Wheeler's man with an office in Camelford, because she didn't know much about him.

"Which leaves us with Bill Rowse!" she declared in such a triumphant manner that Phipps was reminded of a conjurer about to pull a rabbit out of his previously empty top hat.

"Bit of a philanderer?" Bun enquired.

Millie declared that - if it was the practice to award silver cups to the champion fornicator of any particular parish - Bill Rowse's sideboard would be groaning beneath the many tokens of his recognition long before now.

"Known to prefer widows, rather than spinsters. I don't know if you are aware of local customs, but the county was once divided into nine districts called 'hundreds'. St Tudy stands in the Hundred of Trigg . . . and our Bill is generally acknowledged to be the 'prize bull' of Trigg."

"Many offspring?" Bun enquired with one eyebrow raised.

"Countless! Scattered all over, far and wide!" Millie replied.

The sound of a sharp explosion echoed across the lawn.

Bun looked at her sister.

"Third time in less than a fortnight!"

Phipps nodded, her lips tightly compressed.

"We'll have to start drinking it, won't we dear?"

Millie, after several years residence amongst country folk, was quite used to such phenomena, and casually asked if they were having trouble with the home-made parsnip wine.

"Yes." Bun answered with a wry smile.

"The cook must have put too much sugar in the brew." Phipps added with a shake of the head.

"And now we're getting fairly frequent explosions," her sister continued gloomily, "the most recent one happened in the middle of the night."

Millie suggested they bring a couple of bottles down to the Drysdale home during the afternoon, where they were expecting a bit of a get-together.

"Bernard has already 'phoned around to invite the Knightons, together with all other available dinner guests. Suggested they all come along to discuss the shooting over a cup of tea, by which time - if everyone behaves true to form - there should be plenty of red hot rumours flying around St Tudy. So we shall have lots to talk about."

Phipps replied that Bun and herself would be delighted to come, secretly comforting herself with the thought that the Drysdales could hardly serve roasted peacock at four o'clock in the afternoon.

"Good . . . and don't forget your lethal-sounding parsnip wine."

Phipps promised to provide adequate supplies.

Millie, with a sly smile playing round the corners of her mouth said, "We'll have tea first then - after a suitable interval - follow up with a spot of wine tasting. That ought to loosen a few tongues!"

Bassett is Bewildered

By then, Detective Sergeant Thomas Bassett had reached the point where he, too, could have gladly made use of something to loosen tongues after having conducted a short, and seemingly unproductive interview with the late Mr Wheeler's starchy old housekeeper at Bligh's.

Bassett had set his assistant to work in the study, looking through correspondence for anything resembling a written threat, whilst he spoke to Mrs Tregenza.

Questioned about people known to harbour a grudge against her late employer, the woman had taken refuge behind the facts that she had been a staunch Methodist all her life . . . and it was a well-known fact that Exodus stated: 'Thou shalt not bear false witness against thy neighbour'.

Having expressed herself thus, the lady then resolutely refused to commit herself further.

The disgruntled detective sergeant had instructed his assistant to carry on with his search of the deceased's residence, then returned to the churchyard, where he learned that none of the four uniformed men had discovered anything of consequence, so he carried on to the Cornish Arms.

Bassett ordered lunch for six, to be served in a private room.

When the landlord had been invited to comment on Wheeler's sudden death, he had replied that gentleman never came into the pub so he could only repeat parish pump gossip.

This followed the pattern already beginning to establish itself: that their victim did not get on well with his own kind.

59

"Mind you . . . to be fair, I will say that most of the ordinary workpeople found him to be a good boss providing you did your job all right."

"And what about the rest of the folk who attended a dinner party - where Wheeler was present - at Lieutenant-Commander Knighton's home, yesterday evening?"

The landlord leaned forward, across his counter, much as one conspirator would when speaking confidentially to another.

"I'll tell you straight, Sergeant: still waters run pretty deep in these small villages an' goin' by what I've heard in the few years that I've been here - in St Tudy - old Wheeler couldn't have done it better if he'd planned his own murder!"

"Why d'you say that?"

"'Cos most of they there up-country folk, settled in St Tudy since the end of The War, appear to 'ave somethin' to hide. You mark my words: you're goin' to get some mighty funny stories told to you when you ask them there lot where they were when that shot wuz fired!"

"So you suspect one of last night's dinner party?"

"Not necessarily. I'm thinkin' more of their private lives, which they certainly won't want shouted all over the county!"

"Any particular activities in mind?" Bassett asked.

"No names, no pack drill . . . but I asks you: who jumps over their neighbour's back garden hedge when the lights go out? What do they midnight walkers get up to? And are all the married couples makin' a 'go' of things when you scratch beneath the surface?"

Bassett assured the landlord he was a fully trained surface scratcher, then turned to leave, saying he would be back with his constables at one o'clock. The landlord asked him to stay.

"'Ere! How many men 'ave you got working on this job?"

"Six, if you include me."

"Well can't one of you do something about Eric Smitheram an' his blinkin' milk lorry? He's taken to parking up against the churchyard wall at nights - full of empty churns - ready to start his mornin' round of collecting from the farms between 'ere an' the coast. 'Ee d' wake near half the village with his early starts."

"Ever tried telling him about it?" Bassett asked reasonably.

"Ah! Ain't nobody will do that 'cos half are related to him, one way or another. That's why I thought I'd mention it to you. How about you 'avin' a tactful word or two?"

Bassett pointed out he was engaged in a murder investigation, which would always take precedence over matters of a simple public nuisance, then left the bar before its owner could challenge this statement.

Walking past the village shop, the detective turned right to pause near the parish pump, just behind the smithy. Wheel marks clearly showed, cut into the grass beneath the churchyard wall, on the opposite side of the road.

Accepting that working people needed a decent night's sleep, Bassett resolved to speak to Eric Smitheram . . . on the off-chance that some grateful villager might reciprocate by coming forward with information relating to the shooting.

Curling one arm around the pump, the detective idly pushed on the handle until a dribble of water fell from its spout, his mind turning over the publican's gossip.

What if half the married men were out and about chasing other men's wives? Hardly likely to have any bearing on the churchyard shooting. On the other hand: perhaps he should enquire if there were any cottages to let with a view to getting in on the act. Bassett grinned, kicked the pump and set off to see if Polkinghorne had made any progress.

As he walked past Churchtown Cottages, then Virginia House, the detective considered his position. There seemed to be no obvious pointers - let alone clues - to help the investigation.

What if the Chief Constable brought in Scotland Yard?

Well: the first thing would be an outcry from the Police Committee, wanting to know why they should pay for outside help now that they had established their own C I D. And anyway: what could London men do, which couldn't be accomplished by members of a local force pulling together?

It was all very well running comparison tests with spent cartridge cases when you had something to compare . . . but this St Tudy case had only provided them with a dead body.

"And - according to Constable Pope - one set of footprints in the dew-laden grass," Bassett muttered perplexedly.

He shook his head.

Those indentations must have been made by the chap who found the body. Which means that - if no one else walked that way - one could assume suicide . . . until faced with the inescapable fact that both gun and spent cartridge case appeared to have vanished.

He mentioned all this to Polkinghorne, on returning to Wheeler's study, at Bligh's. The younger man suggested that - if there was no further evidence of close contact between killer and victim - it was surely obvious a longer-range weapon must have been used.

Bassett couldn't accept this, pointing out the number of trees both in, and around the churchyard.

"Even with bright moonlight you'd have a Hell of a job to draw a bead on anyone whilst standing in the road . . . or the window of a nearby cottage. But the real stumbling block is accounting for Wheeler's presence, so far from the path, obligingly standing about . . . waiting for his killer to come along and shoot him. Not on, is it Ceddie boy?"

Polkinghorne looked at his watch then gestured towards Wheeler's telephone.

"Tresidder has had enough time to reach Truro and make an external examination by now, Sarge. Why not give him a ring? From what I remember, when I went on the fire-arms course, unburnt powder from the propellent charge fans out from the muzzle of the weapon used, in the shape of a cone."

"Yes. Yes. And from the diameter of the burn mark it is then possible to calculate the distance between gun barrel and flesh. You might have forgotten . . . but I went on the same course!"

Polkinghorne returned to sorting through more papers in Wheeler's desk, while keeping one ear cocked in his sergeant's direction when he was seen to pick up the handset.

Once connected to the pathologist, conversation was brief.

Bassett then thanked Doctor Tresidder and hung up.

"Well . . . ?"

"The gun was held no more than three inches from an ear!"

"As close as that, Sarge?"

"Yes . . . bullet entering one inch in front of the said earhole and leaving from a similar point on the opposite side of the deceased's head."

"Which rules out rifles . . . "

" . . . and leaves us stuck with the problem of: what ever happened to that damned gun, Ceddie boy?"

Polkinghorne reminded his sergeant that the gun could have flown out of the dead man's hand, when fired - especially since he was not a manual worker - for it could be assumed Wheeler's handgrip was not all that strong.

"Which means that gun must be lurking nearby . . . in the grass or shrubbery."

"I shall be calling this chapter in my autobiography 'The Impossible Suicide', when I write my memoirs." Bassett snarled with frustration.

Pointing irritably towards the littered desk top, he then demanded to know if his assistant had found anything to help them in all that lot?

"No significant entries in his diary and no letters containing even the hint of a veiled threat."

"Oh well: keep at it, Cedric. Nearly lunchtime. I'll give you a hand for ten minutes."

The detective sergeant picked up a waste paper basket and unceremoniously emptied this onto a convenient table, then began patiently straightening out scrunched up balls of paper, reading what was written and dropping them back into the wicker basket at his feet.

Halfway through this task, his assistant saw Bassett go rigid.

"Got something?" The detective constable enquired hopefully.

Bassett began frantically scrabbling through the remaining rubbish. An envelope was found, scrutinised, then compared with the sheet of poor quality notepaper.

"Listen to this, Cedric! 'Meet me in the churchyard after you have come away from Knighton's dinner party. Rather urgent. Don't forget to turn up, as you did once before'."

63

"Cheap grey paper and a matching envelope," Polkinghorne observed.

"And nothing like it amongst any of this other junk!"

"Where's it come from, Sarge?"

"Date stamped St Breward, Ceddie."

"Can you make out the date?"

"Day before yesterday . . . and St Breward's only on the other side of the River Camel; a two-mile walk by field and footpath!"

"So it could have been posted by somebody living in St Tudy?"

"Who didn't want his neighbours to know about it," Bassett said grimly, "which chucks out suicide and brings back murder! My head's beginning to buzz. Come on: let's have lunch."

Table Talk . . . Alfresco

Bun and Phipps were lunching alfresco in the lower corner of the rectory lawn, seated in comfortable deck-chairs and shaded by some well-grown fir trees.

Dorothy Nunn and Teresa Lockhart were with them, having 'just dropped in whilst passing', though Phipps was quite unable to imagine where either of their unexpected guests could have possibly been going at an hour when the village shop would have already been closed for lunch.

The first thing each lady had spoken of, once she had received an invitation to stay for lunch and taken a vacant seat, was that afternoon tea party at the Drysdales', which they would be attending later on the same afternoon.

It therefore followed that neither had been going to call at Marsh Cottage - often laughingly referred to as The Peacock Factory - during the midday period.

Which left Phipps presuming they were still worrying about their alibi stories, but she didn't mind because it was so nice to have people dropping in anyway. It made life so much more companionable . . . and one never knew what others might have heard concerning the police investigation!

However, it appeared that her older sister was more concerned about how far she would have to walk, when going down to the Drysdales, for Phipps heard Bun enquiring just exactly where did Millie and Bernard live?

"They always say: 'Bottom of the first hill, on the right, beside the St Mabyn' road. So what would that be . . . Ten minutes?"

65

Dorothy and Teresa both unhesitatingly agreed that anybody could cover the distance from the rectory to Marsh Cottage in that time.

"We'll call for you," Teresa suggested.

"Yes . . . then we can all walk down together," Dorothy Nunn confirmed as she got to her feet and reached over for another cucumber sandwich.

Bun thanked both these ladies for their kind offer adding that, if they were quite sure they wouldn't mind, she would take advantage of their company to help carry down a few bottles of the rectory cook's famous parsnip wine.

"We mentioned the wine to Millie Drysdale, who now wants to have an official tasting ceremony after tea."

"Does parsnip wine mix easily with Victoria sponge sandwich?" Dorothy asked curiously.

"Don't know, old girl. But's it's fast becoming a case of: consume or destroy. Our bottles are beginning to explode!" Bun replied with a sad shake of the head.

Phipps put her own thoughts into words by adding that - in her opinion - life at the rectory had become somewhat akin to living with time-bombs.

Teresa laughed, saying it would be a 'real scream' if their bottles started to go off 'bang' as they were being carried along one of the village approach roads.

"It would certainly shake up all these policemen who have invaded our village, wouldn't it?" She ended.

Poor Dorothy Nunn, of a more timid nature, suggested a programme of defusing - or otherwise making safe - before they set out for the Drysdale's home.

After a period of silence, during which the cucumber sandwiches were cleared, everyone turned their attention towards the fresh strawberry trifle.

Then Phipps restarted conversation by recalling Millie Drysdale's morning visit. "I think she must have discussed everybody of consequence - who could even remotely be affected by Mr Wheeler's death - saying there were a lot of dark horses living in this little village. What do you make of that?"

"Oh you shouldn't take anything Millicent tells you all that seriously," Dorothy Nunn replied nervously. "You'll find out, after you've been here a bit longer . . . "

" . . . that the only people dear Millie does not talk about are Bernard and Millicent Drysdale!" Teresa added drily.

"Does this mean that you think she might deliberately encourage other people into thinking about everyone else's lives; in order to avoid the risk of having to speak about her own activities?" Phipps suggested.

Dorothy responded by saying she had no wish to cast aspersions upon the character of absent friends . . . but Bernard and Millie were people of mystery.

"Rearing a few peacocks for sale can hardly provide an adequate income, yet Bernard never speaks of being in receipt of a service pension - as the Knightons do - nor does he mention having any company directorships."

"I sometimes wonder if Bernard was cashiered," Teresa said.

"Oh really! We've absolutely no grounds for thinking any such thing!" Dorothy Nunn exclaimed.

Phipps smiled inwardly. Dorothy might have spoken with pious emphasis . . . but one could see that she wouldn't mind being proved wrong.

Teresa tossed her head, replying the Drysdales must have got something to hide, or they would be more forthcoming.

"Anyway: Bernard has almost certainly served in somebody's army because Roddy Holbrook says so!" Teresa declared in a most positive manner.

"Why ever should he say that?" Bun asked.

"Because he's in the army himself. And Roddy says that Bernard lets things slip, when he isn't properly on guard: odd words and phrases which are used in the same way as a soldier might express himself," Teresa answered.

"Do you know: I believe Roddy could be right!" Dorothy interrupted with a puzzled frown creasing her face. "I recollect Bernard once using the expression 'spud bashing' when I asked him what Millie was doing."

"Exactly!" Teresa agreed. "We would say: 'peeling potatoes'."

"And Millie does it too: speaks of 'church parade' on Sunday mornings," Phipps added thoughtfully, then felt cross when her sister pointed out these apparent slips of the tongue could just as well be carefully calculated to influence listeners into believing the very opposite.

"What do you mean by that?" Dorothy demanded.

"That Bernard wants to persuade other people - be they friends or merely casual acquaintances - to think he was in the army when all the time he was dodging the column."

Teresa refused to accept this, saying that she took the view Bernard Drysdale was too much of a gentleman to have evaded helping his country in time of war.

Dorothy ruled out the part of a conscientious objector with equal firmness . . . because those sort of men wouldn't have even owned a double-barrelled shotgun - leave alone discharged it when somebody else was exercising dogs in the same field.

Phipps nodded her head, pointing out that there was some truth in Dorothy's opinion because surely conscientious objectors were supposed to be against all forms of violence?

Further argument was prevented by a man's voice calling 'hello' from somewhere near the rectory.

Heads turned, and Phipps saw a black shadow detach itself to begin striding across the lawn. Bun and Phipps stood up, saying it looked as if their curate cousin - young Crispian - had just arrived back from Truro.

The Reverend Crispian Hyde told them to carry on with their alfresco luncheon. He could fetch another deck-chair from the summer house, and he had already made his presence known in the kitchen . . . so food would arrive shortly.

When he joined the party beneath the fir trees, Crispian reported that his wife, Joan, was making satisfactory progress and the most recent operation had been completed without a hitch.

Five minutes later, Mary came out with his lunch tray and Crispian settled down to eat while his companions recounted all the meagre details relating to Everard Wheeler's death.

This provoked the young curate to observe that if Wheeler had been murdered, the killer had risked his neck to little purpose.

"My rector told me that - when Wheeler learned of his enforced leave of absence - he had said he might not be here when the Reverend Salisbury came back to his parish. Apparently, Mr Wheeler was a very sick man."

"But he's always looked sick and ill," Teresa pointed out.

"A man who has endured a great deal of suffering," Crispian observed. "My rector - old Salisbury - told me Wheeler had picked up a dysentery germ whilst serving in South Africa during the Boer War. Never got rid of it. Went out the epitome of a conquering hero, never heard a shot fired in anger, then found himself being returned on a stretcher."

"Yes, I heard that story too," Dorothy agreed. "Some of the older village people say he wouldn't have lived as long as he did if it hadn't been for one of the landed gentry, getting him a position in a neighbouring estate office . . . so that he need not go back to working in the fields."

Phipps wanted to know how he had managed to become a lawyer. She was told a local solicitor was looking for a clerk and gave Wheeler his articles - together with the business - upon retirement.

Teresa asked Crispian if he supposed Wheeler might have done the decent thing and shot himself. Before the curate could give an opinion, Dorothy broke in to remind them there were four policemen still searching the graveyard.

"Which means they haven't found the gun," Bun suggested.

Phipps was all in favour of looking around the churchyard, after the police gave up, but her sister pointed out the gun would have left in the killer's pocket, if the shooting wasn't suicide.

Crispian, about to sink his teeth into a freshly baked tea-cake, wondered if a squirrel had found the weapon and taken it back to its drey. Dorothy presumed he was mixing up squirrels with magpies while Bun was more to the point, telling her cousin that if he couldn't be more helpful than this, he had better retire to the library and read his Church Times.

Dorothy said she would never believe Wheeler took his own life, for the simple reason that it would be more in his nature to stay around, as long as possible, and make others miserable too.

It was no surprise to Phipps that Teresa concurred, then Bun gave it as her opinion that suicide must surely be considered now that they all knew Wheeler had presumably been aware that he was a dying man.

"Who can say how much he was suffering?" She concluded.

"Mmm. Perhaps the pain became too much," Dorothy agreed.

"So he waited until he'd got several of us together - all known to have quarrelled or threatened him - then shot himself, hoping we'd all be suspected of murder," Teresa murmured thoughtfully.

"Sort of . . . go out with a bit of a 'bang?" Crispian asked.

Bun and Phipps glared at him.

Crispian assured them there had been no pun intended.

Conjecture in the Cornish Arms

Detective Sergeant Bassett, walking past the parish pump once again on his way to lunch had, by then, quite made up his mind there would be an early arrest . . . perhaps one of those people present at Dudley Knighton's dinner table on the previous evening. Or maybe some other local resident whom he had yet to meet. But either way, there had to be a killer lurking about in the St Tudy shrubberies . . . and Bassett was utterly determined to find him.

That discarded note and envelope - which had been retrieved from Wheeler's waste paper basket - seemed to prove this beyond any shadow of reasonable doubt, he thought to himself as he accompanied young Polkinghorne through Churchtown and into the Cornish Arms.

Even making allowances for the fact that people soon knew other people's business in any small Cornish village, not every person could have known Wheeler would be invited to break bread with the Knightons.

Furthermore: killer and victim were obviously well-acquainted; because the caution: 'Don't forget to turn up, as you did once before,' clearly implied there had been other meetings take place in secret.

Which begged the question: why so secretive?

Blackmail seemed the obvious choice. Somebody, who had managed to scrape up a little dirt from Wheeler's past, now putting the bite on this respectable country solicitor who had a foot in nearly every committee room for miles around.

71

Upon entering the pub, the detectives were directed through to where they found their uniformed brethren already tucked away in a small back room. Police matters were forgotten as the constables discussed team prospects for various cricket clubs competing in the local leagues.

Constable Bob Kemp, currently stationed in Lanivet, was asking Reg Harrison, a native of Luckett in East Cornwall, how his old village team was shaping.

"Pretty near bottom of its division, according to what I read in the Cornish Times!" He declared provocatively.

"What can you expect?" Reg Harrison replied. "Don't forget: we played St Buryan - top of the league - last week and Roseveare, our best fast bowler, was off sick with a broken wrist. We didn't stand a chance. Young Steve Bolitho caught out their first batsman, before he'd really got started . . . but the next two ran up 190, Not Out!"

"How are things over your way?" Constable Trethowan asked Ivor Joslin - currently stationed in Bodmin - who played for Lanhydrock.

"Us was over to Tideford for our last match an' it only took three men to chalk up 181 runs in 29 overs."

"What about the opposition?"

"Them Tideford crowd were all out for 162 runs."

Bassett pointed out it might be a different story when Lanhydrock played Callington in a fortnight's time.

"They haven't been beaten once this season! I reckon you'll have your work cut out, boy. I've heard it said that their skipper's pretty well up to county standard. He'll have your wickets fallin' like nine-pins."

Joslin, a slow speaker, replied in his deep countryman's voice that Lanhydrock had a few very useful stonewallers.

"Us'll wear 'em down a bit to shake their confidence, then change to more lively batsmen an' knock up a couple of hundred; you'll see!"

"Saving the best 'til last, eh?" Polkinghorne commented, more to show he was there than out of any real interest, because he spent the cricketing months waiting for the next rugby season.

"Yes. Well . . . 'tisn't all done up front, you. Stayin' power has its place in the scheme of things too. Take that match between Bude and Launceston . . . "

And so it went on all through the meal, with each man speaking knowledgeably, if a trifle inaccurately, about all the other cricket clubs from Saltash - on the Devonshire border - to St Just, near Land's End.

A round of half-pints was brought in by the landlord's wife, after she had cleared all their empty plates, then cigarettes were lit or pipes filled.

Cricket being exhausted, the younger constables began discussing some of the village girls they had met in the course of their work . . . and with whom they wouldn't have minded a roll in the hay.

Older married men sat silent, remembering past encounters of a similar nature . . . and the end result: twenty years spent with an overweight, pasty-fed wife who had long ago lost all shape and physical attraction.

Bob Kemp slyly nudged Barry Trethowan muttering, "They'll learn, won't they, boy?"

Barry pulled a long face, sipped his beer whilst considering a suitable reply, then said any of they there youngsters could have a roll in the hay with his missus any time they liked.

He grinned roguishly.

"I'd be glad fer some young feller t' take 'er off me 'ands."

When that subject was exhausted and the younger men fell silent, Bassett and the more senior constables began chatting about variations in the quality and amenities of police married quarters.

Kemp recalled that the handiest billet he'd ever occupied was a large, semi-detached house - number 11A Berkeley Vale - when he had been stationed in Falmouth.

"Just a few yards up the street from the station, with Kimberley Park for the children to play in, not more than five minutes further on up the road."

"But the station's down by the docks, isn't it?" One man asked.

Kemp retorted he was thinking of the police station, not trains.

Eventually, Detective Sergeant Bassett looked at his watch, then glanced around the room.

"Well, come on lads," he called to make himself heard above the noise of idle chatter. "This won't buy the baby a new bonnet! Best finish up your ale, get back to the graveyard and cut a bit more grass for the rector. Last bus for Bodmin goes through the village at four, so you've got less than three hours to find what we're looking for."

Constable Joslin mumbled slowly that - from what he had seen today - there were two persons present who didn't appear to be spending such a great deal of their own time in grubbing around on hands and knees amongst the graves.

Bob Kemp, knocking out his pipe in a large glass ashtray advertising that Guinness was good for him, suggested Ivor must be speaking about the semi-retired folk . . . who no longer wore a uniform, as real policemen continued to do.

Detective Sergeant Thomas Bassett, standing in the doorway which led out through the public bar, turned to observe that he still had a uniform hanging up in his wardrobe.

"And it's got three stripes on the sleeve . . . so let's get on with the job!"

Thoughts of cricket, old wives and merry maidens faded abruptly . . . then Barry Trethowan said talk of Falmouth had reminded him of a very odd case, not unlike their present problem, where some young fellow shot himself but the gun was never found.

"What was that all about, Bob?"

"Before my time, down there, but I was shown the place where it happened: end of the Prince of Wales Pier. They reckoned the gun must have jumped out of this chap's hand - on recoil - and dropped into the river. Divers were brought round from the Dock Company, but they found the mud too deep and had to give up the search without finding anything."

"How did they get on with the Coroner?" Bassett asked.

"Oh they got a suicide verdict, right enough," Barry Trethowan assured his listeners. "There was a note . . . and comparison tests proved it was written by the deceased."

"There's an incident like that in one of the Sherlock Holmes stories," Reg Harrison called out.

When the general laughter had subsided he continued.

"The deceased tied a length of string to the trigger guard of a revolver . . . then shot herself while standing on a bridge over water. A brick - on the other end of her string - pulled the gun clear so that it fell in the water."

This caused another wave of laughter.

"You been doin' a bit of homework, on the sly?" Ivor Joslin laughed mischevously, when the previous hilarity had died down, "Studyin' for promotion to Inspector?"

"You can laugh," Harrison countered without a glimmer of a smile, "but I bet I get a peaked hat before you ever do!"

"Thinking of packing it in, then?" Barry Trethowan enquired innocently.

"No. What makes you say that?" Reg asked suspiciously.

"This reference to a peaked hat . . . thought you might be goin' in for one of they there chauffeuring jobs, boy."

Bassett waited until the following ribaldry had simmered down before observing that he couldn't see how the Sherlock Holmes story fitted into their present circumstances, because they had no marshy ground, stream . . . or even a dung heap near St Tudy churchyard.

"The missing gun could have been thrown clear and dropped into a motorcycle's sidecar," one man suggested.

"Or landed on top of a passing lorry," another laughed.

Bassett pointed out Wheeler's body had been found many feet away from the nearest boundary wall . . . so he was more inclined to blame the midnight fairies.

Polkinghorne reminded everyone of the Guards officer, in trouble with his bookmaker, who took the only way out by shooting himself in an upstairs room . . . yet his service revolver was found on the pavement beneath an open window.

Bassett accepted guns had even been found on the opposite side of the room from where the deceased killed himself, but no amount of recoil could have thrown a gun halfway across the churchyard, so it had to be still buried in the long grass.

"Perhaps Wheeler staggered about for a few minutes, while he was dying," one uniformed constable suggested.

Bassett told him it would have been impossible with a head wound. "You're thinking of body wounds. Some people have been known to crawl a hundred yards before a fatal wound stopped them for good and always, but you wouldn't manage that with a scrambled brain-box . . . so get back to your grass cutting."

Bassett waved his reluctant temporary assistants goodbye, then led Cedric Polkinghorne away in another direction, remarking that they needed more background information about Wheeler.

"I think it's time for us to interview Lady Mary."

Wheeler's Wild Oat

Bun and Phipps, together with several friends, heard all about Lady Mary Holbrook's interview with the detectives, during tea-time chatter at the Drysdale's cottage.

Dorothy Nunn and Teresa Lockhart had called in at the rectory, as promised over lunch, then accompanied Bun and Phipps along the St Mabyn road . . . each gingerly carrying a bottle of the cook's highly volatile parsnip wine discreetly concealed from village eyes in a small shopping bag.

It had been another gloriously hot, sunny day with never a cloud in sight and despite trees casting shade, everyone found the air too close and humid for their walk to be enjoyable.

Few birds sang in the hedgerows, cottagers' dogs and cats dozed fitfully in patches of garden shade, with only the rattle and swish of a horse-drawn reaper and binder disturbing the uneasy peace as a farmer cut his corn in a nearby field.

Then the village children had been let out of school. Their excited shouts and screams carried down the road, though few actually walked in the same direction.

But as the party from the rectory began descending the hill leading to Marsh Cottage, they were overtaken by a farmer's wife driving a governess-cart. She had obviously been up to the shop, and collected several of her neighbours' children from outside the village school, on her way home.

These young passengers sat facing each other on the two side seats of this ancient vehicle, all shouting and waving merrily as the pony jogged past.

"We had one like that in our late father's time at Warningfield," Phipps said wistfully.

"A parish in Sussex," Bun explained to Dorothy and Teresa, "but we never kept a pony once our parents retired to the house on Brighton sea-front. I still miss old Molly."

Phipps shook her head regretfully.

"Having grown up in Victoria's reign," she reminded her two friends who lived in St Tudy, "we find it quite impossible to cultivate a liking for the modern motor car."

"My sister calls me a horse and carriage person," Bun added with a wry smile, "and I suppose I am."

Bun went on to say that the smell of a sweating horse appeared to do no one any harm . . . whereas car exhaust fumes caught at the back of the throat, causing a dry mouth and a nasty cough.

Dorothy agreed with this, drawing their attention to the fact that their clean country air was none the worse for a pony having just passed by. But - if Mrs Trevillion had been driving a car - the smell of its exhaust would have hung about for ages on such a windless day.

Proof of this came a few minutes later, when Lady Mary Holbrook was driven past in Dudley Knighton's station wagon. Dorothy said, "Phew!" waving her hand in front of her nose afterwards.

But Teresa was more practical, pointing out that Dudley really needed his vehicle for carrying all those boxes of day old chicks into local towns, or out to their nearest railway station.

"He could still use a horse and trap," Dorothy commented.

"But it would take him all day to cover a quarter of the distance," Teresa replied.

Bun scowled, as she grumbled that people were all in far too much hurry in the mid-1930s.

"When Mama drove around the parish in her governess-cart we had time to call a greeting to neighbours as we passed . . . admire the flowers in their cottage gardens or pull up to pick nuts or blackberries from the hedgerows. Ever since the nineteen-twenties it's been a case of: why stick to four miles an hour when you can buy a motor car and travel at forty . . . or even worse!"

Dorothy nodded in agreement, saying everything must surely go by in a dizzy blur.

Phipps, knowing her older sister could be a bit of a bore when she fastened onto this controversy of horse versus motor, drew her companions' attention to overhanging hazel branches, growing along the top of a nearby hedgerow, and wondered if this display of partly-formed nut clusters indicated that there would be a good crop for picking during the coming autumn.

Teresa shook her head, remarking that she thought the squirrels always got there first, because she never found a sound kernel in anything picked up from roadside verges.

This provoked Dorothy into recalling how her family enjoyed collecting real walnuts, scattered over her uncle's lawn from a central tree of indeterminate age, when she was a girl.

Then everyone spoke of the enjoyment in gathering sweet chestnuts from the edges of local woodlands, then carrying the spoils home to roast over an open fire on winter evenings, until they reached the bottom of the hill.

They found Bernard Drysdale standing outside his front gate, waiting to greet them, when they reached Marsh Cottage, calling to them not to shake up the wine.

Phipps hastened to assure him there was no sediment in the bottles. Bernard replied it wasn't the state of the wine that worried him . . . so much as the effect sudden explosions would have on his peacocks.

"They'll all take to the woods and we shan't see a single bird for days."

He held the gate open for his guests to enter, saying, "And just in case you have not heard the latest news - concerning the Wheeler shooting - Lady Mary has been entertaining the Bodmin 'Flying Squad'. So she can't wait to tell us all about it."

But as Lady Holbrook explained, when everyone was seated and cups of tea had been passed round, there wasn't much fresh information available even though she'd had the two detectives asking questions for over an hour.

"They wanted to know all about Wheeler's background: family, army service, schools, jobs . . . that sort of thing."

Millicent Drysdale took advantage of her friend's pause to drink some tea, by offering round a large plate of freshly made cucumber sandwiches.

Suddenly, and without the slightest warning, one of the peacocks gave its shrill piercing shriek of 'Pe-haun Pe-haun' right outside the drawing-room window.

Teresa jumped, dropping her sandwiches onto the carpet but Millicent, who was quite used to such discordant outbursts, took little notice.

"I don't know how you manage to get a decent night's sleep, with brutes like that liable to shatter the peace at any moment," Dorothy Nunn muttered with a shake of the head.

"One gets used to the birds," Bernard replied with a shrug, "but they don't have much to say for themselves after lights out. I think they need their beauty sleep just as much as we do."

'There!' Phipps silently told herself. 'Just as Teresa tried to explain it when we were having lunch, earlier today. Lights out! A typical soldier's expression. He must have been in the army!'

Meanwhile, Bernard Drysdale - oblivious of this character analysis by one of his guests - was telling everyone the birds did not make their screeching noise throughout the year.

"Only in the mating season. What you heard, just now, would have been one of our adult males calling to his wives!"

"Wives . . . plural?" Bun asked with raised eyebrows.

"Oh yes," Millicent agreed. "They each need at least five, you know . . . "

" . . . very energetic in the mating season!" Bernard added with a sagacious nod of the head.

Phipps thought Dudley Knighton coloured slightly on hearing this remark, but he quickly turned the subject by asking Lady Mary to continue with her story of the police interview.

The younger Miss Hyde was left wondering if their retired lieutenant-commander was also very energetic during the mating season, as she turned to listen when Lady Mary began speaking.

"Of course, having regard to my present age - which I absolutely refuse to disclose - you'll realise I knew Wheeler when he was a boy." She paused to sip more tea.

80

"The family were poor: eight children, all as thin as weeds, though not half as hardy." Lady Mary continued, "And I seem to remember them dying off during the winter months. Their father was a thatcher. Quite good money when he had work . . . but one cannot thatch in a gale of wind or driving rain, so there were hard times when his entire family existed only one mouthful away from total starvation."

Dudley Knighton suggested this could account, to a great extent, for Wheeler's miserable nature in later life.

"Yes, but his mother had a lot to answer for, too. When she was ready to leave school, she had been kept on as an unqualified assistant. It was a widespread practice, amongst small village schools, before the turn of the century. Governing bodies liked this system because it enabled them to keep staff salary costs at an absolute minimum . . . "

" . . . while the young girls saw it as a cut above domestic service," Bun agreed with the speaker. "We saw the same sort of thing in our late father's parish, back in Sussex."

"Heather Lamb, dear," Phipps recalled aloud.

"Yes. A sickly child . . . but very bright," Bun continued. "Taught the five and six-year olds for many years."

"But the scarlet fever got her in the end," Phipps added.

"Just as well," her sister ended with a shrug. "Not at all fit for breeding purposes."

Lady Mary gave it as her opinion that the same could have been said of the late Mr Wheeler.

"Curiously enough, he became an assistant when it was time for him to join his contemporaries, bird-scaring in the corn fields."

"So he was brought up with ideas above his station?" Dudley suggested. "Used to see it in the navy . . . a bright ordinary seaman who thought himself a cut above the common crew. Usually transferring to the catering branch when opportunity presented him with a vacancy."

Lady Mary nodded, "Everard Wheeler to a 'T'! By the time he was twenty he hardly spoke to those of his own age who were still living in St Tudy . . . and they returned his indifference by ignoring him."

"Poor Mr Wheeler," Phipps murmured, "Loving no one and nobody to love him. How on earth did he become a solicitor?"

"Ah! A long story. I'll have a slice of your delicious Victoria sandwich, if I may, Millie dear."

When she had finished eating and teacups had been refilled, Lady Mary continued by saying it all went back to 1899 and the start of the Boer War.

Young Everard, by then twenty-two, went off to join one of the Yeomanry regiments, going out to South Africa as a would-be conquering hero . . . and being brought home on a stretcher a few months later.

"Was he seriously wounded," Phipps enquired sympathetically.

"Not a scratch. Never even fired his rifle. Caught dysentery."

Bernard shook his head, commenting that was the story of all recent wars since Florence Nightingale went out to Scutari.

"We always lost more men to fever than enemy shot or shell."

Dudley reminded the company there were two kinds of dysentery and it sounded as if Wheeler had picked up the more virulent variety, which would explain his emaciated appearance.

"No doubt about it," Lady Mary agreed. "And if it hadn't been for one of the County families getting him a job in a friend's estate office I dare say Wheeler would have simply died off."

Phipps said their cousin, Crispian, had told them about that.

"But I doubt he mentioned how Wheeler came to leave his office job, less than two years later!"

"A solicitor, looking for a bright young clerk?" Bun suggested.

"Hah! That's all most people know . . . but somewhere there's a Wheeler Minor!"

All heads turned to stare at Lady Mary, some bottom jaws hanging slightly lower than usual. And all remained silent.

"Louisa and I were close friends; used to go riding together. All her sisters were much older and married, so I was her only confidant. It was an era when 'Mothers and Fathers' was a game played in the nursery - with dolls - then forgotten. Neither of us had the slightest idea of what happened on one's wedding night until Wheeler gave Louisa a course of practical instruction."

"So you received a blow-by-blow account?" Millicent prompted.

"More or less . . . but to give credit where it was due: I found Louisa much more easy to understand than those books on sexual matters, written by people such as Doctor Marie Stopes."

"Oh her!" exclaimed Dorothy Nunn, throwing her hands in the air. "Didn't you know she was a specialist on fossil plants and coal-mining? Took her PhD at Munich, becoming the first female science lecturer at Manchester in 1904. Nothing to do with medicine at all!"

"And yet she wrote all those books," Phipps mused.

"Have you read any?" her sister enquired, looking askance.

Phipps coloured up, snapping, "Of course not. You know Mama's views about That Sort Of Thing: if the Bible was sufficient for all her needs, it would serve us equally well."

"Never mind all that," Teresa broke in. "What about the baby?"

"Adopted. Present whereabouts unknown. Would be difficult to trace by now. I gathered it had been farmed out to a retired lady's maid . . . somewhere up-country."

"Boy or girl?" Dorothy Nunn asked.

Lady Mary said she thought it had been a boy.

"That would make him thirty-one or thirty-two, by now," she mumured thoughtfully. "Good God! How time flies! Anyway: that's the truth of the matter . . . as passed on to our pair of detectives. The family he was working for used their influence to place Wheeler with a solicitor at some distance from their home, and the rest of his life is generally fairly well-known."

"Little respect for anyone and always out to make money," Dudley Knighton observed.

"Certainly explains his miserable nature," Bernard added. "A man who lived his life desperately trying to get away from one layer of society . . . but always being refused entry to the world of those above his own pre-ordained station."

Others nodded wisely, saying Wheeler had obviously gone through life bearing an oversized chip on his narrow shoulder.

Lady Mary agreed, but argued he should have been more grateful. "Even when he got poor Louisa into trouble - and could have been thrown out on his ear - her family took care to get him safely settled in another position . . . "

" . . . which, in the end, turned out better than he could have ever predicted," Millicent suggested.

Dudley shook his head, saying chaps like Wheeler were so bitter and twisted that they even resented ultimate good fortune, simply because they've had to struggle so hard, and for so long, before they got it.

Bun wondered if Wheeler Minor had turned out the same; and visited St Tudy to vent his spite on his father.

But Phipps reminded her sister of what Crispian had told them, concerning Wheeler's health.

"Oh yes," Bun looked around to see if anyone else knew what she was going to say. "The story goes that Wheeler told your rector he hadn't got long to live. Made us wonder if he committed suicide, rather than face more pain and suffering."

Bernard glanced at the clock and said, "To Hell with Everard Wheeler . . . let's get to grips with the parsnip wine!"

Plotting and Planning at Pope's

Polkinghorne and Bassett were drinking their afternoon tea
with Constable Pope, who had finally returned from Camelford
Magistrates Court during the afternoon . . . and all agreed that
one could talk about the late Everard Wheeler 'til the cows came
home for milking, without the slightest chance of reaching any
useful conclusion.

Bassett had promptly told Pope of the mysterious letter found
amongst the waste paper in Wheeler's study, then asked the
village constable to suggest any likely blackmailer, currently
resident in the locality.

Not only was Pope unable to oblige, but he had made matters
more complicated by going further, pointing out things could have
been the other way round.

"Wheeler being the blackmailer?" Bassett asked.

"Why not?" Constable Pope replied with a slight shrug. "After
all: he was a nasty enough bit o' work!"

"Well that's right, Sarge," Polkinghorne concurred. "The way
that letter was worded, could have easily meant the writer was
short of cash and wanted more time in which to meet Wheeler's
demands."

The parlour door opened and Mrs Pope came in with more hot
water for the tea-pot. A rich odour of cooking meat wafted
through from the kitchen. Bassett said something smelt good and
asked what the Popes were having for their tea.

"A nice bit o' stewing steak, Sergeant. An' you're both welcome
to stay an' 'ave some, if you like."

The village constable's wife topped up the teapot, then added that her ole man had picked it up in Camelford, after coming out of court, so it was fresh today.

Bassett thanked her, but refused the kind offer by saying that, since there was nothing pressing him at the moment, he was not expecting to work late on his first day in St Tudy.

After she had gone back to her cooking pots, he returned to possible reasons for that churchyard assignation, wondering if it could have been some sort of shady land deal.

"Along the lines of: Jack wants to buy Bill's farm without Charlie getting wind of it, because he'd want it too . . . and competition would raise the asking price?" Pope asked.

"Too theatrical!" Polkinghorne butted in.

"What d'you mean by that, Ceddie?"

"Well . . . anyone concerned with a land deal could make arrangements to meet in normal daytime hours. They wouldn't mess about sneaking into the village graveyard, just before all the family ghosts came out to work the nightshift, Sarge."

After a short pause, to recover from this negative comment, Bassett grumbled that he supposed the letter could have been sent by a village comedian, as a hoax . . . which would explain why it had been screwed up and thrown away.

Polkinghorne accepted this, adding that people usually kept letters at least a few days following receipt, whereas it appeared this particular letter, found in the waste basket, had been thrown there on the same day as it was delivered to the deceased, according to the date on the postmark.

Pope, returning to the possibility that it had been genuine, said the writer couldn't have known what time Wheeler was going to leave Dudley Knighton's dinner party.

"What's that got do with things?" Bassett asked abruptly.

The village constable replied nobody would want to perch themselves on a gravestone - for hours - waiting about in the middle of the night . . . which could have happened if the writer didn't know when the victim would be free to join him.

Bassett thought this over in morose silence, as he consumed a couple more ginger nuts, swilled down with a gulp of tea.

86

Then he nodded to himself as if reaching a conclusion and reminded the other two men of that phrase: 'Don't forget to turn up, as you did once before'.

"In my view - and you may feel free to disagree - this clearly implied at least one previous meeting had taken place."

"Meaning: the letter-writer could have taken it for granted that Wheeler would have turned up at the same time as on the previous occasion?" Polkinghorne asked.

Pope took this reasoning a stage further.

"They could have been using the churchyard for regular meetings . . . in which case it wouldn't have been necessary to mention time. After all: we only know the deceased failed to turn up 'once before'. So what about all the other occasions when he did turn up?"

"Regular meetings could imply making regular payments," Bassett mused aloud.

"Some sort of maintenance . . . like a 'kept woman', Sarge?"

"Not a bloke in Wheeler's position, Ceddie boy. He'd have a bank account . . . so he could have made payments by standing order."

"'Course: there wasn't any mention of money in that letter, was there?" Pope mused aloud.

"Meaning it could have been nothing more than a lovers meeting?" Bassett suggested with a bellow of laughter.

A child's head peered around the edge of the parlour door, to see who was making all this noise. Constable Pope told her to go and play at Auntie Nell's 'til tea-time . . . and take her brother and sister along, too.

When the door closed, Bassett said he couldn't picture the late Everard Wheeler caring for anyone in that way. According to Lady Mary, he was always too busy looking out for his own ends.

"But folk only speak of how he's behaved in recent years," Pope reminded the detectives.

"Meaning there once was a time when he was young and fancy-free?" Bassett asked sceptically.

"According to Lady Mary Holbrook, he sowed a few wild oats shortly after coming home from South Africa," Polkinghorne said.

"Probably hoping to marry into one of the landed families."

"But this makes my very point, Sergeant," Pope asserted.

"That - having once indulged his lascivious passion - he found he'd acquired a taste for sins of the flesh . . . and proceeded to gallop around all the neighbouring parishes as fast as his legs would carry him, giving a repeat performance whenever opportunity offered?" Bassett suggested.

"Well . . . at least once more," Pope reasoned. "Then, perhaps they lost touch."

"The little runt wouldn't marry her . . . so she got hitched to the next best thing when she knew she was going to have Wheeler's child?" the detective sergeant hypothesized.

"And the newly-weds moved away. Chummy could have been a bank clerk . . . " Pope replied.

" . . . or a civil servant," Polkinghorne chipped in, "posted to somewhere up north, on being promoted."

"All of which leaves me wondering why this lost love suddenly reappears in St Tudy," Bassett commented.

"Fallen on hard times," Pope replied. "Then came back to Cornwall, intending to ask Wheeler for help . . . either by way of money, or perhaps she only wanted rent-free accommodation, in which to spend her declining years."

"Which could happen, if hubby's kicked the bucket, Sarge"

"But what about his civil service pension, Ceddie?"

Polkinghorne shrugged helplessly, going on to suggest the poor woman's husband might have got the sack for some reason or other . . . then committed suicide. In which case there wouldn't be any pension.

Bassett accepted this possibility, but went on to remind the other two men that Lady Mary Holbrook had made mention of an illigitimate child - probably a boy - who is presumed to have been delivered up-country, somewhere in Bedfordshire, and brought up by foster parents.

"According to Lady Mary, that lad would be in his early thirties by now, Sarge," Polkinghorne cut in quickly to prove he could count.

"Exactly. Now suppose he found out about his parentage . . . ?"

"How could he do that?" Polkinghorne asked.

Pope thought the foster parents could have told him, when he was old enough, speaking of mysterious estates and a family of land-owners living somewhere in the West of England.

"But how would he find them?" Polkinghorne wanted to know.

"Servant talk?" Bassett suggested.

"Not in those days," Pope objected. "The foster parents would have been too scared of losing their maintenance money. You've got to remember: they weren't just being paid to feed and clothe the boy. They were being paid to keep their traps shut, too."

"Country folk can be very close, when it suits them," Polkinghorne added. "I reckon nobody, up in Bedfordshire, would have ever heard St Tudy mentioned, leave alone the actual name of the real mother's family . . . and they certainly wouldn't have heard of our Mr Wheeler."

"Which means it would take a blinkin' miracle for this kid to make any connection," Bassett grumbled. "Oh well . . . perhaps the Bedfordshire county force will be able to turn up something, if we ask nicely. Job for you, first thing tomorrow morning, Cedric."

The detective sergeant hefted their teapot, decided he could squeeze another cup, and poured out. After taking a couple of gulps, he suggested a change of subject and began discussing where all Knighton's dinner guests reckoned they were when the fatal shot was fired.

"For instance: have you noticed how many of those gentlefolk appear to depend upon the two Hyde sisters for an alibi?"

Polkinghorne replied that the more he thought about it, the less he liked it.

"Something fishy there, Sarge. And didn't you notice how the older woman prompted the younger one, when we enquired about the order in which the guests departed?"

"Yes, I did . . . and that's the pair Eddie Lipscombe and I crossed swords with - over that business in Polperro - not so many moons ago."

"Something to do with a one-legged tramp, wasn't it?"

Bassett gritted his teeth at the memory.

"Yes. And I'll thank you not to remind me of that experience again . . . or it will seriously jeopardise your chances of promotion for at least a hundred years. Now, as to the present: two things bother me: those sisters are almost inseparable . . . so why did one stay behind with the Knightons, when the other walked back to the rectory? And why did that other lot spend the next couple of hours chatting in the rectory when they'd already spent the earlier part of the evening together?"

"Think it's a put up job? Somebody saying they were in one place . . . when all the time they were somewhere else?"

"Something like that, Ceddie boy."

"So it's back to the rectory?"

"Not just yet. Let's be crafty. We'll find it easier to break a single person's alibi, if it isn't true, so let's try our luck with Miss Dorothy Nunn . . . take a chance: tell her she's been observed leaving the churchyard at 11.0 pm and see what happens."

A Vital Clue is Missed

The detectives were aware of something being very much amiss as soon as they passed the Old Clink. Polkinghorne recognised Lieutenant-Commander Knighton's station-wagon as soon as they had turned the corner.

Two wheels rested upon the grass verge, while the others remained on tarmac below the churchyard wall and opposite the parish pump. Bassett glanced inside, saw it was empty and walked on, remarking that - for a naval man - the owner had not done a very good job of berthing his command.

"If he'd parked a warship like that it would have been considered a total constructive loss!"

Polkinghorne presumed his sergeant meant to imply that, in nautical terms, the lieutenant-commander had run halfway up the beach before dropping anchor. He shrugged, agreed it was a funny way to park a car and the two policemen continued in the direction of Miss Dorothy Nunn's cottage.

They discovered 'Sweet Lavender' facing them from the back of a hollow square. This was located just beyond a side road, which took one past the village shop and up to the front door of the Cornish Arms.

A housewife stood in a neighbouring doorway, staring at the tiny two-up-and-two-down cottage, from which raised voices could be heard echoing around the square.

The heavy scent of roses, climbing over a porch on one side of their approach, was momentarily contaminated by the fishy odour of kippers being cooked for somebody else's tea.

Giggling children ducked into their homes, as the two strangers approached, and a cat watched with narrowed eyes when Bassett reached Sweet Lavender's wide open front door. The detective sergeant reached out a hand and rattled the brightly shining brass knocker.

Polkinghorne, now hearing hysterical shrieks of laughter coming from within the building, regarded his boss with an expression of dumb amazement.

"An odd time to have a party . . . with death in the village," he observed.

"Given our victim's miserable reputation, I should think it very likely that some of the residents are celebrating his demise," Bassett replied with a grin.

No one came forward to answer their summons.

Polkinghorne laughed out loud when his sergeant shouted, "Is anyone at home?" Surely: it wasn't so much a case of one person being in occupation . . . as how many?

Then the waiting policemen heard a loud, imperious female voice calling for silence, because she thought she had heard knocking.

This apparently caused fresh shrieks of laughter, which were followed by a more strident female calling, "If it's a ghost . . . tell him to come right in!"

The first speaker replied, "Good idea. Who knows, my dears? He might have a message from Sir Percival. My late husband always declared he'd get in touch once he'd passed over . . . to the Other Side."

Staring past his sergeant's body - which was almost blocking any view of the interior - Polkinghorne watched the figure of a man slowly appear.

To his amazement, the detective constable identified a very unsteady Lieutenant-Commander Knighton. He was seen to lurch in the direction of the doorway with a rolling gait, as if still at sea upon a ship which was proceeding on its course with a heavy list to starboard.

The retired naval officer straightened his back when he recognised the two callers.

"'Wine is a mocker'," he quoted in slurring tones, while continuing to advance by steadying himself with outstretched hands pushing firmly against the cottage walls. "'Strong drink is raging: and whosoever is deceived thereby is not wise'!"

Knighton tripped, thrust one hand forward and succeeded in grabbing the nearby door-post, then clung to it as he got his breath back.

Eventually, looking earnestly at Bassett, he declared, "Many's the time I've used that text at Sunday Divisions . . . but you know: it never did a blind bit of good! Half the crew would always have to be loaded back aboard in a cargo sling after their next run ashore."

Bassett explained his own presence by saying he would like to have a quick word with Miss Nunn, if that was convenient.

"No question of convenience - dear old detective wallah - but more a case of downright impossibility."

Knighton lowered his voice to a more confidential level before adding, "The lady has looked too long at the wine when it was red, as they put it in Proverbs if I'm remembering rightly, and 'encountered its serpent's sting'!"

"Slightly inebriated, sir?"

"Drunk as a fiddler's bitch!"

"Hmmm. Wouldn't be much use trying to conduct an interview, then," Bassett observed.

His informant replied that Miss Nunn was still conscious and able to speak . . . but her intelligence appeared to be suffering from a temporary impairment.

"Difficult to understand what she says, sir?"

"Spouting a load of pure gobbledegook! Doesn't even know where she is. We had to bring her home in the car. Still able to walk, at first, but we should have had to borrow the blacksmith's wheelbarrow if we'd been five minutes later in reaching the parish pump."

"May one ask what you've all been drinking . . . at five o'clock in the afternoon?" Bassett enquired curiously.

"Parsnip wine, lovingly created by dear old Mrs Gregory, the rectory cook. Goes down smooth as silk!"

He paused to hiccup, took a deep breath and continued by saying that there was a sting in the tail.

"It's got a kick like the recoil from a six-inch gun about two minutes later. Absolutely deadly! Poor Dorothy Nunn fell in the fourth round."

Polkinghorne glanced thoughtfully at his watch. Almost another hour before pub-opening-time . . . yet the upper class were pie-eyed and staggering. A example of one law for the poor, but a more flexible ruling for their elders and betters.

The detective studied Knighton's left hand. Its muscles were white with strain, and veins stood up like whipcord, as he held grimly onto that door-post.

Good God! Thought Bassett. The man is hardly able to stand and would probably fall flat on his face if he lost his grip on the cottage woodwork.

The detective sergeant hastily drew back a step, saying he would look in again tomorrow.

Lieutenant-Commander Knighton advised an afternoon call.

Bassett agreed.

He nodded abruptly and turned away, then had second thoughts. "I see you left your station-wagon opposite the parish pump. Might be the cause of an accident . . . with its rear portion jutting out like that. Do you mind if I park it a bit nearer the side of the bus shelter, sir?"

Lieutenant-Commander Knighton told Bassett - in most pleasant tones - that the dear old sergeant could stick the jolly old motor on top of the nearest chestnut tree, for all he cared.

Then the speaker appeared to sag - as if this final effort had totally exhausted all his available strength - took a deep breath, and wobbled away towards the rear of the cottage . . . tottering from side to side as if walking down the corridor of an express train as it crossed points to enter Reading railway station.

The detectives retraced their steps, Bassett muttering that they wouldn't get much sense out of anyone tonight, then pushed the station-wagon into safety beneath the chestnut tree.

Just as they were straightening their backs, the staccato roar of a motorcycle engine was heard approaching the village.

Bassett turned his head in the direction of a road junction - out of sight - beyond Churchtown Cottages.

A heavy, black machine being ridden by a slim, youngish man rounded the nearest corner to take the St Mabyn road.

As it passed, Bassett's jaw dropped open in utter astonishment.

The pillion rider, clinging on with one hand, raised the other to give the detectives a cheery wave . . . at the same time shrieking, "Yippeeeee!" at the top of her voice.

Within seconds this swiftly moving spectacle had passed out of sight, round a bend in the road, just beyond the Old Clink.

"Gawd! Anyone would think it was carnival time," Bassett muttered, still hardly able to believe the evidence of his own eyes.

"I suppose that was Miss Philippa Hyde . . . on the pillion?"

"Riding side-saddle, Cedric? Yes, I suppose so . . . another example of what can happen from drinking too much parsnip wine at tea-time."

"At least it proves she's a lady, Sarge."

Bassett agreed, while pointing out that Phipps appeared to have been riding past on some sort of cut-down park seat, similar to those put out in council gardens for audiences at brass band concerts, rather than something originally designed to be strapped across a horse's back.

"Nice of her to give us a wave, though," Polkinghorne said.

"And you waved back . . . whilst on duty!"

"Well, it don't hurt to be friendly, Sarge."

"I wonder if garden seats constitute a danger to the public, when temporarily affixed to a motorcycle frame?" Bassett mused.

Polkinghorne was spared the problem of answering because a flatbed lorry - fully laden with empty milk churns kept in place by a low chain supported on several iron posts - came into the village from the direction of either Bodmin or Camelford; depending which way one turned at the Methodist church.

The driver stopped in front of the detectives.

A window was wound down, then his head poked out.

Bassett looked up questioningly at the thin-faced creature with sunken cheeks, a sharp pointed nose and ferret eyes; wincing at the sight of a half-smoked cigarette dangling from the lower lip.

"'Ere! 'Ow long're you goin' ter be stuck there, like that?"

Bassett gestured towards Lieutenant-Commander Knighton's shooting-brake.

"Talking about this?" He snapped by way of a reply.

"Well I ain't talking about the Lord Mayor's coach an' four."

"Not ours, chum!" Bassett riposted.

"Well . . . can't you get somebody to move it?"

"Don't see why," Bassett replied.

"Because I parks me lorry there each night! That dang'd car's in my place!"

Bassett strolled casually across to the lorry, introduced himself, then enquired if he was speaking to Mr Eric Smitheram.

"That's wot me mother called me . . . an' she orter know, if anyone did. What d'you want with me?"

Bassett explained about a complaint he had received from the landlord of the Cornish Arms, earlier in the day, without mentioning the party by name. He told Eric that people were saying he disturbed their sleep each morning, when he started on his milk collection round, and asked if he could park his vehicle a bit further away from the village centre.

Eric Smitheram shrugged his skinny shoulders.

"Wouldn't do much good."

His cigarette bobbed up and down in time to the words.

"Why not?" Bassett asked.

"I goes out on the St Mabyn road an' there's nowhere to park out there. An' I gotta git off the road, if I'm staying all night, or I'll need lights on."

Smitheram shook his head.

"Can't 'ave that, Mate! Me battery would be flat in no time an' I'd kick up a darn'd sight more noise if I 'ad to crank up the ole girl by 'and."

Polkinghorne smiled to himself. His well-fed, somewhat over-weight sergeant would make three of this skinny lorry driver. It was impossible for the detective constable to picture them as ever being 'mates'.

He left Bassett to argue the toss with Smitheram and began wandering around the lorry, rattling chains and stanchions.

These held the milk churns in place, so it might pay to see if anything was loose. Then the detective constable looked at the tyres. All had plenty of tread and there were no deep cuts visible in the side-walls. Probably well-maintained, since it was a commercial fleet vehicle, he told himself.

About to turn away, he noticed a short length of thin, brown cord trailing out from the underside, at the rear. Polkinghorne knelt down to look closer and saw that the other end passed through a hole in the steel chassis, where it had been tied in place with a typical 'granny knot'.

Village kids up to some sort of a trick, he thought to himself.

He took out his penknife, cutting the cord but leaving the last eight or nine inches still in place because he couldn't reach that far. The severed length of cord was then screwed up into a ball and tossed over the churchyard wall.

"Damned if I'm going to crawl in any further," he muttered to himself. "So long as nobody's going to get their foot caught in the free end . . . that's good enough for me."

A young boy came out from the back gate of a cottage near the blacksmith's shop. He carried an enamel jug and mooched across to the parish pump for water. Polkinghorne strolled over to ask if he - or one of his mates - had been amusing themselves by tying pieces of string to Mr Smitheram's milk lorry.

The boy shook his head, denying all knowledge.

The detective constable said "Hmmm" in his most ominous manner, then returned to Bassett in time to hear the last part of the conversation about overnight parking.

Bassett said, "Oh well, so long as I've told you - and you knows what people are thinking - I've done me job. If you want the station-wagon moved: I suggest you get down and help push."

Eric Smitheram grumbled, switched off his engine and joined the two detectives. They shunted the smaller vehicle onto the road, then backed it up against the front of the bus shelter, on the other side of the chestnut tree.

All three men parted amicably, Bassett and Polkinghorne strolling round to where they had left their own car and driving home to Bodmin.

During the first part of this journey, Polkinghorne mentioned the brown cord found tied to Smitheram's lorry, suggesting it might have been a bit of fishing line.

"Well: there you are then . . . some of the local kids out to make trouble for Eric. No wonder half St Tudy's up in arms about the noise from that milk lorry. I bet those little beggars tied a tin can - or old rusty bucket - on the back of the vehicle."

"And Smitheram wouldn't notice the extra racket, up in his cab," Polkinghorne mused.

"'Course not, Ceddie . . . because he's sitting right over his engine, isn't he? But it would make a Hell of a din on the road. You didn't find a bucket handle on the end of the cord?"

Polkinghorne said no.

"They break off, if the bucket's badly rusted. I know. We used to do the same thing to the village milk float when I was a kid."

Bassett laughed loudly at the memory, assuring his assistant the pony used to pick up speed 'til he was going down the street like a rocket on Guy Fawkes Night.

Polkinghorne regarded his sergeant with silent wonder.

Bassett observed that milk lorries and rusty buckets were no longer their province, then both lapsed into silence.

Bun and Phipps in the Old Graveyard

By comparison with the detectives' mainly silent homeward journey, Miss Philippa Hyde's sudden return to St Tudy rectory was all noise and chatter.

Captain Rodney Holbrook, proceeding in the general direction of St Mabyn, slowed his motorcycle and turned into the rectory drive. He roared straight through the archway leading into the stable yard and skidded to a dramatic halt beside the disused water trough.

Once the engine had been switched off, Phipps distinctly heard sounds of singing coming from the kitchen quarters of the main building.

"Somebody's happy in their work," she observed, assuming it must be Mavis and Mary, their two maids.

Rodney cocked an ear, then his face took on a thoughtful expression.

"Yes . . . but: Christmas carols? In the middle of summer?"

Phipps replied that it was entirely possible the girls believed in practising well before an event was due to take place.

Her older sister's arrival put paid to this theory.

"We'll be having a rather scrappy dinner! Salad, with cheese and biscuits to follow. Sorry about that."

"Oh! What's wrong? Somebody let the fire go out in our kitchen range, dear?"

"No. Mrs Gregory and the maids have been at the parsnip wine, old girl! Told me they thought they ought to have a taste before it was all gone."

"We must have started quite a panic dear . . . by carrying off four bottles, all at one time, when we set out to spend an afternoon with the Drysdales,"

Rodney Holbrook remarked cheerfully that everyone sounded in good voice . . . if a trifle discordant.

"Must be a powerful brew. When do I get my share?"

Bun suggested that he stay to dinner - such as it was - in which case they could feel completely justified in opening yet another bottle.

"But you'd better walk home, afterwards," Phipps advised seriously.

"Yes. Not a bit of good attempting to ride your infernal machine," Bun added. "That parsnip wine is so powerful that it had poor little Dorothy Nunn talking of dancing a St Bernard's Waltz with one of Millicent Drysdale's peacocks after three small glasses, earlier this afternoon."

"But she collapsed halfway through her fourth," Phipps added with a sad smile.

"Quite lost the use of her legs," Bun explained.

"We really thought we should have had to carry her out to Dudley Knighton's station-wagon . . . " Phipps assured Roddy.

" . . . burbling something ridiculous concerning Peter Piper and pecks of pickled pepper!" Bun observed. "I think she was trying to prove she could still speak . . . but the effort wasn't a great success."

Advancing towards Rodney's motorcycle, the elder Miss Hyde declared she hadn't come out to discuss the effects of the rectory cook's parsnip wine upon lesser mortals, but to take a closer look at this enterprising young officer's latest invention . . . the motorised version of a side-saddle.

Rodney Holbrook, immediately full of disarmingly boyish enthusiasm, described how one of the rear seats had been removed from an old horse-drawn cooks' wagon, which his sergeant had discovered, lying derelict, behind one of the Bodmin Light Infantry barrack blocks. A couple of new fixing brackets had been added, then the cut-down seat was securely bolted onto the motorcycle framework.

"As you can see: it looks very similar to a park seat, but I'd say the army uses much stronger steel than your average Hyde Park deck-chair contractor."

Rodney lifted a green canvas belt, saying that nervous passengers could always buckle this across their lap . . . for additional safety whilst the vehicle was in motion.

"But . . . what keeps one on one's seat?" Bun demanded.

"Gravity! Been around since the world began. Entirely dependable . . . according to Isaac Newton."

Bun replied that she failed to recall any mention of it in the Book of Genesis.

Her sister averred that it must have been present, because otherwise poor old Adam would have simply floated off into space within seconds of God having formed his body from 'the dust of the ground'.

Rodney supported this proposition.

Bun gave a disdainful sniff, clearly still bothered by doubt and dismay, asking what would happen if gravity was cancelled out by centrifugal force . . . when cornering at speed.

"I should rather imagine one's passenger could expect to enjoy the electrifying sensation of free flight . . . before landing on top of the nearest hedgerow," Rodney replied airily.

"In which case, young man, kindly find someone - other than my younger sister - for future experiments!" Bun told him.

Phipps hastened to assure them both that she had felt perfectly safe during her three-mile dash around the local lanes . . . but readily conceded her sense of security might have been less had she been completely sober.

"A couple of glasses of Mrs Gregory's mature parsnip wine does far more for one's self-confidence than a similar quantity of Sunday school lemonade. In fact, I think I can safely state: after two bumpers of Chateau Gregory I'd be ready for anything, dear."

"Then we must certainly open another bottle," Bun declared, "because I had it in mind to take a stroll through the graveyard after dinner."

Phipps regarded her elder sister with amazement.

"Looking for clues?" Rodney enquired with a slight smile.

Bun replied that one never knew one's luck if one did not try, then led the way round to their front door saying that, according to Mavis and Mary, the four uniformed policemen had only searched ground close to the spot where Wheeler's body had been found . . . when they weren't hidden away in a back parlour of the Cornish Arms.

"I thought we might cast a wider net, old girl."

Phipps reminded her sister that the church must stand in at least an acre of ground. Surely she did not envisage hunting through all that?

"No. Of course not, Phippsie. But we can take in a wider circle, beyond where the bobbies spent their time cutting grass and generally prodding about. Who knows? We might turn up something under the nearby shrubbery."

"Such as a missing pistol?" Rodney suggested.

"Stranger things have happened," Bun replied.

"'Seek and ye shall find'," Phipps added brightly. "Matthew seven, verse seven . . . if anybody's interested."

Captain Holbrook drily observed they had better tell their guardian angel to have an evening off-duty, in that case.

"Why's that?" Bun enquired.

"Because I seem to recall something from one of the Psalms about being borne up . . . lest you dash your foot against a stone. Seems to me that's the only way you'll find anything in the long grass: by kicking about with your feet."

Bun asked how Rodney could quote so readily - albeit with only partial accuracy - from the Bible.

"Our Padre - up at the barracks - selected that piece for a sermon about team spirit on a recent church parade. It was my turn to read the lesson . . . hence it's rather stuck in the memory. But - with any degree of luck - I shall have forgotten all about it within another fortnight."

Phipps was just about to reply with a suitable passage from Deuteronomy; 'Therefore shall ye lay up these my words in your heart', when they entered the hall.

Then Bun promptly sent their guest off, to wash his face and hands free of roadside dust, in the downstairs cloakroom.

Phipps took the hint and hurried away upstairs to do the same in their bathroom.

"I've had everything laid out on the sideboard, so don't be long," Bun called after them. "It's buffet style: help yourselves, with a large plate of wholemeal bread to fill empty corners."

Conversation, during this meal, centred upon Wheeler's shooting. But it was only an exchange of known facts and personal opinions, with nothing fresh being produced.

When Rodney uncorked the parsnip wine, Phipps exercised caution by restricting herself to one small glass . . . and even this quantity soon brought a warm glow to her cheeks.

Rodney Holbrook sipped, savoured and swallowed.

"Y-e-s-s. Very smooth indeed," he murmured appreciatively.

Bun advised prudence.

Their gallant captain shrugged this to one side, declaring one developed an early immunity when serving with the British Army out East of Aden.

"Believe me . . . once you've got the stomach used to arrack, it's possible to drink anything," he declared with a superior smile, and was on his third glass before the dangers of Mrs Gregory's parsnip wine became apparent.

Phipps giggled as Rodney rolled his eyes, admitting he now saw the point of not riding home on his motorbike.

Bun told him to leave his infernal machine where it was, outside the old coachhouse door for the night, and pick it up on the following morning.

"Yes, that's right," Phipps exclaimed . . . then you can join us for a prowl around the churchyard," she suggested, "and help look for clues."

"Sorry, but I'm unable to oblige," the young captain replied.

"Afraid you might let the side down . . . by falling over the odd gravestone?" Bun enquired drily.

"No. Of course not. I'm steady as a rock," Rodney answered, deliberately lurching from side to side for the fun of the thing. "But facts are: I promised to spend the evening with my mother."

"Hmmm. Well I suppose we hadn't better tempt you away from the line of filial duty," Bun accepted with a wry smile.

"In which case," Rodney continued after a surreptitious glance at his watch, "I suppose I ought to make a move . . . since I have to walk home."

Then he reached for the wine bottle, pointing out with a boyish grin that there was enough remaining for one more round, and began refilling all their glasses.

Once these had been drunk, Bun and Phipps put on hats and gloves, then all three left the rectory to walk up the road, in the direction of the churchyard.

Rodney Holbrook left the two sisters, when they reached the village school, and carried on by way of the road.

Bun and Phipps branched off to enter the silent churchyard through a gate just beyond the schoolroom door.

Tall beech trees drooped long boughs downwards, in places actually sweeping their leaves through the rank grass beneath, while yew and other smaller species of a more upright growth stood as sentinels between the dozens of dark grey, slate tombstones.

Phipps wondered if they had been planted in this manner deliberately . . . to afford one family group privacy from neighbours - with whom they might have quarrelled - during a lifetime's residence in the parish of St Tudy.

She stopped as her sister paused, resting one arm on a memorial to the late Harry Sloggett - died 1870 - and they surveyed the gloomy scene.

"No wonder those policemen gave up their search, old girl."

"Not much light, is there dear?"

"Shouldn't think we'll do any better than the bobbies. Difficult to know where to start, too."

Phipps, giving consideration to the proximity of nearby buildings standing immediately beyond the church land's boundary walls, suggested their unknown murderer would have been unlikely to leave by the gate through which they had just entered.

"My thoughts entirely, old girl. That cottage on the opposite side of the road: anyone about to go to bed - or getting up in the middle of the night for the usual reasons - would have only needed to look out of a front window to see the fellow escaping."

Bun stood still, staring into the distance.

"Same applies to the other gate, Phippsie. One would come straight out beside that bus shelter."

"With cottages all around . . . "

"Quite! Of course: he could have jumped over a wall . . . "

"That one following the curve of the St Mabyn road?"

"Yes . . . then he could have dodged down Tremeer Lane."

Phipps agreed this was the darkest - and least populated - area, but reminded her sister it was also the greatest distance from the scene of the crime. She felt the ground between where they stood, and Town Farm, might have been used as an escape route.

Bun accepted that several well-grown beech trees on the boundary wall would have given good cover.

"What's more: the St Mabyn road is several feet lower than the churchyard - at that point - so our man wouldn't have been seen by anyone on the pavement. Come on, old girl! It's all part of the process of elimination."

A half an hour later, ruefully surveying the damage to stockings, scratches on both legs and some of her hat decoration which was now fluttering from the low branch of a nearby beech tree, Phipps suggested their activities were fast turning into a process of self-destruction.

The breathless sisters leaned against Henry Bone's gravestone, put up in 1882, considering what they should do next. Bun said perhaps they should do the obvious . . .

"Go back to the rectory?" Phipps enquired hopefully.

"No! Take a straight line. Think, Phippsie! You've just shot somebody. What do you do?"

"Get away as quickly as possible, dear?"

"Exactly. Head for the bus shelter!"

They set out, dodging between headstones of Sleemans, Cottells and Billings, with occasional pauses to examine fresh marks where slate had been recently chipped off.

Bun stopped on the churchyard wall, staring across at cottage windows on the opposite side of the road, near the parish pump.

Phipps disconsolately dropped her own gaze, observing that some builder must have had a load of sand delivered recently.

Like a child with nothing better to do, she picked up a small stone and threw it towards the pile. The top grains of sand, by then dried out from lying in the day's hot sunshine, were pushed to one side . . . allowing the stone to sink beneath the surface.

At the same time, this movement caused a small avalanche to occur . . . which revealed part of another, previously buried object, sticking out, further down the side of the sand pile.

Phipps stared . . . transfixed with silent amazement.

Dark metal. Difficult to be certain in the fading light but . . . ?

She bit her lip. It must be! She turned to Bun, murmuring very quietly, "Unless I'm very much mistaken, dear . . . I'd say that looks like the missing gun."

Shooting in the Rectory Library

Miss Anthea Eulalia Hyde glanced downwards, in the direction indicated by her younger sister.

"Odd shape, old girl. If that's the barrel: pointing toward us, I'd say it looks too blunt. About right for colour I suppose, though never having seen a pistol outside of those Hollywood gangster pictures, one can't be sure."

Phipps screwed up eyes and mouth, the better to concentrate, as she dredged the recesses of her memory in an attempt to visualise such weapons as she might have seen described in Leslie Charteris's books about The Saint . . . or those equally exciting Blackshirt thrillers.

"I think you'll find that's something called a snub-nosed automatic, dear," she finally suggested.

"On the other hand . . . it could be a child's water pistol," Bun remarked drily.

"Oh no dear, surely not . . . ?"

"Well I recall watching a couple of boys chasing each other around the lamp posts on an island platform, when our train stopped in Okehampton, on the way down here from Exeter. They had something very similar . . . but kept filling up from the station fire buckets."

"Whatever's down there looks bigger . . . and heavier, too."

"Well don't take my word, old girl. Go and dig it out! Let's have a closer look." Bun shrugged. "If I'm right, and it is a water pistol, perhaps it would do to put on the white elephant stall at our next church bazaar."

"But I'll get my shoes full of sand!"

Bun pointed to a short length of light branch, obviously torn from the chestnut tree, telling her sister to make use of it and hook the mysterious object free.

"Whose sand is it? D'you know?"

Phipps remembered seeing builder's men chipping away at one of the cottage walls, near the back of the blacksmith's shop, earlier in the week and presumed it would be used there.

"Hmmm." Bun grumbled disapprovingly. "Covering up all that lovely old Cornish stonework with modern Portland cement plaster. A great pity, but there you are . . . it can't be much fun living in a damp cottage."

Phipps agreed with this remark, then left her sister contemplating the scene, and walked over to the top of a flight of stone steps beside the Old Clink.

Once she had got down to road level, a couple of minutes spent in scrabbling about with the broken chestnut branch succeeded in bringing the supposed gun within easy reach on her side of the sand heap.

Phipps bent over to pick it up.

As soon as she felt the weight of the object, she was in no doubt whatsoever that she had found the murder weapon. She looked furtively all around to make quite certain there was nobody else within sight then, reassured upon this point, she removed her wide-brimmed straw hat, concealed the gun between this and folds of her summer frock, then rejoined Bun.

"Well . . . ?"

"I think we'd better go back to the rectory, dear."

"So it's the real thing, is it, old girl?"

"Much too heavy for a child's toy . . . and we can't start playing about with it, out here. Somebody may come along and catch us. And you know what village people are like."

"Yes. Always ready to believe the obvious. Probably think one of us shot Wheeler. Anyway: let's have a quick look."

Phipps passed the gun to her sister, shielding it with her hat.

Bun hefted it, nodded abruptly and jerked her head sideways before handing both hat and gun back to her sister.

"No doubt about it, Phippsie. That's a gun . . . whether it's THE GUN remains to be seen, but let's get away from here," she said, leading them back towards the gate near the village school.

As they passed between the headstones, Bun pointed to various chips taken out of their edges, saying that she now realised how this damage had occurred.

"Our man must have run out this way, gun in hand, and knocked against some of these headstones as he stumbled through the long grass."

Phipps asked her sister's opinion about a short length of brown cord, frayed out at one end, which still remained tied to the gun's trigger guard.

"Probably a lanyard . . . the other end looped around the murderer's neck, to prevent him losing the weapon if he fell."

"Yes. Of course. He knew it would be pitch dark, in all probability, so he'd never find it again. But - running away, with the gun still in his hand - the lanyard must have caught around one of the gravestoves . . . and broken with the force of his speed."

Phipps paused thoughtfully before continuing, "If I'm right, dear, someone is walking about at the present moment with a very nasty skin-burn on his neck!"

"Where the cord cut in, before it broke? Yes. We must have a closer look at our friends, over the next day or two."

"But aren't we going to tell the police, dear?"

"Don't think so, Phippsie." Bun gestured towards the gate. They passed through in silence. There was nobody about, walking in the St Mabyn road. Bun reminded her sister of the penalty for murder . . . to be hung by the neck until dead. "Beastly business! Even when you know it's happening to a distant stranger. Utterly unthinkable when a close personal friend might be involved!"

"You mean Dudley Knighton . . . ?"

" . . . or young Roddy Holbrook . . . or Bernard Drysdale!"

"Yes dear. I see what you mean. And I shouldn't want to do anything which could put a rope around one of their necks. I should have nightmares for the rest of my life. Probably wake up every morning in a feverish sweat . . . right on the dot of eight!"

"Execution hour! Quite. Right or wrong doesn't even enter the argument. Being hypothetical: suppose it was Dudley who fired the shot? I dare say he would have had a perfectly sound reason for taking such drastic action."

Phipps nodded. He was ex-navy . . . and an officer too. He would have been well used to considering all possibilities before ordering his men to take any particular course of action. She was sure he would never act rashly, on the spur of the moment. In which case: concealing the murder weapon could be regarded as a life-saving action. No different from giving artificial respiration to a drowning man. Bun was right - as always - and whichever way one regarded Mr Wheeler's death . . . his killer was hardly likely to go out and shoot somebody else in a couple of days time, or even one day next month.

Phipps expressed complete agreement with her sister.

They walked on in silence for a while then Bun remarked that, in her opinion, where an extreme case left one with little alternative to implementing the death penalty, a man ought to be shot . . . by a proper firing squad, in order to lend a measure of dignity to the proceedings.

"No one hangs dogs or horses. They'd be taken to court for cruelty to dumb animals if they did that sort of thing!"

Phipps suggested that it might be extremely difficult to hang a horse - in the middle of a farmer's field - after it had broken a leg while trying to jump a ditch.

"My very point, Phipps!" her sister replied irritably. "When all else fails one gives one's dumb friend a quick bullet . . . so why treat members of one's own species differently?"

She went on to say that, in her opinion, public executioners were a particularly loathsome bunch of creatures. And did Phipps know they had an inalienable right to strip the body of clothing afterwards?

Phipps did not know this, saying she had never possessed a reason for acquainting herself with such facts.

"Oh yes! Take the case of Robert Snooks: robbed the mail between Hemel Hempstead and Berkhamsted at the beginning of the last century."

Phipps intimated that she didn't think she had heard of him.

"Hung at Boxmoor," her sister replied. "Near the scene of his crime to deter others . . . then the hangman began stripping the body when it was all over. Disgusting!"

Phipps agreed, asking her sister how she came to be such an obvious authority on this subject, since it had all happened a long way from Sussex . . . where they had spent most of their own lives until retiring to Devonshire.

"It was that time you had the German measles. Mama sent me off to stay with our Uncle Hector, when he had the living of Nettleden . . . a small village to the north of Berkhamsted. The gardener told me."

"Probably using the late Mr Snooks as an example of what happens to thieves . . . after he caught you eating your way through all the fruit in the vicarage gardens, dear."

Bun replied tartly that a mouthful of cherries or strawberries was not in the same category as a sackful of registered letters.

"Anyway: the hanging part didn't shock me half so much as being stripped naked afterwards. By then, even Nanny Hudson didn't see me in the totally unclothed state!"

They turned off the road to enter the rectory.

Once inside the house, Bun went round to make certain their servants had all retired to bed.

Phipps took the gun straight into the library, where she found Sooty the cat curled up in a corner of the settee, quietly dozing, with one eye open to watch her approach.

She gently scooped Sooty off into her arms, and carried her away to a bedroom for safety's sake, at the same time looking to see if Cousin Crispian had returned from his evening visit to a sick parishioner.

All was well. They had the rectory to themselves.

The sisters met again beside the library table, thoughtfully regarding the automatic pistol which lay before them, while two oil lamps cast menacing shadows all round the remainder of this large room.

"Have you realised . . . that thing is probably still loaded?"

"With bullets, dear?"

"Certainly not with a handful of Dolly Mixture, old girl."

"Then hadn't we better get them out?"

Bun replied she would make it her first job.

Phipps watched her sister's large, capable hands working over the weapon's surface, clearly trying to find some part which either hinged or slid open . . . and obviously having no idea whatsoever of how to get inside the weapon.

Phipps tried visualising a scene from one of the American gangster films which she had seen at the Regal, in Exeter, shortly before they came down to St Tudy. The private eye had taken a similar gun from a desk drawer, did something - though she couldn't remember what - then pulled at the handle part, looked, nodded, and slapped something back into place with the heel of his left hand.

She was about to tell her sister all about this - because she thought it might be of some help - when there was a loud 'bang'.

The sharp, acrid smell of gun-smoke stung her nostrils.

Both sisters looked up at the ceiling.

There were no holes to be seen in the white plasterwork.

Phipps began anxiously clutching at her body, grabbing handfuls of flesh and squeezing hard in an effort to find out if she had stopped the bullet . . . quite convinced that she was going to find her life's blood slowly seeping away through her clothing at the very next moment.

Bun, with a very shaky voice, asked, "Are you all right?"

"Yes. I think so , dear. At least: my frock isn't soaked in blood, as far as I can tell. Just as well, too! It was new, this spring, bought specially for our church garden party. You must have missed me . . . but please don't try again!" Phipps ended on a note of rising panic.

Bun observed that she quite understood her sister's anxiety, but reminded her that ladies of their standing did not indulge in wanton fits of hysterics. That sort of dramatic behaviour was reserved for kitchen maids who dropped Crown Derby teacups on the still-room floor. "Just try to remember: one of our maternal ancestors was a Baronet!"

Phipps retorted that would not make her bullet proof.

"Well I couldn't help it! The damn'd thing slipped. I grabbed at it because I didn't want it damaging the library table. Must have caught the trigger against something . . . "

" . . . such as your finger, dear?"

Bun replied icily that if her younger sister thought she could do better, she was very welcome to give an immediate demonstration of her superior knowledge.

Phipps, disinclined to risk a bullet puncturing her tender skin, accepted that it was necessary to render the weapon harmless and encouraged her older sister to try again . . . then slipped unobtrusively beneath the library table, where she hoped to remain out of harms way.

The top of this solidly-crafted piece of furniture was about an inch and a half thick. Surely well-seasoned English oak would be capable of stopping any stray bullets? And I'm not being a craven coward, she comforted herself, because if that gun goes off again it stands to reason Bun won't be holding it in such a manner that she gets shot. The barrel will be pointing away from her body and therefore towards that of any stray observer.

Phipps listened apprehensively. Muffled sounds, of a solid object bumping against the wood above her head, were followed by several sharp metallic 'clicks'. She crouched lower, inwardly flinching with fear as her sister grunted . . . indicative of considerable human effort being expended by pulling, or pushing at something which was refusing to yield.

Then there was another explosion!

Phipps jumped - as if stung by a wasp - bumping her head on a cross-bar which supported the table top.

"There! You've done it again!" She screeched.

"I'm well aware of that," Bun replied shortly, "and if your sole contribution is going to be confined to making statements of obvious fact, I should prefer a restrained silence."

Phipps scrambled out from her refuge and picked up the gun.

"You should pay more attention to detail, next time we go to see a gangster film," she snapped. "The bullets are all hidden away in the handle." She turned the weapon upside down, in order to squeeze and fumble about near the butt's base plate.

Within seconds, to her delight - and inexpressible relief - the interior pulled clear to reveal several live bullets still clipped into place on a length of sliding metal.

The look of astonishment on her sister's face added to the younger woman's feeling of satisfaction, and she was quite unable to resist giving a dismissive shrug of the shoulders.

"Easy when you know how, dear! I think you were playing about at the wrong end." Phipps shook her head, lips compressed disapprovingly. "I wonder you didn't injure yourself! Come on: let's get the door and windows open to blow away your gun-smoke before Cousin Crispian returns."

"Hmmm. Safe now . . . is it?" Bun asked as she picked up the gun and gave the trigger an experimental squeeze.

There was an immediate explosion!

Bun dropped the weapon and stepped backwards, white faced.

"I thought you said that thing was safe?"

Phipps didn't answer. She was too busy feeling for signs of personal punctures or loss of blood . . . though she gained some degree of reassurance from the fact that she felt no pain.

Finally, she collapsed into the nearest armchair, trembling all over. When she found her voice again, she explained that there must have been one round left in the barrel.

"Why didn't you take it out?"

"Because I didn't know it was in there! Anyway: it's all your own fault. Really Bun . . . I am surprised at you! Fancy pulling the trigger, just to find out if the gun was safe!"

"Know a better way, old girl?" Bun asked grimly, starting to walk across the room. Near the other armchair she suddenly fell to the floor, giving a strangled cry of shock and pain.

Phipps, presuming her sister had shot herself in the foot, though she couldn't think how, squeaked, "Oh my God!" and struggled to her feet.

But, to her relief, she found nothing visibly wrong. Bun explained that she had caught a foot on something round, which caused a momentary loss of balance.

"Of course. That gun's what they call an automatic: reloads itself after every shot . . . "

" . . . which means the spent cartridges are scattered in all directions? We'd better find them before our cousin, or one of the maids does so. Which means that was part of the reason for so many policemen spending all day in our churchyard, Phippsie."

"I think they were disappointed too, dear. Perhaps we should send them one of our cartridge cases . . . just to cheer them up. After all: we don't want them losing interest in the case, do we?"

Bun thought it might be amusing but warned her sister to wipe all surfaces of both paper and envelope - as well as the brass cartridge case - to remove any possible traces of finger prints.

After sitting down, to get her breath back, Bun raised the subject of finger prints again. "We must have the murderer's!"

"Somewhere on the remaining bullets?" Phipps suggested.

"Yes. Useless bothering with the outside of the gun: everything will have been scoured clean by that sand . . . but you're the only person to have handled those live bullets. So any other prints must be from the man who loaded them into the weapon."

Phipps agreed, but questioned how one obtained fingerprints.

"Some sort of powder, old girl. Easy enough to find out."

"Ask a policeman?" Phipps suggested sweetly.

"No! Take the bus to Bodmin. Browse around their public library. Sure to be something helpful under 'Crime'."

Phipps, feeling thrilled to bits, said it was a good idea but, for the present, hadn't they better find those empty cartridge cases and also discover where the three bullets had gone?

Their three brass cartridges were found easily enough, but whereabouts of the bullets took longer. Finally, it was decided two had become embedded within the wood framework of a settee, whilst the third had made a neat round hole in the wall plaster. Phipps dug this out with a nail file, then filled the cavity with screwed up tissue paper before smoothing the surface with a thick mixture of flour and water paste.

Meanwhile, Bun attended to the settee's 'entry wounds', by darning over both with suitably coloured mending wools and embroidery silks brought down from her workbox.

Then Phipps removed both gun and cartridges to her travelling trunk - which had a stout brass lock - safe from prying eyes.

Bun was just completing her repairs to the settee fabric, when their curate cousin returned . . . and asked what was going on.

"Roddy Holbrook: smoking! Burned a hole. Just darning over, to make things tidy," Bun explained.

Crispian, sniffing the remains of gunsmoke still hanging in the air, said he didn't think much of Roddy's choice in cigarettes, 'terribly strong tobacco', then went off to the kitchen, soon rejoining his cousins with a plateful of bread, cheese and pickle.

Seating himself at the library table - how Phipps thanked their lucky stars its surface bore no traces of bullet scars - Crispian told them he had just heard an interesting story, whilst visiting Mrs Skinner: crippled with arthritis, who hadn't walked for years.

A grand-daughter had called in - young Elsie, housemaid at Town Farm - who told them she had seen Mr Bernard Drysdale dodging amongst the graveyard headstones last night.

"And what was she doing . . . out so late?" Bun enquired.

"Wasn't out. Indoors. Her bedroom's in the attic. Overlooks the church grounds," Crispian explained.

Phipps stared enquiringly at her sister.

Bun murmured, "So Bernard is now Number One Suspect."

Bassett Quizzes the Schoolchildren

Detective Sergeant Bassett was presented with a short, freshly polished brass cartridge case, when he returned to St Tudy on the following morning.

Constable Pope told him it had been found on a seat in the church porch by Mr Hyde, the curate, when he arrived to say a quick prayer before breakfast.

Detective Constable Polkinghorne watched as the object was passed from one hand to another, inwardly flinching at the inevitable destruction of any traces of a fingerprint which must now be taking place.

But when Bassett handed it to him, the constable realised this particular cartridge case had recently been cleaned with Brasso, so all traces of prints would have been obliterated long before it reached the police.

He glanced across at Pope, to see him giving Bassett a white paper bag, with printed lettering advertising Barnecutt's Pasties. There was a Wadebridge address on one side . . . and childish handwriting on the other.

"'For the police'. Hmmm. Any note with it?"

Pope breathed in, compressed his lips and shook his head.

"No Sergeant, nothing else."

"Obviously written by some kid," the detective sergeant said with a dismissive shrug."

"Could be a practical joke, I suppose," Polkinghorne mused.

"But on the other hand," Bassett suggested, "perhaps the little beggar did find this in the churchyard grass . . ."

" . . . then took it home, without telling anyone else, and gave it a ruddy good shine with some of his mother's cleaning rags," Pope observed gloomily.

Polkinghorne disagreed, saying he couldn't imagine any village boy doing that. "First thing he'd do, Sarge, would be to pass it round all his mates to show 'em that he was so much smarter than they were."

"What's your idea then, Ceddie?"

"That first chap on the scene - who found the body - also found the cartridge case."

"Slipped it into his pocket as a souvenir, d'you mean?"

"Reckon so. Perhaps he has access to Brasso in the place where he works . . . in use for cleaning the brasswork on harnesses. Then, come evening, he heard our chaps had been looking for something in the churchyard grass, realised he shouldn't have gone off with the cartridge case . . . "

" . . . and became scared he'd get into trouble," Constable Pope concluded with a smile.

"So he thought he'd best send it back to us, under the cover of darkness?" Bassett suggested.

Pope shook his head, maintaining he'd seen enough of his own children's scribbles to feel certain that the writing on this paper bag was also the work of a school kid.

"Perhaps a girl, Sarge."

"Maybe an older sister," Polkinghorne cut in hopefully.

Pope nodded vigorously.

"Well . . . that's right. Young brother finds our cartridge case and takes it home. 'Big Sis' sees him playing about with it, realises it's connected with the churchyard shooting and drops it in the porch, next morning."

"Which means questioning all the village children," Bassett grumbled with a sigh of despair.

The three men were talking in Constable Pope's kitchen.

Polkinghorne looked up at the clock on the mantelpiece.

"Eight forty-five. The kids won't even be in school for another quarter of an hour . . . then we've got to give 'em time for morning prayers, Sarge."

118

"All right! That gives us time for another cup of tea. Put the kettle on, Constable."

Pope did so and passed the biscuit tin.

Twenty minutes later, as the detectives approached the village school, they became aware of a sing-song drone becoming louder and louder.

This reached a crescendo with 'Eight tens are Eighty', then tailed away with increasing rapidity through 'Eight elevens are Eighty-eight' to stop abruptly at 'Eight twelves are Ninety-six'.

"They won't be sorry to have that interrupted," Bassett observed, jerking his head sideways at the classroom windows on turning towards the entrance door. "Multiplication tables were the bane of my life, at that age, and I wouldn't mind betting that this lot feel the same."

Once inside the classroom, Polkinghorne diplomatically stood to one side while his boss explained the purpose of their visit to the teacher.

Letting his gaze wander round the crowded room, he noted that most of the little girls stared back with frank, wide-eyed interest; whilst their brothers all attempted to avoided his mild scrutiny by looking down at their desk-tops rather than catch his eye. Some sneaked sideways glances at other little boys . . . who appeared to be wriggling about very uncomfortably on their polished wooden benches.

There was a brief moment of complete silence, when the teacher told her class why the policemen were present, then Polkinghorne saw little girls put hands to mouths, turning to face each other, hair falling down over their eyes as they bent their heads to discuss matters in great secrecy.

Little boys remained stricken dumbly silent, stealing shifty glances towards friends . . . or malevolently scowling at enemies of the moment.

Polkinghorne paid particular attention to one lad, until he remembered where they had met each other once before: at the parish pump, on the previous evening. He had come out for water, so presumably lived in one of those cottages near the blacksmith's forge.

I wonder if he did tie that brown cord on the back of Smitheram's milk lorry? But further thought on this subject had to be shelved as one of the little girls raised a hand.

"Please Miss: I saw John Frances with a Barnecutt's bag, the other day."

"Didn't at all!" Piped up one of the little boys. "Don't listen to 'er, Miss. She'm a liar!"

John Frances was told this was not the correct way in which to speak of other people . . . and he must not shout in class.

Then he was ordered to stand in the corner.

Another, smaller girl, came to the aid of the first speaker, saying that John Frances had brought his lunchtime sandwiches in such a bag. Others, their memories jogged by these statements, joined in with delighted cries of, "Yes. That's right, Miss. I see'd 'im too!"

"Last Wednesday, it was."

"No. Thursday . . . when our milk was late."

And: "'Twasn't at all. 'Twas Tuesday, 'cos we 'ad our nature walk an' ate our sangwiches in Farmer Sobey's water medders, down beside the stream."

"Ooo yes, Miss! And I saw John Frances throw his bag in the stream. 'Ee shouldn't orter 'ave done that, should 'ee?"

End of the John Frances lead, Polkinghorne thought wryly.

He listened with waning interest as other little girls made similar accusations . . . which were then denied with equal vehemence by the little boy allegedly concerned.

Denunciation, swiftly followed by repudiation, passed to and fro across the classroom until everyone had had their say.

But the Bodmin detectives failed to learn who was responsible for delivering the cartridge case to that seat inside the village church porch.

When all were finally reduced to a simmering silence, the teacher told her charges that she wished to look inside their desks and asked for lids to be raised.

"Girls an' all, Miss?"

"Yes please, Alice. Everyone. Now! At once!" She ordered with a brief accompanying handclap.

Polkinghorne took his eyes away from the colourful tonic sol-fa wall chart which had been claiming his attention, to glance along the rows of raised desk-tops.

All up?

No. Not quite!

The school mistress was walking slowly towards a small boy, with dark curly hair, who had failed to obey her instructions.

He didn't look more than six years of age, and was sitting forward on his bench, head bowed, shoulders heaving slightly and tears squeezing from his eyes to trickle down fiery red cheeks like water from a mountain spring.

Every child in the class turned to stare.

The young teacher asked what was wrong, as she gestured for the child to open his desk. The lad refused, muttering that he couldn't. He'd got something there.

Teacher raised the desk-top to peer in . . . then swiftly thrust an arm beneath the lid.

Polkinghorne wondered if she was about to produce the missing gun . . . a dead rabbit or a live mouse. But she only displayed a home-made catapult. He looked across at Bassett and the two men exchanged shrugs of disappointment.

"I'll speak to you about this later," the mistress said, "but for the present: you had better take yourself out to the lavatories before you wet your trousers and disgrace yourself completely!"

From the ungainly manner in which this lad stumbled away, Polkinghorne surmised the teacher's instruction had been issued about two minutes too late.

No further contraband items were discovered. Finally, the young woman told a monitor to go around and collect all the English exercise books. These were then handed to the detectives so that handwriting could be compared with the note on Barnecutt's food bag.

Immediately, there was an urgent request from one of the older girls who asked to be excused. Permission was given without argument. The mistress then riffled through the pile of books, selected one, opened it and placed the food bag on a page facing the owner's handwriting.

Polkinghorne, looking over Bassett's shoulder, could see little ground to doubt who had written 'For the police'. The school teacher said quietly that this book belonged to the girl who had just rushed out.

"Jean Tamblyn, but I shouldn't have thought . . ."

"Like the Canadian Mounties . . . we always get our man, even when she's only a schoolgirl," Bassett replied with a grin.

Polkinghorne, wincing at this heavy-handed humour, shook his head with embarrassment.

His sergeant shrugged indifferently.

The three adults remained grouped together, on the low platform in front of the class, waiting for several minutes. Then the six-year old boy returned.

He was asked if he had seen Jean Tamblyn.

"Please Miss . . . she's run 'ome!"

Johnnie Tamblyn Helps the Police

Bassett and Polkinghorne found Mrs Harry Tamblyn in Chapel Cottages, a short terrace of four dwellings built facing the road, just before it divided at the Methodist Church; one branch leading towards Camelford whilst the other took people towards Bodmin.

The detective constable remained silently watchful while his sergeant introduced them, then went on to explain the reason for that police search, trying to find a brass cartridge case, throughout most of a previous day.

"To our surprise, one of the correct shape and size has made an appearance in the church porch, early this morning."

"Aw . . . but what's this got to do with me?"

"We have reason to believe your daughter - Jean - may be able to help us. Could we come in and have a chat about it?"

Polkinghorne thought it would be more kindly to soften the blow, of having two policemen on her doorstep, by adding a few words of sympathy.

"She's drawn attention to herself by running out of school, this morning. I hope she got home safely?"

"Aw 'ess . . . she'm 'ome, right enough, but I doubt you'll git any sense out of the maid."

"A bit worried, is she?" Bassett enquired with a short laugh, as they were shown into a spotlessly clean parlour: obviously used for weddings, funerals and precious little else.

"She'm fair frit to death! But it wad'n 'er as found that there brass thing."

"Oh?" Bassett said with a raised eyebrow, stretching out in one of Mrs Tamblyn's best armchairs, and privately thinking this must be where the preacher is placed after conducting the latest family burial service.

"Naw . . . she telt me it were our youngest: Johnnie."

"Did Jean say where the lad found it?"

"'Ess. Up in the old graveyard . . . beside the parish church."

The two detectives exchanged a glance of satisfaction.

"And when was this, m'dear?" Bassett asked mildly.

"Why yes'day mornin' . . . afore all you lot come and started messin' about in the grass under they there beech trees."

"Wasn't Constable Pope keeping an eye on things?"

Mrs Tamblyn shook her head.

"Not by what our Jean telt me. Said they 'ad the place to themselves . . . so there weren't nobody there to stop 'em poking around."

Polkinghorne cut in to suggest the two children must have been out pretty early.

"Oh ah. 'Bout eight, I should think. I 'ad to pack 'em off like that so's Jean could leave the boy with 'er gran for the day, afore she went on t' school."

"Going out later, yourself?" Bassett enquired.

"'Ess . . . but not for pleasure! I 'ad to 'elp bury me aunt, over to Laneast."

Mrs Tamblyn shook her head at the very thought, adding that it was some old job to get there.

"But I was lucky in the morning: got a lift in Mr Snell's cattle lorry. 'Ee farms at Lower Stone and 'ad to take some pigs over to Launceston market, so 'ee dropped me off at them crossroads up on Laneast Downs. I only 'ad t'walk 'alf a mile."

Bassett philosophically let the loquacious housewife ramble on about the difficulties of cross-country travel in that part of Cornwall.

Polkinghorne realised the sense in this forebearance. When one needed co-operation from a member of the public, a talkative person was worth ten others pretending they had been born deaf mutes.

Eventually, Mrs Tamblyn completed the saga of her ordeal by country buses, when returning to St Tudy, and Bassett was able to redirect her attention towards facts concerned with the discovery of their cartridge case.

The detectives were informed that her daughter Jean had heard people speaking about a shooting, up in the old graveyard, as she passed them grouped around the parish pump, behind the blacksmith's shop. There was nobody about, up near the church, so the two children had gone over for a look, 'cos they didn't see no harm.

"And did Jean describe anything?"

"'Ow d'y'mean, sir?"

"Did she tell you what they did . . . or what they saw?"

"Well . . . they did'n do nothing. Just looked . . . "

" . . . and saw . . . ?" Bassett prompted.

"The grass 'ad all bin trampled down in one place, under they there beech trees; an' that's where our John picked up that old brass thing. But it weren't stealing," Mrs Tamblyn hastened to add, "'cos it were just lying there!"

Polkinghorne nodded his head sympathetically.

"Looking as if nobody wanted it . . . just a bit of litter?" he suggested.

"Well that's right. They kids didn't think nothin' more about it. Young John picked it up 'cos it were all bright and shiny . . . an' put it in 'is pocket."

The detective constable felt the poor woman was now close to tears - which could be embarrassing all round - so he hastened to offer reassurance.

"We're not saying the children did anything wrong, m'dear."

"No. Nothing like that," Bassett added, shuffling uncomfortably in his seat. "But we should like the little boy to show us exactly where he found that cartridge case. Perhaps Jean could come over with us . . . just to confirm where she was standing, at the same time? Then she could bring her brother home before going back to school."

"But what about that there Miss Cook - the school teacher?"

"Well . . . what's this to her?" Bassett asked indifferently.

"She'm a right tartar, where absence is concerned. She'll play 'ell with my girl . . . for running off like she did!"

Polkinghorne stepped into the breach, telling Mrs Tamblyn he would slip back to the school and explain everything, while the two children were showing his sergeant where they had been wandering about during the previous morning.

The woman went upstairs to fetch Jean and Johnnie, who had taken refuge together in one of the bedrooms.

While they waited, the detectives talked over this latest development. Polkinghorne realised the children must have passed through the churchyard when the village bobby was away, and said so.

"Yes. Sloppy business, all round. But what can you expect, Ceddie boy? Even if Pope had tried to get reinforcements, he would have still needed to leave the scene of the shooting in order to reach a telephone." Bassett shrugged helplessly. "Just one of those things sent to try us."

"Ah well . . . could have been worse. At least the girl had sense enough to pass over that cartridge within twenty-four hours."

"Now all we've got to do is find the gun, then our new-found friend - the County Pathologist - can run a comparison test."

"And if marks made by the firing pin and ejector mechanism match those on our specimen, we've won, Sarge!"

"Always assuming we can find the previous owner . . . and prove he fired the fatal shot!"

"That'll be one of them dinner party guests, I reckon."

"Or any other unknown person . . . living anywhere else in the British Isles, Cedric!"

Bassett gave his assistant a very twisted smile, reminding him that detectives had to keep an open mind.

"But not that open!" Polkinghorne retorted.

Further comments had to be postponed because Mrs Tamblyn returned with the children. Once introductions were over, all four set off for the church.

Four-year old Johnnie walked along with his head up, as bright and chirpy as a cricket; whilst his sister Jean kept her shoulders hunched forward and head bent downwards.

It's almost as if she's conscious of the family disgrace she had brought on them, through being escorted back to school by two hulking great policemen, Polkinghorne thought to himself.

As they passed the right hand turn-off for Wheeler's house and Dudley Knighton's chicken farm, a woman - draped over her cottage half-door - called out, "What 'ave you two children bin up to? Them's policemen, you're with!"

Then she asked the detectives: "Arrested 'em, 'ave 'ee? Goin' to lock 'em up in the Old Clink? I'd put the pair of 'em in the stocks, if we 'ad any!"

Johnnie smiled and waved.

His sister blushed scarlet, maintaining a tight-lipped silence.

Polkinghorne was about to shout a reply to Jean's tormentor, when his sergeant called back, "They're helping us with our enquiries, m'dear."

"Oh! Anything I can do, me 'andsome?" the woman laughed. "I'd be glad to give someone like yourself a helping hand."

Bassett waved negatively, without slowing his pace.

Then they were walking through a pungent miasma, which Polkinghorne recognised as coming from the scorched hoof of a cart-horse, standing outside the blacksmith's shop. He must be having new shoes fitted, in readiness for bringing home this year's corn crop, the detective thought.

As they passed by, he marvelled that such a small man could manage to control such a large hoof. Must be quite a bit of weight in that, he thought. As if reading his mind, Bassett said he wouldn't care to have one like that standing on his corns for any length of time.

Polkinghorne agreed.

The party turned across the road, just afterwards, and saw three women - all carrying enamel jugs - gossiping together beside the parish pump.

They became silent and watchful as Bassett led the way into their churchyard, just beyond the chestnut tree.

"You don't want to worry about them, girl," he advised Jean Tamblyn. "Better they were home, getting their husbands' dinners, instead of minding other people's business."

"They ain't got no cause to look at me like that!" Jean Tamblyn responded with sudden spirit. "My Ma says Mrs Bell's old man is always in an' out of court! He don't do no regular work, neither. Gets his money by catching rabbits . . . an' pheasants too, when he thinks 'ee can get away with it."

"Bit of a poacher, eh?" Bassett asked with a smile.

"Never done nothing else, as far as anyone in St Tudy knows."

Once under the spreading arms of the beech trees, her brother Johnnie led them between headstones dedicated to the memory of Masters and Billings to stop at a square of short-cut grass. Polkinghorne watched as the little boy looked about for a moment . . . lost and trying to get his bearings. Then he trotted over to one side and stuck his finger into the ground.

"Here Mister!"

Bassett asked if he was sure.

The lad replied, "Yes."

This was instantly confirmed by his sister. Jean said she remembered waiting near that dark grey, slate headstone which was standing all by itself, just in front of a large bush.

Bassett asked how the lad managed to find such a small object as a cartridge case, before the grass had been cut.

"I dunno," Jean replied with a hopeless shrug. "He was just poking about over there . . . where the body had been lying."

"You didn't actually see him pick it up?"

"No . . . but he didn't go anywhere else, sir. Just bent down, picked up something, then came over to show me what he'd got in his hand."

Polkinghorne thought this would be sufficient to satisfy an Assize jury and was about to walk on towards the school, when Johnnie was heard muttering about a gun.

Bassett asked his sister what this was all about.

She shrugged, as if it were of no importance, telling the detectives that her brother claimed to have seen a gun in that pile of builder's sand, near the bus shelter.

"Did you see it too?"

"No. I'd gone into school. This was later in the morning. Me gran brought John up to the village with her for company.

Johnnie Tamblyn Helps the Police

"When the policemen were cutting grass in the churchyard?"

"I 'spose so. It was when Gran come over for her News Chronicle. M' brother stopped to build a sand castle . . . while Gran went round to the shop."

"I did! I did!" The girl's little brother shouted, jumping up and down to emphasise this point. "I found a gun . . . just like the big boys have when they're playing at cowboys and Indians. But I couldn't make it go 'bang'," he ended sadly.

"Just as well, I'd say," Bassett commented before reminding his constable to get on round and square things with Miss Cook, the school teacher.

When Polkinghorne returned, he found the Tamblyn children holding hands beneath the chestnut tree, and his boss groping about in a huge pile of white sand which probably originated in the china clay country, out on the edge of Bodmin Moor.

"Can't find nothing. We'll have to go through this lot with a fine sieve. Slip across to them builders and ask to borrow one, together with a couple of shovels."

"Aw heck! That'll take us all morning!"

Polkinghorne turned to cross the road, grumbling there must be all of five tons lying there, when his sergeant called him back.

"I reckon we've finished with these children, Ceddie boy. Give 'em a couple of pennies for sweets and let 'em know we're glad of their help."

The detective constable did as he'd been instructed, noting the little boy's grey socks - shrunk short from too many trips to the wash tub. The same could be said for his jersey, while those grey flannel shorts were a couple of sizes too big . . . obviously bought with a view to having the lad grow into them.

Jean's dress, whilst plain, had quite a bit of wear remaining, but was already too tight, giving this garment a skimpy appearance. The girl would need a new one, come autumn, if normal decencies were to be observed he thought, passing over a silver threepenny bit.

Then Polkinghorne wished he had not been so generous. They would probably be afraid to spend so much money on themselves, all at once, and take the coin home to their mother.

The two detectives spent the rest of their morning working through the sand pile, with a hot sun burning down upon their bent backs. The sergeant assured his constable that the boy had told him he had definitely seen a gun; described as being browny-black, very heavy - like mother's clothes iron - and flat.

"So we're looking for an automatic?"

"Yes. Young Tamblyn said he found it buried in sand near the top of the pile. He was afraid to take it home. Scared one of the big boys might have lost it . . . and he'd get beaten up if they saw him carrying it away. So he left it here. Just covered it with more sand and went off home with his dear old gran!"

"So you think he found the murder weapon?"

"No doubt about it. Toy pistols aren't all that heavy. I reckon our man has come back and collected it after we all left the village, yesterday evening. But we'll have to go right through this pile, in case I'm wrong. Can't have one of the villagers finding the gun, then ringing up Bodmin police headquarters."

Polkinghorne agreed that could be most embarrassing.

Bun Studies Fingerprinting

Bun and Phipps were also feeling hot and bothered by midday. They had risen earlier than usual and managed to finish their breakfast before Cousin Crispian appeared, then hurried up to the village bus stop just in time to catch the first service for Bodmin.

This had set them down at the bottom end of town, near an imposing granite building where the judges stayed when the Assize Court was in session on the opposite side of the road.

Enquiring their way to the public library, they had been directed towards a narrow street of small shops . . . and told to keep going - for about a mile - until the road got wider, when they would see the building on their left hand side.

Upon reaching their goal, they found a notice on the door which advised them the library would not be open to borrowers until nine o'clock. Bun led the way across the foot of a very steep hill, to sink down on a conveniently situated public bench at the back of the next pavement.

"Going to be another lovely day," Phipps observed.

Bun declared she was sweating like Farmer Giles' cart horse.

"I thought those shops would never end, dear."

"Y-e-s. One of those typical Cornish miles . . . which seems more like two, when one comes to pace it out."

To their further chagrin, neither lady could find any book which was of the slightest use, when they were finally able to get into the library and browse around its shelves. Recent murders were well-documented, as were classic crimes of earlier years, but fingerprints only appeared to receive a passing mention.

"No real forensic detail," Bun sighed with frustration, returning yet another volume to its resting place.

"I don't suppose there's much call for text books on that sort of subject dear," Phipps pointed out.

"Only one thing for it, old girl . . . Plymouth!"

"But how on earth . . . ?"

" . . . do we get there? Haven't the least idea. We'll ask the librarian. He ought to know."

He did.

Mr N G Pentecost explained that there were two different railway stations serving the town, but they would find the Great Western much the better route for Plymouth.

"You walk straight down through the main shopping street, until you reach a small triangle of raised ground on your right. That's a very small car park in front of the Assize Court."

"We know," Bun replied with deep feeling, "we've just come up from that part of town."

"Oh well . . . you won't have any trouble in finding the station, because it's at the top of the first hill . . . on your way to Lostwithiel."

Phipps timorously enquired if it was very far . . . to Lostwithiel?

"About six miles . . . "

Bun let out a strangled gasp.

Mr Pentecost took pity on her, explaining that they wouldn't have to walk that far. The station was located opposite the barracks . . . no more than a half a mile from the Courts.

To Phipps' complete surprise, she now heard her sister explain that her verruca would never allow her to walk that distance. Bun reached into her purse, withdrew tuppence, which she gave to the librarian together with a request that he 'phone for a taxi.

"Tell the driver we'll be waiting outside, on one of those public seats."

"I didn't know you had anything wrong with your feet, dear," Phipps murmured sympathetically, once they had regained the pavement. "Which one . . . ?"

Bun replied that she did not have a verruca . . . but thought it wise to invent one.

132

"Whatever for?"

"To ensure Mr Pentecost didn't refuse to make the 'phone call, on the grounds that public libraries were not designed to provide those sort of facilities." Bun glared. "Being a stranger in this town, how could I know where to find an outside call box?"

Phipps pointed further up the pavement, to their left.

"I think that red-painted, square-shaped kiosk standing beneath the fish and chip shop signboard might be what you wanted."

Bun leaned out, looking further along the pavement.

"Well . . . you may be right. But how was I supposed to know it was there, when I was inside the library? In any case, you know my views on public telephones, Phippsie . . . germs!"

Their taxi arrived within minutes and, after its two passengers were seated, drove straight up the hill beside the library.

Bun asked their driver if he was going in the right direction, because they had been told to walk down through the town, in order to reach the Great Western railway station.

"Yes. I'm taking you round the back way . . . over what we d'call The Beacon. Gives you a brave 'andsome view of Bodmin. An' all inclusive! No extra charge, m'dears."

And he was right, because Phipps could see much of the town was spread out before them, on her left, as their taxi followed a dipping, curving road around one of the hilltop contours. Then it descended to thread its way along a narrow, winding lane, eventually joining a major road right in front of the boundary wall surrounding the Duke of Cornwall's Light Infantry barracks.

Once they had paid the driver and purchased day returns to Plymouth, Bun and Phipps had another, longer wait on the station platform, before a tiny engine, pulling one coach, drew in to stop before them. Two old women, carrying large wickerwork market baskets, descended and hobbled away. The guard threw out four flat wooden boxes containing fish, then loaded some luggage being sent on in advance.

Bun and Phipps climbed aboard and settled themselves into window seats. Doors slammed, whistles blew, brake rods creaked, the coach jerked with an accompanying hiss of steam from the engine, and they were off.

They soon discovered their train meandered around the beautiful Cornish countryside at little more than a fast walking pace for the next three miles. Unfortunately, much of the line ran through deep cuttings, so wide views were often obscured. Finally, they rounded a curve, to stop in Bodmin Road station.

This appeared to be surrounded by rhododendrons, but there was no time to stand and stare. The Paddington express stood waiting on the other side of their arrival platform. The two sisters hurriedly crossed over to this train. No sooner were they seated, than it pulled away.

"I suppose this is how the 'boys' went across to fight in Flanders," Phipps murmured thoughtfully, "marched over the road from Bodmin Barracks . . . and then it was non-stop to Dover."

" . . . with two thirds of them never setting foot on English soil again," Bun concluded with a catch in her throat.

As the express hauled them along a track bordered by more rhododendrons on the right - with a wooded river valley to be seen occasionally beneath the left hand embankment - Bun observed that this train was making considerably better speed than the local 'Puffing Billy'.

"One felt it would have been possible to walk the same distance in very little more time," she concluded.

Phipps smiled. "But think of your verruca, dear!"

Bun relaxed, leaning her head back against the seat cushion as they slowed to a crawling pace and trundled across the Largin Viaduct. A long, slow climb soon followed - during which the express passed through Doublebois station without stopping.

Phipps was staring out of a carriage window, idly watching green fields slip by, when she became aware that they were being hauled across another high viaduct. Staring down at the valley beneath, she saw a single line track on which a one-coach local train was moving.

"Bun, isn't that line rather familiar?"

"Hmm?" her sister muttered, leaning forward to see better. "Oh yes . . . the Looe branch line. We were on it a month or two ago, when we took Brother Theo's children to Polperro. So I suppose we'll be pulling into Liskeard shortly."

134

Their train stopped within a couple of minutes, with doors opening, passengers boarding and porters shouting 'Liskeard! Change here for Looe! London train. Plymouth next stop!'

Once moving again, Phipps continued to watch the Cornish countryside unfolding beyond the trackside, whilst her sister rested against the cushioned back of her seat.

The express rushed through Menheniot station, then the one serving St Germans, with no more than a whistle blast to indicate their presence. It crossed the River Lynher, then raced onwards between cornfields and meadowland as far as Wearde Quay, before slowing down to crawl through Saltash.

"Wake up, Bun!" Phipps called excitedly. "We're just about to cross the Royal Albert Bridge, into Devonshire."

Bun replied that she'd seen it all before . . . but nevertheless stretched to see all the naval warships, moored further downstream, before their train disappeared into the dreary cuttings which carried the line through to North Road station.

On leaving their carriage, Bun made a serious mistake. Thinking the railway station must be near the City centre, she led Phipps out onto the street without asking directions.

"How do you know which way to go?" her sister asked.

"Simple! Those buses on our side of the main road are displaying 'Plymouth' destination signs. All we have to do is stroll quietly along in the same direction."

A half an hour later, both sisters were hot, fractious, and completely lost. Bun finally gave in and hailed a passing Luxicab. Within a couple of minutes Phipps found herself being set down before the main entrance to the City library.

"Thought we must be somewhere close," Bun murmured complacently as she led them upstairs, following wall arrows to the Reference Room.

Phipps let her tight-lipped silence indicate disbelief.

She arrived to find herself in a large open space filled with rows of tables and chairs. More than half were occupied by young students who were industriously copying notes from books open before them. Shelves lined the surrounding walls on three sides, with short island fitments jutting out into the room.

Bun said it might be inexpedient to ask the duty librarian outright for a book on the technique of taking fingerprints.

"I shall simply request directions towards the section dealing with crime and criminals. Then - if anyone asks why I'm interested - I shall tell them I'm writing a murder-mystery," she explained to Phipps.

But nobody questioned the purpose of her enquiry.

The librarian instructed his junior assistant to take the two ladies across to the relevant bookshelves, then turned back to his senior assistant and continued discussing the possible social significance of John Betjeman's poetry.

Phipps let her sister wander around by herself, preferring to browse along a shelf labelled MEDICAL SPECIALITIES, in the belief that she might discover something of use if they ever came across a dead body.

The word FORENSIC caught her eye.

It appeared as part of the title of a hefty volume bound in red leather. She lifted it down, riffled through some of the pages, then hurriedly replaced it.

Whole-plate pictures - in colour - of naked human bodies laid out on what were obviously mortuary tables, made her feel decidedly queasy.

Revealing photographs of heads which had been battered to death by that Penny Dreadful favourite, the blunt instrument, were even more disgusting.

One could actually see their brains!

Then she noticed a book devoted to VENEREAL DISEASE.

The words rang a bell. Yes! She could dimly recall having heard that expression used in connection with fallen women, but she had never known exactly what it meant. Now was the time to find out more!

It must take many forms . . . to merit such a thick volume, she concluded, glancing at the back page to see it bore the number 450. Then she turned to the illustrated pages and found herself confronted by paintings of male genitalia in the final stages of corruption and necrosis.

A shiver of pure horror ran down her spine.

Fancy carrying something like that around in one's trousers!

Slamming the book shut, she hastily pushed it back into place on its shelf . . . then stole guilty sideways glances to right and left, whilst uncontrollably blushing the deepest possible shade of crimson.

After such a disagreeable experience, PROBLEMS IN OBSTETRICS or SURGICAL TECHNIQUES FOR THE GYNAECOLOGIST held no attraction for her enquiring mind. Phipps continued to stare at the bookshelves until she had recovered some composure, then turned round to look for Bun.

Her sister was seated at a table, head bent over an open book, making notes as industriously as any student. Phipps was about to walk over and join her, when she realised a tall young man, who had just passed behind Bun, was turning to retrace his steps, quite obviously interested in what she was reading.

Phipps remained where she was, partly shielded by a fitment which jutted out into the room. He had a very short haircut above a shiny, smooth-shaven face . . . and looked vaguely familiar.

The young man paused briefly behind Bun's chair, smiled secretively, then went out.

Phipps raised the matter when she rejoined her sister, but Bun said she had been much too interested in what she was doing to bother about wandering strangers.

"And it's all here!" She whispered. "The different types of powder; how to dust it onto suspect surfaces; together with diagrams of all main skin patterns. Fascinating, old girl! By the way: did you know fingerprints were first used as a means of identification out in India?"

Phipps declared she had always believed the French were first.

"No! You're thinking of the Bertillon system . . . identifying criminals by means of anthropometric measurements."

"They mention that in your book, do they, dear?"

"Only a passing reference. That system was superseded by fingerprinting . . . probably about the same time as our police adopted it, in 1901."

That's Bun all over, Phipps thought: once she starts on something - and gets her teeth set well in - there's no holding her.

"How very interesting, dear," she whispered back by way of further encouragement.

"Oh it is! I shall be here for ages. Why don't you go out and have a look around the shops? Those sandals you're wearing are about ready for the jumble sale."

Phipps pulled a long face, but accepted that she would have more variety to choose from in the Plymouth stores, than would be found amongst smaller - one old lady and a cat type shops - to be found in most of the Cornish market towns.

"All right. I'll come back and collect you in an hour's time."

Once in the street, Phipps decided it was time for a pot of tea and biscuits. So she went into the first suitable place she came to: a baker's shop with its own cafe on the floor above.

If this had been on the ground floor she would have seen The Man From The Library and gone elsewhere. But as it was, she had already climbed the stairs and half-crossed the floor to a vacant table, then sat down before looking round at the other occupied tables.

This was when she saw that young man who had been prowling past her sister in such a suspicious manner. He was sitting on the far side of a bentwood hatstand. When she recognised him, Phipps changed to another chair which faced in the opposite direction.

This reaction was purely instinctive. After all: if she failed to place the young man, when she first caught sight of him in the Public Library Reference Room, there could be little - or no reason - to fear his presence. But there was no escaping the fact that his proximity made her feel decidedly uncomfortable.

A waitress approached and Phipps gave her order, then sneaked another look at the man. Undoubtedly above average height - this was apparent even though he was seated - but it was the ultra-clean face which really bothered her. Odeon Cinema managers, the Station Master at Paddington, and Brighton undertakers looked like that. Come to think of it . . . so did a lot of the younger policemen!

But I don't know any Cornish policemen - other than those investigating Mr Wheeler's death - and one or two down in Polperro, she thought to herself . . . then it all came back.

She had been walking up to the village shop, when she passed their local bobby . . . in the company of The Man From The Library.

So he is a policeman, Phipps concluded. What rotten luck: Bun choosing this particular morning to visit Plymouth!

Now, in her mind's eye, she could see that picture quite clearly. The two men were walking down the St Mabyn road, when I passed them, last week, so they could have seen Bun on the rectory lawn. No wonder he recognised her today and took an interest in her library book!

Phipps could not help shuddering. This young man would now go home and tell Sergeant Bassett all about her sister's curious interest in fingerprinting techniques. Which could result in an embarrassingly difficult interview when Bun and herself returned to St Tudy. She took out her compact and studied the young man with the aid of a mirror set in its lid.

Yes! It was him, all right!

And now he was getting to his feet: coming over to speak!

Phipps replaced the compact in her handbag, seized a spoon and began stirring her tea . . . despite the fact that there was no sugar in the cup. She felt less self-conscious appearing to do something useful even if - in reality - her action was useless.

Anything was better than simply sitting and waiting in dread.

She felt him stop beside her chair.

Her stirring ground to a halt.

He introduced himself as Sergeant Kenneth Symons, stationed at Torpoint, and asked if she was enjoying her stay in St Tudy.

"We passed each other when I was over there to visit an old uncle of mine who hasn't been very well, lately. Constable Pope told me you and your sister were related to the new curate."

Phipps gestured for him to sit down. What else could she do? There was no reason to shout 'Go away. my mother told me never to speak to strange young men'. In any case: at her age, forty-four next birthday, she was grateful if any young man bothered to notice her . . . let alone stop to speak.

However, Symons declined, saying he was due to appear in Court - as a witness - immediately after lunch.

"Anything exciting?" Phipps asked, more for the sake of showing polite interest than really caring about how this young man would be spending the remainder of his working day.

"A Dockyard Matey, up for stealing twenty fathoms of best quality manilla rope. When arrested, he told me his wife needed a new clothes-line!"

"But you're with the Cornwall County Constabulary, surely?"

"Yes, but Chummy stole the rope in Devonport, then took it home to his cottage at Torpoint, which is where I came in."

There was a short exchange of further small-talk, before Symons went off to Court, leaving Phipps glumly sipping her tea.

She had posted one of those brass cartridge cases - fired from the automatic - in a Plymouth collecting box less than an hour earlier . . . addressed to Bodmin police headquarters.

Now the police would know she was in Plymouth at the time!

Miss Nunn's Guilty Secret

The younger sister's fear was confirmed by Mavis - one of the rectory housemaids - when Bun and Phipps returned to St Tudy, late in the afternoon.

They met her carrying a shopping bag which gave out dull 'clinking' sounds, halfway between her place of employment and the Cornish Arms.

"Good Heavens, girl!" Bun gasped, "Surely you haven't been selling Mrs Gregory's parsnip wine around the village?"

"No Miss . . . but she said she fancied a change an' sent me over the pub to get her a couple of bottles of Guinness."

"Hmmm. Any further developments concerning the shooting?"

"You're both wanted by the police!"

"Did they enter carrying handcuffs?"

"No Miss . . . but they said they'd be back tomorrow, when I told them you were gone into Bodmin for the day."

"How did you know that?" Bun demanded. "I don't recall mentioning a destination, this morning."

"Didn't have to . . . old Mrs Bray - lives in that little cottage up past the new graveyard - was on the bus an' heard you ask for Bodmin."

"And hastened to spread the news," Bun sighed.

"Anything else?" Phipps enquired.

"Your friend - Miss Nunn - is in trouble!"

"Oh dear. What's she done now?"

"Well . . . according to Mr Daniels, the Wadebridge coalman, they detectives questioned her nearly all afternoon!"

"Oh poor Dorothy," Phipps exclaimed. "But do go on Mavis. What else did Mr Daniels have to say?"

"He told Cook they went into Miss Nunn's cottage just as he was delivering to the Watsons - big house, same side as the church - an' didn't come out again 'til he'd nearly finished his round."

After Mavis had gone on her way, Bun consoled her younger sister by pointing out that it was far too early for Sergeant Bassett to have received their anonymous gift of a brass cartridge case, because it couldn't have been posted in Plymouth until midday, or slightly later.

"As for that unfortunate meeting with Sergeant Symons if - as you told me - he is stationed at Torpoint, and was going to attend Court during the afternoon, it is hardly likely that he has been in communication with Bassett, as yet."

"Well . . . you never know what the police are getting up to," Phipps replied in worried tones.

Her sister said that they all knew their British policemen were wonderful - visiting Americans told them so on every possible occasion - but they couldn't be in two places at once.

"Not even Jesus managed to pull off that miracle."

"Then whatever can it be, dear?"

"Don't know. One way to find out though . . . "

"Yes . . . ?"

"About turn! We'll pay a call on Dorothy Nunn."

Phipps noticed that children playing outside cottage doors fell silent, as Bun and herself drew nearer to Sweet Lavender.

Two small girls, who had been skipping, gathered up their rope and hid behind an older sister. Three little boys, who had been playing some form of 'tag', abandoned their game and dived headlong through a convenient hole in the nearest hedge.

"One would think Bubonic Plague had broken out," Bun sniffed derisively, "and we are the suspected carriers."

Phipps commented that there was certainly something in the air, recalling how children - in the Sussex village where they had grown up - behaved like this immediately following the sudden death of a near neighbour . . . unnaturally quiet and subdued.

She glanced hurriedly at nearby windows. None had drawn curtains, so sudden death was not the reason for this present exhibition of self-restraint.

When they reached Dorothy's cottage door, Tiddles - sitting hunched up on the step - let out a plaintive 'yowl'.

"He sounds hungry, dear. You don't suppose . . . "

"Certainly not! Why should she? In my experience, old girl, perpetual worriers like the Dorothy Nunns of this world do not do away with themselves . . . they sit tight and pass their burden on to somebody else. Anyway: we'll soon know the worst," Bun concluded, stepping firmly up to the cottage door and giving its brass knocker a brisk rat-a-tat-tat.

Phipps, who was standing a little further back, saw a lace curtain beginning to quiver. Must be something very serious, to make the poor soul's hand shake as much as that, she thought.

This was confirmed when the cottage door was finally opened.

Dorothy Nunn had been crying!

Red-rimmed eyes - sunk back into dark sockets - stared out from a white face. Muscles twitched, in what Phipps took to be a valiant attempt at smiling, then Dorothy extended a shaking hand and invited them inside.

But this was done by gesture, rather than words, one hand limply waving whilst the other grasped a door jamb as a means of self-support.

Dorothy collapsed into a deep armchair as soon as they reached her living-room . . . lips moving but no words becoming audible.

Tiddles weaved around, brushing first against one person's legs, and then another's, mewing plaintively as he did so.

Phipps observed the half-empty tumbler, standing in the centre of an adjacent wine table, and wondered if it contained gin.

Dorothy disabused her by weakly murmuring, "Water. I can't seem to manage anything else. I feel terrible . . . and if other people get to know . . . I shall have to leave the village!"

Bun agreed that she looked dreadful, but suggested a decent cup of freshly-brewed tea could make all the difference to Dorothy's present fragile state.

"Phipps! Slip out to the kitchen and put a kettle on the stove. Better feed the cat, while you're out there too, and make some toast. No butter!"

Phipps did as ordered, keeping one ear permanently cocked towards the open doorway in case she missed anything. But she gathered - from the lack of voices - her sister was doing nothing to encourage confidences at this early stage.

When Phipps returned to the invalid's presence - to fuss over and persuade with kindly insistence - Dorothy managed to eat her dry toast, after first sipping a cup of tea down to the dregs.

Then she became tearfully thankful.

Bun cut short this useless display of gratitude, saying it was nothing. Phipps silently agreed, After all: she was the one who had made the tea and toast . . . while her big sister (in every sense of that word) had merely occupied the other armchair and given their patient moral support.

Dorothy blew her nose, drank more tea, cleared her throat, sat up straighter . . . and let them into her guilty secret.

Mr Plummer - "I call him Edwin" - was the same age as herself and now living alone in Little Apples. This was a cottage situated in a derelict orchard, reached by a narrow lane that separated their village shop from the Cornish Arms.

"His wife died shortly after I moved into St Tudy. Consumption and, what with one thing and another . . . "

"Two lonely people drawn together for mutual comfort and support," Bun suggested diplomatically.

"Something like that," Dorothy agreed with a wan smile.

"But how on earth did you manage to keep it quiet?" Phipps enquired breathlessly.

"Lie of the land! My garden backs on to Edwin's crab apples. Impossible for neighbours to see who is moving to and fro on a dark night . . . "

"And you both have convenient holes in the boundary hedge?"

Dorothy gave a guilty smile and nodded her head.

After sipping her tea, she continued, "It all began when Edwin caught the 'flu. I used to slip over - last thing in the evening - to make certain he had everything he needed for the night."

"Such as plenty of soft handkies and lemon drinks." Phipps suggested diplomatically.

"And a bit of 'Vick' rubbed well into his manly chest?" Bun suggested helpfully, with one eyebrow raised and looking towards Phipps with a significant expression on her face.

"Yes. Well . . . we won't talk about intimate details. Anyway: when Edwin was convalescing, I fell into the habit of spending most of my evenings with him . . . and it has gone on like that ever since," Dorothy ended with another guilty smile.

Phipps asked why they did not marry.

Dorothy admitted Edwin constantly asked her to do so.

"Then why not . . . ?" Bun wondered aloud.

"Practical considerations. Edwin's home is very spartan. You know what men are like . . . "

"All those cold showers, when away at public school, makes 'em frown on creature comforts . . . "

"Exactly! So you can understand how little I want to give up my own lovely little home."

"And there's hardly enough room for two, is there dear?" Phipps suggested in what she hoped was a tactful tone of voice.

Bun told Dorothy that she had made her point . . . in which case: what had suddenly gone wrong?

"The police have found out! A neighbour must have seen me!"

"Your private 'Lover's Leap', couldn't have been so secret as you thought," Bun observed.

Dorothy agreed, saying it made her flesh positively creep to think of the eyes of another watching . . . and all that horrid sniggering which must have been going on in the village.

"So what happened when the detectives called?" Phipps asked.

"I told them how I had walked up to the rectory, gone on to my own place to see that Tiddles was all right, then returned, escorted by Captain Holbrook all the time, and remained at the rectory with you - Phippsie - and Teresa Lockhart, until about twelve-thirty."

"The sergeant seemed happy enough when we told him that."

Dorothy sniffed. "He told me to tell the truth!"

Bun heaved a sigh of despair.

145

Phipps gave a gasp, "And you did so?"

"There didn't seem any other way. The sergeant said I'd been seen elsewhere in the village, so I couldn't have been at the rectory."

"Policemen's double-talk: all my eye and Betty Martin!" Bun snapped irritably.

"You should have maintained a dignified silence," Her sister added primly.

"But I didn't know what to do! I've never been questioned by the police before this."

Bun nodded sympathetically. "Quite understand, old girl. No previous experience . . . so you couldn't be sure it was bluff."

Dorothy agreed that such a thought had not entered her head.

"Guilty conscience: so you believed the worst. When it's very possible nobody has ever seen you visiting Edwin by the . . . "

" . . . back door?" Phipps put in brightly.

"Well: most of the villagers are very nice to one's face, but who knows what they might be saying when out of earshot? And you must remember . . . there are at least four cottages overlooking my garden."

"So you could have been seen from a bedroom window?" Bun mused aloud. "And I suppose that's where you were when Wheeler was getting himself shot, amongst the tombstones?"

Dorothy nodded with silent guilt.

"And you told the police EVERYTHING?" Phipps asked.

"I couldn't very well see any alternative."

"Oh well . . . never mind dear. I'm sure the detectives won't tell anyone else, since you were nowhere near the churchyard when the fatal shot was fired." Phipps consoled their troubled friend.

Dorothy replied that she hoped not . . . because she wouldn't be able to continue visiting Edwin if she knew all the village was watching, then laughing at her behind her back. She would have to sell Sweet Lavender and move elsewhere.

"I'm so sorry to have caused so much trouble," she ended.

Phipps listened to her sister reassuring poor Dorothy in a surprisingly kindly manner, considering what a mess she had landed everyone else in, with her latest statement to the police.

At times like this Phipps could see some point in Roman Catholicism. One of their flock would have simply unburdened herself through the confessional . . . instead of making her guilty admissions to crafty Detective Sergeant Bassett.

But Phipps did not voice these thoughts aloud because her older sister could be rather stuffy where Popery and the Church of Rome were concerned.

Then Dorothy, obviously relieved that the Hyde sisters were prepared to be so tolerant and forgiving, revealed that most of her physical sufferings should not be blamed upon the police.

"I woke up - this morning - with the most terrible headache, and I was sick, too! Nothing to do with the time of the month. And I haven't eaten field mushrooms or shellfish . . . so it must have been that parsnip wine."

"One glass too many?" Bun enquired pleasantly.

"I hadn't been keeping count!"

"Perhaps you should have done, dear," Phipps suggested.

Dorothy retorted that - as far as she was concerned - even one glass would be too many in future encounters with that brew.

"Smooth as a liqueur . . . with a kick like a mule!" Bun exclaimed with genuine enthusiasm. "Can't beat the old country recipes: open fermentation, with baker's yeast floating on slices of wholemeal toast. Just like Mama used to make."

"Yes, that's true," Phipps said with a sigh for times long past. "We used to help make all the hedgerow wines, back in the old days, when we were growing up in Papa's Sussex parsonage. But we weren't allowed to taste it . . . so we used to slip downstairs during the night, dip a kitchen cup into the brew, drink it down as fast as we could, then dash back to the nursery before we got caught. I used to sleep very soundly after sampling our three-week-old bramble wine."

Her sister inclined her head in the direction of the mantelpiece clock, saying they ought to be leaving before Cousin Crispian sent out a search party.

On their way down to the rectory Phipps said she didn't like the sound of things. Her sister believed there would be nothing to worry about: provided everyone else stuck to their original stories.

"The detectives will think people have been trying to shield Dorothy, because of her embarrassing position, and take no further action."

But there was more disconcerting news, when the two sisters were talking with Crispian over dinner, for he mentioned seeing the detectives sifting through a pile of builder's sand near the church.

Phipps shuddered to think what might happen to them if Sergeant Bassett ever discovered they had found the gun he must have surely been looking for. But how did he know where to look? Probably worked it out, just the same as Bun did!

Then there was more bad news.

Crispian spoke of finding the pasty bag in his church porch.

"And what d'you think was in it?" Without waiting for any answers, Crispian added brightly, "A brass cartridge case!"

Bun and Phipps stared at each other over their soup plates.

Phipps silently extended two fingers.

Her sister nodded grimly.

Discussing the Way Ahead

"One shot . . . "

"One death too, as far as we know, old girl!"

"But two cartridge cases . . . "

"So the first shot missed," Bun suggested.

The sisters had retired earlier than usual, the moment their cousin was safely tucked away in the library to write his Sunday sermon, and both maids were known to have gone for a walk.

Bun and Phipps wanted to take advantage of the long, light, summer evening to try their luck at fingerprinting.

Whilst the older woman assembled her notebook, the recommended powders and a soft brush - normally used for cleaning her camera lense - Phipps removed the empty magazine from their automatic. She ranged the remaining live bullets beside it, complaining that she felt they were wasting their time.

"I think we should be making our get-away, dear."

"Nonsense! I've just spent the best part of a day finding out how to set about this. I'm certainly not going to let myself be put off by fear of what tomorrow may bring!"

"But that's just it, dear!"

"Mmmm? What's 'it'? Can't you be more precise, Phippsie?"

The younger sister sighed with exasperation.

"That sergeant from Torpoint - who was looking over your shoulder in the library - is bound to tell our Bodmin detectives that he's seen you studying a text book on fingerprinting techniques in Plymouth. Then Sergeant Bassett will receive our cartridge case in a packet bearing a City postmark!"

"And come round to the rectory at a fast gallop to give us the third degree . . . whatever that might be, old girl?"

"Yes dear. Frankly: I'd feel very much happier if I were packing an overnight bag . . . and catching the next cattle boat sailing for Egypt."

When asked why she chose that country - since Argentina was generally said to be the refuge of preference by most criminals on the run from their home police force - Phipps explained how she had recently read a most interesting travel article in The Lady magazine . . . all about sketching on the Upper Nile.

Bun said - very tongue-in-cheek - that she had no idea regions of the Upper Nile had so much to offer.

"Oh yes. It's becoming very popular. Though the writer did suggest one should be prepared to stay away for most of an English winter . . . three months minimum, while those able to manage six would find plenty to interest them for that length of time. And - more to the point - we don't have an Extradition Treaty with King Fuad."

Her sister, by then fully engaged in dusting everything about the pistol and its cartridges with fine powder, which was carefully brushed away to reveal faint patterns of loops and whorls, muttered that six months in that fly-ridden country was - in her view - a course of last resort.

"Best to brazen it out here, Phippsie."

"But we seem to be in danger of losing control of the situation."

"Nonsense! Forewarned is forearmed! The police can't possibly prove it was you or I who posted that second cartridge case: only make wild guesses which would never be accepted as evidence by the Court of Assize."

The younger sister took this point, but said she still could not help feeling that the net was closing in upon them.

"Can't see why, old girl."

"Because, my dear sister - if Sergeant Bassett sieved through all that sand by the bus shelter - it would seem likely that he must know something we don't know!"

"Very likely," Bun replied as she paused to admire her handiwork, "but there's no direct connection with either of us."

"Somebody must have seen me pick up that gun!"

"Rubbish! You kept it covered with your hat. Furthermore: not a living soul came out for water; or to walk round to the pub."

"What if someone, passing in the road, heard the sound of all those shots coming from the rectory?"

"We'll blame the parsnip wine! Mrs Gregory has already lost three bottles . . . and you can hear the noise they make all over the building when one blows up."

"So: why does Sergeant Bassett want to see us again?"

"That silly business with Dorothy Nunn, I expect. He'll give us a pretty stiff telling-off, for making up a false story to support her alibi. Wag the warning finger! Issue threats of prosecution for wasting police time. Nothing we can't handle . . . after all's said and done: we are not exactly without previous experience of their methods."

"First: that body in Topsham," Phipps recalled, "then the lack of a body, down in Polperro." She nodded her head. "Mmmm. I see what you mean, dear."

"Good! So when they come bouncing in tomorrow - full of self-importance - just smile sweetly, say you're sorry . . . then pass around the tea and biscuits. That should keep 'em happy."

Sounds of an approaching motorcycle diverted their attention at that moment.

Phipps looked out of the window to see the rider park his machine and stare up at the house.

"It's Roddy Holbrook, dear. I suppose he's heard about the detectives questioning Dorothy Nunn. I'd better go down and keep him away from Cousin Crispian. You know what clergymen are like, when disturbed in the middle of writing a sermon."

"Take your time. I'm just finishing something. Won't be long."

Phipps met Roddy in the rectory garden, explained that her sister would join them within a few minutes, then encouraged him to stroll about admiring the shrubbery.

Roddy told her he had only just heard the latest rumour. Men from 'B' Company had spent all day at the ranges, on Dartmoor, so he had been kept late to check their ammunition returns after they had arrived back in barracks.

151

"I had dinner in the Mess. Came over to the village quite a bit later than usual. Nipped into the Cornish Arms - avid to hear all the latest gossip concerning The Great Investigation - and learned the bobbies have been applying thumbscrews . . . to poor old Dorothy Nunn?" he ended questioningly.

Phipps mentioned their visit to Sweet Lavender and hearing Dorothy's admission that she had broken down during the police interview.

"Changed her alibi, has she?" Roddy asked anxiously.

"Yes . . . but Bun doesn't think this will affect anyone else. Now that Dorothy has said she didn't come round to the rectory with you, the police are powerless . . . "

" . . . because they know she can't tell them what the rest of us were doing! Well: thank God for that! The lady - whose honour I'm protecting - happens to be married to my adjutant!"

"Oh dear. I suppose you'd be drummed out of your regiment, if anyone got to hear of this flirtation?"

"Not in the case of Nobby Hurst. He's Divisional Welterweight boxing champion! I'd be invited to step into the ring for a lively ten rounds, without the option. Traditional presentation of the loaded service revolver would, in comparison, be like taking the easy way out!"

Phipps offered words of sympathy, then asked Roddy if he knew why the builder's sand had been sieved.

"One of the village kids found a cartridge case before the policemen arrived, took it home and polished it up with mum's Brasso. Big sister saw him, put the cartridge case in a bag, wrote a few words, then raced round and left it in the church porch. But I'd have thought you knew all this . . . ?"

"No. We've both been away all day . . . up in Plymouth. I bought myself a new pair of sandals," Phipps explained, lifting a foot to give it a twiddle and show off her footwear. "Our cousin mentioned finding a cartridge case, over dinner, but that's all we've been told."

"Yes. Found on a porch seat, when he was on his way to bid the Lord goodmorning, by all accounts. It seems the child also told our 'tecs he'd seen a gun . . . "

" . . . in that pile of sand?"

"Right first time! Ten out of ten. Public house opinion has it that our killer ran through the graveyard, then jumped down into that pile of builder's sand, where he dropped his gun, then made off into the night."

"And the gun?" Phipps asked anxiously.

"Disappeared without trace!"

"But . . . if this little child saw it . . . ?"

Roddy Holbrook sniffed at a flowering shrub, said it reminded him of tom cats, then addressed himself to the question.

"Popular belief favours the idea that our killer is a local man who returned for the gun much later . . . when he thought the coast was clear. You didn't see anyone lurking about - or pick up any discarded pistols - when you and your sister were over there, flitting amongst the headstones like a pair of ghosts on an early evening haunting shift, by any chance?"

"Oh no dear," Phipps replied quietly . . . taking care to avoid looking at her escort whilst telling such a bare faced lie.

Fortunately for her peace of mind, Bun waved from the steps shortly after this and Phipps headed back towards the rectory drawing-room, with Roddy following a few paces to the rear.

Once they were seated, Bun apologised for her earlier absence, then handed Roddy a large glossy photograph, asking if he had ever seen it - or any person in the group - lurking around in the village.

Phipps craned her neck to see what this was all about, then sank back into her chair feeling quite bewildered. Why on earth was her sister showing Roddy the most recent picture of their eldest brother with his wife and family? When one remembered their usual place of residence was located in Lewes, Sussex, it was hardly likely Theo and company would be known in St Tudy.

As she expected, Roddy told them everyone in the photo were strangers. "Why do you ask? Suspects?"

"Don't know. I found it in the churchyard. Thought it might have been dropped by our murderer . . . but it was more probably lost by one of the village children. I'll ask, up at the school, next time I'm passing that way."

Phipps opened her mouth to speak, received a warning glare from her older sister, and promptly lapsed into silence.

Bun hastily asked Roddy Holbrook if Phipps had told him all about Dorothy Nunn's paramour.

"Yes. Though as names go: Edwin Plummer doesn't seem to indicate a chap with a terribly romantic nature. But then: I could be unfairly prejudiced. Once knew a lay preacher called Edwin: short, fat and nauseatingly obsequious."

Phipps, who already knew Mr Plummer by sight, told them he was a fairly average sort of man, though he obviously would not see forty-five again and therefore lacked the glamour of virile youthfulness.

"I suppose, with his orchard backing onto Dorothy's land, one could say their's was a liason of convenience."

Rodney nodded acceptance, reminding them Miss Nunn earned her living by writing for women's magazines.

"I expect this dalliance helps broaden her experience. Jolly useful when turning out the odd love story. Probably gives it that desired ring of authenticity."

Phipps was pleased to hear her sister spring to Dorothy's defence, saying she was satisfied the involvement went quite deep. Anyone could see - with only half an eye - that Dorothy Nunn was living an otherwise lonely existence.

"In fact, I would go so far as to say: if she could only face up to the idea of having a man about the house throughout the twenty-four hours of the day, I am certain they would marry and regularise their present situation."

Phipps turned to Roddy, reminding him of what Paul the Apostle once wrote to the Corinthians: "'I say therefore to the unmarried and widows, it is good for them if they abide even as I. But if they cannot contain, let them marry'."

"Yes . . . well come down from your pulpit, old girl." Bun told her younger sister. "Let's be practical: 'Without counsel purposes are disappointed', as they say somewhere amongst all those dreary Proverbs. Rodney! Have you spoken to the Knightons or Teresa Lockhart?" Bun asked.

"No. Came straight round to confer with you first."

"Good. We'll stick to our original story. Which means: we all tell the police we knew of Dorothy's nightime escapades. But we agreed to say she was with Tess, yourself and Phippsie to help spare her embarrassment . . . when they called to ask questions concerning her whereabouts at the time of the shooting."

Rodney said he would go round and tell the others right away.

"'For an oppressive policeman is more feared than any man-eating tiger'. Misquotation from Confucius. Actually: he was criticising the government."

"Don't we all," Bun murmured resentfully.

Rodney got up and walked towards the door.

Bun told him to drive carefully.

Phipps pointed out an accident - at this stage - could make life even more difficult for friends and acquaintances.

"You might get a bump on the head," Bun explained, "forget all our carefully thought out arrangements . . . and tell the truth!"

"Then we should all be most embarrassed," Phipps observed, walking out to the porch with their visitor.

On returning to the drawing-room, she demanded to know what her sister had been trying to do with Theo's family photo.

"Obtain a nice clear set of young Roddy's fingerprints. Process of elimination, old girl! If we play the same harmless trick on all the men - present at Dudley Knighton's dinner party - we might find one of them provides us with identical prints to those I've managed to bring up on parts of the gun and ammunition!

"And he will be our murderer, dear?"

"Of course . . . and all the rest will be in the clear."

"Then what happens?"

"Nothing."

Phipps considered this briefly before suggesting they appeared to be making a lot of effort with very little purpose at the end of it. Her sister rejected this, saying the whole business was proving a most stimulating intellectual exercise.

"You're hardly likely to receive an honorary BSc if nobody knows of your success, dear! And it's not something you can boast about in public because, if our murderer realised you knew of his guilt, we might find ourselves the next victims!"

155

Bun retorted there was no reason to lose a night's sleep worrying about that possibility, because nobody else would ever know the results of their investigations. She then led the way upstairs to begin dusting their brother's photograph with powder. She scrutinised the resultant fingerprints, showing her sister various differences to those on the murder weapon.

Despite inner apprehensions, Phipps became intrigued as Bun drew her attention to the loops and whorls in the original skin patterns, soon asking who was next on the list.

"I thought: Bernard Drysdale."

"Ah yes! The man of mystery . . . with an unknown past."

"Exactly. We don't know where he comes from, or anything about his family background."

"There could be a hidden connection with Wheeler?"

"Something like that, old girl. So, tomorrow morning: Marsh Cottage, here we come!"

Bassett Reviews the Evidence

Detective Sergeant Thomas Bassett found himself faced with several choices, when he arrived at Bodmin police headquarters, on the following morning.

The post mortem on Everard Wheeler had revealed an inoperable tumour; a Mrs Vickery - of Town Farm - had rung up to say that her housemaid now declared she had seen a man prowling about the churchyard, at the time Wheeler was shot, and thought he looked like that Mr Drysdale who ate peacocks; and the morning mail had produced a small cardboard box, bearing a Plymouth postmark.

When opened . . . a brass cartridge case had fallen out. A scrap of plain brown paper followed, bearing the printed message: 'FROM A WELLWISHER. ST TUDY.'

Polkinghorne, after examining the cartridge case, observed that it was the same calibre as the one found by the Tamblyn child, but wondered how two shots came to be fired when there was only one bullet hole in Wheeler's brain box . . . and, according to their pathologist, powder burns indicated the gun had been held close to the victim's head.

"So the killer couldn't have missed with the first shot."

"And what about this 'phone call, Cedric?"

"Town Farm . . . overlooks the churchyard. We'll have to interview this girl, Sarge."

"Gloomy enough under those trees in daylight. I'd have thought it was impossible to tell the difference between a ghoulie and a ghostie in the middle of the night."

"Probably this housemaid's one of those empty-headed village girls who wants to get into the limelight," Polkinghorne suggested.

Bassett took up this theme, supposing that the girl had probably eaten too much cheese for supper.

"And ended up having bad dreams on going to bed, Sarge?"

Bassett admitted his own thoughts ran along similar lines but, just to be on the safe side, he felt it might be wiser if they could interview Mr Drysdale first.

"To prevent him being warned, in advance, by local gossips?"

"'Ess me dear!" Bassett replied, lapsing into broad Cornish.

He flipped over some papers.

"This makes interesting reading, Ceddie . . . if you've got the stomach for intimate physical detail."

Polkinghorne observed that he had stood the test well-enough when acting as Coroner's Officer at post mortems in the past.

His sergeant handed over the pathologist's report. After several minutes scrutiny, the detective constable dropped this onto his desk, tapping his finger on the papers.

"Makes you think, don't it, Sarge?"

"That bit about the tumour . . . a damned good reason for committing suicide."

"Say's here: no more than three months left to live."

"Funny thing is: Wheeler must have known. There'd be pain, surely? Yet MacIlroy, the village doctor, made no mention of it. Job for you, Cedric. Give him a ring. Prod his memory!"

Bassett shook his head sadly.

"What a pity we never found a gun beside the body. With death only a few weeks away, any coroner's jury would have returned a suicide verdict . . . even without the traditional farewell note."

"Didn't you tell me the landlord of the Cornish Arms suggested something like that?"

"Yes. Said Wheeler couldn't have planned the shooting better if he'd pulled the trigger himself."

Bassett screwed up his eyes to help concentration then added, "His exact words - as near as I can remember - were: 'You're goin' to get some mighty funny stories when you asks them where they were when that shot was fired'!"

"Who . . . and why?"

"The up-country folk. Seems some of them play a bit fast and loose when the sun goes down. 'Musical Beds' without the music! The landlord warned me I'd get some very unlikely alibis."

"Such as our little Miss Dorothy Nunn . . . and her doleful boyfriend, Edwin Plummer, Sarge?"

Bassett agreed with a wry smile, adding he had gained the impression that some of the married couples were also playing How's Your Father . . . which meant - with no evidence to support a suicide theory - they were still faced with murder.

"So you think Wheeler got to hear some of his old sparring partners were night-time hedge-hoppers and might have been trying to use this knowledge for his own ends?"

"I've heard it said - at inquests - that some folk go a bit funny in the head when they know they're going to die. I think our landlord, over in the Cornish Arms, felt Wheeler was the sort of chap who resented fancied slights for a very long time."

"Yet he couldn't have set out to embarrass the two-timers: by getting them all together just before he blew his brains out, because the gun would be near the body," Polkinghorne reasoned.

His sergeant accepted this, but pointed out - since it must have been murder - they would have to keep grinding away at the dinner party guests.

"Including the Miss Hydes?"

"No! We're going to play this hand with cards held well up to the chest. We'll see what everyone else comes out with, at first. Unless I'm very wrong . . . those Hydes are the linchpins, helping to hold together other people's alibis."

"Like Miss Nunn's 'fairy tale'?"

"'I was at the rectory with Captain Holbrook'," Bassett mimicked disparagingly. "Well: dear Captain Holbrook should be at his office desk . . . in the Bodmin Barracks, by now. So pull yourself together, Ceddie boy, 'cos we're off to join the army!"

As they were walking out of the headquarters building, a man entered, saw Bassett and asked if he was enjoying his new job.

"Ah! Ken Symons. Haven't seen you for a while. Where are you stationed nowadays?"

Sergeant Symons mentioned Torpoint, spoke of a coming interview with the Deputy Chief Constable, then advised Tommy Bassett that he had a rival working on the St Tudy case.

"Oh yes. Who might that be?"

"Lady by the name of Hyde. Staying in the rectory. I saw the younger sister back-along, when I was down visiting an old uncle of mine. Shouldn't have known who she was, but I was with Pope and he told me. The older one was crossing the stable yard, which can be seen from the road, when we reached the rectory."

"Look . . . I'm on a murder investigation, Ken. Does this story have any place in the current enquiries?"

"Judge for yourself. I had to go to Court, up in Plymouth, yesterday . . . "

"Oh my God!" Bassett groaned.

"That's right, Tommy," Symons laughed. "I saw the pair of them. Had a quick word with the younger one in a cafe. Pretty little thing, isn't she? Anyway: I first noticed the older woman up in the reference room of Plymouth City Library . . . reading a text book all about fingerprinting!"

Detective Sergeant Thomas Bassett ground his teeth.

"I've crossed swords with that pair once before . . ."

"A story which got around the county force," Symons grinned.

"Yes. That crazy search for a one-legged, ginger-haired tramp! So you think those sisters are taking a hand in my murder, now?"

"I only collect the evidence. You're the best person to judge its worth Tommy, old son."

Bassett asked what time Ken Symons had seen the two sisters.

"Older one: twelve - twelve-thirty. Younger one, in a cafe, about one. Important, is it?" Symons asked curiously.

"Damn' right it is!"

Turning towards Polkinghorne, Bassett asked if he had noticed any postmark on the packet in which their cartridge case had arrived, as he was unwrapping it.

"Time-stamped at 1.30 pm , Sarge."

"Remember the date?"

Polkinghorne thought for a few seconds, then nodded.

"Yesterday. So one of those Hydes sisters could have . . . "

160

"Not could!" Bassett snapped at his assistant. "Damn'well did! And we'll never be able to prove it."

"What about fingerprints?" Polkinghorne asked.

Bassett shook his head, saying that the brass had been wiped as clean as a whistle.

Sergeant Symons, sensing that his presence was no longer required, patted Tommy Bassett on the shoulder, telling him not to have a nervous breakdown . . . because there was always room back in the uniformed branch for a good man, such as himself, then went on his way.

Polkinghorne suggested 'phoning up the Plymouth sorting office to find out when the time-stamps were changed.

Bassett asked what good that might do.

"Well - if they change it at two hourly intervals - that would help narrow down the period when the packet was posted."

"The Miss Hydes may appear to be a couple of dotty old dears, but believe me . . . they've got all their wits about 'em!"

Polkinghorne remained thoughtfully silent for a few moments, then pointed out that the packet could just as easily have been posted for a friend.

"Captain Holbrook, for instance?" Bassett prompted.

"Why not? If they are friendly enough to cook up a false alibi for Dorothy Nunn . . . "

" . . . they wouldn't think there was anything suspicious in being asked to post something in Plymouth, so's it would get to its destination quicker?"

"Exactly."

"Yes . . . but whoever posted that packet would have seen the address. And in any case: why should Captain Holbrook send us a brass cartridge case?" Bassett asked.

"To muddy the waters? You said yourself that he's stationed in Bodmin Barracks. Well then . . . "

"Unlimited access to ammunition!"

Detective Constable Polkinghorne remained expectantly silent.

His sergeant nodded slowly and thoughtfully, lips pursed to give greater gravity to his deliberations. Finally, he arrived at a conclusion and looked up.

"Nothing much to stop young Holbrook slipping a handful of empty cartridge cases into his pocket, after a day spent out at the ranges, is there?"

"And we all know what young officers are like, Sarge."

"Blinkin' overgrown schoolboys!"

"So this could be his idea of a practical joke, couldn't it?"

"With one - or both - of those Hyde sisters only too damn' willing to help."

"Of course . . . both cartridges might have been fired by the murder weapon, Sarge." Polkinghorne added cautiously.

"We'll soon sort that out. Send the second cartridge case down to Truro. Ask Tresidder to compare any marks with those found on the Tamblyn cartridge case. If he gets a match, we'll know they've both been fired by the same gun . . . and that's when we go calling on the Miss Hydes!"

Bassett turned round to re-enter the building.

"Get yourself back to the office, Ceddie boy, and start putting things in motion, whilst I slip up to report progress - or the lack of it - to our Super."

When Bassett came down to the CID office, he found his second assistant, Detective Constable Edward Lipscombe had returned from some other enquiry and was now holding the fort.

He had the telephone handset up to one ear, but gestured for Bassett to take it, whispering 'Truro' by way of explanation.

The sergeant found Doctor Tresidder was calling.

He said that he had looked at the Tamblyn cartridge case, since sending his post mortem report up to Bodmin, and reached the definite conclusion that it had been fired, then ejected, from an automatic pistol. This would have normally been loaded with ammunition of 7.65 millimetre calibre.

"Ah . . . more or less what we expected."

"Yes . . . but not very helpful if you can't find the gun."

"We're working on it, sir. By the way . . . I shall be sending another cartridge case down, today."

"From the scene of the shooting?"

"That's for you to tell me, Doctor! Frankly: I don't know where it's come from. Turned up in the morning's mail."

Doctor Tresidder assured Bassett that he would carry out all possible tests to obtain a match, then rang off.

Polkinghorne returned at this point, carrying three mugs of tea and a plate of biscuits.

Bassett repeated his conversation with their pathologist.

"At least this seems to add substance to young Johnnie Tamblyn's statement . . . that he saw such a weapon in the building sand."

"Yes. Pity we failed to find it," Bassett commented ruefully. "How about your 'phone call to Plymouth?"

"The time-stamp was changed at a quarter to twelve."

"So the younger Miss Hyde could have posted our second cartridge case between the City Library and that cafe, where Ken Symons saw her. Useful information, if we need to put the pressure on, when questioning those Hydes, but that's about all," Bassett grumbled before sinking his teeth into a rich tea biscuit.

Then another thought struck him. Swallowing hastily, he asked Polkinghorne if he had spoken to the other - local - doctor.

"Old MacIlroy? Yes."

"Any luck?"

The detective constable shook his head.

"Says it's all news to him, Sarge. Assured me this was the first he'd heard about any tumour. But he did say Wheeler was a very 'close' patient."

"Meaning . . . ?"

"MacIlroy said he thought it very possible the deceased would have made use of his local doctor for coughs and colds, but gone to a more fashionable practice when he found himself threatened with anything of a more serious nature."

"Lack of confidence in the country doctor?"

"That . . . and the very understandable desire to keep his illness a secret. You know what village life is like . . . "

"Slip and fall over at the bus stop . . . and you're suffering from a broken ankle by the time the story reaches the parish pump," Bassett said with a shrug. "So what's the next step? Check with the out-patients' department, up at the hospital?"

"MacIlroy suggested a couple of surgeries here, in Bodmin."

Bassett asked if his assistant had managed to make contact with these people.

"Yes, but I've already tried with no success. Neither of them has any patient called Wheeler."

Bassett expressed the opinion that it probably wouldn't matter who Wheeler had consulted . . . only that he had kept the whole business a closely guarded secret.

"Because if his neighbours knew he was at death's door . . . "

" . . . there wouldn't have been any point in shooting the little squirt, no matter how unpleasantly he might have been acting towards the killer."

"On the other hand, Sarge . . . it could have been an uncontrollable desire for vengeance," Polkinghorne suggested.

"No! You're clutching at straws."

Bassett finished his tea and stood up. "Come on, Cedric. It's high time that we had our chat with young Holbrook."

Policemen versus Peacocks

Bun and Phipps had also finished their elevenses - tea and biscuits served on the rectory lawn - and were making themselves presentable, before strolling down the St Mabyn road as far as Bernard Drysdale's home.

Phipps nearly bumped into her sister's broad back, as they left the rectory. Bun had suddenly come to a halt on the top step, just outside their front door, and was throwing out her matronly bust to inhale noisily.

The sun had risen hours ago, but Phipps presumed the clean country air still retained some of its invigorating freshness.

"Like wine!" her sister exclaimed between deep breaths.

Phipps said she hoped it wouldn't have the same effect on Bun's constitution as Mrs Gregory's lethal parsnip brew wrought upon poor Dorothy Nunn.

Following her sister's example, Phipps also took a few deep breaths, before observing that it was such a pity the glorious Cornish countryside felt so 'close' and airless by midday, during the summer months.

"Cousin Crispian should have found himself a job in one of the coastal parishes, then we could have always enjoyed a cooling sea breeze when we came to visit."

"Yes . . . but not much in the way of shade, old girl. Haven't you noticed that there aren't many tall trees growing near the north coast? Mostly stunted oak or hawthorn, permanently bent over towards the east, due to being constantly pounded by westerly gales sweeping in from the Atlantic."

Phipps admitted it had been a bit of a shock - when the Knightons had driven them up to Bude - to see all the hedgerow trees leaning across the road.

"Quite different to what we were used to in Sussex, where so many villages are tucked away in sheltered valleys."

Following her older sister around the short gravel drive, towards the county road, Phipps pointed to a small, dark cloud of intense physical activity.

"The gnats are flying high, dear. A sure sign of continued fine weather for the harvest."

As if on cue, a carter came out from the farm yard beyond the opposite hedge. He led a team of heavy draught horses down the road for a short distance before turning into a field, where he could be seen hitching up to the reaper/binder, in readiness for another day's corn cutting, as the Hyde sisters passed by.

Bun gestured towards a beautiful, well-grown Rhode Island Red cockerel, which was eagerly pecking up fallen grain from a roadside verge.

"I suppose that's the bounder who woke me at four o'clock in the morning!" She muttered irritably.

Phipps observed that the bird would make someone a fine Christmas dinner . . . though she wouldn't care to pluck and draw the poor creature herself.

Once the village outskirts had been left behind, their conversation reverted to the task ahead. Phipps said she quite understood this business of elimination, but still found it difficult to believe a nice person - such as Bernard Drysdale - could shoot another in cold blood.

Bun reminded her that officers and gentlemen had been known to shoot the odd German, during the course of war. And there had been that nasty business of the discharged shotgun, when the late Mr Wheeler had been exercising his dog.

"In any case, Phippsie . . . we know very little about any of these people."

"Mmmm. Only what they see fit to tell us."

"And where the Drysdales are concerned: that isn't very much!"

"You think there could be hidden depths, dear?"

166

"Why not? Lots of people have something they'd rather not discuss in public. No reason why Bernard should be any different. He's very pleasant, I grant you . . . but I dare say the same might be said of the Public Executioner, when off duty, and look at the way he earns his living!"

They turned a final bend, towards the bottom of the hill, and saw Marsh Cottage nestling beneath green trees, just beyond the side of their road.

So cosy and homely, Phipps thought to herself . . . then she realised the peacock on the opposite side of the tarmac was viciously attacking something as if its own survival depended upon a successful outcome.

When they had drawn nearer she saw, to her horror, that the bird had a small snake curled around its cruel beak. As she watched, the peacock banged its victim repeatedly against a large stone jutting from the hedge, causing the snake to writhe and twist itself into even tighter knots.

Then the bird shook its head violently.

The snake dropped to the ground . . . and the peacock darted forward to gobble it up!

The Hydes told Millicent Drysdale all about this unequal contest, after they had exchanged the usual greetings, upon arrival. Phipps was surprised to be informed that all the birds were brought up as naturally as possible. In summer months this meant they were completely free to roam at will, more or less living off the land.

"They'll eat almost anything," Millie told the two sisters, "berries, insects, chickweed and meadow grass . . . with small rodents, worms, frogs or snakes for the meat course. I expect Homer found himself a grass snake."

Phipps stared in disbelief.

Her sister raised an eyebrow. "Homer?"

"Comes of having a classical education," Bernard explained, having joined them. "We name all our birds after characters in Greek Mythology . . . or their poets."

Phipps thought this was nice . . . and did the birds answer to their names?

"Oh dear, no!" Millicent laughingly replied, "But it's more natural than shouting 'Come in Number Seven. Time for your bran mash'."

"Or: 'Come in bird number Twenty-four. Your time is up. We need a hot dinner'," Bernard added.

Phipps shot an anxious glance towards her sister.

Bun mouthed a silent 'Ooooh', by way of reply.

"So what's the latest news on the village grapevine?" Bernard asked once they had gone inside and were all seated in the Drysdale drawing-room.

"According to our curate cousin; who told us that he heard this story from Elsie Skinner; who works at Town Farm . . . with a bedroom window overlooking the churchyard . . . you head the list of suspects!"

Phipps winced with embarrassment.

This was just like Bun! Straight and to the point. No tact whatsoever.

Bernard asked what he had done to deserve this honour.

"Allowed yourself to be seen - dodging about amongst the gravestones - at approximately the time that shot was fired."

"So I can expect Bassett and his bloodhound at any moment?" Bernard asked with a carefree laugh. "Perhaps you should excuse me, while I pack my toothbrush and a change of underwear, before they come dragging me off into durance vile."

"Perhaps you'd be good enough to take a look at this, before you leave," Bun said, hastily digging into her handbag, "if you can spare a minute."

Phipps watched in silence as Brother Theo's family photo was handed over and Bernard was asked if he recognised anyone.

He did not. He showed it to Millicent, who also shook her head, then the photo was returned. Phipps almost giggled at the careful manner in which her sister slipped it between sheets of tissue paper - concealed within her handbag - to avoid smudging Bernard Drysdale's fingerprints.

Wondering if the gun she had found could have just possibly been his property, Phipps casually mentioned Captain Holbrook's story about the Bodmin detectives sieving building sand.

"Apparently, one of the village children is said to have seen something which looked like an automatic, on the morning of the shooting . . . but before the police arrived."

Bernard only laughed, admitting he had seen the two men sweating like cart horses when he strolled up to the village shop for his morning newspaper.

"I wondered what was going on. Now I know. Most amusing."

Which means he's either as innocent as the proverbial new-born babe, or a jolly good actor, Phipps thought to herself.

Then there were sounds of a motor car drawing up.

Everyone turned to stare across at the window, wondering who had arrived.

Millicent crossed the room, to take a closer look.

"Oh my God! It's the police!" she gasped.

Bernard, Bun and Phipps joined her.

But before anyone could get out of their vehicle, a large peacock ran across the grass, screeching angrily, flew up with both feet outstretched in front of its body, and began fiercely clawing the car window in a fit of obvious rage.

Phipps could now see Detective Sergeant Bassett's normally placid face quite clearly. It appeared to express acute anxiety.

"That's Horace," Bernard commented dispassionately. "He's not exactly one of natures philosophers. Everlastingly taking running jumps at things he sees as a threat."

"We always have to lock him up in the nearest shed whenever the coalman's due to call," Millicent added. "That silly bird's got himself into the most embarrassing habit of pecking the poor man's derrière!"

"Frightfully dangerous when the fellow's got a hundredweight of best Derby Brights on his back," Bernard said with a shake of the head. "If that lot dropped on Horace . . . well, the poor creature wouldn't even be fit to eat."

Bun and Phipps exchanged startled glances.

"The real point is," Millicent hurried to explain, "he's only ten. In the prime of life. We don't want to lose him just yet!"

Bun drew her sister back from the window, because she didn't want the detectives to see them.

Bernard said there wasn't any need.

"The sun's shining right into their eyes. They can't possibly recognise people inside the cottage."

"It would appear Bassett and friend are trapped," Bun observed wonderingly.

"Oh they are!" Millicent said very positively. "If they dare to set foot outside their car Horace will draw blood!"

"And you mustn't think, just because we don't ride to hounds, that we are in any way averse to indulging in blood sports, especially where uninvited policemen are concerned," Bernard added with a laugh.

"But we'll have to do something," his wife retorted.

"All right Millie, so we shall . . . but not just yet. Let 'em sweat! After all: they aren't here by invitation . . . only a couple of gate-crashers," Bernard replied with a wolfish grin.

Bun declared she was beginning to find those two policemen a bit of a bore.

"Our police can be a great disappointment - where crime is concerned - because they ask so many questions, but never reply to any of mine. Ah! Your Horace is warming to his task," she ended.

All heads turned around to look out of the window once again, eagerly watching the furious peacock fly up to land on the roof of the police car.

This vehicle had been designed as an open tourer, though the county police authority decreed that its folding canvas roof should remain permanently in place when on official business.

Phipps wondered how long this sagging material could withstand such a heavy body performing the avian equivalent of a paso doble and asked its weight.

"Something over twenty pounds," Bernard replied, chuckling with delight as the detectives hunched forward, necks twisted, to eye ominous bulges in the underside of their fragile roof.

All four continued to watch as Horace pounded steadily to and fro, hoarsely shrieking 'Pee-haun' over and over again, while swishing his yard and a half of tail feathers around in a constant swirl of evil temper.

Phipps caught her breath in suppressed excitement as his dark metallic green-blue head flashed in the sunshine, before lunging downwards in an attempt to thrust that wicked beak through the roof canvas.

"Go on! Give it to 'em, Horace!" Bernard encouraged quietly. "This makes me think of the time Atlas ripped a sleeve off that moth-eaten old tramp's coat."

Millicent said she was reminded of Apollo tearing Bernard's shirt whenever her husband went too close to any of his concubines. "Stupid bird! I mean to say . . . what could Bernard possibly do with a peahen?"

Phipps was sorely tempted to respond 'Eat it', but tactfully restrained herself and remained silent.

Then Horace, after another vicious lunge, broke the canvas.

Millicent said Bernard really must do something.

Bernard replied, "Plenty of time for that. I prefer to wait until that bird's had time to cool off. I don't want him venting his spite on me."

"You'll end up having to buy the police a new car!"

"We can afford it. All our birds are fully insured for this sort of occurrence. Have been, ever since Dionysus went on safari to Tremeer Manor, found the ornamental gardens to his taste, and ate the ruddy lot." Turning to Bun and Phipps he declared, "More trouble than a tribe of Tipperary Goats!"

Sounds of men shouting reached the watchers. Bun declared she never thought she'd live to see the day when she would hear a couple of full-grown policemen calling for assistance.

"Well . . . they are human, dear," Phipps murmured. "It's just that they're trained to hide their feelings."

"Not doing a very good job at that, right now, old girl!"

Phipps caught sight of Detective Constable Polkinghorne trying to attract their attention by waving frantically.

He had good reason to be so agitated, she thought, for Horace had managed to enlarge the hole in the roof so that he was now able to poke his head inside. Phipps watched, heart in mouth, as that evil questing head swung from side to side, beak snapping wildly all the while.

171

At this point, Phipps saw Bassett slide off his seat to take refuge beneath the dashboard, and Bun wondered aloud why he didn't make a run for the cottage.

"Too risky," Bernard told her. "Imagine twenty pounds of angry bird hitting you between the shoulder blades. You'd be knocked flat . . . and he'd have the shirt off your back before you could get up again. Then he'd start on your flesh! Remember: they eat meat. Even eat their own chicks!"

Phipps shivered with revulsion.

Millicent said very firmly that Bernard had had his fun, but now he really must effect a rescue.

Muttering 'Spoilsport', he set off to help as instructed.

His wife said she must make haste to put the kettle on and brew a strong pot of tea.

"So good for shock. By the way . . . if you don't particularly wish to stay and chat with our 'Bodmin Bobbies', you can always leave by the footpath fields."

Bun and Phipps agreed this would be much more tactful than answering yet more questions. Millicent led them through her back door, indicated a path screened by tall bamboos, and told them to cross a couple of fields then turn right, for the road.

The Irish Connection

Meanwhile . . . over in their police car, the two detectives were no longer on speaking terms.

Polkinghorne had been amused when the enraged peacock first launched his attack. He could see history in the making. One of those charge-room legends which are passed on from one generation of policemen to the next.

He even got as far as imagining the day of his retirement, when questioned about the most memorable experience of his entire career, he would answer quite casually, as if it had all been part of the day's work: 'That time I was attacked by an insane peacock'.

However, when the wretched bird's head finally pierced their canvas hood, the detective was suddenly afraid of sustaining actual physical injury. Suppose that material split, depositing a peacock on his lap, in a maelstrom of clutching claws and ruffled feathers?

"Why don't you sound the horn, Sarge?"

"Because I don't want to make matters worse!"

"We could attract attention from inside that ruddy cottage and get help!"

"And upset this mad bird even more?" Bassett demanded. "No thank you, Cedric!"

Polkinghorne lapsed into temporary silence thinking, once again, of the terrifying spectacle of those fearsome claws scratching at the car's side windows. They could take a man's eye out with a single swipe! And half his face with the second one!

173

And now there was this ever-searching beak to contend with, constantly snapping about, just above his head. A chap could lose an ear. At moments like this, one needed the benefit of good leadership. A superior with sufficient strength of character to lead the troops forwards from the front . . . and not go cowering down underneath the car's dashboard! Confining his encouragement to issuing instructions from a place of relative safety.

Finally, just as Polkinghorne began steeling himself into making a run for the cottage, hoping the peacock's trapped head would prevent it following, he saw Drysdale approaching the car.

Then relief turned to stark panic.

The property owner merely gave the terrified occupants of the police car a cheerful wave . . . and calmly walked straight past, disappearing into a nearby barn!

Polkinghorne decided there comes a time in the life of every living creature when personal survival must take precedence over tribal loyalties. Hopefully calculating that he might have several precious seconds in which to make his escape, before the peacock realised his prey was getting away, the detective constable furtively released his door catch.

Then - gripping the edges of his seat with both hands - he took a deep breath and launched himself outwards. Landing in a huddled bundle, Polkinghorne was aware that the bird had stopped to take in this new development.

Without wasting a split second, he scrambled to his feet, dashed across the road, and lumbered hell for leather towards Marsh Cottage as fast as his big flat feet would carry him.

The front door opened before the constable . . . just as he was preparing to crash through with the force of his own bodily mass and terminal velocity.

Polkinghorne threw himself into the building.

To his immeasurable relief, he heard the door slammed shut.

After recovering both physical poise and mental equilibrium, he assumed his official role by sternly asking Millicent Drysdale, "Are you aware that it is an offence to allow wild animals, in your care, to roam at will . . . if they are known to be a possible source of danger to other persons or domestic pets?"

To Polkinghorne's amazement, the lady of the house simply introduced herself, offered him a nice cup of tea, freshly made no more than a couple of minutes before his sudden - and totally unexpected arrival - then enquired sweetly if he took sugar.

"Two lumps please," he mumbled.

He was handed cup and saucer, shown into a sitting-room, and left to his own devices.

The detective constable crossed to look out of a window.

Drysdale was now returning to the scene . . . carrying something which looked remarkably similar to a small round, red-leather, African native's war shield. He approached the police car with caution, keeping the shield between himself and the peacock, which now had its head free and was eagerly looking about for its next victim.

The bird flew down to ground level, shook its ruffled feathers, then rushed at Drysdale to make savage darting pecks, always being thwarted by the owner's adept use of the shield.

"Come on man!" he shouted at the cowering figure of Detective Sergeant Bassett. "Now's your chance! Make a run for it . . . but hurry. I can't hold this bird for long."

Polkinghorne smiled mirthlessly as he watched his sergeant scramble out of the car and hurry towards the cottage.

Drysdale shouted and waved his free arm at the peacock, then retreated.

Apologies, official cautions, assurances for the future and solemn warnings were exchanged over cups of tea.

Afterwards: questions were asked and official eyebrows raised on hearing some of the answers.

As regards to guns: an ex-service .45 revolver was produced without argument . . . together with a box of ammunition and the necessary firearms certificate.

Detective Sergeant Bassett told the Drysdales that their story would be cross-checked, then left the premises.

He drove to the top of the hill, then pulled over to park in a field gateway. Cigarettes were produced, lit, and both men inhaled deeply. Letting his own breath out with a rush, Bassett told his assistant he didn't want another morning like this again.

Polkinghorne, relieved that their relationship was back on normal lines, agreed wholeheartedly.

"There were moments, back there, when I could see us getting early retirement, Sarge . . . due to injuries sustained in the course of duty," he muttered.

Bassett replied that he had almost given up all hope of living long enough to draw his retirement pension at one point, when that dreadfully questing beak first succeeded in breaking through the car's roof canvas.

"But who would have ever guessed that Drysdale is a war hero?" Polkinghorne said after a few moments of thoughtful silence. "I felt proper embarrassed when he brought out all them medals as proof."

"Member of the aristocracy too!" Bassett ruminated.

"But that almost rules him out of the case, doesn't it? I mean: with all his family living up north there can't be any prior connection between them and the deceased, can there?"

Bassett shrugged. "Probably not. You can see why he's living down here, using an assumed name though . . . officer in the Black and Tans . . . "

" . . . with Sinn Fein putting a price on his head!"

"Pity about his marriage going on the rocks," Bassett murmured thoughtfully, "but what can you expect?"

Polkinghorne agreed that Drysdale shouldn't have married an Irish wife. "Pull of the land, Sarge. Family estates taking preference over a wandering life and possible insecurity. Now look at the mess he's in . . . "

" . . . a Roman Catholic spouse, with no chance of a divorce."

"Yes . . . a bit stupid though. You can almost say his present problems are his own silly fault."

Bassett heaved a sigh. "Well I know one thing, Ceddie boy. I wouldn't have been so daft as to marry an Irish girl, then join the Military Police and spend the next six months helping to lock up all her friends and relations in Mountjoy Prison."

"No wonder he sleeps with a loaded revolver beside his bed!"

"Yes. But - on the other hand - I suppose he didn't see much alternative, once The War was over in France and Belgium."

Bassett shrugged his shoulders, going on to point out that being a younger son, with little prospect of ever succeeding to the title, and no money in his own right, the formation of The Black and Tans must have seemed like the answer to all life's problems: a new career, together with the chance of marrying into a landed Irish family.

"The security of a comfortable home, where his wife and children would always feel at ease," Polkinghorne mused.

Bassett shook his head. "Typical of his class, really. School, college, commission. As he said himself: if he'd come back to England it would have been a case of teaching in some prep school . . . "

" . . . or selling Encyclopaedia Britannica on the doorsteps of those new housing estates around the outskirts of London."

"No wonder he stayed in Ireland and hung on to his commission," Bassett observed.

Polkinghorne accepted this, but pointed out Drysdale shouldn't have married into an 'enemy' family.

"That's like some of our own chaps . . . go on a course up-country, fall head over heels in love with one of the local girls, and the next thing you know: they're coming back to Cornwall as man and wife. I don't go much on mixed marriages, Sarge. Cornwall's different from Up There . . . and Them Up There's very different to Us Down Here. It's like oil an' water . . . they don't mix!"

Bassett ignored this, changing the subject slightly to say that he really thought they had uncovered a bigamist, when Drysdale mentioned still having a wife in Ireland.

Polkinghorne agreed with a grin, admitting that he'd been about to issue the customary caution, prior to taking the fellow into custody.

"Then he goes an' spoils everything for you, by explaining all about the present Mrs Drysdale!" Bassett laughed.

"Yes . . . proper let-down, finding out she's only a widowed sister."

"He's a clever devil, though," Bassett mused thoughtfully. "To combine a change of name with pretending to be married."

Polkinghorne accepted that if anybody, from his Irish days, was out looking for him they'd never connect that Black and Tans officer with this present day peacock grower.

"Makes a change from Captain Holbrook, anyway: playing fast and loose with the wife of a fellow officer at the barracks."

"D'you know, Cedric . . . I almost burst out laughing when that bounder told us the other fellow is a regimental boxing champ!"

"Then cheerfully admitted telling us a cock and bull story about going to the rectory, after Knighton's dinner party, because he wasn't much good with the gloves . . . "

" . . . and can't run very fast either!" Bassett shook his head. "I don't know . . . you can't beat the gentry for keeping calm in a tight corner."

He glanced at his watch, then shuffled himself up straight once again. "I reckon we've just about got time to have a few words with that milkmaid - or whatever she is - round at Town Farm, before we go to lunch."

This proved to be a perfectly straightforward interview.

Polkinghorne took notes while his sergeant questioned young Elsie Skinner, who told them she slept in an attic room. Being directly below the roof, it was very hot at this time of the year and she had been unable to sleep, on the night of the shooting.

"So I got up an' 'ung me 'ead out the window . . . to get a bit of breeze, like. An' that's when I saw 'im. It were some quiet: except for they ole screech owls. An' no lights anywhere. Then I see'd this shadowy figure - with a funny pointed 'at - dodging about between the gravestones."

"Sure it wasn't a ghost, m'dear?" Bassett asked.

"Oh no-o-o-o . . . 'cos it were a black shadow, an' ghosts are all white," Elsie explained seriously.

"And why did you think it was Mr Drysdale?"

"'Cos of 'is funny pointed 'at! Just like that ole tweed thing, Mr Drysdale wears."

"A deer-stalker?"

"Dunno 'bout that. Ain't no deer round 'ere. Tell 'ee what: that fellow Sherlock Holmes wears one just like it, in the films."

"Anything else you can remember, Elsie?"

"He were fairly tall . . . and normal . . . not fat. But I'm certain it were Mr Drysdale 'cos 'ee's the only chap in St Tudy who do wear a funny pointed 'at."

"Couldn't have been a woman?"

"No-o-o-o. They don't wear 'ats like that."

"Now . . . about that shot . . . ?" Bassett asked hopefully.

Elsie replied that she hadn't actually heard it, because she must have fallen asleep. But she woke up later, looked at the clock beside her bed, and found it was midnight.

"What happened next? What did you do, this time?"

Elsie shrugged. "Just turned over an' went back to sleep."

Bassett thanked the girl and led the way out to their car, saying they would check with the village bobby, but he thought Elsie Skinner was telling the truth.

"The fact that she didn't hear the shot proves it, Sarge. If she was making up her story as she went along, she wouldn't have missed out on the one chance to pretend she'd heard something nobody else had heard."

"What about her waking up at midnight?"

"Could have been restlessness, due to the heat, but you'll notice she didn't wake up any more. Maybe the room became cooler, as the night wore on . . . "

" . . . or maybe it wasn't the heat, that woke her, but the sound of the shot! If she was properly asleep, she wouldn't know what had disturbed her. Take cats, trying to get the lid off your dustbin. You're asleep. You wake up . . . then you hear yowling as they fight it out for first pick at your fish an' chip paper. And next morning, you find the dustbin lid lying on the cobbles. But you can't actually recall hearing the 'clang' as it hit the deck."

"That would account for nobody coming forward to tell us they heard the shot," Polkinghorne murmured. "But this all brings us back to Drysdale again. His story is that the pair of them went in to have a nightcap with Lady Mary Holbrook, after giving her a lift home. If young Elsie's right, he must have slipped down to the churchyard from there . . . but why?"

"Best not to bend our brains any more until we've heard what Lady Mary has to say upon that subject," Bassett counselled.

The Detective Sergeant looked at his watch, noted that it was getting near their time for taking an official meal break and asked his assistant if he fancied a proper meal.

"Meat an' two veg?"

"On expenses, of course . . . with a bit of figgy duff to follow."

"Won't get that in the Cornish Arms, will we?"

"Thought we might go to a nice little cafe I know, bottom of the main street, in Camelford."

"What if the guv'nor finds out, Sarge?"

"We can interview one of those auctioneers, present at Knighton's place, for Wheeler's last supper."

"Good idea," Polkinghorne agreed, as Bassett drove off.

They had to pass Jack Wills' office, in order to reach the chosen cafe. Bassett's brain had just registered the words Auctioneer and Valuer - above a window full of property particulars - when he caught sight of the Hyde sisters.

They were walking up the pavement and could have been approaching the estate agent's premises. Unfortunately, there was a lorry following close behind the police vehicle, which made it inadvisable for Bassett to stop and see where they went. He drove on, gripping the steering wheel until his knuckles whitened.

"Now what the Hell are they up to?" he wondered aloud.

Bun and Phipps' Round Trip

As it happened, Bun and Phipps were making the best of the remainder of that day by going out and about, adding to their collection of fingerprints every bit as eagerly as keen stamp collectors are reputed to search for 'penny blacks'.

Following their hasty exit from Marsh Cottage, they had gone back to the rectory and compared specimens of the Drysdales' fingerprints on their brother's family photograph, with those on their gun and cartridges.

"No resemblance whatsoever," Bun declared, "which lets both Bernard and Millicent off the hook."

"And poses the question of: what shall we do for the rest of the day?" Phipps asked her sister.

Bun thought it might be best if they left the village, in order to further postpone being questioned by the detectives about their activities whilst in Plymouth.

Phipps agreed and, after giving the matter some thought, suggested a roving commission which should allow them to combine the business of detection with the pleasure of riding around the beautiful Cornish countryside.

"What do you have in mind, old girl?"

"Well . . . I thought that if we go up to the village straight away, we should be in plenty of time to catch the country bus on its first return trip from Bodmin to that old stagecoach inn, now called the Wellington Hotel, down in Boscastle."

Bun enquired why they should want to visit Boscastle.

"We don't, dear. But that bus goes through Camelford . . . "

181

" . . . where a brief visit to Jack Wills' office should enable us to obtain a decent set of his fingerprints for elimination purposes or otherwise."

"We can then ask our way to the Southern Railway station, taking a chance on how frequently the trains run, and buy two tickets for Bodmin via Wadebridge . . . "

" . . . where we then pay a similar visit to Bill Rowse's office?" Phipps suggested with a tight little smile.

Bun nodded, going on to say that they could return home via another train - or a bus, whichever ran to the most convenient time table - by way of Bodmin and the country bus service.

She carefully cleaned off both the surfaces of her test photo, then the sisters hurried up to the local bus stop, beside the main entrance to the old churchyard.

Later, everything was going precisely as the sisters had planned when they were spotted by Detective Sergeant Bassett, on his way to lunch.

Phipps thought she recognised the car.

Bun pointed out that it was a common enough make, which meant that one could expect to see plenty of summer tourists passing along a main road in similar vehicles, so there was nothing to worry about.

They entered the Camelford estate agent's office and, after reminding Mr Wills that they had met at a dinner in St Tudy, Bun cheerfully explained that she could be interested in buying a small cottage in the district . . . providing the price was right. In which case: could he let her have particulars of any property which might prove suitable.

Mr Wills could, and did so.

Phipps watched approvingly as her sister placed the sheets of property details straight into her handbag with the greatest care, to lessen the chance of smudging the obliging estate agent's fingerprints.

However, when asked the way to Camelford railway station, the Hydes were told it was out in the country . . . a couple of chains short of two miles distant.

To Phipps' relief, her sister very sensibly asked for a taxicab.

The driver set them down outside a handsome stone bulding, surrounded by fields. Phipps admired the distant patchwork of meadows and hedges which criss-crossed this striking rural scene for several miles, before being obscured by a mid-summer heat haze shimmering between land and sky.

Bun muttered something which sounded vaguely poetic, about places where time stood still, sheep panted with the heat, milch cows dozed peacefully 'neath oak and chestnut, and all the railway staff appeared to be asleep, as they sauntered into the tiny booking-hall.

Firm rapping on the office shutter, followed by cries of 'Are you there?' eventually caused a porter to come in from the direction of the platform.

His shirt sleeves were rolled up above bony elbows, his tie was twisted and gravy-stained, whilst his waistcoat was unbuttoned, thereby displaying a grubby shirt.

"I bin out-along, waterin' me plants," he explained. "Wanter go somewhere, do 'ee?"

"Only if you have a train available," Bun replied equably.

Phipps smiled to herself as this little man pulled out his pocket watch, looked at it, then screwed up his sharp-featured rat-like face, indicating concentrated thought, before saying that the ten o'clock off Exeter - a stopping train to Padstow - would be coming through in five minutes time.

Bun told him she would like two singles to Bodmin.

Phipps drifted away to the nearest platform, thankfully sitting down in the shade and sighing with contentment. Such a peaceful scene, she thought to herself.

Even the carters in a nearby cornfield were lying against a convenient hedge, washing down lunchtime sandwiches with the contents of half-gallon stone cyder bottles, the clatter of their reaper/binder stilled and no other strident mechanical sound to be heard for miles.

Hitched to a nearby oak tree, Phipps saw the two horses also making a meal of things, dipping into their nosebags, then munching noisily whilst enjoying a well-earned midday rest from their daily task of pulling the machine which cut the corn.

There was a farm on the other side of the station crossroads but, as far as she could determine, all the livestock must be fast asleep. No cock crowed, nor bullock lowed.

Then, in the distance - some miles away - she noticed a plume of white smoke, or steam, travelling slowly along a fold in the ground. This, she presumed, would be their train approaching down a cutting from the previous station.

Bun joined her and they crossed to the down platform, where several crates of lettuce and four large chip baskets full of ripe tomatoes stood ready for loading into the next train, doubtlessly bound for shops in Wadebridge or Padstow.

"I saw a notice advertising seven-day tickets for ten and sixpence, in the waiting room," Bun told her sister when they had sat down on a bench seat.

"Travel anywhere from Padstow to Bude - by Southern Railway trains - and as often as you like," Bun continued. "It might be an idea for us, if we can ever find the time to explore further afield."

Phipps recalled seeing that London weekend tickets were available for threepence under two pounds but, as she said to Bun, one didn't fancy going up to Town during a heatwave.

Further desultory conversation ceased when the porter crossed to their platform. Shortly afterwards, they heard the sound of a whistle, then a tired-looking engine pulled two very dirty, smoke-grimed, green-painted carriages into Camelford Station.

"Padstow train!" The porter shouted, although there were no other passengers waiting. "Stopping at Delabole, Port Isaac Road, St Kew Highway and Wadebridge change for Bodmin North."

Bun and Phipps climbed aboard as the porter handed containers of market garden produce into the guard's van. Then doors slammed, whistles blew, brake rods creaked, their coach juddered and the train lurched away down the track.

Once they had settled into the otherwise empty compartment, Phipps asked her sister if she thought it had been altogether wise to tell Mr Wills they were going to Padstow . . . when they only intended to visit Wadebridge. Estate agents all knew one another and Mr Rowse might hear of their calling on Mr Wills and wonder why they needed to lie about their proposed itinerary.

Bun replied that - contrary to what they had been taught at nanny's knee - real life experiences showed there was little purpose served by telling the truth when a convenient lie would do just as well. In her opiniou, truth should be reserved for more important occasions than five minute chats with estate agents.

"As Pontius Pilate once remarked, 'What is truth?'"

Phipps could think of no answer to that.

She watched her sister go through the same routine with Bill Rowse - as had been practised on Jack Wills - upon their arrival in Wadebridge.

Then they ate a very late lunch in a restaurant adjacent to the imposing town hall, before strolling back to the station and boarding the next train for Bodmin North.

This was the Southern Railway's station, located on the opposite side of town from Bodmin General and the rival GWR.

"Did you see the way that man Rowse was looking at you?" Bun asked, as they watched the broad plain of the river valley give way to steep-sided fields and woodland.

"Made me feel as if I was wearing an invisible frock, dear!"

"He reminds me of Algy Hackett, the Hampshire Selbornes' dreadful cousin. He stared at me so intently, on one visit, that I felt I had to slip upstairs and put on an extra petticoat!"

"Brutally ravished with every passing glance! The younger girls could thank their lucky stars the Good Fairy wasn't present to give Algy ten wishes . . . or there would have been ten fatherless children born nine months later," Phipps observed.

This set the tone of conversation for the remainder of their journey to Bodmin, as they reminisced about hunt balls and country house parties attended prior to 1914. But they had to sit apart on the Boscastle bus, for there were no empty double seats.

Phipps squeezed herself in - beside an elderly, very overweight countrywoman who sucked peppermint-drops throughout the journey - and spent her time trying not to breath too frequently.

Once back inside the St Tudy rectory, Bun led the way up to her bedroom. She immediately got out her fingerprint outfit, to make tests on those sheets of property details which they had collected from the Camelford and Wadebridge estate agents.

Phipps stole sideways glances, as she wet her handkerchief and wiped bird droppings from her sister's dressing table.

Bun was making fast work of dusting paper surfaces, having become familiarised with the necessary routine by now.

Then - quite suddenly - she stopped.

Phipps held her breath.

Her sister straightened up, staring ahead, deep in thought.

Phipps saw her shake her head, before bending to look again.

Then she turned, a dumfounded expression on her face.

"I believe I've found our murderer, old girl! Come and look."

"Goodness me! Who is it?"

"I haven't the slightest idea!"

Roddy Holbrook's Revelations

Miss Philippa Hyde crossed the bedroom to look at a sheet of duplicating paper, bearing details of Miss May's Cottage, Foxes Row, in the parish of St Teath. This was one of the properties being offered for sale by Jack Wills of Camelford.

'"A detached country residence in excellent structural repair, sited within a large garden which might be described as being more in the nature of a small paddock. The property is within easy walking distance of village shops and the parish church.' Yes. It sounds very nice, dear. Are we thinking of buying it?"

By the way in which her sister shook her head, Phipps realised she was displeased.

"Never mind about all the old 'guff,'" Bun instructed with a wave of the hand. "What about those fingerprints?"

Phipps stared closer at the details of Miss May's Cottage, was unimpressed but had more sense than to pass an adverse judgement. All those black smudges, thickly over-laying one another and bordering each side of the paper. How did one ever learn anything from this mess? She accepted the magnifying glass, which Bun thrust into her hand with some show of impatience, and looked again.

To her delight, Phipps now discovered that she could make out very faint patterns of whorls and loops, but most of those smudges still remained featureless to her untrained eye.

Bun next directed her sister's attention towards fingerprints which had already been discovered on the automatic and its ammunition.

Phipps dodged between these and Jack Wills' sheet of cottage particulars. Mmmmm. Very faint, in places, but none the less similar for all that.

"Here . . . and here," she murmured, pointing to some impressions on the edge of the paper.

"Identical!" Bun stated triumphantly.

"Absolutely! But what about all these other marks, dear?"

"The large ones are clearest, but there's none on the gun."

"And these very small marks?"

"Made by the office girl. I looked at her hands while Jack Wills was speaking to you about that awful house on the edge of Delabole slate quarry. She had fingers as thin as pencils. I wondered if she was old enough to have left school."

"Oh I think so, dear. Her face had a very 'knowing look'," Phipps replied, then pretended to study the sheet of paper once again . . . whilst thinking over the available evidence.

The large, very clear prints would have been made by Jack Wills. They had definitely been impressed by a large hand . . . and she had noticed the Camelford estate agent had what might be called countryman's hands. More suited to holding the plough than an office pen or pencil.

"But how do you explain the murderer's fingerprints, Bun?"

"Ah! Glad you asked that question, Watson," her sister replied with a grimly self-satisfied smile.

Phipps suggested her clever sister get to the point at issue.

"The curious fact that they only appear on one sheet of paper, when we obtained particulars of three other properties from Wills, led me to one conclusion. That estate agent must have shown it to somebody else. Mr 'X' looked at it, then gave it back."

Phipps assured her older sister that she was wonderful and had obviously missed her true vocation . . . then sweetly pointed out that any man - normally resident anywhere in the country - could have dropped into the Camelford office, picked up the relevant sheet of particulars, looked . . . then cast it to one side and gone on his way.

"You mean a summer visitor?"

"Yes dear."

Bun's face registered glumness, but she soon rallied round to say that it was just possible a constructive distortion of the known facts might yet yield the desired results, though she had to admit she would be trying a long shot.

"You mean you are going to tell somebody another of your skilfully crafted cock-and-bull stories?"

"Something like that, old girl. I shall telephone Jack Wills to say we are interested in Miss May's Cottage, but do not wish to waste our time viewing the property if he already has other people lined up and about to make an offer."

Bun paused to think, before adding brightly, "I shall say there are some pencilled calculations on the back of his 'particulars' sheet, which lead me to believe another would-be buyer must be very keen to proceed."

She picked up the agent's business card, looked at it, then at her wristlet watch, and finally walked towards the door saying that she would try ringing his home number . . . since there was just time before their own dinner would be served.

Later, on her sister's return, Phipps observed symptoms of dejection.

Bun came into the room, closed the door and sat down with a puzzled look on her face.

Phipps asked, "What's up, dear? Has the donkey kicked over your apple cart? Been told to mind your own business?"

"Au contraire. Wills was most forthcoming."

Bun picked up her magnifying glass and re-checked the suspect's fingerprints yet again. Then she pursed her lips, tapped the polished top of her dressing-table several times - obviously in deep thought - and ended up by looking at the ceiling.

After another pause, she turned towards Phipps.

"According to everything Jack Wills passed on to me, there would appear to be only one possible explanation . . ."

"Which is . . . " Phipps enquired eagerly.

"The late Mr Everard Wheeler shot himself!"

"But that's impossible!" Phipps exclaimed.

Her sister shrugged dismissively, saying that facts were facts and could not be successfully disputed.

Phipps reminded her sister that she had discovered that gun several yards away from where the body was found!

"One cannot blow one's brains out, one minute, then throw the gun away with the next breath. If one has aimed straight and true, there won't be any more breathing!"

"Can't help that, Phippsie. Wills assured me the only person to have shown any interest in Miss May's Cottage was Wheeler. He called in at the Camelford office on the day before our dinner party at Knighton's place . . . mainly to discuss valuation of that piece of land Dudley was interested in buying."

"Then how did his fingerprints get on our sheet of particulars?"

"Wills told me he had a telephone call . . . and Wheeler looked at details of one or two properties while he waited. Miss May's Cottage was one of them. Wills said he had only recently taken instructions for the sale . . . and the sheets of particulars were actually lying on the corner of his desk."

"Right under Wheeler's nose, in fact?"

"Quite! Which proves some of our fingerprints were made by Wheeler."

Phipps accepted this point . . . then went on to say it was just possible that Wheeler had owned the gun, but somebody else had stolen it.

"We don't have any fingerprint on the trigger, thanks to our attempts at unloading the weapon, only on the bullets and slide which contained them."

Bun muttered something about killjoys and wet blankets, but her sister was spared further chastisement by the sound of a gong. Phipps glanced at her watch then suggested dinner was being served earlier than usual.

"Cousin Crispian is driving down to the hospital, at Truro, for a couple of hours . . . to hold hands with poor Joan."

As they walked downstairs, Bun said that she didn't wish to upset her sister's digestive system . . . but during her conversation with Jack Wills, he had also mentioned being questioned by the two detectives from Bodmin.

"He said Sergeant Bassett particularly asked after us."

"So nice to be wanted," Phipps answered wryly.

"Yes . . . but not by the police!" Her sister replied tartly.

Phipps heard more disquieting news after dinner, when Bun and herself were taking their coffee out on the lawn. Sounds of an approaching motorcycle were soon followed by the appearance of young Roddy Holbrook.

"Hello. Sorry to barge in . . . but I've rather let the side down."

"Nothing too dreadful, I hope?" Bun asked, offering coffee.

"Yes. 'Fraid so. Been consorting with the enemy. Giving aid and comfort! So I thought I should pop round . . . to let you know which way the wind blows, and all that sort of thing."

Phipps experienced a sinking feeling, despite the fact that she had just eaten a substantial four course meal.

Roddy sipped his coffee, then turned round to look behind at the rectory frontage, observing that he had never noticed the windows were leaded before this.

"Well-proportioned panes, too. Quite belies the inescapable fact that the jolly old place was only put up in 1909 . . . as witness the date on that granite tablet, up there beneath your eaves."

Phipps saw her sister rolling her eyes skywards, before telling their visitor to stop waffling and get to the point.

"Frightfully sorry. Thought the odd spot of social chit-chat might help ease the strain somewhat. Fact is: I've been bamboozled by the bobbies. Those two Bodmin bounders dropped into my office - up at the barracks - today."

Roddy shook his head at the disagreeable memory.

"Must have known we were due a GOC inspection at any moment. Hoping to catch me on the hop: with my mind chock-full of 'matters militarily'."

Bun told him to spare them further quotations from Gilbert and Sullivan.

"Like me to cut the cackle and get to the gristle? Right-ho! It's about that alibi you were kind enough to cook up."

"You've been rumbled?"

Rodney Holbrook inclined his head in graceful admission.

"Sergeant Bassett, I suppose?

"Hole in one! Bowled me a googly! Oldest trick in the book. Much afraid your's truly fell for it hook, line and sinker."

"But what - precisely - did they actually do?" Bun asked.

"Said I couldn't possibly have been in the rectory, at the time stated, because I had been seen by a constable on foot patrol, speeding down Lower Bore Street."

"Is there such a place?" Phipps asked, trying to be helpful.

"Oh yes . . . in Bodmin!"

"And, having been correctly brought up to believe honesty is the best policy, you told Bassett it couldn't have been you . . . "

" . . . because I was in the lounge bar of the Royal Talbot, down in Lostwithiel, with Annabel Rycroft."

Bun suggested Bassett had then asked for the lady's address.

Roddy Holbrook gave a crestfallen nod.

"Had m'mind on other things . . . those cursed ammunition returns. D'y'know: the workshops people pinch our empty cartridge cases to make cigarette lighters, which they then sell for beer money. Terribly unfair . . . I get the blame when my numbers don't tally."

"How did you explain your lady-love?" Phipps asked.

"Admitted she was married. Sort of threw myself on their mercy. Made a plea for absolute discretion on the grounds that my life would otherwise be endangered."

"St Matthew warns against false prophets who arrive in sheep's clothing, but inwardly are ravening wolves," Bun reflected.

Rodney assured her the apostle knew what he was talking about. Detective Sergeant Bassett's bite was definitely worse than his 'Baaa'!

"By the way, I called on Teresa Lockhart before coming here, but the 'Terrible Tecs' had got there earlier. Poor old Tess told me she's been doing a bit of courting on the QT. Doesn't want the Aged Parent to hear about it . . . him being permanently on the sick list, 'cos it might worry him . . . "

" . . . so that's why she came running to us for an alibi," Bun murmured to Phipps, with an understanding nod.

"'Fraid so," Rodney agreed, "and my own mother's no better!"

"But we heard the Drysdales gave her a lift home, then went in for a nightcap and stopped talking 'til after the time that shot was thought to have been fired," Phipps exclaimed with surprise.

"Bernard stopped . . . but Millicent went home."

Bun raised both eyebrows. "You surely don't mean . . . ?"

Rodney Holbrook replied that he wouldn't care to say what he meant, because it was a subject to which he had not given much thought. However, the circumstances were exceptional, in this particular case. It therefore followed - in his opinion - that any adultery which might have taken place, was entirely excusable.

"Bernard - not his real name - has a rather formidable millstone round his neck for the rest of his 'born and natural'. A Catholic spouse who doesn't believe in divorce."

Phipps, completely bewildered, pointed to the fact that Bernard and Millicent attended the parish church together.

"No reason why they shouldn't, m'dears," Rodney smiled. "They're both straightforward C of E . But Millie is not the spouse of whom I speak, only a widowed sister."

"So she isn't called Drysdale?" Bun stated rather than asked.

"A nom de guerre . . . as one says."

"And what about the Knightons? They asked to be included in any useful alibi story, if we had one available."

Rodney looked thoughtfully down at his feet.

"Bit awkward. I mean to say: no gentleman cares to discuss this sort of thing when there's ladies present. Let's just say that our Lieutenant-Commander is still a lively Jack Tar . . . after the jolly old bugler has blown 'Lights Out'."

"From which," Bun observed, "I suppose you imply that Patricia Knighton has lost the urge to continue with marriage consumation manoeuvres?"

Rodney Holbrook inclined his head to signal 'Affirmative'.

A short, silent pause followed this disclosure, then Phipps observed that - under the present circumstances - she felt quite sorry for the poor old rector of St Tudy . . . preaching God's word whilst being surrounded by so many unrepentant sinners.

Rodney let out a bellow of laughter.

Upon recovering his poise, he gave Phipps a knowing look.

"I shouldn't worry too much about the Reverend Arthur Salisbury, if I were you."

"Not the rector, surely . . . ?" Bun interjected.

"Vile rumour has it that he only avoided divorce through adultery on numerous occasions, during the course of a singularly active life, through close friendship with a retired district nurse."

Rodney Holbrook coughed with embarrassment, stared at the ground, then looked up at the the nearest tree.

"She was said to be a wizard with her trusty knitting needle."

Bun remonstrated, reminding Rodney of the rector's heart condition, which had forced him to take extended sick leave.

After glancing about, to make certain none of the domestic staff were within earshot, Rodney said that - from all he had heard, the reverend gentleman was enjoying his proverbial 'droit de seigneur' with a not unwilling housemaid, when he experienced his seizure.

" . . . and Doctor MacIlroy only sent him off to recuperate in order to get him away from Mavis and Mary!"

Bun said firmly that Captain Holbrook should take his leave, if he was going to regale them with stories from the officers' mess. Rodney accepted dismissal with good grace, but looked back over his shoulder, as he turned into the stable yard.

"I didn't hear that in the mess," he called. "I was in the public bar of the Cornish Arms at the time!"

The Parsnip Wine Strikes Again

Phipps stared blankly across the rectory lawn, from the relative security of her deck-chair. Was it all really true? What she had listened to when young Roddy 'spilled the beans' about what had been going on in the village. Did their new-found friends all behave in such a wanton manner?

Of course, her sister had reminded her on a previous occasion, when they had been discussing family backgrounds, that so very little was actually known about even one single person amongst their St Tudy acquaintances. 'Only what they see fit to tell us', had been Bun's very words.

Yet they are all such nice people, Phipps thought to herself, being considerate neighbours and jolly good company in any social situation.

Then there was the implied suggestion that Lady Mary was not above cutting fast and loose . . . and she wouldn't see her fiftieth birthday again!

Oh well, at least I'm nearly ten years younger . . . so there might be hope for me, too! Maybe we should buy a cottage and settle in St Tudy, Phipps wondered. Who knows, perhaps there's magic properties in this Cornish country air, or very active minerals in the water?

She glanced across at her sister. Bun appeared to be lost in silent reverie. Phipps could not help thinking that her sister had been too severe with young Roddy. Sympathetic understanding was called for.

"A bit of a shock, wasn't it?" she said, to re-start conversation.

195

"Mmmm? Oh . . . yes. Rodney Holbrook makes St Tudy sound like a second Babylon!" Bun paused for reflection, then added, "Rather apt, when one thinks about it, I suppose: all being written down in The Book of Revelation!"

Phipps smiled, recalling the subject matter of Chapter Seventeen. However, she was quite unable to visualise Lady Mary Holbrook, widow of a King's Messenger, clothed in scarlet and purple; or timid little Miss Dorothy Nunn decked out in gold, precious stones and pearls.

As for picturing either of these otherwise respectable ladies seated on a scarlet beast - which had been stuffed full with the names of blasphemy - and was reputed to have seven heads and ten horns well . . . it simply did not bear thinking about.

In any case, Dorothy had not become drunken with the blood of saints and martyrs . . . but with Mrs Gregory's parsnip wine. Ah! Now that was an idea. Phipps told her sister she would just take their coffee tray round to the kitchen.

"Oh! Then I'll ask a small favour, old girl. Perhaps you'd run upstairs and bring out my cardigan. This evening air can feel rather damp after sunset."

When Phipps returned, she was carrying a silver tray on which a freshly opened bottle of parsnip wine and two clean glasses were set out.

"A little natural stimulation to help constructive thoughts," she explained, handing her sister the requested cardigan.

Bun stood up, asking her sister to help move their table and deck-chairs into the centre of the lawn. "We have important matters to discuss and there's always a chance of those maids overhearing if we remain near the windows."

When they were settled, Phipps suggested pouring the wine.

"Do you think that's wise?" Bun asked. "I don't want to end up like poor Dorothy Nunn."

"As young Roddy said, apropos something else: 'exceptional circumstances', dear."

"Drink too much of that stuff and you'll obtain exceptional results, old girl. Tell me: did you believe what Roddy had to say about his mother? Bit far-fetched, to my mind."

The Parsnip Wine Strikes Again

Phipps handed her sister a glass of parsnip wine, observing that Rodney Holbrook was an officer and a gentleman. In her opinion, his sense of decency, combined with natural restraint, lent honesty to his statement.

Bun was quick to point out that he certainly wasn't practising restraint when speaking about the rector. Speaking frankly, she suspected more than a little exaggeration.

"Well I'm inclined to believe him, dear. Because, in my view, Mavis and Mary sometimes exhibit too much self-confidence for eighteen-year olds!"

"You're an authority on the subject, old girl?"

"Perhaps that's too strong a phrase . . . but I've watched that pair walking through the village once or twice and - by the way they act when there's boys about - I'd say they know quite precisely how many beans make five. Though I must admit . . . I never thought the rector was the one who had been giving them their 'arithmetic lessons'. By the way, have you thought any more about those fingerprints?"

Bun replied she was glad to be reminded of them, because she had bought a fresh film to use in Cousin Crispian's German camera.

"I'll just pop upstairs and take pictures of the gun and prints before the light fails."

Phipps watched her sister stride off so purposefully across the rectory lawn, drank some more wine, topped up both glasses, then lay back in her deck-chair to dream peacefully of a similar evening in the summer of 1910.

She had been staying with the Broughams of Hartley Wintney. One of the young men had met her as she explored the shrubberies. Phipps shook her head regretfully. Her first kiss, and she couldn't remember his name!

Never mind . . . she still remembered the kiss. Sounds of movement indicated her sister's return and brought Phipps back into the present.

"I've been thinking, old girl," Bun said, pausing to sip from her wine glass. "In connection with the known fact that we have Wheeler's fingerprints on the automatic . . . "

197

". . . coupled with the statement by one or other of the Knightons, that Wheeler suggested most of the guests for that dinner party," Phipps reminded her sister.

Bun glared, then finished by saying that she now wondered if the wretched man had planned his own death?

"But do we have other evidence to back up this theory?"

"What young Roddy told us, earlier this evening."

"About all the goings-on, after the lamps are lit, in St Tudy?"

"Exactly, Phippsie! The fact that Roddy knew about the rector and the housemaids proves you can't keep anything secret in a country village."

"So you think Wheeler was well aware of the embarrassment that would be caused to all concerned . . . in the event of police being called in, to investigate a violent death?"

"Yes . . . unlikely though that may sound." Bun answered with a dismissive shrug.

Phipps agreed, saying it sounded like something out of an Agatha Christie who dunnit. To be frank: she thought it more probable that Wheeler was blackmailing one or more people known to be indulging in these midnight frolics. Somebody objected and shot the wretched man with his own gun.

"What's known as poetic justice, dear."

Bun pointed out that blackmail only succeeded when the victim did not want some dark secret becoming public property. However, according to Roddy Holbrook, most of the clandestine liasons appeared to be common knowledge in St Tudy . . . even if the principal participants lived in blissful ignorance of this fact.

"Bernard Drysdale's marriage doesn't fall into the same category though. Suppose Wheeler had threatened to disclose his whereabouts to the deserted wife?" Phipps asked.

"But Bernard's fingerprints are not on the gun!"

"Because he wiped them off! Wheeler's prints appear on the bullets because - since he was the gun's owner - he was also the one to load it. So Wheeler's prints survive . . . but everything else has been wiped clean after the fatal shot was fired."

"And how did Bernard obtained possession of the gun?"

"Stole it during a social call?" Phipps suggested hopefully.

Bun curtly reminded her about the shotgun being discharged when Wheeler had been exercising his dogs near the Drysdale peacocks.

"Hardly likely to be dropping in for a chat over tea and crumpets after that, Phippsie."

"Perhaps Dudley Knighton was the thief. He could have called on business - having already planned to kill Wheeler - so that he could buy the neighbouring meadow cheap from the executors of the estate. Then taken the gun from its drawer whilst Wheeler was out of the room for some reason or other."

Bun reminded her sister that if Rodney Holbrook was to be believed, they could presume the lively Lieutenant-Commander would have been comfortably closeted with one of the neighbourhood wives, by the time Wheeler was being shot.

"In any case, Phippsie, one has to address the question of how would Dudley Knighton have persuaded Wheeler to meet him in the churchyard? And another thing: how could Dudley have known his proposed victim owned an automatic pistol?"

"That's easy! It could have been mentioned in the course of a conversation months ago. You know the sort of thing: 'Lots of burglaries, lately, hereabouts.' Answer: 'Well they won't catch me napping. I sleep with a loaded pistol beside the bed'."

"Which means Dudley would have had to dash upstairs to search the bedrooms. Not on, old girl."

"He could have said he wanted to spend a penny!" Phipps snapped in reply.

"More likely to be directed to the downstairs cloakroom! No good, old girl! You're clutching at straws.

"Yes . . . well - according to Exodus - brick-makers found straw pretty useful stuff! You may recall that the poor old Israelites found life extremely difficult when Pharaoh cut off their supplies. And - come to think of it - Moses wasn't much help either."

Bun looked sharply towards her sister, asking what on earth she was babbling about. Receiving no answer, for Phipps was busy refilling their wine glasses, Bun paused, thought, nodded and muttered, "Oh yes. That story about the Jews working as slaves in Egypt. Only metaphorical! Very tenuous connection."

She reached out a hand and drank some more wine, then held her glass up to the failing light.

"Beautiful clarity. Not a trace of sediment, either."

"So smooth too. And no burning sensation, at the back of the throat, as it slips down," Phipps agreed appreciatively.

"Unlike some of the cheaper whisky blends, old girl." Bun shook her head. "Can't think how Dorothy got into such a state."

"I know! They had to almost carry her out to Dudley's station wagon," Phipps reminded her sister.

Bun shrugged. "Probably drank too much, too quickly, on an empty stomach. I like Dorothy but one has to face the obvious: she's not a very 'worldly' sort of person. Though I dare say she writes a pleasant enough love story."

"Of course, our housemaids were no better: singing Good King Wenceslas at the top of their voices . . . a couple of days before the Feast of St Swithun!"

Bun swallowed the remainder of her wine at a gulp, then refilled both glasses once more, reassuring her sister that such young country girls wouldn't know how to drink good wine.

"Dash it all, Phippsie, they were swigging the stuff from tumblers as if it was a half a pint of near-beer shandy!"

The sisters continued discussing their investigation in a desultory manner, pausing to refill their wine glasses from time to time, content to enjoy their own company whilst watching bats from the rectory stable dart to and fro above their heads, in the gathering dusk.

Phipps briefly upset their mental tranquillity on one occasion, by reminding her sister they were almost certain to receive another visit from the detectives, on the morrow . . . which might be expected to prove acrimonious.

But the older woman cheerfully brushed fear aside by saying they would put the blame where it belonged . . . squarely upon the shoulders of those misguided folk who asked for help in establishing false alibis.

"Yes. That's right, dear. After all: we never took the initiative, did we? Others asked . . . "

" . . . and we complied, like the good Christians that we are."

The Parsnip Wine Strikes Again

"Ready to lend a helping hand to friends in need," Phipps replied happily. She seemed to remember that most of the falsehoods had been invented - with great enthusiasm - by her older sister, but had more sense than to say so. Instead, she confined herself to suggesting, "So it's all their own fault . . . for seeking to deceive?"

"Absolutely, old girl."

Phipps attempted to look at her watch, some time after the wine bottle had become empty. "Goodness me! Too dark to see where the hands are. I suppose we ought to be thinking of getting off to bed," she observed . . . but received no answer.

She stood up, intending to stretch herself by raising both arms above her head, but found her knees too rubbery. Afraid of losing her balance, Phipps resumed her seat.

As she slid down the deck-chair canvas, she wiggled her feet, then raised and lowered her legs alternatively to make quite certain everything was in working order. But when she tried to stand, once more, she still found her knees unable to bear her weight. Her head felt distinctly odd, too.

No pain . . . just a peculiar numbness.

Phipps looked across at her sister, intending to say that, from personal research, it would appear as if a stomach full of food was by no means an adequate prophylaxis, where Mrs Gregory's parsnip wine was concerned.

To her amazement, Phipps saw that her sister's head hung down, resting sideways against one shoulder. The eyes were closed, mouth open with bottom lip pouting truculently, and one arm drooped slackly . . . with its hand resting on the grass.

Bun's knees, instead of being together, splayed outwards. The ample bosom heaved . . . and noises which sounded like a cross between a snort and a snore issued forth with each exhalation.

"Oh well . . . " said Phipps, conscious that her own face had gone rather flaccid, "We shall just have to wait until Cousin Crispian gets home from the hospital."

And with this resigned thought, she slid even further down the deck-chair canvas, closed her eyes and went to sleep.

When she awoke, she found it was quite dark.

And there was something making a slight noise, behind her. A fox . . . or badger? She swivelled round. A man's dark shape was approaching across the lawn.

"Hello Philippa. Dozed off, did you?"

It was Cousin Crispian.

Phipps told him she appeared to have been sitting awkwardly and one of her legs had 'gone to sleep'. Could he perhaps help her up to bed?

"It really is quite terrible: pins and needles all the way up to my knee!" She explained, hardly expecting for one moment to be believed, with that empty wine bottle on the table.

When she had managed to struggle to her feet, Phipps was relieved to find that her knees were now just about able to support her, providing she kept a very firm hold on her cousin.

Crispian, like the good Christian he was, helped her to cross the lawn and climb the stairs without making any comment.

Phipps went into her bedroom, shut the door and flopped onto her bed fully clothed . . . feeling extremely thankful she had not been reduced to crawling all this way on her hands and knees.

"So embarrassing if one of the maids tripped over me," she murmured, before drifting away into a dreamless slumber.

Running Around in Circles

Detective Sergeant Thomas Bassett's sleep was anything but a carefree slumber. Admittedly, his bedroom had soaked up the heat of the day, which may have caused restlessness in the most phlegmatic of men . . . but Bassett had a disturbed mind to contend with in addition to summer night-time temperatures.

It had been a very long day, which became progressively worse as the evening wore on, and his thoughts kept him wakening off and on throughout the night. Not exactly nightmares . . . but certainly very bad dreams.

Finally, at five o'clock in the morning, Bassett gave up this unequal struggle. He got out of bed, grumbling to himself, washed and shaved, ate a scrappy breakfast, then walked out through the deserted streets of Bodmin. He turned off, at the county police headquarters, and headed for his CID office desk.

Sitting down with a sigh bordering on despair, he drew a clean sheet of paper onto the blotter, hoping that writing up reports might help unburden his mind and thereby clear his head.

The previous afternoon had started quite pleasantly.

He and Polkinghorne had called upon Jack Wills, the auctioneer and licensed valuer who used to act for Wheeler in his land deals, at the Camelford estate agent's office.

The man had behaved in a completely open and co-operative manner, when asked his whereabouts on the night of the shooting. Wills explained that he was a keen sea-angler. He had driven straight over to the north coast, on leaving Lieutenant-Commander Knighton's home.

Asked what he had been going to do at this time of night, Wills replied that he was intending to fish the last hours of the incoming tide.

He told the detectives that he had parked his car at the top of the harbour slipway, in Port Isaac; called in at the Golden Lion Inn for a drink - where he chatted with old Len Trevorrow - then collected rod, line and bait from Arthur Curtis's cottage and went afloat. He had stayed out in his dinghy 'til about 2.0 am.

Once back in Camelford's main shopping street, Polkinghorne had suggested it was a lovely afternoon for driving around the Cornish countryside at the County's expense, so Bassett had motored over to Port Isaac, seeking confirmation of Jack Wills' story.

As expected, both Trevorrow and Curtis agreed that they had spoken to the angler, who was well known to both of them, shortly before closing time.

Strolling about on the harbour beach, now uncovered by the low tide, Polkinghorne had got into conversation with fishermen unloading crabs from a small lugger.

One of them remembered helping Jack Wills pull his dinghy up the public slipway some time early that same morning. He couldn't be exact . . . but reckoned it must have been shortly after high water.

A passing glance at tide tables, conveniently displayed in the tiny harbour office window, together with various Notices to Mariners, showed Bassett this had occurred at 1.32 am.

So everything Wills had told them proved to be correct.

After a pot of tea, in a tiny cafe overlooking the harbour, Bassett had suggested they carry out the same check on Bill Rowse, who had an office in Wadebridge.

This had turned out to be very much a wink-and-nudge farce.

Rowse, asked where he went after leaving the Knighton home, commenced by saying he had dropped in on a client to give a valuation for purposes of probate.

"At gone eleven o'clock . . . nearly midnight?"

"Oh yes, Sergeant," Rowse had replied, very much tongue-in-cheek. "We have to be there when the client needs us."

"From which: am I to gather your client who required such urgent personal attention was a lady, sir?"

"That's right. We do a lot of probate valuations for wives who have suddenly become widows. Don't know what's wrong with the men around these parts. I suppose their womenfolk must wear 'em out," Rowse had replied with a leer.

"Well . . . if we could have the lady's address?" Polkinghorne had suggested.

Rowse shook his head, giving a shark-like smile.

"Sorry. Can't oblige. I'm sure you chaps can understand?"

"Your 'professional' services would no longer be required by many of the ladies, if you were unable to guarantee discretion?" Bassett had suggested rather than asked. "Merry widows have to feel their secret's safe with you, sir?"

"Or they wouldn't wish to 'make merry' any more," Rowse had answered with a wry smile.

Bassett then abandoned this line of questioning, simply enquiring what time Mr Rowse had got home to his own bed?

"About a quarter past one. The Missus looked at the clock and made her usual comment. You've only got to drop in on Peggy. She'll confirm it."

"Will she be at home, later this afternoon, sir?"

"Yes. You know where we live, don't you? A few hundred yards along the St Teath road . . . Banfield's Barn. My property backs onto Dudley Knighton's chicken farm."

The detectives had taken their leave, returned to the car, and driven back to St Tudy.

As expected, Mrs Peggy Rowse had instantly confirmed her wandering husband's time of return to the matrimonial home, but then spoilt everything.

Bassett asked if she usually woke up when her husband came in late.

"Oh no. He goes his way an' I goes mine. But I didn't get to bed myself 'til near quarter to one."

"Any reason why you were up so late, on this particular night?" Bassett enquired, more from force of habit than any expectation of a surprise answer.

"My friend and neighbour - the Lieutenant-Commander - spent the latter part of his evening with me. We're very good friends, Dudley and me."

Bassett had thanked Mrs Rowse and left Banfield's Barn.

Once alone in the county road, Polkinghorne had stared at his sergeant.

And Bassett had rolled his eyes skywards.

"Here we go again, Ceddie boy!"

"Round in ruddy circles, Sarge?"

"Looks very much like it. Come on!"

"Which way now?"

"Knighton's place, of course!"

However, when faced with this fait accompli, Dudley Knighton had readily admitted he was not in his own home at the time previously stated. His wife had then confirmed this, saying that she had simply gone to bed, and read her library book, after their dinner guests had all departed.

Back in the police car, Bassett grumbled, "Once again we come back to those Hyde sisters . . . "

" . . . and from what we've just heard, Miss Anthea Eulalia certainly didn't stop at Trickey's Meadows, as she told us at the beginning of all this, Sarge."

"I tell you, boy . . . that pair are a blinkin' menace!"

"So what's it to be: next stop the rectory?"

Bassett shook his head, saying that he thought it best to clear up the matter of Mr Drysdale's whereabouts on the night in question by visiting Lady Mary.

However, when they called at the Holbrook residence the two detectives were informed that Lady Mary wasn't at home, though she was expected to return within the next half an hour.

Walking back towards their car, Bassett murmured, "Who can we upset for five or ten minutes? Any ideas, Ceddie?"

"Teresa Lockhart's alibi was supported, in part, by young Holbrook."

"And if that young bounder wasn't with her . . . ?"

" . . . how could she have been with him?"

"Right. We'll give her an anxious five minutes. Come on!"

Behaving true to form, Bassett employed his usual subterfuge by telling the girl that she had been seen walking through the village at the same time as she was supposed to have been sitting quietly in the rectory with all her friends . . . such as Captain Holbrook and Miss Philippa Hyde, to say nothing of poor little Dorothy Nunn, "Who we now know wasn't there at all."

To Polkinghorne's amusement, Teresa caved in without a struggle, saying yes, she had been out walking because she didn't feel very sleepy.

"Then why tell us differently?" Bassett asked mildly.

"Because next morning, when I heard Wheeler had been shot, I realised the police would be coming round to ask us all where we were at the fatal moment . . . and I couldn't see any way of proving that I wasn't in the churchyard."

"Quite sure?" Bassett prompted the young lady.

She shook her head violently, as if to emphasise this point.

"No! Never went near the place."

"What made you think of asking the ladies at the rectory to vouch for you," Polkinghorne enquired, more from idle curiosity than any real need to know, one way or the other.

"Oh well . . . they're so much older that I am . . . and quite obviously respectable," she ended with a slight shrug.

Polkinghorne glanced at his sergeant's impassive face, thinking Bassett would have given a different opinion, then set about asking Miss Lockhart to describe what really happened.

"I called in at the rectory, told them how worried I was because it was so jolly difficult to prove a negative, and the older sister suggested I say that I spent the remainder of the evening over there. I agreed. I mean . . . there didn't seem any harm in it. After all: I didn't shoot Wheeler. Haven't got a gun. And wouldn't know how to use it in any case."

"Those Hydes!" Bassett gritted when he and Polkinghorne were back in their car.

"And they seemed so harmless, Sarge . . . "

" . . . when all the time they're nothing but a Public Nuisance!"

Bassett started the engine, engaged gear and drove back to Lady Mary Holbrook's residence.

She was home by then, received them in her drawing-room, and confirmed Bernard Drysdale's revised alibi . . . then icily pointed out that - apropos what the housemaid at Town Farm had been spreading round the village - policemen also wore something which might be described as a 'funny pointed hat'.

"Not a great deal of difference between your helmets and a deer-stalker when seen in silhouette - beneath trees - on a dark night," she reminded the detectives sententiously.

Bassett thanked Lady Mary and left.

By then beginning to tire, the detective sergeant drove round to Constable Pope's police house.

When told of Lady Mary's opinion, regarding pointed hats, he freely admitted he was in the habit of urinating under the churchyard trees whilst out on night patrol . . . and saw no particular reason why he should discuss this matter at any great length with other people.

"Yes . . . well . . . not as bad as some of them town chaps," Bassett replied placatingly. "I've known of blokes, out on night beat, who didn't think twice about relieving themselves up a back alley . . . "

" . . . or doing it in somebody's flower garden," Polkinghorne joined in.

"Hence that expression: 'watering the daisies'." Bassett said.

Mrs Pope came through with tea and fresh-baked heavy cake, so that the detectives didn't get back to their office in Bodmin until just before eight o'clock in the evening.

Bassett found an urgent message awaiting his attention.

REPORT TO ME IMMEDIATELY!

C. Hawken Supt.

Fearing trouble, and preferring to take any dressing-down in private, the detective sergeant told his assistant to wait, then made his own way up to the superintendent's office.

Hawken told him to sit, then handed over a report which had finally come through from Bedfordshire County Police. It stated that the name of the elderly couple, who had become foster parents of Wheeler's illigitimate child, was POPE . . . and the child had been MALE.

Superintendent Hawken told his sergeant that he had looked up Constable Pope's record and there appeared to be nothing to connect him with an earlier life in Bedfordshire. Then asked Bassett for his own observations.

"First I've heard of this, sir. Trouble is: there might be something in it. I've just come back from St Tudy and Pope admits to being within the churchyard boundaries, that night!

"At about the time Wheeler was supposed to have been shot?"

"Yes."

"Doing what?"

"Having a Jimmy Riddle, whilst on foot patrol in St Tudy village, between the hours of 10.0 pm and 2.0 am."

Hawken slammed his hand down on the desk.

"That settles it! He must come off this case, just to be on the safe side. We'll send him down to St Just . . . the one near Land's End, tonight! I'll 'phone him and tell him to pack a bag. We're a man short of established strength, so he won't suspect anything's wrong. You take the car back to St Tudy, collect Pope and run him over to Bodmin Road railway station. Then stay with him until his train leaves, to make sure we know he's gone."

Bassett stopped to reassure his assistant that the guv'nor wasn't after their blood, then hurried out to the car and drove away. He finally got home to bed at 10.30 pm.

And now it was another day.

Polkinghorne arrived at his usual time to find Bassett carefully re-writing certain pages of the previous day's reports, and was told to get on with up-dating Miss Lockhart's story.

The morning mail brought another pathologist's report, stating the second cartridge case had definitely been fired by the same gun as the first - obtained from the Tamblyn child.

"Looks as if the Miss Hydes are next on the list for a gruelling interview, Ceddie boy," Bassett observed maliciously.

"A bit of luck your mate - Sergeant Symons - seeing them up in Plymouth," Polkinghorne answered with a grin.

"Yes. I'm really looking forward to hearing their account of how they found that cartridge case," Bassett laughed mirthlessly, "and why they thought of sending it to us."

Polkinghorne pointed out an expert could prove they sent that object to the police, by comparing the name, address and note 'From a Wellwisher. St Tudy' with their own handwriting. "By the way, Sarge: have you thought about checking up on who wrote that letter we found in Wheeler's place?"

"Constantly! Been keeping my eye open for similar styles of handwriting everywhere. Funny thing is: the only samples which I've seen - that appear anything like the same - are entries in Wheeler's own desk diary. Which makes it look as if Wheeler wrote the blinkin' note himself, requesting a meeting in the churchyard."

"Perhaps he was writing it for somebody else, Sarge."

"You're forgetting the matching envelope. That note came through the post. So Wheeler was the recipient, not the writer!"

The Murder Weapon Identified

Detective Constable Cedric Polkinghorne finished up-dating his report on Miss Teresa Lockhart's activities, after she had left Trickey's Meadows, following the end of Dudley Knighton's dinner party. Then he sat quietly sucking the end of his pen for several minutes.

"Sarge . . . "

Bassett looked up enquiringly.

" . . . about Constable Pope."

"Oh yes, and what's your latest thoughts on that subject?"

"He's about the right age to be Wheeler's illegitimate son. Didn't we ought to compare his handwriting with that note from Wheeler's waste paper basket?"

Bassett shook his head.

"Been done, Ceddie boy. 'Course, I thought of it, but old Charlie Hawken beat me to it. Got the note and envelope out of our case file - along with Pope's original Incident Report - while we were out joy riding; his words, not mine! Showed them to me when we were discussing this business, last night."

"Well . . . ?"

"No similarity whatsoever. On the other hand . . . "

The detective sergeant paused to rummage in his desk drawer, eventually producing a torn half sheet of paper. This was laid out beside the note and envelope originally posted in St Breward.

"I found this memo in one of Wheeler's law books, back at Bligh's. It looks as if he had been checking clauses in a conveyance . . . so this must be his normal handwriting."

" . . . or his clerk's!" Polkinghorne cautioned.

Bassett declared that as far as he could tell, it was the same, or at any rate very similar - to what he had already seen in Wheeler's journal and account books.

"If you take a look, Cedric . . . "

Polkinghorne got up and moved around his sergeant's desk.

"Now: you can see Wheeler's script was very distinctive . . . "

"All sloping slightly to the right, Sarge."

"With 'A's and 'O's thin ovals, rather than full rounds."

Bassett slid the envelope which had been through the post alongside the torn memo sheet.

"They're both similar," Polkinghorne admitted.

Bassett then slid the note, requesting the churchyard meeting, into place on the other side of the memo.

"Quite a bit different, Sarge . . . as if the writer's attempted to round out those vowels."

"Exactly! Makes me think the sender tried to disguise his style when writing the note . . . "

" . . . but forgot all about it by the time he got to the envelope?"

"Yes. See . . . I reckon he had to stop and think what he was going to put down in the note, whereas the address was familiar to him. He could write it without a moment's thought, and obviously dashed it off at normal writing speed . . . "

" . . . without realising what was happening, Sarge. So he's ended up with words produced nearer to his natural style!"

"Same as he would have done if he hadn't been trying to disguise his hand in the first place!" Bassett said triumphantly.

The detective constable let this sink in before he spoke again.

"Suppose you're right . . . Wheeler wrote the note, then drove across to St Breward and posted it to himself . . . why?"

"To make any person - carrying out an investigation - believe he was meeting somebody at the time of his death. Send us off on a wild goose chase: checking up on all his fellow guests; which we have done."

"And asking apparently innocent people a lot of embarrassing questions," Polkinghorne observed.

"Which we have also done," Bassett reminded his assistant with a grim nod.

"But he couldn't know . . . "

" . . . when he was going to be shot?" Bassett gave a smug leer.

Polkinghorne spread his hands wide apart, palms upward.

"Oh yes he could, Ceddie boy . . . if he intended to pull the trigger himself!"

Polkinghorne reminded his sergeant that this question of suicide had been discussed before but - with no gun found beside the body - no coroner would ever accept this possibility in a month of Sundays.

Bassett shrugged his shoulders, replying that they had already eliminated most of the dinner guests, with the exception of those two meddlesome old maids who were staying at the rectory, and Mr Danvers.

"We'll drop in for a chat with the old man, though I don't see him in the position of number one suspect, even if he is the only one left for us to check out. So who else could have fired that blinkin' gun?"

"Could have been done by a passing tramp."

Bassett told his assistant that he was wrong on two counts. In the first place: Wheeler's gold watch and chain, wallet and fountain pen hadn't been removed. So it wasn't murder for criminal gain and secondly: British tramps did not - as a general rule - carry around automatic pistols.

"Might do . . . if he was an ex-soldier. It could be a souvenir from Flanders, Sarge."

Bassett declared this to be wishful thinking, on the part of his detective constable, because a tramp would have sold anything of value for food - or beer money - long before the summer of 1935. In his opinion it was far more likely that Polkinghorne's wandering tramp found the gun, after Wheeler had shot himself, while walking through the churchyard.

"But what was he doing there, in the middle of the night?"

"Looking for somewhere to sleep, maybe. Who cares? I say he would have made off with the gun, hoping to sell it in the first junk shop he came to, next day."

"But what about the Tamblyn kid? He said he saw a gun in that building sand . . . on the following morning!"

Bassett shrugged, telling Polkinghorne that perhaps his imaginary tramp had seen somebody else - maybe Teresa Lockhart - walking along the road, and thrown the gun into the sand because he was afraid of being arrested and charged with shooting Wheeler.

The detective constable reminded his boss that the average tramp wore lots of clothing; several coats, whether it was winter or summer, so he could have effectively concealed the gun before leaving the scene of the crime.

Bassett pointed out their mythical tramp could have still feared he might be stopped and searched.

Polkinghorne decided to abandon tramps in favour of a local person having found and removed the gun.

If they accepted that the deceased had committed suicide, had a local resident come along, found the gun and hidden it in that sand pile, fully intending to recover it when all the fuss of discovering Wheeler's body had died down?

"Just an ordinary working man who fancied the weapon for what it was: a souvenir . . . a collector's item?" Bassett asked.

"Or something with which to rob a bank in six months time," Polkinghorne suggested with a smile.

"Or shoot his wife!" Bassett responded.

"Bill Rowse!" Polkinghorne laughed.

His sergeant doubted this, saying Rowse would be too smart for that. Not the sort of bloke who would shoot his unpaid housekeeper . . . because who would then wash his clothes, cook his meals and generally look after his home?

"Yes. We've all met his kind in police work, Sarge," the detective constable replied with a knowing nod.

"One hundred per cent self-centred."

"Every time! Perfectly happy to do as they please while there's a little woman in the background. But, if he got rid of the wife, it would be an entirely different story for Rowse. I reckon some of those widows he's so very fond of playing games with - during the hours of darkness - would start clamouring to marry him."

"Which would completely spoil his fun!" Bassett laughed.

Polkinghorne said it had often seemed to him that blokes, with as little moral principle as Mr Bill Rowse, enjoyed more licentious freedom in the married state, than did other men who were still single.

"Ah well . . . haven't you noticed, Ceddie? Some women, especially widows, seem to like that sort."

" I can't think why, myself."

"Neither can I . . . but never mind the why's and wherefore's. Time we got back to business!"

"What about having another chat with Penrose?"

"That fellow who found the body in the first place?"

"Yes Sarge. I mean to say: he might have found the gun right beside the deceased . . . "

" . . . and stuck it in the sand pile with a view to picking it up later?" Bassett shook his head, reminding his assistant that the village bobby had interviewed Penrose on two separate occasions, first . . . shortly after the body was moved round to Doctor MacIlroy's surgery; and again, after that first cartridge case turned up in the church porch.

The detective sergeant turned over several reports then read aloud, '" . . . denied touching the body or removing any other object from the scene of the incident'. ANY OTHER OBJECT, Ceddie! I think we've got to put ourselves in Penrose's boots."

"Meaning that he feels duty-bound to report what he's found, yet knows he mustn't be late for work," Polkinghorne suggested.

"So what does he do, Ceddie?"

"Rushes round to the village police house as fast as his little legs would carry him, says his piece, then nips off to his place of employment."

"Well there you are: Penrose didn't look further than the body on the ground, so I think we'll count him out."

"What about somebody else going through the churchyard? Between the time Penrose left and Pope arrived?"

"But Penrose didn't speak of seeing anyone else."

"Well - if we're right about Wheeler's death being suicide - his gun must still be in the village, Sarge."

215

Bassett replied that very likely it was, but he couldn't carry out a house to house search because there wasn't an ounce of real evidence to support any application for warrants.

"A magistrate would throw me out with a flea in my ear!"

Polkinghorne observed it was a pity they had lost Constable Pope, because there was nobody quite so well-placed to pick up the odd bit of parish pump gossip as a village bobby.

"I don't reckon you ought to have made so much fuss about that coincidence of identical surnames. Pope's a very common name. They're dotted about all over the country."

Bassett agreed, but reminded his assistant that transferring Pope to St Just had been their super's idea.

"Which reminds me: you've got an urgent call to make as soon as Somerset House is open for business. I want you to ring up and check out both names. The real mother's surname is somewhere in Lady Mary's statement."

By the time they reached morning tea break, Polkinghorne had all the facts. There were definitely two entirely different men. The illegitimate one had kept his mother's surname after all. He had remained up-country - marrying an Aylesbury girl in 1930 - and moving house twice in the following five years. His second child had been born in Abingdon, Berkshire, whilst the birth of a third had been registered in Swindon, Wiltshire.

"Better watch out!" Bassett warned with a laugh. "He's coming this way! And what about poor old Constable Pope?"

"I took the Somerset House information to the Assistant Chief Constable. He cross-checked with our man's personal file and found everything correct. That was a false alarm."

"Bah! Just like old Charlie Hawken to go into a panic over nothing. Let's hope Pope likes being stationed at St Just for a few years. Personally: I shouldn't care to spend the winter in those parts. Gale force winds coming at you from three thousand miles of Atlantic Ocean, where there's nothing to stop 'em! Enough to blow a chap off his regulation big black bicycle!"

The telephone rang.

Bassett answered it, and Polkinghorne took this to be the right moment for going out to wash up their teacups.

On his return, the detective constable was told that Doctor Tresidder had come up with more information gleaned from the cartridge cases.

"I 'spect you saw odd numbers and other marks stamped on by the manufacturer?"

"Yes . . . round the rim, on the base."

"Well our clever pathologist has a friend in the War Office. This bloke put our man in touch with another chap in the Ordnance Corps. And he says that both cartridges were made by the Deutsche Waffen and Munitions Fabriken AG, of Karlsruhe!"

"How the Hell could he know that?"

"Apparently those marks are some sort of commercial code. Even gave the area: Baden, and the date: July, 1917. The Ordnance chap simply looked 'em up in some reference book. Anyway: that's fact! Then Tresidder went on to offer his opinion, strictly off the record for the present, that the automatic we are looking for is almost certainly an 'ACP Dreyse'."

"That weapons course. At the police college, Sarge! I remember seeing a Dreyse on display in their museum. Widely issued to German police forces before The War."

Bassett consulted his notes. "Yes . . . made by Rheinische Metallwaren and Machinenfabrik of Sommerda from some time in 1907 or '08. Trouble is . . . they were later issued to army personnel when the Luger factories couldn't keep pace with demands following losses on the Western Front. So any of our chaps - fighting in France or Belgium - could have found a Dreyse and stuck it in his knapsack as a war souvenir."

Polkinghorne recalled more facts from his weapons course and asked why the gun couldn't have been made in Spain or Italy.

"Tresidder's relying on the ammunition markings. Has to be part of a German Army issue. So . . . what could be more natural? You've found your gun and then you pick up a box of ammunition in the same place. Of course you're going to have that as well. But - in any case - even if the finder only picked up a gun, it could have had a fully loaded magazine."

"And a German police-issue weapon wouldn't have been loaded with German War Department bullets?"

"Exactly!"

Polkinghorne grumbled that it would still be like looking for a needle in farmer Giles' haystack, because any amount of troops from English country parishes joined the army and served in France from '14 to '18.

Detective Sergeant Bassett said that he would leave that worry for another day. He knew where he could find the Miss Hydes.

"We'll nip out to St Tudy rectory and see what they have to say about posting cartridge cases in Plymouth!"

"Perhaps we'll find that's another curious coincidence."

"And just what d'you mean by that, Constable?"

"Them being in Plymouth - at the same time as your mate Sergeant Symons - when some unknown person posted that damned cartridge case to us. Anyway, upsetting a couple of old maids won't help us find that missing automatic."

"No . . . but it will make me feel better. Get the car!"

Hangover Hall

Bun and Phipps were also preparing to set forth on further perambulations by mid-morning, though separately, rather than in each other's company as would more often be the case.

Both had slept much later than usual.

Phipps had been the first to regain consciousness, but she couldn't make out where she was. Then - to her suprise - when she sat up on the bed she made the discovery that she was still fully dressed. Folding her arms around her body, she held on tight. To her relief, she felt quite solid . . . so it wasn't a bad dream.

However, cohesive thought was proving difficult.

And her head felt 'funny' too.

Happily . . . she discovered that she felt no pain.

But her mind was quite blank, as if she'd been anaesthetised.

The physical need to slake a raging thirst encouraged her to attempt standing on the bedside rug. That wasn't a great success. She felt rather giddy. Phipps held on to the end of her bed for some time before gently easing her feet into slippers and tottering downstairs.

Since she was respectably dressed - if a trifle rumpled - she instructed Mary to serve tea and toast on the lawn.

No butter, by specific request.

While she waited, sitting quietly in her deck-chair with one leg crossed over the other and her right foot swinging free, a young robin flew down to perch on her toe, head cocked perkily to one side, obviously hoping for a feed of crumbs.

"You'll have to come back after Mary's brought my toast out, dear," Phipps told the bird gently, wishing she could pick up the tiny bundle of speckled brown feathers and stroke them with a finger.

She felt despondently 'empty' and sorry for herself. Comfort could only be obtained by close physical contact with another living creature. She would have gone in search of Sooty, the rectory cat . . . but felt too fragile to walk any great distance.

Bun did not put in an appearance until Phipps was pouring herself a very weak fourth cup of tea, having twice added water to the pot.

The older sister slumped down heavily in a deck-chair.

Phipps glanced at her watch.

Nearly nine o'clock!

"Welcome to Hangover Hall," she said.

Her older sister merely grunted.

"It doesn't look as if that cockerel disturbed your beauty sleep, this morning, dear." Phipps observed with a wry smile.

"The Devil himself would have had his work cut out, old girl. I've been dead to the world all night. Can't remember a thing. And now I'm dying of thirst!"

Bun made a gesture towards her sister's cup and saucer.

"Never mind what Nanny Hudson used to tell us - about catching all those germs if we ever drank from somebody else's cup - pass over yours. I can't wait for one of those maids to bring out my tray."

Phipps did as instructed and watched her sister gulp down most of the tepid liquid.

Then Bun pointed towards the toast. "Are you actually eating that . . . without even a scrape of butter to help it down?"

Phipps nodded as she chewed.

"Then all I can say is: you're a better man than I am, this fine morning, Gungha Dinn."

Phipps acknowledged this compliment with a gentle inclination of the head. When she had swallowed her food, she replied that this may well be so . . . but she certainly wasn't feeling strong enough to control a wild elephant . . . or even a tame mouse.

Bun suggested it was unlikely that her sister would encounter such a beast on the rectory lawn, in St Tudy, so why mention elephants?

"Because he was an elephant boy, dear."

Bun shook her head, saying that Gungha Dinn had been a water carrier, in her childhood, but let's not get into an argument over tame mice or other irrelevant trifles.

Later, as feeling and mental ability showed signs of gradually returning to normal, both sisters agreed Mrs Gregory's parsnip wine could kill - if taken in sufficient quantity - and resolved upon total abstinence for the remainder of their stay.

Further discussion was cut short by the sound of a motor car pulling up in the road, beyond their garden hedge. Then a door slammed and footsteps could be heard, scrunching down the rectory's gravel drive in their direction.

"Oh dear!" Phipps exclaimed, weakly wringing her hands together as anxiety took over from concious thought and reason. "I do hope this isn't another visit by those two detectives. I'm simply not fit enough!"

Bun added that the same could be said about herself.

"But you never posted anything in Plymouth!"

The number of times poor Phippsie wished she had not posted that wretched cartridge case to the police! Well she certainly wasn't up to the ordeal of parrying their questions today.

She looked around wildly. Just her luck!

They were sitting too far out in the lawn for her to be able to hide herself in the shrubbery.

Nothing for it but to sit and wait for the inevitable.

However, Phipps was soon relieved of all anxiety, because it was the trim figure of Millicent Drysdale that stepped gaily round the rhododendrons - up by the gate - and crossed the grass towards where the two Hyde sisters were seated.

"Oh! You gave me quite a 'turn', Millie!"

"Sorry about that, Phippsie, but Bernard had to go into the bank - Bodmin - so I got him to drop me off by your gate. I've left him gossiping with one of your 'earthy' neighbours."

Bun turned listlessly to say, "Welcome to Hangover Hall."

221

"Oh dear! Like that, is it?"

"'Fraid so . . . " Bun replied, her voice trailing off as if the words had been spoken with a final breath.

"Truth to tell: I'm simply dying to know how the pair of you got on with the CID boys yesterday . . . since they were both still in one piece when they finally finished giving us a Cornish version of the Third Degree," Millicent said with a light laugh.

Bun waved a hand towards an empty deck-chair.

Millie sat down.

"One thing's for sure:" she rattled on with hardly a pause in which to draw breath, "Sergeant Bassett, and Poor Dumb Friend, won't feel very chummy towards peacocks for many a long day to come! So . . . what happened to you?"

"Oh we decided to make ourselves scarce. Managed to catch the bus and went for a circular mystery tour," Bun replied.

"How thrilling! Where did you end up?"

"Back here, eventually . . . but we made our first stop in Camelford. Had a stroll through the main shopping street . . . "

" . . . and popped into the estate agent's," Phipps joined in.

"Yes. Happened to see a nice looking little cottage: quite near here, as a matter of fact, and asked for details," Bun concluded.

"Ah! Thinking of settling down in Cornwall now, are you?" Millicent shook her head and rushed on without waiting for an answer. "A bit embarrassing for us, though . . . thanks to those blasted detectives. Cat's out of the bag, and no mistake!"

"About you being Bernard's sister?" Bun enquired.

"Yes. But there's much more to it than that. The poor boy joined the Black and Tans, after the war in France came to an end. He was an officer in one of their special squads. Not very popular with the natives, as you may imagine! So now he's in hiding, with a price on his head. As a wife, I was part of his disguise, because the real one's still living in Tipperary."

Bun suggested the Drysdales might have been overdoing their precautions, since the Irish Troubles had all happened more than twelve years previously.

Millicent replied that the Irish Republican Army was still very much in existence.

"Why - only recently - I heard on the wireless that they were over here, in London, putting bombs in our pillar boxes!"

"Yes. I seem to recall something about that," Bun agreed.

"Uproariously hilarious . . . if it wasn't for the fact that people get so horribly injured when they go off 'Bang'."

Bun accepted that the thought of a solid cast iron, red-painted Victorian post box disappearing in a puff of smoke made one think more of pantomime than political vengeance.

Phipps enquired after Dudley Knighton and his wife, saying that they must surely be feeling more embarrassed than anyone.

Millicent Drysdale shook her head.

"Shouldn't think so. I expect most of our little social circle had some idea about 'difficulties' . . . and Dudley's solution. I know I did. Pat and I had one of those chummy all-girls-together sessions, over the kitchen sink on one occasion. Like most of us, who grew up around the turn of the century, I gather she didn't know much about The Joys of Married Life . . . until she was married!"

"And when she found out . . . ?" Phipps prompted.

Millicent twisted her face in dumb resignation.

"Let's just say she lacked any real enthusiasm for extending her singularly painful experience into the habit of a lifetime! I gathered that - since Dudley left the Navy - he's entered into one of those deliciously private arrangements with a conveniently placed female neighbour."

Phipps, looking at her sister, said they all knew how easily such compromising balancing acts became public knowledge, when one was living in a small community. If others knew what was going on - after Evensong - the story must have surely also reached the late Mr Wheeler's ears.

Bun caught Millicent's eye and told her Phipps and herself had been tentatively considering the possibility that the wretched man had committed suicide.

"After getting you together at Dudley Knighton's dinner party," Phipps explained, "in the hope that you'd all be most frightfully embarrassed by any police investigation."

"Yes. I know. Others have raised that very same point, too. Teresa Lockhart, for one," Millicent said, shaking her head.

Phipps admitted it seemed improbable, at first.

Millie Drysdale nodded agreement, saying that she had not been at all keen on the idea, when first mooted, "But now that it turns out everybody else had something to hide . . . "

" . . . it begins to make more sense, dear?" Phipps suggested.

Bun asked what Millicent thought: about no gun being found.

"Beside the body . . . " Phipps prompted.

Millicent replied that neither Bernard nor herself regarded a missing pistol as negating this proposition. Anyone could have picked up the weapon and made off with it: hidden beneath a coat or tucked into a trousers' waistband, because modern automatics were fairly small . . . when compared with the Wild West six-shooters of a previous century.

"And they can weigh as little as a couple of pounds . . . or even less!" Millie concluded by raising her eyebrows.

"Yes. We know," Bun replied, glancing towards her sister, who appeared to be turning a delicate shade of pink.

Phipps, wishing to bring about a change of subject, asked if Bernard Drysdale intended to remain in St Tudy.

"Oh yes," Millicent nodded firmly. "Awkward at first, but people soon forget. We'll be nothing more than a nine days wonder within a very short time, totally eclipsed when the next village maiden is known to be heavy with child . . . at the same time as the unfortunate creature is lamentably short of a husband."

Bun agreed this was the most sensible course to follow, especially since they had done nothing to be ashamed of, in the eyes of reasonable-minded people.

"Mind you," Millicent cautioned, "one wonders how much longer the men will be with us."

"Hitler?" Phipps suggested.

Millicent nodded.

"Mmmmm. Dudley says the Germans appear to be getting restless. He's almost sure there'll be another war before long."

Bun mentioned having read, in the Telegraph, that several British battleships were being re-fitted.

Millicent said they had heard much the same when on board Royal Sovereign, with the Knightons, for the Spithead Review.

"How on earth did you manage that?" Phipps enquired.

"One of our older cousins is an admiral. There was also talk of a more general re-armament, when we were all having tea."

Millicent gave a sad little laugh.

"As far as my poor brother's concerned: I really do believe he would feel safer - back in the army - than living here, in St Tudy. You see: there's always that outside chance of being recognised by some itinerant Irishman who knew Bernard when he was serving in the Black and Tans."

Discussion of the Abyssinian situation followed, for Mussolini was carrying out manoeuvres in Northern Italy and war was expected to break out almost any day now. When this subject was exhausted, Millicent stood up, saying there were one or two things she needed to pick up from the village shop.

She got to her feet and started to walk away, then turned back.

"Nearly forgot! We're having you all down to dinner - the same old crowd - day after tomorrow. Keep it free!"

Bun got to her feet, as soon as they were alone, asking her sister to have one of the maids bring them a fresh pot of tea.

"I shan't be more than a minute or two. Just want to go upstairs and remove my fingerprint film from Crispian's camera. Thought you might take it into Bodmin for developing and printing."

Phipps exaggerated her weak and frail expression into one of complete and utter dejection.

"No need to look so droopy and pathetic, old girl! Like the chicken that fell in the sewage pit. You'll be sitting in the bus for most of the time, keeping yourself out of the way, just in case those detectives come looking for the busy little bee who sent them that second cartridge case, from somewhere in Plymouth!"

Phipps took the point and agreed to carry out her sister's errand without further demur.

Later, when she was about to set out for the bus stop, Phipps asked Bun what she intended doing for the rest of that day.

"Thought I might take a quiet stroll as far as St Breward. It's a village about a couple of miles away, by public footpaths. I need to get some fresh air, old girl, and be by myself to think about everything. D'y'know: I still feel a bit 'woozy'!"

Phipps agreed that wide open spaces should effect a cure.

"I'll pack up our pistol too, and get that out of the way. Thought I'd send it back home to Tozers Quay, in Topsham."

"Certainly better than leaving it lying about, down here. Only needs one of those maids to find it . . . !"

" . . . and the news will be all around the village quicker than you can say 'Postman's Knock'."

"Worse than that dear . . . think of trying to explain what we've been up to, when Sergeant Bassett comes to call."

"Which is the whole point in getting rid of the thing. And of course, I can't send it through the St Tudy post office because everyone knows who we are . . . and that girl behind the counter will remember the weight."

"Probably think it strange that you are posting a parcel to yourself too, dear."

"Quite."

"But you could come into Bodmin with me."

"Too late. We'd miss the bus. I haven't even got the gun packed up yet." Bun shook her head decisively. "No. I'll have to walk over to St Breward. No reason for any of the Cornish CID to be wandering about out there, right on the edge of Bodmin Moor."

An Afternoon Out in St Breward

It was yet another of those gloriously hot sunny mornings when people wishing to publicise Cornwall as a holiday venue rush about taking photographs of country or seaside scenes, for use in the production of picture postcards.

Detective Constable Cedric Polkinghorne, at the wheel of the police car, was driving along a main road past Racecourse Downs just outside Bodmin, heading in the general direction of Launceston.

Low hedges, topped with stunted gorse or wind-blown hawthorn, protected sheep grazing in adjoining fields from straying onto the roadway.

In the distance - ahead and to his right - the rounded humps of Hawk's Tor and Temple Tor shimmered in the heat haze, beneath a cloudless blue sky.

This is the life for me, he thought, all the joys of the open road with none of the costs coming out of my own pocket. Just as well, too. I could never afford to buy a car for myself. Not on a policeman's pay. Last time I looked in a showroom, they were asking all of a hundred pounds for one of them there little old Austin Sevens or Morris Minors!

Earlier, his sergeant had directed Polkinghorne into Honey Street at the lower end of Bodmin, after they were once clear of police headquarters.

Bassett bought a couple of pasties from their favourite baker, regardless of the continuing hot weather, then ordered: "Next stop: St Breward!"

"But when . . . and where do we eat, Sarge?"

Bassett told his assistant that they would have lunch on the downs, far from the maddening crowd, then procede towards the village of St Breward, where they would call in at the post office to see if anyone could remember Wheeler posting that letter requesting a meeting in St Tudy churchyard, then they would be able to carry on over there . . . in time for afternoon tea . . . on the rectory lawn.

A nice round trip which should take up most of the afternoon, Polkinghorne told himself with silent satisfaction, cheerfully remembering that Summer visitors would gladly pay seven and sixpence each for a coach seat, to make the same journey; but Bassett and himself would be able to enjoy all this wild Cornish countryside for nothing.

A few miles further on, the detective constable turned off the main road, to follow a narrow, un-fenced, winding strip of tarmac on his left. This cut across the close-cropped moorland grass of Manor Common.

Dried out rivulets and tiny ponds were marked by tussocks of tall-growing wiry grass, untouched by the moorland ponies, now keeping a cautious eye on this year's foals - browsing beside the road - as Polkinghorne drove by.

Small groups of sheep and their fat lambs could also be seen laying about in distant hollows, sheltering beneath the limited shade of stunted gorse bushes and panting with the heat from midday sunshine.

Grubby, off-white mounds of china clay waste reared up in one direction, whilst the constable could see a granite 'Cheese Wring' standing out on a nearer hillside, backed by ancient granite quarries, sorry memorials to a once thriving business that were now standing derelict and abandoned.

After a long country mile, their car reached a road junction where the wooden arms of a moorland fingerpost pointed to Treswigga and Deacons; Carbaglet and Newton; with the way to St Breward straight ahead.

Bassett pointed out the square block of a church tower on the skyline, a couple of miles further on.

Polkinghorne raised his eyes to look beyond the slopes of rough grazing, where huge rounded lumps of granite outcrop showed amongst clumps of bracken, which was already beginning to turn brown, due to the lack of rain.

"That must be the village, behind those trees near the church," he said with a shudder. "Just imagine living out here, Sarge."

"Middle of winter . . . with a couple of inches of fresh snowfall covering the entire landscape, so's you wouldn't know road from moorland!"

"And then having to carry out your normal bicycle patrol all round the ruddy parish, Sarge!"

"Yes. There's a lot of worse places on the beat than Bodmin main street, when the pubs are chucking out on Saturday nights, Ceddie boy."

A horse and rider crossed the road ahead.

Shortly afterwards, Polkinghorne had to brake sharply to avoid a pair of sheep. These animals displayed a mulish determination to throw themselves beneath the car, as they were approached, but quickly bundled across to the opposite side of the road when given the right of way.

Several turns later they drove down a slight hill with open common to the right but an enclosure on their left.

Polkinghorne noticed, with a grin, that there was a rook or magpie standing, as if at sentry duty, on the top of every single wooden post which had been driven in to support the sheep netting.

Flat, open ground flanked a swiftly flowing river of brown water, at the bottom of the incline.

"Pull up! This'll do us!" Bassett exclaimed. "We'll take our mealbreak before these pasties get cold."

"Pretty, isn't it, Sarge?" his assistant said, nodding in the direction of a hump-back bridge.

Four weathered granite piers supported slabs of similar material which had been covered with a thin layer of tarmac, in much the same way as icing is used to cover a cake.

A group of moorland ponies stood in the centre of the river, having come down through a well-trodden slipway.

These animals seemed to spend their time bending down to drink occasionally, but otherwise staring silently towards the detectives who had, by then, stretched out on a small plateau of short-cropped grass, situated between the road and the higher side of the river bank to eat their lunch.

"Where are you going for your holidays this year, Ceddie?" Bassett asked by way of making idle conversation when they had finished eating their pasties.

"Somewhere off King's Ash Hill, in Paignton. A wooden chalet in one of those new holiday camps which are being built in South Devon."

"Sounds like a confidence trick to me, Cedric," his sergeant cautioned. "I've been up there: to a family funeral. Blinkin' great cemetery, but I didn't see no holiday camps! What's wrong with a week at Newquay?"

"No thanks!" Polkinghorne exclaimed in a voice which clearly brooked no argument. "I've been stationed there. Lively enough in summer, but a chap could fire a gun up the main street on a winter's evening and wouldn't hit as much as a stray cat, leave alone one of his own kind staggering home from the pub. I've been put off Newquay for life!"

Bassett said the place he liked least was Camborne, with all those abandoned mine buildings surrounding the town.

"But I'd go back there tomorrow if promotion to inspector depended upon it."

Following more desultory conversation, Bassett looked at his watch, saw that it now showed a quarter to two, and declared that it was high time they got going again.

"Then we ought to reach St Breward post office just as they open up for the afternoon," he said.

They eventually reached a road which zig-zagged up towards the church, just beyond a fingerpost pointing to The Candras. On driving to the top of this short hill, Polkinghorne found the low, granite-built Old Inn nestling close to the graveyard. Further along this road, a large circular yellow enamelled Automobile Association nameplate, edged in black, had been fastened to a cottage wall. It stated St Breward was 235 miles from London.

Seeing neither shop nor post office, Bassett made enquiries at the public house, where he was directed back down the hill.

Polkinghorne drove them past grim, granite-faced cottages to a junction just beyond the Methodist Church. A post box, let into the granite wall of a low building on his right, indicated they had found the post office.

He parked at a wider part of the road, and was just about to get out of the car, when Bassett grabbed his coat.

"Stay where you are! Slide down in the seat. Sit on the blinkin' floor, for all I care. Just make yourself inconspicuous. Didn't you see her?"

Polkinghorne acted as instructed but, since he had been looking in the other direction when parking their car, didn't know what the fuss was all about and asked his sergeant.

"Anthea Eulalia Hyde! She was sitting on that low wall, in front of the post office. Must have been waiting for them to open because she's gone inside . . . carrying a parcel. Now why would she come over here when there's a post office in St Tudy?"

"Perhaps she doesn't want anyone knowing she's sending it. Could be her sister's birthday present . . . if ladies still have birthdays at that age, Sarge."

Bassett admitted this might be the answer, but doubted it.

"You mark my words, Cedric: she's up to something fishy!"

Cedric suggested Sarge had 'got it in' for Miss Hyde.

"And why not? Look at the number of hours we've wasted, because of those duff alibis . . . which wouldn't have happened if the Miss Hydes hadn't been so obliging to all their mates. Then again: we haven't sorted out the mystery of the second cartridge case yet. Bet you a pint to a pasty they're at the bottom of that."

"Perhaps they've found the gun this time."

"Impossible! We've all scoured the place, and found nothing."

Polkinghorne pointed out that the Tamblyn boy had told them that he had found a gun. What if the Hyde sisters had got to that sand pile before them?

"We'll soon find out!" Bassett snarled. "We'll wait until she's pushed off. Then I'll question the post bloke about Wheeler's letter and ask about Miss Hyde's parcel at the same time."

"I don't want to sound like a wet blanket, Sarge, but how are you going to see what's in that parcel . . . got X-ray eyes?"

"Congratulations, Ceddie boy!" Bassett exclaimed, slapping his assistant on the back. "You're one step nearer promotion to sergeant. I know you're trying to be funny, but you've just given me a damned good idea . . . Bodmin Hospital!"

"The X-ray department?"

"Why not? Look out! The door's opening! She's coming out!"

The two detectives watched Miss Hyde step into the road.

To Bassett's relief, she appeared not to notice the police car, which was a perfectly ordinary hooded tourer with no words of identification painted on its bodywork.

Miss Hyde turned to her right and walked off down the hill without as much as a stealthy backward glance.

Bassett waited until she was out of sight, then pulled himself up from the car's floor to straighten his back and shake any creases out of his trousers.

"We'll give her a couple of minutes before getting out. She may have left her gloves, or something, and have to come running back," he said. "I don't want her catching me whilst I'm looking at her parcel. I wonder what she's up to now?"

Chickens Coming Home to Roost

Phipps could hardly eat any breakfast, on the following morning, because of all her anxieties. And the very atmosphere itself was full of foreboding, too.

When she had glanced out of her bedroom window, on rising earlier, she had found the landscape blanketed by a pall of dense black cloud which showed little or no sign of movement in the apparently windless sky.

Few birds sang.

They knew the weather was on the change.

There was thunder in the air!

Would all the milk turn sour?

Phipps went down to breakfast, expecting there to be storms indoors as well. Ever since their ill-fated Plymouth excursion, she had been living in constant dread of being questioned by the Bodmin detectives and endlessly regretted sending that wretched cartridge case through the post.

But how was she to know that one of the village children had found the right case? And how could she have possibly foreseen a meeting with anyone in the Cornish police force who knew her by sight . . . when wandering around Plymouth City streets?

A day of disaster, if ever there was.

So much for her silly idea of playing a joke on the CID! But there you are, she told herself, policemen - by the very nature of the job - tend to take life rather more seriously than do middle-aged ladies of good family, who are living a life of relative idleness, supported by a quite substantial private income.

However, there was one small grain of consolation . . . her older sister's equally unfortunate performance during the previous afternoon.

When Phipps thought about that . . . well!

It made her own exploits in Plymouth pale to insignificance.

How could Bun - usually so depressingly sensible - have set out to tempt providence in such a deliberate manner? It reminded Phipps of when the Devil invited Jesus to throw himself off the temple roof, and let angels carry him safely to the ground, to establish beyond all reasonable doubt that he really was the Son of God.

The response had been 'Thou shalt not tempt the Lord thy God'. Substitute 'the Cornwall County Constabulary' and that text would fit the present situation admirably!

Phipps, reflecting on how she had spent the previous day, felt almost virtuous.

On arrival in Bodmin, she had found a photographer who was prepared to develop and print her sister's film that very same afternoon. Upon receiving payment - together with a few pence extra for postage - he guaranteed to put everything in the mail before the last collection took place.

Phipps had thanked the man and wandered back to that nice cafe, just below the Assize Courts for a light luncheon, completely satisfied with a job well done.

On her return to the rectory, late in the afternoon, she had felt somewhat crestfallen at the way her sister had thanked her in a most casual manner.

Then horrified, when she heard of Bun's afternoon activities.

To avoid any unfortunate meeting with members of the Cornwall CID, wandering abroad when they should be safely shut away in their office, her sister had telephoned the Bodmin Police Headquarters, before starting out on her walk to St Breward, simply asking if Detective Sergeant Bassett was available, then wanting to know where he might be found when told he was out.

The man on the police switchboard had informed her that all members of the department were out. One detective constable was attending an inquest at St Columb.

" . . . and the other two?" Bun had prompted the telephonist. "There are three in that department . . . aren't there?"

The man answered that this was correct, but the others: a constable and their sergeant were driving out to St Breward, and would be going through to St Tudy, after concluding their enquiries in St Breward.

Bun had then asked if her informant could give her any idea when he expected the last named persons to be back at the Bodmin Police Headquarters.

"They have only just left - not more than ten minutes ago - the man on the switchboard had replied, so he wouldn't expect them back in the CID office until well on towards the end of that afternoon . . . if at all.

"So I looked at the clock," Bun told her sister, "then calculated that, providing Bassett stopped for lunch whilst on his way, he should reach St Breward in the early afternoon. I therefore abandoned all thought of posting the automatic pistol in favour of preparing a special parcel which would be of similar shape, size and weight."

"But still addressed to yourself . . . at Tozers Quay, Topsham?"

"Naturally," Bun answered with one of her superior smiles.

"So you hurried over to St Breward . . . ?"

"No." Bun answered with a shake of the head. "Took my time, actually, old girl. Then, upon my arrival outside the post office, I perched myself on a low wall opposite the building and composed myself to await events."

"But how did you know Bassett would pass that way?"

"Because it was the only exit road leading directly from there towards St Tudy. I knew Bassett and companion would have to come down there . . . and they did!"

"After a long wait, uncomfortably perched on a cold stone wall?" Phipps queried. "Nanny Hudson wouldn't have approved!"

Bun retorted that she had not been there long enough to get piles . . . as their old nursery governess would have suggested, because the detectives turned up just as the shops were re-opening after their lunch hour. The driver obviously saw me, drove on to a wider part of the road and stopped."

"But they could have been going to stop there in any case," Phipps commented, by way of indicating this did nothing to imply that they were in least bit influenced by her sister's presence.

Bun's lip curled disdainfully as she replied that dear Phippsie would not have made that sort of remark if she had been there and seen for herself. Both driver and passenger had slid down in their seats, immediately they stopped the car, as if trying to pretend they were not there.

"Hmmm. Yes, that was silly," Phipps observed. "So they had decided to keep you under observation. I expect they wondered why you were sitting on that wall . . . so far from St Tudy, dear."

"No doubt. Anyway - to cut the long story short - I thought: that settles it!"

"So what did you do?" Phipps asked, now all agog.

"Walked across to the post office, went inside, and registered my parcel!"

Phipps then wanted to know why it had to be registered.

"Two reasons. To draw attention to both myself and the parcel. Make it appear to be important. Also: it would take longer for the postmaster to deal with . . . so he would be more certain to remember me, if questioned later."

"Bassett didn't come in, whilst you were there?"

"No. The pair of 'em remained skulking in their car."

Phipps, somewhat disappointed, had asked if that was all.

Her sister laughed, saying she had left the post office and walked down the hill - as if returning to St Tudy - but sat on another garden wall to admire the view as soon as she was out of sight of the police car. After a few minutes, during which that vehicle had not come down behind her, she had crept up to a point where she could see it . . . still parked in the same place.

"And . . . ?" Phipps asked breathless with excitement.

"Nobody in there, old girl! But it didn't require a degree in applied psychology to work out where Bassett and his pet bloodhound had gone."

"Into St Breward post office?"

"Yes. Just to be absolutely certain, I strolled up and snatched a brief glance through a corner of their window."

"And you saw Bassett?"

"Yes. Leaning over the counter, talking to the fellow who had attended to me no more than a few minutes before. Looked as thick as thieves, plotting to steal the emperor's crown jewels!"

"I hope nobody looked round and saw you staring in at them."

Bun replied that she had not remained at the window more than the split second it had taken her to recognise the actors and commit the scene to memory.

She had then hurried away, down the hill, until she reached a five-bar gate. She had opened this and gone into a field, waiting behind a reasonably thick hedge which screened her from any persons - or vehicles - proceeding along the road.

"The police car was driven past at quite a speed, some fifteen or twenty minutes later . . . "

" . . . which proves the detectives questioned that post master about you and your parcel . . . "

" . . . and means we are under surveillance, old girl!"

Poor Phipps . . . having questioned her sister about the parcel's contents, had hardly slept a wink for worrying about the outcome.

Absolute proof of trouble to come, at the rectory, was provided next day by a small paragraph in their Western Morning News.

BOMB SCARE

Police officers were called to St Breward sub-post office yesterday, when a stranger posted a suspicious package.

Mr F C Scoble, sub-post master said it was very heavy. It might have been an IRA bomb.

Detective Sergeant T Bassett took the package to the East Cornwall Hospital at Bodmin.

It was examined in the X-ray department by Dr H O Greene who found the suspect package contained . . . horseshoes.

Cousin Crispian laughed uproariously after reading this.

Phipps gave Bun her meaningful 'well-you've-done-it-now' look.

Bun told her to stop looking as miserable as a pickled walnut. No laws had been broken and the village blacksmith had been paid five shillings for his horseshoes.

"But there's such a thing as wasting police time!"

"Up to Bassett if he wants to X-ray people's parcels, old girl."

"Well I think you're about to have the opportunity of discussing that with him, in person, dear! Their police car has just pulled into our drive. I'd say you've got some chickens coming home to roost!"

Discussing Guns and Horseshoes

Bun and Phipps found their two policemen waiting in the library, where they had been conducted by Mavis. Detective Sergeant Bassett apologised if their call was being made at an inconvenient time, but went on to explain that there were one or two points which he needed to clear up.

"Ah! So you've solved the mystery," Bun suggested brightly.

"Not entirely, Miss Hyde," Polkinghorne replied.

His sergeant added, "Let's just say that if we could find the necessary evidence to back up inspired guesswork . . . we should probably be able to convince a coroner's jury."

"Of suicide . . . of course." Bun stated rather than enquired.

"Ah-h-h-h-h! Now this is a very interesting remark," Bassett observed thoughtfully. "May one ask why you speak in such a positive manner?"

"Because everything points in that direction," Bun responded.

"After all," Phipps joined in, extremely thankful that neither detective had appeared to be interested in herself . . . or that unmentionable trip to Plymouth, "Mr Wheeler would have been aware, by then, that he was going to pass on . . . "

" . . . and he was well-known for having gone through life with a giant-sized chip on his shoulder . . . " Bun added.

Detective Sergeant Bassett, ignoring the astonished expression on Polkinghorne's face, butted in with, "Now just a minute! Just a minute, if you please, Miss Hyde!"

"Y-e-s-s . . . ?"

"Let's take this a bit slower, shall we?"

239

"It is hardly likely to alter the final outcome."

"Nevertheless . . . I should be grateful if you would tell me how you come to know about the deceased's fatal illness."

Phipps remained silently watchful whilst her sister explained how the late Mr Everard Wheeler was said to have discussed the matter of his failing health with the old rector.

" . . . who mentioned it to his curate?" Polkinghorne suggested.

"A perfectly natural thing to do!" Phipps retorted.

"Yes, wasn't it?" Bassett sighed with resignation.

"Part of his parish business . . . "

" . . . knowing when to expect the next customer for a funeral?" Bassett interrupted Phipps.

Phipps replied distantly that she would not have phrased it in that manner.

Ignoring this rebuke, the detective sergeant rushed on to point out there was surely no need for the Reverend Crispian Hyde to tell everyone else in the parish of St Tudy.

Bun responded in a mild manner but with an icy tone of voice, that Cousin Crispian had not - as far as she knew - spoken of Wheeler's condition to anybody . . . until the nasty little man had been found dead in the churchyard.

"So it wasn't a breach of confidence!" Phipps told Bassett.

"Oh well . . . I suppose it makes a change from hearing the latest news by way of the postman or milkman," he observed. "But why mention that chip on the shoulder?"

Bun recounted what she had heard from Lady Mary Holbrook, concerning the dead man's early life. Then she suggested they all sat down.

Once all four were relaxed in the rectory's most comfortable armchairs, Bun continued by telling Bassett to work it out for himself, observing that - regardless of Wheeler's possible unsuitability for the position of bridegroom to a daughter of the local aristocracy - the wretched man was a fellow human being.

"One presumes he loved the girl and, when she was sent away, felt robbed of both a wife and child."

Bun paused for effect before concluding, "His only child . . . as things turned out."

240

"Which caused a life-long resentment of those better off than himself?" Bassett nodded and continued, "Yes. I must admit my colleague and I have - from time to time - begun thinking along similar lines."

Phipps had difficulty in hiding a smile as that colleague, right on cue, also nodded his head.

Bassett continued by saying that a certain 'helpful' villager had also pointed them in the right direction.

Bun raised an eyebrow in unspoken query.

"Oh nothing to do with your cousin or the rector. Just a trenchant remark concerning people who played midnight leap-frog, over their neighbours' garden hedges."

Bun grimaced understandingly.

"A fruitful source of possible scandal if a jealous person were to draw public attention towards all these 'goings-on'," she said.

"And that poor little Dorothy Nunn gave you proof!" Phipps exclaimed, in a tone of voice calculated to clearly indicate her disapproval of the detectives' methods.

"Aided and abetted by Captain Holbrook . . . " Bassett commenced with hands held open to indicate helplessness.

" . . . his mother, lady Mary . . . " Bun prompted.

" . . . and nearly everyone else who attended Dudley Knighton's dinner party!" The senior detective concluded.

After pausing for breath and glaring at the two sisters he said, "Which brings me to that unlikely story you told us, when we first met, about several of those dinner guests spending the remainder of that particularly memorable evening with yourselves - here - at the rectory."

Phipps shivered with fear at what might be coming next.

But her sister merely shrugged her shoulders, pointing out this was 'old hat' now that those alibis had been proven false.

"What could we do?" she asked reasonably. "We are strangers in St Tudy. All those people had been hospitable to us in one way or another. And they were all perfectly decent, law-abiding citizens, as far as we were aware at the time."

"I know . . . so you felt it would have been difficult to refuse their pressing requests for help," Bassett accepted with a shrug.

Bun added that it would have seemed churlish, to say the least.

Phipps turned her attention towards Detective Constable Polkinghorne, as he morosely observed that such unthinking actions wasted a considerable amount of police time . . . which had to be paid for out of rates and taxes levied against everyone in the county.

His sergeant told Bun and Phipps that he supposed their irresponsible conduct might be excused under the circumstances: their common membership of the same church. "I expect you felt it was your Christian duty to help those in need."

"Yes. Actually that was our prime motivation . . . though I should have hesitated to express myself in those precise terms for fear of sounding pious," Bun replied evenly.

"Yes . . . well . . . "

Here it comes, Phipps thought, inwardly bracing herself.

" . . . we now have more serious offences to consider," Bassett went on. "Did either of you ladies send us an empty cartridge case, which could have been fired in an automatic pistol, by means of the Royal Mail, while on a recent visit to Plymouth?"

Bun shook her head, giving a negative answer with a clear conscience, since she knew full well that her younger sister was the guilty party.

Phipps, hoping against hope that this would be the end of the matter, flinched as the detective sergeant turned to face her.

"Did you do it?"

Holding her breath, whilst she thought of the best way in which to phrase a not completely untruthful reply, Phipps saw Bun get to her feet, saying that perhaps it was time she ordered the tea and biscuits, because it appeared as if their interesting discussion might continue for some time to come.

With infinite relief, Phipps heard the detective sergeant thank her sister . . . as he layed back in his chair to await Bun's return from the kitchen quarters.

Then new worries presented themselves. Phipps could see that Bassett's wandering eye had stopped, seemingly fixed on a spot of mould which was now growing on the library wall, just behind Polkinghorne's head.

She hoped he would not recognise that almost perfect circle for what it was . . . the entry hole - now plastered over with a water and flour paste - of a bullet fired from an automatic pistol. But, oh dear, it did look so very much as if a .38 bullet had passed that way.

Bassett shook his head slightly, then turned back to look directly at Phipps, once again.

She saw his lips twitch.

Then a near-smile flitted across his round face.

"Give it up, dear!" he murmured in a voice which sounded as if it were tinged with sorrowful regret. "We know you did it."

Was he speaking about that shot fired into the wall . . . or the fact that she had posted the cartridge case? Phipps wondered in speechless panic.

"How could you? You weren't there," she replied, satisfied this would serve very well to answer either activity.

Bun, who had returned, stopped in the doorway.

Bassett ignored her, staring intently at the younger Miss Hyde and saying to Phipps, "Ah-ha! But you were, weren't you, my dear?"

"That's a filthy trick to play on anyone!" Bun exclaimed as she came further into the library and resumed her seat.

"It always works, though," Bassett responded with a shrug and a slight smirk.

Phipps almost burst out laughing at her sister's comment of, "There's only one answer to that, my dear man . . . horseshoes!"

To the younger woman's disgust, Bassett never turned a hair.

"Oh yes. Good of you to mention them, Miss Hyde. I might have forgotten, otherwise. You're a collector, are you?"

"On occasions . . . if I come across something which might be suitable for our kitchen ceiling beams, back in Devonshire. Cart-horses' shoes are much too big . . . though I must admit one, fixed to an outside cottage wall, doesn't look at all out of place."

There was a knock at the door.

Relieved at this chance to move, thereby getting away from Bassett's accusing gaze, Phipps jumped to her feet and opened the library door to let Mavis enter.

The maid was carrying a heavily laden tray. This was set down upon a big table near the window, then the girl withdrew.

Phipps poured tea and passed round the cups, together with a plate of assorted biscuits.

Returning to her chair, she watched Detective Sergeant Bassett crunch a couple of ginger nuts as if they were dog biscuits, wash them down with huge gulps of tea, then look straight at Bun.

Exhibiting an earnest expression, with which he obviously hoped to encourage confidences, he told her that he could take a joke as well as the next man but death by shooting was by no means funny.

"You and your sister, in my opinion, have caused my department a great deal of wasted time."

"I'm sure I don't know how we could have done that."

"Guns and horseshoes!"

"I fail to understand the purpose of that terse remark."

"Weight! Weight and size, Miss Hyde. My constable and I sat up half the night discussing an embarrassing five minutes at the East Cornwall Hospital . . . "

" . . . and did you reach any satisfactory conclusion?"

How can she be so composed and pretend indifference? Phipps wondered, anxiously nibbling a petit beurre and worrying about what was coming next.

Bassett gulped more tea, then explained that he and Polkinghorne thought it strange to learn Miss Hyde should have carried a parcel of horseshoes all the way to St Breward, when she could have posted them more conveniently in St Tudy, as she passed the village post office.

"However: taking into account the fact that you telephoned Bodmin to ask for me at eleven o'clock . . . and the village blacksmith said he sold the horseshoes at five minutes past eleven, one can suppose you purchased those horseshoes with a deliberate intention of making a fool of me!"

"Rubbish! How could I possibly know you were going to X-ray my parcel?" Bun replied sharply. "I used the public call box to enquire after you because I wanted to know when the inquest on Wheeler would take place."

Bassett retorted that he failed to see the connection.

"Quite obvious surely?" Bun continued. "I chanced, in passing, to see some nice horseshoes thrown out on the blacksmith's scrap pile and bought them for our cottage in Devonshire. By the time I had finished packing them, our post office had closed for lunch. So I took them with me on my country walk."

"That's not true! Our switchboard man told me your call was made from a private telephone . . . which means you made a special journey: TO the blacksmith AFTER you called Bodmin and found out I was going to St Breward."

Wagging a cautionary finger at Bun, he said, "You laid in wait for me! I saw you! On that wall. By the sub-post office!"

Phipps, quaking inwardly at what might happen next, watched Bassett lie back in his armchair, slowly drinking the remainder of his tea with a very smug expression on his face . . . whilst Bun, having been caught out, remained huffily silent and disconcerted.

In the midst of this hiatus, Phipps heard a tap on the library door. Then Mavis entered to say that one of the village boys had called, wanting to speak to a policeman.

Bassett jerked his head.

Polkinghorne stood up and followed the maid outside.

He returned in less than two minutes, walked straight across the room to where his sergeant was seated, and appeared to drop something into Bassett's hand.

Phipps studied the detective sergeant's changing expression as he looked into his carefully cupped hand.

Initial curiosity slowly changed to one of calculating appraisal.

Almost sniggering, he then stood up.

"Going out for five minutes . . . but keep the pot warm. I'll be ready for another cup of tea when I come back."

Phipps smiled as Polkinghorne followed his master out of the library . . . like the good dog being taken on his favourite walk.

"I wonder if he'll stop at every lamp post?" she murmured.

"Eh? What?" Her mystified sister asked.

"Oh . . . nothing dear," Phipps replied, straining her ears to hear if the front door closed. The moment she heard the distant 'clunk' of wood against jamb, she hurried across the room.

245

First: she craned her neck to look out of the library window.

"They're both walking off - towards the road, dear - and there's a boy with them," she said.

Bun jumped up, threw open the door, and called, "Mavis!"

The maid hurried through the hall from the direction of the kitchen, where Phipps concluded Mavis had been telling the cook of current events beyond the green baize door.

"Yes Miss?"

"What's happening? D'y'know where those policemen went?"

"Up to the churchyard. That was Bobby Richards, just called. Said he'd found another of they old cartridge things."

Phipps experienced instant relief. If there were more to be found elsewhere, perhaps Bassett wouldn't bother her again over that one she had posted in Plymouth.

Bun waved her hands at Mavis.

"Don't just stand there, waiting for a pat on your head, girl! Get your coat on! Go after them! But make it look casual. See if you can find out where that boy found this new cartridge case, then come straight back here!"

Back to the Churchyard

Little Bobby Richards, strutting with self-importance, led the Bodmin detectives into the churchyard.

Bassett was quite contented to follow three paces behind, allowing Polkinghorne to walk beside the lad and ask further questions.

The detective sergeant preferred to review progress.

And he had not exaggerated the facts when he told the Miss Hydes that he had spent half the night in discussing their silly trick with those horseshoes.

He and Ceddie Polkinghorne had abandoned the CID office in favour of a small back room down at the Hole in the Wall public house.

Not a good place to be - on Saturday nights - after soldiers from the barracks had been let loose with a week's pay burning holes in the pockets of their walking-out trousers, but quiet enough on mid-week evenings.

Polkinghorne had been prepared to laugh off that silly business up at the East Cornwall Hospital.

Well . . . it was all right for him.

But he wasn't the one who had to approach a supercilious young doctor about the possibility of X-raying a parcel thought to contain a bomb or an automatic pistol.

And then, after watching me make a complete fool of myself, the best Ceddie Polkinghorne can manage is a misquotation from some obscure 18th century poet about the Devil finding work for idle hands.

Bassett smiled at the memory of those grammar school English lessons when his master, Mr A J Candy - popularly known as 'Old Sugar' - used to declaim:

'For Satan finds some mischief still

'For idle hands to do.'

whenever he caught a lad playing the fool behind his back, during lesson time.

Then - his thoughts returning to the present - Bassett changed the smile for a malevolent scowl.

That horseshoe parcel couldn't possibly have been made up as a spur-of-the-moment joke, but must have been the end result of a long, and careful thought process.

He had said as much, down at the Hole in the Wall.

But Ceddie Polkinghorne wasn't having any.

He had suggested that Miss Anthea Eulalia Hyde had simply nipped up to the village and bought a few discarded horseshoes as soon as she knew where Bassett was going to be found, during the remainder of that day.

"To give you a bit of a surprise, Sarge."

Bassett had argued his assistant was missing the point which was: why telephone Bodmin in the first instance? Certainly not to find out the time and place of Wheeler's inquest . . . because at least three people, from the village, would be summoned to attend: Doctor MacIlroy, the sexton and that farm-hand who discovered the body on his way to work.

In such a small place as St Tudy, the news would be all round the cottages within thirty minutes of the principal witnesses receiving official notification.

Which proved Miss Hyde had not been telling the truth.

On the previous evening, Bassett had been dogmatic upon this point . . . that their meddlesome old maid had wanted to find out where he was and the blethering idiot, on the police switchboard, had been daft enough to tell her.

But this didn't get away from the perfectly reasonable probability that Miss Hyde had been planning something before she even thought of putting through that telephone call to his office in Bodmin.

Polkinghorne had readily accepted that their confiscated parcel was about the same size and weight as one which might contain an automatic pistol . . . but insisted this was merely fortuitous coincidence.

Bassett had opted for the alternative possibility.

Deliberate intent!

Suppose Miss Hyde had already packed up a pistol - the one he and his assistant had been searching for, on the day when they were sieving that damned great pile of sand - then called Bodmin to make sure she wouldn't meet the detectives whilst on her way to the post?

If one took it for granted that she wouldn't wish to post such an easily remembered parcel in St Tudy - where she and her sister were now well-known - then St Breward was her obvious second choice. Another village, within reasonable walking distance, and possessing a sub-post office.

As Bassett had then pointed out to Polkinghorne, over their third glass of ale, this could mean the horseshoe parcel was a cobbled together substitute . . . as soon as she knew she would probably be seen - by the two detectives - while in the vicinity of St Breward.

Furthermore: if Miss Hyde had been setting out on a completely innocent country stroll, as she now claimed, she wouldn't have needed to start lying in her teeth when asked for a few simple details.

Liars - no matter how well-bred - were people setting out to conceal something!

And what could she want to conceal? Bassett gritted his teeth. A gun . . . that's what! But he knew he'd never get a search warrant on possibly fallible guesswork. Hard evidence was needed. Then he recalled noticing that curious, tiny circle of green mould on the library wall.

By God! I've got her!

I've seen many a damp wall in my time, he recalled, with patches of green mould growing over the surface plaster. But that stuff needs damp, ill-ventilated conditions. Something not present in the rectory library.

The detective sergeant walked on, deep in thought, for several paces, then gritted his teeth and nodded to himself.

Mould spreads outwards from the scource of moisture, he told himself. Never shows up as a single, isolated green spot, unless some grubby kid has wiped a jammy finger on the wall . . . or a small hole in the plaster has been patched with a substance which can encourage such a growth.

For example:

I am a housewife living in an old house. Accidentally, I knock against a wall with something heavy . . . chip a bit of plaster, then have to effect repairs with what I've got in my kitchen.

Something capable of sticking and binding, then setting and staying put.

Bassett tried recalling his mother's kitchen, on a baking day, then gave a satisfied nod.

Yes! White of egg . . . mixed with pastry flour.

Or perhaps I simply use an odd bit of pastry which fell on the floor when I was making the pasties. It looks much the same as putty so I bung it in the hole, smooth it over with a knife dipped in hot water . . . and Bob's your uncle! All done.

Manfully resisting any inclination to leap in the air, execute an entrechat, throw his arms about, or bellow 'Eureka' at the top of his voice, Detective Sergeant Bassett stolidly followed little Bobby Richards and Polkinghorne through the churchyard grass, until they stopped beside a row of slate headstones.

The boy pointed to fresh damage on some of their otherwise perfect edges, where triangular fragments were now missing. He told the detectives that he first thought this had been caused by somebody knocking against the edge of the slate with an iron bar, or similar object.

Then, happening to scuff the grass about with his foot - for no particular reason - he discovered something lying there. He had bent down to part the rank grass with his hands, and found this brass cartridge case.

"Right there, sir," he said, pointing to the spot.

Bassett gave the lad a couple of coppers for Wall's ice cream, not so much by way of reward as to get rid of him.

Once the two detectives were alone, Bassett pointed to the line of sight from this spot towards the building sand.

"You know what happened, Ceddie boy . . . ?"

"The killer ran out this way. His gun knocked against the gravestones, causing subsequent vibration to release the trigger mechanism, and another bullet was fired."

Polkinghorne paused in thought for a few moments, then added that the weapon must surely have a very sensitive trigger.

"Yes. Either an old weapon which has seen a lot of use, or a new gun . . . where somebody has filed the mechanism to achieve what's known as a 'light pull'. No wonder the blighter stuffed it into our sand pile . . . firing without warning, like that!"

Polkinghorne suggested the bullet might have hit one of those cottages on the opposite side of the road. Bassett led the way across, but examination of exterior walls and questioning the occupants yielded no further evidence.

No one remembered hearing any sound of a shot, but three people complained about the milk lorry, saying that it was more noisy than usual.

It was alleged that there had been some backfiring as Eric Smitheram started up.

"He oughter take that dang'd thing into the garage! 'Ave 'is valves ground in properly," one man suggested. "I know about engines an' if that lorry ain't put right we'll git no sleep!"

Bassett asked Polkinghorne for his views as they walked back towards the rectory. The detective constable pointed out back-firing would have masked the sound of a pistol shot . . . but Eric Smitheram didn't start work until 6.30 am; whereas Wheeler, according to the medical evidence, was dead by midnight.

"Not on, is it?" Bassett asked with a resigned shrug.

"Unless our killer sat beside his victim for six hours, offering up prayers for his immortal soul . . . "

" . . . in which case: Pope would have seen him when he dodged in to water the daisies."

The two men continued in silence for a while then, when almost level with the rectory gates, Bassett remembered that spot of green mould, spoke of his suspicions and gave instructions.

"Cedric . . . when we get back in the library, I want you to remain standing. If you look at the wall - behind that chair where you were sitting, you'll notice a small circle of green mould."

Polkinghorne said he'd already noticed the spot.

"Good! Now I want you to stare at it. Go up close . . . so that those Hydes are in no doubt about what's receiving your attention. Give it a minute or two, while I begin questioning them again, then brush the mould with your hand."

"How about if I pretend to taste it with the tip of my tongue?"

"Yes . . . that ought to shake somebody!"

"Then sit down . . . after giving you an ominous nod, Sarge?"

"Excellent! You'll make inspector's grade yet, Ceddie boy."

Logical Deduction is Applied

Mavis had returned to the rectory whilst the detectives were calling on cottagers living in premises located between the smithy and the village shop.

Carefully obeying the older Miss Hyde's instructions - that she should act in a casual manner - the rectory housemaid had kept to the road throughout, instead of taking the short cut along the churchyard path.

There, she had observed, from a safe distance, little Bobby Richards leading the Bodmin detectives through the gate beside the village school. Then she had continued around the road, skirting the outside of the churchyard, to pass Town Farm and the Old Clink, where she stopped once again to loiter in the vicinity of the parish pump.

This position gave Mavis a clear view straight across to that row of headstones, where Bobby was now showing the detectives the exact spot where he had discovered the most recent cartridge case to have been found amongst the tombstones.

She remained where she was as the two men knelt down, apparently examining the edges of several slate slabs and feeling for damage, before standing up, exchanging a few words, then coming out in her direction.

Mavis had then walked quickly towards the first turning on her left . . . heading for the village shop. She paused, trying to appear just like anyone else by looking in the window . . . while constantly stealing guarded sideways glances back over her right shoulder.

Once she was satisfied that neither policeman had followed her, Mavis hurried across the wider road - as if making for the churchyard gate - then dodged down the narrow footpath, beside the Watsons' large garden, in order to by-pass the church. This enabled her to re-join the back road just before it reached the village school.

Knowing the coast was clear, she now felt safe to enter the churchyard. Mavis walked as far as the tower end of the main building, then crept carefully round to make certain the detectives had not returned.

No one in sight.

The rectory maid walked across to the rows of headstones where she had seen the village boy stop and point out something to the detectives.

However, she did not need to make a very close examination, to see that there were small triangular nicks, where pieces of material had been recently chipped off the upright edges of two adjacent slate slabs.

And the grass was well trampled down all around them.

Mavis nodded to herself, full of self-satisfaction, and hurried back to the rectory where she reported to the older Miss Hyde, before rushing through to tell Mary and the cook.

"Saved your bacon, Phippsie," Bun remarked as soon as the maid had gone out and closed the library door.

"I certainly hope so . . . but what makes you so sure?"

Bun rolled her eyes ceilingwards, heaved a sigh, then told her younger sister that it stood to reason.

"If that boy can find a small object - such as a brass cartridge case - in all that rank grass around those headstones . . . "

" . . . so can I, dear?"

"Can't think of any reason why you shouldn't, old girl."

"Yes . . . I see."

"Thought you might . . . with a little persuasive guidance."

"So when they come back to question me, I simply say that I found my brass cartridge case in the same place as this boy has apparently just found another?"

"That's right," Bun smiled encouragingly. "Go on . . . "

"I decided to post it anonymously . . . but why?"

Bun heaved another sigh of despair.

"Because - being a lady - you didn't wish to put yourself in the position of very possibly having to give evidence during the course of a notorious murder trial."

"Well that's nothing more than the truth," Phipps replied. "I shouldn't care to appear in a court . . . but I don't think I shall mention this little boy, and where he found his cartridge case. The detectives might think I was making up my story . . . because, being down here, I couldn't possibly know where that child found anything up there."

Bun thought about this for a few moments, made up her mind and nodded aggreement.

"Good point, old girl. Just mention the two gravestones showing recent damage . . . "

"Little notches chipped out of their edges . . . as if something had struck them?"

"That's right." Bun paused, then laughed. "D'y'know Phippsie, if our universities handed out honorary degrees to people who most distinguished themselves by displaying outstanding ability to pervert the course of justice, we'd be in line for a brace of PhDs!"

Phipps suggested that such honours were already frequently conferred upon certain types of professional gentlemen, such as famous lawyers and politicians.

Her sister agreed this was so . . . but she had been thinking more along the lines of some form of recognition for enthusiastic amateurs, such as themselves.

They lapsed into reflective silence for a while.

Then another thought struck the younger sister.

"Bun dear . . . what about the gun?"

"Oh I don't know," she replied with an indifferent shrug. "A bit of the old thrust-and-parry ought to keep 'em guessing. You must remember . . . they don't know we've found Wheeler's automatic."

Phipps was about to warn her sister of the dangers involved when 'playing' with detectives - because they were not fish and Bun lacked previous angling experience - when she was stopped short by hearing a prolonged ring on the front door bell.

"Oh dear. They're back again!" Phipps muttered.

"Round Two coming up!" Her sister confirmed drily.

Within half a minute, Mavis was showing Bassett and Polkinghorne into the library.

Bun asked the girl to bring a fresh pot of tea, for the original was now cold, then settled herself into an armchair.

Phipps and the detective sergeant did the same, but the younger woman suddenly began to feel distinctly apprehensive when she saw that Polkinghorne had remained on his feet, and was now staring around at the library walls . . . as if looking for something.

Bun expressed the hope that their meeting with the village boy had proved to be of some use.

"Oh yes. Very interesting indeed," Bassett answered without giving anything away.

Phipps remained silently watchful of Detective Constable Polkinghorne's movements.

Was he really looking at those dreary mezzotints of minor country houses . . . or the walls, themselves?

Vaguely, as if in a dream, she heard Bassett say something about Wheeler's death and murder. Then her sister's reply, which included the key word: suicide.

But, by then, Polkinghorne had stopped quite still, and was fixedly scrutinising one small area of one particular wall.

It was a blank space . . . except for a very small repair which had been carried out on the night they found that gun in the building sand . . . and Bun shot a hole in the plaster!

Phipps became completely mesmerised.

She heard nothing else.

She saw nothing else.

It was as if the clock had bust its spring and suddenly stopped ticking. Time itself was standing still.

Had she retained the power of general thought, Phipps might have realised this was how the rabbit feels on coming face to face with a hungry weasel beneath the autumn bracken.

But free thought had been replaced with naked awareness.

Discovery was imminent!

Phipps silently watched as the detective constable reached out a hand and began gently brushing it over the surface of her bullet hole repair work.

Now he was putting that same hand thoughtfully up towards his partly open mouth!

The tip of a pink tongue emerged to taste questioningly.

Oh, why did we have to use cornflour? Phipps reproached herself.

Anyway, he doesn't appear to like the taste, she thought with some measure of relief. But then - he wouldn't - would he? She hadn't put any sugar in the paste mixture.

Polkinghorne grimaced, lowered his hand, gave the green mould a final long, calculating stare, then walked slowly back to the vacant armchair and sat down . . . nodding in a most meaningful manner towards Bassett.

As for Phipps: the clock had begun to tick. Life continued.

Her eyes now took in the larger scene, whilst ears picked up nearby sounds of speech.

She gathered Bassett was explaining how the police now knew, quite by chance, that the gun with which Wheeler had been shot had - in all probability - been the deceased's own property.

The detectives had paid a call on Mr Danvers, that same morning, in the course of a routine enquiry. During their brief conversation, the old gentleman had mentioned of how his gardener, Jim Bascombe, had served in France during the latter part of The War.

This man had apparently brought home a number of souvenirs from the battlefield and pride of place in his collection had been an automatic pistol. Bascombe had spoken of how he removed it from a dead German unteroffizier, who had been serving in a Bavarian machine-gun company during the 1917 offensive.

"Bascombe worked part-time for both Danvers and Wheeler," the detective sergeant continued. "And eventually told Danvers, in the course of general conversation, that he had sold his automatic to Wheeler. Even remembered the maker's name: Dreyse. Very popular with the German police."

Phipps, almost blushing, recalled seeing that word on her gun.

She coughed gently and took out her handkerchief to wipe her nose, by way of hiding her face. Glancing across at Bun, she saw that her sister was remaining completely impassive.

"But how can you be sure that gun shot Wheeler?"

"Cartridge cases, Miss Hyde," Bassett replied. "All three were fired from the same weapon . . . because microscopic marks have proved to be the same on each one. Also: numbers stamped on their bases are the same, and this particular ammunition was definitely issued to the German army during 1917, for use in Dreyse automatics . . . so where's that pistol?"

Phipps made a noise halfway between a squeak and a gulp.

Bun answered blandly that she, and her sister, had been asking themselves that very same question.

Bassett remarked, with matching nonchalance, that he and Polkinghorne believed the gun had been found by one of the ladies present.

Bun wondered how they had reached such an odd conclusion.

"That silly joke with the horseshoes! It took us a long time to work out, but we came up with the correct answer eventually."

"And what might that be? Or are we not allowed to know?"

"Put simply: we concluded posting rusty horseshoes was a waste of money . . . and registration completely ridiculous! Which made us think you wanted to draw attention to your parcel. I mean to say: a few horseshoes could have been wrapped up in old newspapers and tucked away at the bottom of a suitcase, when the time came for you to go back to your home in Devonshire; now couldn't they Miss Hyde?"

Bun observed that, for a short story, Bassett appeared to be on the verge of writing his first novel.

Bassett retorted that it would never sell.

"Too improbable . . . like your own activities. Anyway: we thought you must have really been going to post something else. An object of value which was too dangerous to keep in the rectory . . . in case one of the maids found it."

"Anything else, or have we reached the end?" Bun enquired.

"We then considered your timing," Bassett continued blandly. "regards the telephone call and when you bought the horseshoes."

"We believe that you bought those horseshoes immediately after learning that we were heading for St Breward," Polkinghorne joined in provocatively. "And also after finding out the weight of a Dreyse automatic pistol . . . by putting it on your kitchen scales."

"Which is . . . ?"

"A fraction over two pounds . . . and your horseshoes weighed two pounds, five and a half ounces according to St Breward post office scales!" Bassett smiled in triumph. "What a coincidence!"

"A well-chosen word, Sergeant," Bun replied drily.

"We believe that's what we were meant to think. We believe you arrived at that particular weight for your horseshoe parcel after first ascertaining the weight of the real thing."

"Imaginative Poppycock!"

"We prefer to call it 'Logical Deduction'."

Phipps decided she might as well call it 'Six Months Without The Option' . . . or 'A Christmas In Holloway Gaol'.

To her horror, Detective Sergeant Bassett now turned to face her, asking where she had found her cartridge case.

"Oh . . . er . . . in the churchyard," she replied in an almost unintelligible gabble, being caught completely off her guard.

"Sure it wasn't discovered under an armchair . . . in here?"

Phipps asked, in a very weak voice, "Why should that be?"

"Because I reckon a firearm has recently been discharged in this room!" Bassett replied shortly.

He pointed to where Polkinghorne had been examining the library plaster. "I suggest that little spot of green mould, up there, covers the entry point . . . where a bullet struck home."

Bassett shook his head at the thought, telling both sisters they were lucky one of them hadn't ended up by accidentally killing the other.

"That gun's got a hair trigger!" He almost shouted. "A good hard knock will cause it to fire then, because it's an automatic, it cocks itself on the recoil . . . all ready to fire again. I expect one of your maids will remember hearing the noise of a report, when we question them."

There he goes again, Phipps thought to herself, making use of the Dirty Tricks Department.

"You needn't think that threatening the mistress with lots of extremely embarrassing questions being put to the servants, will get you any further in your investigation," she snapped petulantly.

Then bit her lip with sudden anxiety.

Next thing - she thought - will be Mavis and Mary rushing out, joyously repeating every single word all round the parish by nightfall!

It came as no surprise to Phipps when she saw her sister's jaw tighten into an expression of grim resolve.

"There's no need to involve those girls. They couldn't tell you anything. Not present at the time." Bun shrugged resignedly. "The gun is hidden in the bottom of one of our suitcases, under lock and key. Since you can't possibly use it to hang one of our friends, I'll bring it down."

Detective Constable Polkinghorne stood up.

"No need for an escort," Bun said. " I know my way . . . and I'm a bit too old to start jumping out of bedroom windows like Errol Flyn, that American fellow, does in those Hollywood films."

Bassett and the Hydes Pool Evidence

"I've got a good mind to report the pair of you for suppressing evidence, wasting police time . . . and keeping a dog without a licence!" Detective Sergeant Bassett exclaimed after he had finished examining the automatic pistol which Miss Hyde had brought down from her bedroom, and listening to her account of where and how it was found.

Phipps was outraged, retorting that he was being ridiculous.

"We don't own a dog . . . so there, now!"

"Which means you haven't got a licence to keep one," Bassett snapped back.

"Of course not!"

"Well . . . ask yourself this: how would you stand - in the eyes of right-thinking people - if my assistant or I were to 'plant' a stray in your stables, one weekend?"

"If we liked the little animal, we should immediately purchase a dog licence at the village post office," Phipps told him.

Bassett gave a sharklike grin.

"And what's that supposed to mean?" Phipps demanded.

"That you couldn't obtain a licence after midday - on Saturday, m'dear - because the post office would be closed!"

"That's monstrous!" Phipps protested.

Bun shook her head, looking first at Detective Sergeant Bassett and then at her sister.

"Oh come off it, old girl! Can't you see this stupid man's pulling your leg?"

"He's not smiling" Phipps observed, "only baring his teeth!"

261

"As far as I can see, there's not a great deal been happening to cause genuine smiles-all-round, at the present moment, is there?" Bassett suggested blandly.

"Oh I don't know, about that," Bun replied. "From where I'm standing it looks very much as if - providing you keep your wits about you - that you will both come out of this little mystery covered in glory."

"After spending nearly a week carrying out investigations around St Tudy . . . only to discover that everyone's been making a complete fool of us?"

"But my dear man:" Bun exclaimed, "your superiors won't know that, will they?"

"And a good job too!" Bassett retorted grumpily.

Bun gave it as her opinion that he would drive back to the county police headquarters, in Bodmin, that evening having - to all intents and purpose - solved one of the most difficult cases of suspected murder to have ever cropped up in the entire country.

Bassett admitted it had proved to be a bit of a puzzle.

"Yes, of course it has," Bun agreed in soothing tones, "but there can be only one conclusion . . . which will result in people at your headquarters - who really matter - taking this as proof of your outstanding ability."

Bassett glanced across at Polkinghorne . . . who simply rolled his eyes in disbelief.

"Oh yes," Bun continued with confidence, "the way I see things: your future with the Cornwall CID is now assured."

Bassett muttered that this case could hardly be said to be solved when they had not - as yet - found the person who fired the fatal shot.

The elder Miss Hyde smiled reassuringly at her younger sister, then turned her attention back towards Bassett.

"But you have, my dear man!"

Bassett made a sarcastic remark to the effect that she must be psychic but - if she could see into the immediate future with such unparalleled clarity - perhaps she would be good enough to tell him all about it.

Bun shrugged her shoulders dismissively.

"His body's lying in the mortuary, down at Truro."

"You mean that Wheeler did it all by himself?" Polkinghorne asked incredulously.

His sergeant heaved a sigh, then admitted he and Polkinghorne had eventually found themselves thinking along similar lines, but realised that they lacked conclusive proof.

"There's no real evidence which will stand up in court," the detective constable pointed out.

Bun nodded pleasantly at Bassett.

"I think I can help you, over that particular hurdle. One moment, if you please."

Phipps watched her sister get to her feet and head for the library door wondering - somewhat apprehensively - whatever Bun was going to do now.

Bassett looked at his assistant and raised his eyebrows.

Polkinghorne replied with a grimace indicating doubt.

However, they were not kept in suspense for long because Bun returned in less than a couple of minutes.

Her sister instantly realised that she was carrying the Bodmin photographer's envelope in one hand.

Phipps studied the changing expressions which crossed Bassett's face, as Bun laid out her set of fingerprint photos, then drew the detective's attention to a number of similarities between certain patterns on a white paper background, and others which had been made on brass cartridge cases, or the clip which had contained them, in the automatic pistol.

"Nice and clear," Bassett muttered to himself, with what Phipps took to be grudging admiration. "You must have used a very good camera."

"Good sets of prints, too," Polkinghorne added after leaving his chair to stand behind his sergeant.

"Yes. A bit smudgy, here and there round the edges, but they'll do," Bassett acquiesced. "How did you managed to bring them up so well?"

Bun and Phipps, speaking alternatively, told the detectives all about their visits to friends with a family photo; then calling on the two estate agents.

Bassett remarked upon the amazing coincidence of the way in which Wheeler's fingerprints had been obtained.

Bun had the good grace to readily admit that she had simply been very lucky in obtaining a sheet of cottage particulars which had previously been handled by Wheeler.

"And you found out how to bring up these fingerprints, then photograph them, by simply looking through a book in Plymouth City Library for a couple of hours?" Bassett stated rather than asked, ending with a disgruntled snort.

"Well we couldn't have asked at our nearest police station, now could we?" Phipps suggested pertly.

To her delight, the detective sergeant responded with a bellow of laughter, telling her she would have probably found herself being locked up in the County Asylum . . . as a potential fruit-and-nut-case.

"Which wouldn't have been any help to you," Bun said.

"And you've done all this without telling anybody else?" Bassett asked the two sisters.

Phipps silently shook her head.

Bun replied, "That's correct, Sergeant. So you're quite safe to inform your superintendent this has all been due to your own efforts . . . aided and abetted by Constable Polkinghorne, without whose assistance . . . "

Polkinghorne almost purred.

His sergeant muttered "Yes. Of course."

Bassett bent his head over the photos once again then, after some more time spent in silent thought, whilst he pretended to examine the fingerprints obtained from that sheet of property particulars collected from the Camelford estate agent's office, the sergeant pointed out that - in his opinion - a coroner was unlikely to accept suicide as the strongest possibility.

Bun demanded to know why not.

Phipps bit her lips in agitation.

Polkinghorne shrugged helplessly.

Bassett reminded the two sisters that - according to their present story - they had found the gun in a pile of building sand, many yards away from the victim's body.

Phipps agreed this was correct.

Whereupon Bassett asked how did one explain this to one's superior officer . . . leave alone the coroner?

"We could always say we found it closer to the scene of the shooting," Bun suggested, very straight faced.

This met with no response.

"If that would be of any help to you," she added in her most persuasive tone of voice.

"No we could NOT!" Phipps snapped with exasperation.

Her sister raised her eyebrows questioningly, clearly feeling affronted by this sudden outburst.

Polkinghorne suggested that the younger Miss Hyde sounded very positive . . . in a negative sort of a way.

Bassett told his assistant to stop trying to talk in riddles.

Then he turned his attention towards Phipps, enquiring what was standing between herself and a 'little white lie'?

"One has to take the oath before giving evidence, once the case gets to court," she answered with an embarrassed grimace. "And neither my sister nor I could possibly tell such a deliberate lie after doing that!"

"Because you wouldn't go to Heaven," Bassett added drily.

Bun told her sister to stop talking like old Nanny Hudson, adding that her suggestion was only made from a general desire to be helpful.

Bassett, with a sigh, observed that there were times when their desire to help had made this investigation somewhat more difficult for himself and Polkinghorne.

Then suddenly, the detective constable - who had been examining an odd length of brown cord which seemed vaguely familiar - asked why it had been included with the automatic and remaining live ammunition.

"Oh, I thought you'd better have it." Bun answered offhandedly.

"One end was tied to the gun, when I dug it out of that pile of sand," Phipps added.

"Yes. We presumed it to be part of a lanyard," Bun continued.

"We actually tried looking at our friends' necks," Phipps told the policemen, "to see if any man showed signs of skin-burn."

Bassett asked why?

Polkinghorne looked blank.

Phipps rushed on to say, "Well . . . it must have taken quite a lot of sudden force to break that cord. It's quite strong stuff, you know. So we thought it would have cut into the flesh and left a nasty mark for days afterwards."

"But you didn't have any luck?" Bassett enquired.

Bun shrugged apologetically.

Phipps reminded the detectives that most of their male friends were gentlemen who wore collars and ties everywhere, except in their baths or beds.

"So - not helping scrub backs in their bathrooms . . . " Bun said.

" . . . nor sleeping with any of them," Phipps added with an accompanying blush, "we were unable to discover any signs of recent injury."

"But I still don't see how you can say Wheeler's death could have been suicide," Polkinghorne joined in with a puzzled expression on his face.

Bun waved a hand dismissively.

"Our first thought too . . . before gathering all this finger-print evidence . . . "

"Which proves Wheeler did fire the gun . . . " Basset murmured thoughtfully.

"Exactly," Bun continued with her explanation. "You see: we were misled after finding those nicks chipped out of a couple of gravestones . . . "

"Yes." Bassett nodded, "We've just been up there, looking at the self-same thing."

"We know," Phipps said with a smile.

"But you weren't there," Polkinghorne observed with a puzzled frown.

"Or were you?" Bassett demanded suspiciously.

"Not at all. We sent one of the maids to keep an eye on you." Bun replied.

"No sense in employing servants if one does not make use of them." Phipps added pertly.

Bassett shook his head in despair, then told Bun to continue.

266

"Well . . . my sister and I first thought the murderer had run out between the gravestones, caught a loop of his makeshift lanyard on one of them, which dragged the gun out of his hand to hit against the slate . . . thereby causing the slight damage we've just been discussing."

"And this shock broke the cord . . . " Bassett prompted.

" . . . at the same time causing the gun to fire," Polkınghorne added, by way of demonstrating he was a pretty good chap too, when it came to this theory stuff.

"I thought the murderer had then got rid of the gun," Phipps joined in, "by burying it in that pile of building sand . . . after he had jumped down into the road somewhere close to where Smitheram's noisy milk lorry is parked at night."

"But later, knowing Wheeler had shot himself, we concluded a passer-by had picked up the gun and moved it."

Bassett said he had thought so too, at one time.

Then Polkinghorne reminded his sergeant of that occasion when they had spoken to the driver of the milk lorry.

"I found a similar length of cord tied to one of his chassis members."

"Oh yes," Bassett prompted with little interest.

"Well I cut it off, close to the tail-board, in case somebody caught their foot and tripped. I told you on the way back to Bodmin. Remember . . . ?"

"Yes. All right. I know what you're talking about: old rusty buckets tied to the backs of vehicles," Bassett began remonstrating, then he suddenly clapped a hand to his head.

"My God! We've done it, Ceddie boy!"

"If you're thinking what I'm thinking . . . ?"

Bassett answered that he was sure this was the case.

While Bun and Phipps looked on with blank facial expressions.

"The way I see it," Bassett expounded excitedly, "a length of cord had been tied between the milk lorry and the automatic's trigger guard. Wheeler had then knelt down, committed his soul to his Maker and shot himself. The milk lorry had been driven away - some six hours later - whipping the weapon across the graveyard . . . where it hit against some of the headstones."

267

"Causing it to fire again . . . as witness that cartridge case which the young village boy reported finding today," Polkinghorne joined in enthusiastically.

"Only one snag," Bassett grumbled. "We haven't got a long enough length of cord."

Polkinghorne declared that they could easily find the rest, since it must have broken off somewhere on Smitheram's milk collection round.

"Then you're going to have a long walk, Constable, to find it."

Bun, feeling sympathy for the detective constable, who obviously did not look forward to searching many miles of Cornish roads and hedges, reminded Bassett there was another way of proving relevance.

"Jack Wills acted for Wheeler when he was engaged in his land deals. And Wills is a keen sea-fisherman. He mentioned it in the course of that evening we all spent around at Dudley Knighton's place. So why not telephone Wills?"

"He might be able to give us a lead," Polkinghorne suggested.

Bassett, after asking permission to use the rectory telephone, sent his detective constable away to try his luck.

When Polkinghorne returned, Phipps saw his face was absolutely wreathed in smiles.

He told them Wheeler had been in the Camelford estate office on the day he died, already proven by Miss Hyde having obtained a sheet of property details handled by the dead man, and Wills definitely remembered Wheeler asking his advice on the breaking strain of fishing cord.

"What's more . . . he actually asked where he could buy the stuff in hundred yard lengths! I tell you, Sarge, we're home and dry! Wills gave Wheeler the name and address of his own supplier - a marine chandler - down in Port Isaac!"

"And . . . ?"

"I got his number from Wills and rang this chandler bloke. He remembered the sale. Told me he couldn't very well forget it. The customer looked more like a doctor, solicitor or local preacher than a fisherman. You see: this particular cord is a firm favourite with the longline men."

"Proper job!" Bassett exclaimed triumphantly. "A few samples, sent down to our pathologist at Truro - for comparison under his microscope - will clinch it!"

Polkinghorne looked uncertainly at his sergeant.

"Well . . . what's biting you now, Constable?"

"Should we . . . ?" Polkinghorne shifted his eyes from side to side, indicating the two sisters, " . . . that letter?"

"Oh: St Breward!" Bassett laughed. "Yes. Why not?"

The detective sergeant turned towards Bun, explaining how they had discovered a note in Wheeler's waste paper basket, asking him to meet the writer in the churchyard after he left the Knightons' dinner party.

"A matching envelope bore the St Breward post mark, hence our visit to the village postmaster . . . "

"Who remembered Wheeler posting the letter himself!" Polkinghorne added.

Bassett went on to say that most of the village sub-postmasters cleared their own boxes and date stamped the contents.

"The bloke at St Breward had just cleared his box when he saw Wheeler arrive and drop an envelope in. Thinking it might be important - Wheeler being a well-known solicitor - the postmaster went out and got it."

"Then, seeing that Wheeler had posted a letter to himself," Polkinghorne added as he took up the story, "this chap we spoke to in St Breward scratched his head and thought the old solicitor was going barmy."

"Point is: he remembered," Bassett interrupted his assistant, "and I'd say this is pretty vital evidence of Wheeler planning that whole evening's charade," the detective sergeant concluded with a satisfied grin.

"So it was as we suspected," Bun observed. "Wheeler assembled local people who had been in some sort of disagreement with him and had something to hide, then shot himself . . . "

" . . . presumably with a twisted smile on his miserable little face," Bassett broke in with a bitter laugh, "knowing his old sparring partners were going to have a difficult time finding alibis for the time of his death."

"But now we've found out about him buying that fishing cord, everything's nicely sorted out," Polkinghorne observed.

"Yes." Bassett agreed. "First, he knew he was going to die; so he buys his gardener's pistol; then gets Knighton to throw what amounted to the Last Supper. Afterwards, Wheeler ties one end of his fishing cord onto the milk lorry, then makes the other end fast around the trigger guard of his gun. Step two: he blows his brains out. Step three: the lorry drives off, next morning, thereby dragging the gun between those damaged headstones, causing it to fire again. This also breaks the cord. Then our gun flies through the crisp morning air to land in that sand pile.

"All part of a grand plan," Bun murmured.

"Aided and abetted by our summer visitors: the Miss Hydes!"

"I think everyone should help the police," Phipps said sweetly.

"Thank God they don't!" Bassett declared with deep feeling.

In The Final Analysis

"So that's all there was to it? Wheeler took his own life?" Millicent Drysdale exclaimed, "With no mystery whatever?"

"Just a common or garden suicide?" her brother grumbled. "How singularly disappointing!"

It was the evening of Millie's dinner party, down at Marsh Cottage, and most of the guests who had been present at Dudley Knighton's home during the previous eventful week were now gathered together to discuss Everard Wheeler's sudden end.

Miss Anthea Eulalia Hyde had just finished telling everyone a carefully revised and thoroughly expurgated version of how the two Bodmin police detectives had finally reached this surprising conclusion.

She had begun her story at that point where they had dropped in at the rectory, to thank the two sisters for sending in a cartridge case, which they had picked up whilst looking at old gravestones in the village churchyard.

"Phipps had posted it anonymously," Bun told her audience.

"One wished to avoid publicity," Phipps said demurely.

"Naturally, we didn't wish to be involved," Bun declared with a completely straight face, "but the Boys from Bodmin recognised her writing, by comparing the name and address on their postal packet with signed statements taken in the village. Very clever!"

"Too clever by half," her sister murmured wryly.

"Then, whilst we were giving them tea and biscuits in the library, to our utter amazement, a village boy turned up with a third cartridge case!"

"Of course," Phipps interjected at this point, "you'll have heard all about that by now, thanks to the local grapevine working overtime."

Bun drank some tea because her throat was beginning to feel quite dry, then took up the story once again, saying that what her friends were unlikely to know (because we only made up this bit some time later, she thought wryly) is that - after the boy had gone - our detectives searched through nearby long grass, and that was when Bassett stumbled over the gun!

"Complete with this odd, frayed bit of fishing line still tied onto its trigger guard," Phipps added with a facial expression which said more clearly than a dozen well chosen words 'well what do you think about that?'

"Of course," Bun continued, "that reminded the constable he'd seen a similar piece of cord tied onto the back of Mr Smitheram's milk lorry."

"After that, as you can guess," Phipps joined in with a dismissive shake of the head, "it was as good as all over, bar the back-slapping congratulations. "

Bun took up the narration once again.

"Yes. They 'phoned Jack Wills, who remembered Wheeler asking questions about fishing line, and he put them onto the chandler down in Port Isaac."

"Fortunately, he was able to describe a professional gentleman, who bought a hundred yards of longline cord, well enough for all of us to recognise this customer as having been the late lamented Mr Everard Wheeler," Phipps explained.

"Hardly 'lamented'," Millie and Dudley Knighton said in unison.

"And as you probably know . . . Mr Danvers had already told the police about his gardener selling Wheeler a German automatic pistol, brought home from Flanders," Phipps reminded their listeners.

She thought it was a pity not to mention the pile of building sand . . . but, owing to a previous agreement made with Detective Sergeant Bassett, it had been decided that a few minor alterations to the known facts would help reflect greater credit upon himself and Polkinghorne.

At the same time - and by way of slight compensation - all thoughts of charges concerning the suppression of evidence would then be conveniently forgotten.

As Detective Sergeant Bassett had pointed out: this would spare the sisters from the misery of celebrating next Christmas inside Holloway Gaol.

"But what about that story the Tamblyns have been putting about?" Dorothy Nunn asked.

"Telling everybody their child found a gun in a pile of building sand, near the bus shelter?" Bun asked.

"Yes . . . because after all's said and done, everyone saw those two detectives sieving and shovelling over there," Dorothy reminded them. "On it for ages, working under a scorching hot sun. Did a most thorough job."

Bun shrugged, replying that one shouldn't place too much reliance upon the words of small boys. She didn't expect that silly child could tell the difference between a gun and short length of discarded scrap iron.

"Not only that," Phipps added, "but he found the first cartridge case and carried it home . . . "

" . . . so why didn't he add the gun to his collection at the same time, if there really was one?" Bun asked reasonably.

Phipps nodded dismissively.

"Simply childish imagination!"

Bun assumed what her sister always thought of as being her schoolmarm face.

"You can take it from me . . . there never was a gun in that building sand," she stated in her most positive manner.

Then G G Danvers said that he couldn't understand about the letter. Surely Wheeler had relied too much on pure chance, screwing it up into a ball, as if it was a bit of rubbish, then dropping it in his waste basket?

Bun shook her head, smiling understandingly.

"No! That was just one facet of his meticulous planning."

"Can't see it, m'dear."

"If you remember: Wheeler spent a good deal of his working life listening to evidence being given in magistrates' courts."

"And what is the connection?" Danvers pressed.

"He was a man who - unlike most of us - was completely familiar with all aspects of police procedure," Bun explained patiently. "He knew that, in cases of suspicious death, no stone would be left unturned. Which means all waste paper baskets, dustbins and even the ashes in the grate would be minutely examined. By screwing up that letter he made it appear completely genuine."

"As if he was angry with the writer," Dudley Knighton broke in, "which is exactly the way I treat communications from my local Inspector of Taxes."

Bun smiled acknowledgement.

"Precisely what our Sergeant Bassett thought when he found the note . . . then spent the remainder of the week trying to decide which one of you was the writer!"

"Thinking he would have been the person who met Wheeler in the churchyard and bumped him off," Teresa Lockhart exclaimed. "Beastly little man, giving us all this trouble."

Phipps inclined her head sympathetically, observing quietly that this was precisely what the late Mr Everard Wheeler had intended.

"His way of having the last word," Bun suggested.

Then Patricia Knighton brought up the subject of horseshoes being sent through the Royal Mail, having read about that mysterious parcel which had been handed in at St Breward village post office, during the course of this investigation.

Bun, keeping faith with arrangements previously made between Detective Sergeant Bassett and herself, extemporised by saying this had been just a bit of incredibly bad luck . . . as far as the CID was concerned.

"Bassett told us all about it. He was in St Breward to check on Wheeler's letter, which had been posted over there. When the detectives went in, to question the local postmaster, the silly old fool presented Bassett with this heavy parcel, saying that it had been registered by a dark-haired man who spoke with a pronounced Irish accent." (And no one in St Tudy can prove otherwise, Bun thought to herself.)

Millicent nodded her head, reminding everyone they must have all seen accounts of the IRA blowing up London pillar boxes in recent weeks.

"Well there you are . . . " Bun hurriedly agreed, hopefully concealing her secret relief at getting out of this awkward situation so easily. "Bassett simply tried to help the postmaster."

"He told us that this poor man was in a complete state of panic," Phipps added for good measure.

Then Captain Rodney Holbrook gave Bun a nasty jolt, when he expressed surprise that two detectives confided so much in a couple of ladies who were really only summer visitors.

"It's the atmosphere," Phipps replied earnestly. "We were all sitting in the library . . . surrounded by shelves full of sermons in bound volumes, bible commentaries and other religious works."

"Makes one think in terms of the confessional," her sister added with a knowing nod. "But you must remember, Roddy, we were never told anything which would not be made public knowledge by coming out at the inquest."

"Oh yes," Phipps joined in, "you'll be able to read exactly the same in all the local newspapers, later on."

After a silent pause, Dudley Knighton turned to the Drysdales, saying one thing still puzzled him. How did Wheeler manage to find out they were brother and sister? And who could have told him about Bernard's time in the Black and Tans . . . to say nothing of that Irish wife?

"Gross abuse of professional confidence! Wheeler acted for the vendor when we bought Marsh Cottage. I thought it best if both our names were on the deeds . . . in case anything happened to me, so he knew that part before we even arrived in St Tudy."

"And as regards our family connections," Millicent joined in, "we own three villages, up North. Anyone could drop in at the local pubs, buy a few drinks, bring the conversation round to the sons of the Big House and hear all about Bernard's adventures since flying the nest."

"Everard Wheeler always was a clever devil," Lady Mary observed. "What you suggest fits his character to a 'T'. I never took to that man." She shook her head. "Didn't care for the eyes."

"Always made me think of snakes!" Teresa Lockhart muttered.

"Well he's gone now," Millicent declared brightly, "so let's hurry up and forget he ever happened. I'll just pop out to the kitchen and see how our bird's getting on, in the oven."

Bun and Phipps exchanged furtive questioning glances.

Bernard Drysdale noticed and hastened to reassure them.

"No need to look so worried!"

Millicent agreed. "It's not a peacock called Nemesis . . . "

" . . . only a turkey . . . name of Timothy," Bernard explained.

Phipps, still horrified at eating a bird which she had known by its christian name, because this made the whole matter so very personal, decided to restrict herself to vegetables and chipolata sausages . . . since she wouldn't know the name of the pig.

We hope you have enjoyed reading this book. For details of others in the series: drop us a line at Treviades Press, Falmouth, Cornwall TR11 5RG.

Love,

Bun and Phipps